The Western Writers series is edited
by Bill Pronzini and Martin H. Greenberg.

Also in the series

The Best Western Stories of Wayne D. Overholser
Edited by Bill Pronzini and Martin H. Greenberg

THE
Best Western
Stories
OF

Steve Frazee

Edited by BILL PRONZINI
and MARTIN H. GREENBERG

SOUTHERN ILLINOIS UNIVERSITY PRESS
Carbondale and Edwardsville

Edited by *Dan Seiters*

Designed by *Design for Publishing, Bob Nance*

Production supervised by *Kathleen Giencke*

Library of Congress Cataloging in Publication Data
Frazee, Steve, 1909–
   The best western stories of Steve Frazee.

   (The Western writers series)
   Bibliography: p.
   Contents: The fire killer—The man at Gantt's Place—Learn
the hard way—[etc.]
   1. Western stories.   I. Pronzini, Bill   II. Greenberg,
Martin H.   III. Title.   IV. Series: Western writers
series (Carbondale, Ill.)
PS3556.R358A6   1984   813w.54   83–18052
ISBN 0–8093–1175–7

87 86 85 84   4 3 2 1

Contents

Acknowledgments

"The Fire Killer." Copyright © 1951 by Popular Publications, Inc. First published in *Argosy* as "Nights of Terror."

"The Man at Gantt's Place." Copyright © 1951 by Popular Publications, Inc. First published in *Argosy*.

"Learn the Hard Way." Copyright © 1952 by The Hawley Publications, Inc. First published in *Zane Grey's Western Magazine*.

"Great Medicine." Copyright © 1953 by Flying Eagle Publications, Inc. First published in *Gunsmoke*.

"The Bretnall Feud." Copyright © 1953 by Popular Publications, Inc. First published in *Argosy*.

"The Luck of Riley." Copyright© 1953 by Steve Frazee. First published in *Dime Western*.

"Singing Sands." Copyright © 1954 by Popular Publications, Inc. First published in *Fifteen Western Tales*.

"The Man Who Made a Beeline." Copyright © 1954 by Popular Publications, Inc. First published in *Western Story Magazine* as "Next Stop—Hell."

"The Bounty Killers." Copyright © 1955 by Male Publishing Corp. First published in *Swank* as "I'll Kill You Smiling, John Sevier."

"Due Process." Copyright © 1960 by Steve Frazee. First published in *Ellery Queen's Mystery Magazine*.

"My Brother Down There." Copyright © 1953 by Mercury Publications, Inc. First published in *Ellery Queen's Mystery Magazine*.

Introduction
A Decade of Excellence
By Bill Pronzini

In their entry on Steve Frazee in *Encyclopedia of Frontier & Western Fiction* (McGraw Hill, 1982, a good but not infallible reference work), coauthors Jon Tuska and Vicki Piekarski dismiss the substantial Frazee *oeuvre* in a single sentence: "[He] attempted to give all of his Westerns a strong historical flavor, but his weakest area was in his highly romanticized and questionable treatment of Native Americans." This statement is misleading, inaccurate, and grossly unfair, and neither it nor its implied dismissal should be allowed to stand unchallenged.

A strong case can be made, in fact, that during the decade 1951–60, when most of Frazee's fiction was published, no one wrote better or more uncommon popular (or "formulary") Western novels and stories. Testimony in evidence includes a score of published novels, several of which were filmed and several of which made reviewers' "best of the year" lists (e.g., his 1958 book about a mountain man, *Rendezvous*, has often been favorably compared to A. B. Guthrie's *The Big Sky*); first prize in an annual contest conducted by *Ellery Queen's Mystery Magazine* for a modern Western crime story, "My Brother Down There," which was later selected by Martha Foley for inclusion in her *Best American Short Stories of the Year;* and an impressive array of other short fiction, the most accomplished of which appears in this collection.

Yet Frazee has never received the critical attention his work deserves, despite being highly respected by his peers in the Western Writers of America, a professional organization for which he served as president in 1954 and vice-president in 1962; by aficionados and general readers of the genre; and by members of the Western Heritage Foundation, who voted him their Western Heritage Award in 1961. Perhaps one reason for this critical neglect (and misinterpretation) of his talents is that much of his short fiction was published in obscure magazines, and many of his novels appeared under the imprint of the lesser paperback houses. Another probable reason is that while his work is sometimes humorous (the short stories "Due Process," and "The Luck of Riley," and the 1960 novel *More Damn Tourists*), more often it is quite grim—particularly when he employs the theme of man's struggle for survival against the savagery of nature and of his fellowman—and uncompromising in its depiction of the harsh realities of the frontier. Reasons these may be, but they are not valid ones.

Nor are the contentions of Tuska and Piekarski. Is Frazee's work romanticized? Yes, in the sense that *all* popular Western fiction, to one degree or another, is a romanticized version of life in the Old West. That does not mean it is lacking in insight or fundamental truths. Frazee at his best may not be in the same class with Eugene Manlove Rhodes, Ernest Haycox, Dorothy Johnson, and Jack Schaefer; but his stories, like theirs, leave one with a feeling that yes, this is the way it must have been a century or more ago.

Is his treatment of Native Americans questionable? Hardly. Frazee's portrayal of the Indian way of life and of the relationships between red men and white during the nineteenth century is often cruel, bitter—but in no way are anti-Amerind sentiments expressed or implied except by individual characters for specific fictional purposes. Considering the nature of his protagonists, and the time frame in which they lived, they express a considerable amount of compassion for Native Americans. This compassion (as well as the cruelty and bitterness) can be found in two of the stories in these pages: "The Man Who Made a Beeline" and "Great Medicine." The second of these stories is particularly good, and contains a liberal measure (ironically enough) of what its Blackfoot warrior protagonist refers to as "the weakness of mercy."

To ignore the work of Steve Frazee is to do it and the author a grave injustice. And to blithely dismiss it as unimportant and unworthy is to not understand it at all.

Charles Stephen Frazee was born in Salida, Colorado, on September 28, 1909. He worked at mining and heavy construction jobs beginning in his teens and continuing until 1936, while at the same time he pursued his formal education. He received an A.B. degree from Western State College in 1937, was married to Patricia Thomass that same year, taught high school journalism for four years, became the father of a son and a daughter, returned to construction work as a superintendent in 1941, and entered the United States Navy in 1943, serving for the duration of World War II. From 1950 to 1968, he was building inspector for the city of Salida; he also has served as a director and president of the Salida Building and Loan Association since 1956.

Throughout the 1950s, while pursuing his writing career, he and his family lived in a log house in Salida. It is a measure of the man that he built this house himself and patterned it after the mountain cabins of the nineteenth century. Perhaps it is also a measure of the man that when he began writing fiction in the late 1940s, his avowed aim (as quoted in a biographical sketch on the jacket of his first major novel, *Shining Mountains*) was "to write honest Westerns," and that he has succeeded in this aim according to his own personal code and vision.

By the early 1950s Frazee was regularly selling stories to the pulp magazines and to other markets, drawing heavily for material on his mining experience, his knowledge of wilderness skills, and the history and geography of his native state. Not all of these early stories, nor all of his later work, were historical or formulary Westerns; he also wrote adventure fiction, crime fiction, and occasional fantasy and science fiction—most of these, too, drawing on personal experience and Colorado history. An adventure story, "When Earth Gods Kill" (*Adventure*, November 1952), for example, deals with modern hardrock mining and underground engineers; and a crime story, "The Thin Edge" (*Detective Fiction*, November 1952) features a present-day railroad telegrapher in a small Colorado town.

Western stories did comprise the bulk of his early output, however. These found homes in such magazines as *Adventure, Argosy, Gunsmoke, Fifteen Western Tales, Zane Grey's Western Magazine,* and *Western Story.* The best of them—"The Man at Gantt's Place," "The

Fire Killer," "Learn the Hard Way"—are represented in this collection.

Shining Mountains (Rhinehart, 1951), Frazee's second published novel and the first to appear under his own name, was a major book club selection and immediately established his reputation. Like much of his fiction, it deals with the twin themes of men battling each other and the wilderness: in this case, two hostile factions, one of veterans of the Union Armies, the other of veterans of the Armies of the Confederacy, are forced by circumstances to band together just after the end of the Civil War on a search for gold in the rugged Colorado Rockies. Again to quote Frazee from the biographical sketch on the dust jacket: "No great historical figures stride through *Shining Mountains*. Just the men and women I knew twenty-five years ago in Summit County. . . . Their words were the words of men and women and not the dull, dubious words you find in written history."

Other novels followed rapidly, nearly all of them Westerns of one kind or another. One exception was *The Sky Block* (Rinehart, 1953), a chase/adventure story in the mode of Geoffrey Household and John Buchan, set in a remote section of the Rockies and involving the search for a hidden meteorological "doomsday device" implanted by "a foreign power." Despite its melodramatic components, and its overtones of the anti-Communist extremism of the McCarthy era, Frazee's handling of the theme minimizes these sensational aspects and makes the novel a successful entertainment of its type.

Another departure from the nineteenth-century Western was the novelized version of "My Brother Down There," published as a paperback original by Fawcett Gold Medal in 1957 under the title *Running Target*. Some of the power of the novelette is diluted by expansion, but this tense, bitter tale of a manhunt in the Colorado wilderness, in which both the hunters and the hunted are dominated by the primitive elements in man's personality, is nonetheless quite good in its longer form.

Of Frazee's traditional and historical Westerns, several are outstanding. *High Cage* (Macmillan, 1957) is the gripping account of what happens when five miners and one woman are snowbound at an isolated mountain gold mine. This story again utilizes the themes of the atavistic struggles of man against man and man against the elements. A superior example of suspense writing, the novel offers some of the most effective descriptions of high-mountain blizzard conditions and wilderness survival to be found in popular fiction of any type.

Desert Guns (Dell, 1957) is a powerful character study set in the Great Southwest of the 1850s, relating one man's "epic struggle against the land, his enemies, and his own devouring greed," as the publisher's blurb on the front cover rather aptly states it. The mountain-man novel, *Rendezvous* (Macmillan, 1958), tells a tense story of the days of the Rocky Mountain fur trade and of the courage and perseverance of a trapper named Mordecai Price and the inhabitants of a wilderness wagon train under his charge. *Smoke in the Valley* (Fawcett Gold Medal, 1959) chronicles the life and times of a family of settlers in the hills of Colorado just after the War Between the States—a much better historical family saga than most of those that have achieved bestseller status in recent years at twice the length.

A Day to Die (Avon, 1960) relates the story of a bloody 1869 war between the United States Cavalry and several united Indian tribes (Cheyenne, Sioux, Crow, Blackfoot, Apache). Much of this novel is told from the point of view of a Cheyenne warrior named Iron Buffalo, and certainly is not unsympathetic to Native Americans. Such passages as the following from its final pages again belie the "questionable treatment" claim of Tuska and Piekarski: "Peace was now something that only the Big Bellies and the women would talk about. . . . Unless the Indians wanted to die in places where there was no air to breathe, no land to ride across, no game to hunt and no far places to look upon, they would have to fight—even as the Shawnees and Delawares had fought before the many-shooting guns. If freedom came from dying, then freedom was worth the price, Iron Buffalo thought."

These are just a few of the excellent novels Frazee produced during his one prolific decade. Others include *Many Rivers to Cross* (Fawcett Gold Medal, 1955); *He Rode Alone* (Fawcett Gold Medal, 1955); *Cry Coyote* (Macmillan, 1955); *Hellsgrin* (Rinehart, 1960); and *More Damn Tourists* (Macmillan, 1960), a contemporary novel set in a small Colorado town and quite funny.

One other Frazee book of note from this period is his novelization of John Wayne's *The Alamo* (1960)—a film Brian Garfield, in his *Western Films: A Complete Guide*, refers to as "childish and boring" and a "soggy dirigible." The novel version bears no resemblance to the film; it has the virtue, as the film does not, of being historically accurate. "I was able to get all of Amelia Williams' work in the 1934 Texas State Historical Associations quarterlies," Frazee says, "one of the finest pieces of research I have ever seen. She had gone through thousands of records to come up with a critical study of the siege and of the personnel and of the historical problems relating to the Alamo. I also had the rather skimpy writings of men from the Mexican Army. Of course I had to use literary license in depicting the actions and thoughts of individuals, but the whole picture, day by day and bit by bit, was as accurate as it could be drawn at this late date."

After 1960, owing to extended service as a probation officer, Frazee published just two more Western novels, *A Gun for Bragg's Woman* (Ballantine, 1966) and *Fire in the Valley* (Lancer, 1972). The former title ranks with the best of his work in the fifties, and is particularly interesting and unusual because its central character is a woman. Much lighter in tone than most of his novels—and quite amusing on the whole—it details free-spirited Casey Leclair's efforts to tame a family of thieves and toughs in the mountains of Cimarron in 1886.

The balance of Frazee's post-1960 writings include a nonfiction book for young readers, *Where Are You? All About Maps* (1968); a suspense novel, *Flight 409* (1969); and several juvenile novels, including *Year of the Big Snow* (1962) and *Killer Lion* (1966).

All told, he has published 53 books and close to 100 short stories—again, the great percentage of them having appeared in the 10-year period between 1951 and 1960. No fewer than 11 of his works, both long and short, have been purchased for feature films; and another 9 were adapted for television. He also cowrote the screenplay for the film *Running Target*.

The best of the films based on Frazee's fiction is probably *Many Rivers to Cross* (1955), from the novel of the same title. Starring Robert Taylor, Eleanor Parker, and James Arness, the film emphasizes comedy much more than does the novel, but is still a mostly faithful adaptation. *Running Target* (1956), from the novelized version of "My Brother Down There," is likewise a faithful adaptation and is quite good, despite a B-movie cast (Arthur Franz, Doris Dowling) and a low budget.

Less successful adaptations are *Wild Heritage* (1958), taken from

Smoke in the Valley; High Hell (1958), an updated, soap-opera version of *High Cage,* far inferior to the novel; and *Gold of the Seven Saints* (1961), also inferior to its source, the novelette "Singing Sands." The other films based on Frazee works are not worth mentioning. The author himself, in fact, has expressed a desire not to be identified with them at all.

The stories in this collection span exactly the full length of Steve Frazee's decade of excellence, 1951–60. Some were first published in pulp magazines; others in such digests as *Gunsmoke, Zane Grey's Western Magazine,* and *Ellery Queen's Mystery Magazine;* still others in men's magazines of the period. All are well-crafted; at least four— "My Brother Down There," "Singing Sands," "Great Medicine," "Due Process"—are exceptional. And all reflect his major fictional strengths, of which there are five.

First, there is his ability to tell a convincing, satisfying, and unusual story, even when employing stock Western situations (something he does not do often). "The Fire Killer" combines the search for a gang of rustlers with the hunt for a strange, savage creature that kills with brute strength and leaves tracks unlike those of any known animal. "The Man Who Made a Beeline" tells the story of a wholly different "hardship" from the norm faced by two settlers in an isolated mountain valley. "Due Process" is a delightfully good-humored tale of the shooting of a bully and the efforts of a bunch of cowhands to disburse his "estate." Similarly good-humored is "The Luck of Riley," in which a man named Riley Winslow learns some fundamental verities about Dame Fortune.

"The Man at Gantt's Place" has all the elements of the standard "oater": a land struggle between cattlemen and cattlemen, as well as between cattlemen and nesters; a young man's coming of age; gunfights, tough lawmen, a crooked ranch foreman, and a steely-eyed gunman. Yet Frazee mixes these elements in ways that are not quite conventional, so that the whole becomes much more than the sum of its parts.

A second Frazee strength is his understanding of the nuances of character, of what motivates people, of the good and bad that exist side by side in the human animal, of the conflicts that rage between enemies and friends alike. He is not afraid, as lesser Western writers are, to portray genuine and deeply felt emotion. It is precisely this strength that transforms such simple stories as "The Bretnall Feud" (two brothers who hate each other and take opposite roads in life), "The Bounty Killers" (a pair of professional manhunters on the trail of a wanted man), "Singing Sands" (man's lust for gold), and "Learn the Hard Way" (a budding young outlaw's day of reckoning) into powerful and convincing studies.

His third strength is the ability to vividly and realistically depict a variety of Western settings and to do so in such a way that the settings become primary characters in their own right. The eerie Big Ghost Basin of "The Fire Killer," the high mountain country of "My Brother Down There," the vast northern plains of "Great Medicine," the awesome sand dunes of "Singing Sands"—all these places, and more, come alive through his word-portraits.

The ability to build and maintain suspense is Frazee's fourth strength. Once begun, such stories as "The Fire Killer," "The Bounty Killers," "The Bretnall Feud," and "My Brother Down There" are not easy to put down. We *must* find out what happens next.

And finally, Frazee's fifth strength is his prose style. Always terse, smoothly constructed, evocative, it takes on at times a kind of dark, rough-edged lyricism, as in these random examples:

When the wind was at its strongest he never heard the singing. The sounds came only with diminishing winds or when the blow was first rising. High-pitched music skirling from the ridges, running clear and sharp, then clashing like sky demons fighting when the wind made sudden changes. Anderson heard the singing at times when he stood at the foot of the dunes in still air, sensing the powerful rush of currents far above.

Sometimes, crouched in the doorway of his hut, he watched the queer half daylight of the storms and read strange words into the music. There was something in the sounds that wailed of lostness and of madness, of the times after centuries of rain had ceased, when the earth was drying and man was unknown. ("Singing Sands")

Habit and training made Lew weigh the forces that pushed him. He remembered the fine green lines of evil in Trey Martin's face. A man could become another Martin too easily. ("The Man at Gantt's Place")

If Melvin had been here just to fish and loaf, to walk through the dappled fall of sunshine in the trees, and—yes, to be caught away from himself while watching the endless workings of an ant hill; to see the sun come and go on quietness; to see the elk thrusting their broad muzzles underwater to eat; to view all the things that are simple and understandable. . . . then, he knew, he would be living for a while as man was meant to live. ("My Brother Down There")

Kaygo lay there for an hour. He was not asleep. He moved occasionally, but mostly he lay there looking at the sky and clouds.

He was wallowing in freedom; that was it. Damn him! He would not do what fugitives are supposed to do. He insisted on acting like a man enjoying life.

My brother down there, Melvin thought. Yes, and I'll kill him when he comes near enough on the saddle of the mountain. ("My Brother Down There")

The best Western stories of Steve Frazee are very good indeed. And because they are, perhaps *The Best Western Stories of Steve Frazee* will help to bring him the critical attention and respect he deserves as one of our most accomplished contemporary writers of popular Western literature.

THE
Best Western Stories
OF
Steve Frazee

The Fire Killer

Young Bill Orahood, the Sky Hook owner, was waiting for Ken Baylor where the trail forked near the fall-dry bed of Little Teton Creek. Orahood was mostly arms and legs and a long neck. Without a word he swung his chunky sorrel in beside Baylor and they rode toward Crowheart.

They went a quarter of a mile before Orahood blurted out the question that everyone in the Crowheart country was asking: "What do you suppose got Paxton?"

Baylor shook his head. Maybe Doc Raven knew by now. Raven had not been in town late yesterday afternoon when a drifting rider brought Bill Paxton's body out of Big Ghost Basin.

"You saw Paxton?" Orahood asked. "After—"

"Yeah." It was something to forget, if a man could.

A mile from town they caught up with big Arn Kullhem. A wide chunk of a man, his flat jaw bristling with sandy stubble, Kullhem looked at them from deep-set eyes and did not even grunt when they spoke. His Double K lay right on the break into Big Ghost. More than any rancher, he had suffered from what was happening down in the basin.

Bridle bits and saddle leather and hooves against the autumn-crisp grass made the only sounds around them until they came to the top of the last rolling hill above Crowheart. Then Kullhem said, "Doc Raven didn't give us no help on them first two."

Bill Paxton was the third man to die in Big Ghost. First, an unknown rider, and then Perry Franks, Kullhem's foreman. Both Franks and Paxton, one of the twins of Crow Tracks, had staked out in

1

the basin to get a line on the shadowy men who were wrecking the Crowheart ranchers. If they had died from bullets, Baylor thought, the situation would be clear enough.

"Who's going to stay down in the basin now?" Kullhem growled.

Orahood and Baylor looked at each other. Strain had been building higher on Orahood's blistered face the closer they rode to town. He and Baylor glanced over their shoulders at the hazed ridges that marked the break above the gloomy forests of Big Ghost.

Up here the grass was good, but when the creeks ran low, cattle went over the break to the timber and the swamps in the basin—and then they disappeared. Big Ghost was an Indian reservation, without an Indian on it. Fearful spirits, the ghosts of mutilated dead from an ancient battle with Teton Sioux, walked the dark forests of the basin, the Shoshones said. Even bronco Indians stayed clear of Big Ghost.

The cowmen had no rights in the basin; they had been warned repeatedly about trespassing on Indian land, but their cattle were unimpressed by governmental orders. That made the basin a wealthy raiding ground for rustlers from the west prairies, who came through the Wall in perfectly timed swoops.

For a time the Crowheart ranchers had checked the raids by leaving a man in Big Ghost as lookout. Franks, then Bill Paxton. Baylor knew there was not a man left up here who would volunteer to be the third lookout in Big Ghost—not unless Doc Raven could say what it was a man had to face down there.

They crossed Miller Creek, just west of town. A man on a long-legged blue roan was riding out to meet them. Baylor looked up the street at a small group of men in front of Raven's office, and then across the street at a larger group on the shaded porch of the Shoshone Saloon.

Kullhem spat. "You still say, Baylor, that Baldray ain't behind all this hell?"

"I do." Jim Baldray, the Englishman, owned the I.O.T. His range was fenced all along the break, with permanent camps where the wire winged out. Baldray had the money to keep his wire in place. I.O.T. stuff did not drift down into Big Ghost. There was nothing against the Englishman, Baylor thought, except a sort of jealous resentment that edged toward suspicion.

"You and your brother-in-law don't agree, then," Kullhem said harshly.

Pierce Paxton, the twin brother of the man now lying on Raven's table, was not Baylor's brother-in-law yet, but he would be in another month.

Hap Crosby met them at the lower end of the street. He was the oldest rancher in the country. Sweat was streaking down from his thick, gray sideburns. He looked at Baylor. "Baldray's here. Pierce wants to question him—if Raven don't have the answer."

All the Paxtons had been savagely impatient when anger was on them. Pierce, the last one, would ask questions, answer them himself, then go for his pistol. Baldray would be forced to kill him. Pistol work was the first custom of the country the Englishman had learned; and he had mastered it.

"All right, Hap." Baylor looked up the street again. He saw it now. He should have seen it before: the tension there on the Shoshone porch was as tangible as the feel of the hot sun.

"Did Doc—has he—" Orahood asked.

"No, not yet," Crosby said curtly. "Baldray's drinking with that drifter who brought Bill Paxton in."

"Does that mean anything?" Baylor asked evenly.

"I didn't say so, did I?" Crosby answered.

Four other ranchers were waiting with Pierce Paxton at the hitch rail in front of Raven's office. Paxton did not look around. Sharp-featured, tense, his black hat pushed back on thick, brown, curly hair, he kept staring at the doorway of the Shoshone. He was wound up, dangerous. He was fixing to get himself buried with his brother that afternoon, Baylor thought.

Slowly, sullenly, Arn Kullhem said, "By God, I think he's right."

"How far would you go to back that?" Baylor asked. "Across the street?"

Kullhem's deep-set eyes did not waver. "I wonder sometimes just where you stand in this thing, Baylor."

Old Crosby's features turned fighting-bleak and his voice ran hard with authority when he said, "Shut up, the both of you! We got trouble enough."

It was the slamming of Doc Raven's back door, and then the whining of his well sheave that broke the scene and gave both Baylor and Kullhem a chance to look away from each other.

The ranchers stood there in the hot strike of the sun, listening to the doctor washing his hands. Orahood's spittle clung to his lips, and a grayness began to underlay his blisters. A few of the loafers from the Shoshone porch started across the street.

Doc Raven came around the corner of his building, wiping his hands on his shirt. He was a brisk, little, gray-haired man who had come to the country to retire from medicine and study geology.

"Well?" Kullhem rumbled, even before Raven reached the group.

Raven shook his head. His eyes were quick, sharp; his skin thinly laid and pink, as if it never required shaving. "He was smashed by at least a dozen blows, any one of which would have caused death. His clothing was literally knocked from him, not ripped off. I can't even guess what did it."

The sweat on Crosby's cheeks had coursed down through dust and was hanging in little drops on the side of his jaw. "Maybe a grizzly, Doc?"

Raven took a corncob pipe from his pocket. He nodded. "A silver bear would have the power, yes. But there isn't so much as a puncture or a claw mark on Paxton."

"No bear then," Orahood muttered.

Raven scratched a match on the hitch rail. "It's like those other two cases. I don't know what killed any of them."

With one eye on Pierce Paxton, Baylor asked, "Could it be he was thrown from a cliff first, then—"

"No," Raven said. "Those granite cliffs would have left rock particles ground into the clothes and flesh."

Pierce Paxton had turned his head to watch the doctor. Now he started across the street. Baylor caught his arm and stopped him.

"No, Pierce. You're off on the wrong foot."

Paxton's face was like a wedge. "The hell! How much of *your* stuff was in Baldray's holding corral that time?"

Baylor said, "You know his men had pushed that stuff out of the wire angle. There was a man on his way to Crow Tracks to tell you when you and Bill happened by the I.O.T."

"That's right, Pierce," Crosby said.

"Say it was, then." Paxton's lips were thin against his teeth. "I want to ask Baldray how it happens he can ride Big Ghost, camp out there whenever he pleases, and ride out again, but Franks and my brother—"

"I ride it, too," Raven said.

Paxton backed a step away from Baylor. "They know damned well, Doc, that you're just looking for rocks!"

"Who are *they?*" Kullhem asked.

"That's what I'm going to ask Baldray." Paxton knocked Baylor's hand away and started across the street. One of the loafers had already scurried inside. Baylor walked beside Paxton, talking in a low voice. The words did no good, and then Baldray was standing in the doorway, squinting.

The I.O.T. owner was a long, lean man, without much chin. He wore no hat. His squint bunched little ridges of tanned flesh around his eyes and made him appear nearsighted, almost simple. The last two to make an error about that expression had been drifting toughs, who jeered Baldray as a foreigner until they finally got a fight out of him. It had lasted two shots, both Baldray's.

Baldray blinked rapidly. "Not you also, Baylor?"

Paxton stopped, set himself. The Englishman stepped clear of the doorway.

"Baldray—" Paxton said.

Baylor's rope-scarred right hand hit Paxton under the ear. The blow landed him on his side in the dust. Crosby and Doc Raven came running.

"Give a hand here!" Raven said crisply. Two of them stepped out to help carry Paxton away.

"The hotel," Crosby said. He looked back at Baylor. "I can handle him now."

Baldray smiled uncertainly. "Come have a drink, men!"

Across the street, the little knot of ranchers stared silently. Then Kullhem swung up, and said something to the others in a low voice. Orahood was the last. Baylor went into the Shoshone.

The gloom of the big room reminded him of the silent, waiting forests of Big Ghost. He stood at the bar beside Baldray, who was half a head taller. Kreider, who had found Bill Paxton at the edge of the timber in Battleground Park, took his drink with him toward a table. A man in his middle twenties, Baylor guessed. The rough black beard made him appear older. Just a drifting rider?

Baldray poured the drinks. "Hard business, Baylor, a moment ago. I would have been forced to shoot him."

"Yeah." Baylor took his drink.

"Raven found nothing?"

"Nothing—just like the two others. What do you make of it, Baldray?"

The Englishman's horsy face was thoughtful. He smoothed the silky strands of his pale hair. "A beast. It *must* be an animal of some kind. As a young man in Africa I saw things you would not believe, Baylor; but I still contend there must have been credible explanations. . . . And yet there are strange things that are never explained, and they leave you wondering forever."

There was a hollow chord in Baldray's voice, and it left a chill on Baylor's spine when he thought of Big Ghost and of the way Bill Paxton had been smashed.

"The rustlers always did steal in and out of the basin, of course," Baldray said. "They nearly ruined me before I fenced the break and hired a big crew. You fellows made it nip-and-tuck by keeping a scout down there, but now with this thing getting your men . . ." Baldray poured another drink.

The "thing" rammed hard at Baylor's mind.

"Isn't it sort of strange that this animal gets just our men, Baldray? After this last deal we won't be able to find a rider with guts enough to stay overnight in the basin. That means we'll be cleaned out properly."

Baldray nodded. "It does appear that this thing is working for the rustlers—or being used by them, perhaps. The solution, of course, is to have Big Ghost declared public domain."

"Fifty years from now."

"It's possible sooner, perhaps." Baldray's face took on a deeper color. "Fence. I'll lend what's needed for thirty miles. Damn it, Baylor, we're all neighbors."

He had made the offer before and Kullhem had growled it down in rancher's meeting. Fencing was not all the answer for the little owners. It was all right for I.O.T. because Baldray could afford a big crew, and because the cattle of other ranchers were drifting into the basin. Shut all the drifting over the breakoff, and then the rustlers would be cutting wire by night. The smaller ranchers could not hire men enough to stop that practice.

Baylor looked glumly at his glass. The immediate answer to the problem was to go into Big Ghost and find out what was making it impossible to keep a lookout there. He walked across to Kreider.

"Would you ride down with me to where you found Bill Paxton?" No man could simulate the unease that stirred on Kreider's dark face. "You figure to come out before dark?"

"Why?"

"You could tell that this Paxton had been in his blankets when he got it. He shot his pistol empty before. . . ." Kreider took his drink quickly. "No, I don't guess I want to go down into the basin, even in daylight—not for a while." He looked at Baldray. "You don't run stuff down there, do you, Mr. Baldray?"

Baldray shook his head.

So the Englishman had hired this man, Baylor thought. There was nothing unusual about that, but yet it left an uneasy movement in Baylor's mind. "You're afraid to go down there, huh?" he asked.

Kreider stared into space. "Uh-huh," he said. "Right now I am." He was still looking at something in his own mind when Baylor went out.

She was young, with red-gold hair and an eye-catching fullness in the right places. She could ride like a demon and sometimes she cursed like one. Ken Baylor looked at his sister across the supper table at Hitchrack, and then he slammed his fist hard against the wood.

"Sherry!" he said, "I'll paddle your pants like Pop used to if you ever even think about riding down there again!"

"Can it. Your face might freeze like that."

Baylor leaned back in his chair, glowering. After a few moments he asked, "Where was this moccasin track?"

"By a rotted log, just south of where Bill Paxton had camped."

No Indian. Raven sometimes wore moccasins.

"There was a mound of earth where Bill's fire had been. Smoothed out."

Kreider had mentioned the mound, but not the smoothness. "At least, that puts a man into it," Baylor said.

Sherry gave him a quick, narrow look. "You felt it?"

"Felt what?"

"A feeling that something is waiting down there, that maybe those Shoshone yarns are not so silly after all." She hurried on. "Sure, I know whatever it is must be related in some way to the rustling, but just the same. . . ."

After a long silence she spoke again. "No one would go with you, huh?"

"Orahood. Just to prove that he wasn't scared."

After he left Crowheart that morning Baylor had found the ranchers meeting at Kullhem's. If it had not been for Crosby, they would not have invited him to get down; and even then, desperate, on the edge of ruin, they had been suspicious, both of Baylor and each other.

"Old Hap Crosby wasn't afraid, was he?" Sherry asked.

"No. But he wasn't sure that getting this thing would cure the rustling. He favored more pressure on the Territorial representatives to have Big Ghost thrown out as reservation land. Then we could camp down there in force."

The others had ideas of their own, but threaded through all the talk had been the green rot of distrust—and fear of Big Ghost Basin. Baylor told Sherry about it.

"Damned idiots!" she said. "In their hearts they know that Baldray—or no other rancher up here—is mixed in with the rustlers!"

Baylor hoped it was that way. He got up to help with the dishes, stalling to the last. They heard Gary Owen, one of Hitchrack's three hands, come in from riding the break.

"Take *him*," Sherry said. "He's not afraid of the devil himself."

Baylor nodded.

"I'm going to Crowheart," Sherry said. "If Pierce still wants trouble with Baldray, it will start in town—except that I'll see it doesn't start." She rode away a little later, calling back, "So long, Bat-Ears. Be careful down there."

Owen's brown face tightened when he heard the "down there." He was standing at the corral with Baylor. "You headed into the Ghost?" he asked.

"Tonight."

"Saw two men on the Snake Hip Trail today, a long ways off." Owen removed his dun Scotch cap, replaced it. He lit a short-stemmed pipe. "Want me to go along?" He forced it out.

Baylor tried to be casual. "One man will do better, Gary."

"Say so, and I'll go!"

Baylor shook his head. They could not smooth it out with talk.

Three times the ranchers had gone over the escarpment in daylight, ready for full-scale battle. On the second try they had found horse tracks leading away from cattle bunched for a drive through the West Wall. Crosby claimed the rustlers had a man in the basin at all times, watching the break. Baylor thought so, too. But the idea had been lost in the general distrust of each other after the third failure.

Baylor was not thinking of men as the neck of the dun sloped away from him on this night descent in the huge puddle of waiting blackness. The night and Big Ghost were working on him long before he reached the first stream in the basin.

He stopped, listening. The tiny fingers of elementary fear began to test for climbing holds along the crevices of Baylor's brain. He swung in the saddle, and when he put his pistol away he told himself that he was a fool.

Shroud moss hanging across the trail touched his face. He tore at it savagely in the instant before he gained control. He came from the trees into the first park. War Dance Creek was running on his right, sullenly, without splash or leap.

All the streams down here were like that. Imagination, Baylor argued. He had come over the break unseen. The moss proved he was the first one down the trail in some time. *The first rider, maybe. What is behind you now?* Before he could stop himself, he whirled so quickly he startled the dun.

Back there was blackness, utter quiet. He strained to see, and his imagination prodded him. There was cold sweat on his face. He cursed himself for cowardice.

Where the trail crossed the creek, he would turn into dense timber and stake out for the night. He was here, safe. There was nothing he could do tonight. In the morning. . . .

It was night when the Thing got Paxton. . . .

The dun's right forefoot made a sucking sound. The animal stumbled. There was no quick jar of the saddle under Baylor, and he knew, even as he kicked free and jumped, that the stumble had been nothing, that the horse had bent its knee to recover balance before he was clear of leather.

Baylor stood in the wet grass, shaken by the realization of how deeply wound with fear he was. The dun nosed him questioningly. He patted the trim, warm neck and mounted again. If there were anything behind him, the dun wold be uneasy.

"*. . . there are strange things that will never be explained, Bay-*

lor. . . ." Baldray had said that in the Shoshone, and now Baylor was sure he had not been mocking him or trying to plant an idea.

Baylor spent the night sitting against a tree, with his blankets draped around him. The dun was tied on the other side of the tree. Baylor's carbine was close at hand, lying on the sheepskin of the saddle skirts. The carbine was too small of caliber, Baylor thought, too small for what he was looking for. What *was* he looking for?

Out of the dead silence, from the ancient, waiting forest, came another chilling question. *What is looking for you, Baylor?*

The night walked slowly, on cold feet. It passed at last. Baylor rose stiffly. He ate roast beef from his sack, and finished with a cold boiled potato. Raven was the only other man he knew who liked a cold spud. Raven had come to the Crowheart country just about the time cattle rustling began in earnest, after a long period of inactivity.

The nameless fears that had passed were now replaced with the suspicions of the conscious mind.

Early sunlight was killing dew when Baylor rode into Battleground Park. He picked up the tracks of Sherry's little mare, coming into the park from the Snake Hip Trail. Owen had seen two riders on the Snake Hip the day before, but there was no sign that they had come this far. He followed Sherry's trail straight to where Paxton had been killed.

Baylor studied the earth mound over the fire site. It was too smooth, and so was the torn ground around it; and yet, the earth scars still spoke of power and fury and compulsion. An ant hill made a bare spot in the grass not fifteen feet away. Paxton would have used that. Because of the nature of his business here he would have had it figured in advance.

Baylor picked up a tip cluster of pine needles. He stared at the spruces. Their lower branches were withered, but here was broken freshness from high above. He went slowly among the trees close to the fire site. Here and there Paxton had broken dead limbs for his fire, but there was no evidence that anything had come down from the high branches.

He tossed the tip cluster away and went south of the camp to the rich, brown mark of a rotted log. There were Sherry's tracks again, but no moccasin print.

Out in the grass the dun whirled up-trail. Baylor drew his pistol and stepped behind a tree. A little later Baldray, wearing a fringed buckskin shirt, rode into the park with Doc Raven.

"We knew your horse," Raven said. He was wearing Shoshone moccasins, Baylor observed.

Baldray's face turned bone-bleak when he saw a jumper fragment on a bush. "Oh! This is the place, eh?" He swung down easily. "Let's have a look, Raven."

The doctor moved briskly. "The devil!" he muttered. "See how the fire has been covered." His smooth, pink face was puzzled. He picked up the piece of jumper. "Good Lord!"

Baldray's heel struck the tip cluster of pine needles and punched them into the soft earth. "Did you discover anything, Baylor?"

"Nothing." Baylor shook his head. Raven's saddlebags appeared to be already filled with rocks. Gary Owen said the doctor started at the escarpment and tried to haul half the country with him every time he went out. "You fellows came down the Snake Hip?"

Raven was studying tree burls. "We started in yesterday," he said, "but I had forgotten a manual I needed, so we rode out last evening." He looked at Baldray. "You know, James, in the big burn along the cliffs I've seen jackpine seeds completely embedded in the trunks. I have a theory—"

"Rocks, this time," Baldray said. "If you want to look at that quartz on the West Wall before night you'd better forget the tree seeds." He blinked. "Tree seeds? Now isn't that odd?"

When the two men rode west, Baylor stared at their backs, not knowing just what he thought.

Baylor spent the day working the edges of the swamps along lower War Dance. Cattle were wallowing everywhere. He was nagged by not knowing what he was looking for; he had expected to find some sign where Paxton had been killed, at least the moccasin track.

At sunset he came out in the big burn. Several years before, Indians had thrown firebrands from the cliffs to start a fire to drive game from the basin. The wind had veered, and the fire, instead of crowning across the basin, had roared along the cliffs in a mile-wide swath. That cured the Indians. Evil spirits, they said, had blown a mighty breath to change the wind.

With the bare cliffs at his back, Baylor looked across the spear points of the trees. The parks were green islands, the largest being Battleground Park, where Paxton had died. The Wall was far to his right, a red granite barrier that appeared impassable; but there were breaks in it, he knew, the holes where Crowheart cattle seeped away.

About a half-mile air-line a gray horse came to the edge of one of the emerald parks. Bill Paxton had ridden a gray into Big Ghost. Kreider had brought out only the rig.

Once down in the timber, it took an hour of steady searching before Baylor found the right park. The limping gray knee-high in grass was Paxton's horse, all right. It saw Baylor when he led the dun from the timber. It snorted and broke like a wild animal for cover. There was never a chance to catch it.

Baylor recoiled his rope, listening to the gray crashing away like a frightened elk. The horse had not been here long enough to go mustang. The terror of the night the Thing had got Bill Paxton was riding on the gray.

Night was coming now. Gloom was crouched among the trees. The little golden sounds of day were dead. *You are afraid, Big Ghost said. You will be like Paxton's horse if you stay here.*

Baylor went through a neck of timber between parks. In the dying light on lower War Dance he cut his own trail of the morning. Beside the dun's tracks, in the middle of a mud bar, he saw a round imprint. He hung low in the saddle to look. A man wearing moccasins had been on his trail. Here the man had leaped halfway across the mud bar, putting down only the toes and the ball of one foot to gain purchase for another jump to where the grass left no mark. The foot had slid a trifle forward when it struck, and so there was no way to estimate how large—or small—it had been.

Baylor was relieved. He could deal with a man, even one who used Indian tricks like that. If this fellow wanted to play hide-and-seek, Baylor would take him on—and catch him in the end, and find out why the man had erased the track that Sherry had seen.

Dog-tired, he made a cold camp far enough from War Dance so that the muttering water would not cover close sounds. He freed the dun to graze, ate a cold meal, and rolled up in his blankets. A wind ran through the timber.

Baylor rolled a smoke, and then he crumpled it. The scent of tobacco smoke would drift a long way to guide a man creeping in. *No man killed Paxton or the others.*

Baylor lay wide awake, straining at the darkness, for a long time, until finally he slept from sheer exhaustion.

The morning sun was a wondrous friend. Baylor slopped the icy water of the stream against his face. The dun came from the wet grass and greeted him.

He rode south, then swung toward the Wall, crossing parks he had never seen before. He took it slowly, not watching his backtrail. In the middle of the day, after crossing a park just like a dozen others, he dismounted in the timber and crept back to make a test.

For an hour he waited behind a windfall. The first sound came, the breaking of a stick on the other side of the tiny green spot. Baylor had been half dozing by then. Too easy, he thought; something was wrong. He heard hooves on the needle mat.

He had expected a man on foot. He crawled away and ran back to the dun, placing one hand on its nose, ready for the gentle pressure that would prevent a whinny. A little later he heard sounds off to his left. The man was going around, sticking to the timber. Slowly Baylor led his horse to intercept the sounds. The other man came slowly also, and then Baylor caught the movement of a sorrel, saw an outline of its rider.

He dropped the reins then and went in as quickly as he could. He made noise. The dun whinnied. The other rider hit the ground. A carbine blasted, funneling pulp from a tree ahead of Baylor. He shot toward the sound with his pistol. The sorrel reared, then bolted straight ahead.

It flashed across a relatively open spot. It was Pierce Paxton's stallion. "Oh, God!" Baylor muttered. "Pierce."

"Pierce!" he yelled.

There was silence before the answer came. "Baylor?" It was Pierce Paxton. He was unshaven, red-eyed.

He said, "Who the hell did you think you were trying to take!"

Baylor put his pistol away. "Moccasin Joe. Who were you shooting at?"

"Anybody that tried to close in on me like that!" Tenseness was still laid flat on Paxton's thin features. "Who's Moccasin Joe?"

Baylor told everything he knew about the man.

Paxton shook his head, staring around him at the trees. "It's not Raven. I've been watching him and Baldray from the time they went across Agate Park."

"Why?"

Paxton stared. "You know why." He rubbed his hand across his eyes. "I think maybe I was wrong. We lost two men down here, Baylor, but Baldray and Raven never had any trouble. Now I know why. They got a cabin hidden in the rocks near the wall. They don't stay out in the open." Paxton saw the quick suspicion on Baylor's face.

"Uh-huh, I thought so too, at first, Ken. I thought they knew what's loose down here, that they were hooked up with the rustlers. I watched them for a day and a half. All they did was pound quartz rock and laugh like two kids. They may be crazy, Baylor, but I don't think they're hooked up with the rustlers."

Paxton rubbed his eyes again. "Made a fool of myself the other day, didn't I? What did Sherry say?"

"Nothing much. We both made fools of ourselves a minute ago, Pierce. . . . Let's catch your horse."

The stallion had stopped in the next park west. Paxton went in and towed the horse back on the run. It saw the dun and tried to break over to start trouble. Paxton sawed down brutally on the bit before he got the horse quieted. That was not like Paxton. The nights down here had worked on his nerves, too.

They went back in the timber and sprawled out. Paxton lay with his hands over his face.

"How you fixed for grub?" Baylor asked.

"Ran out yesterday." Paxton heard Baylor rustling in his gunny sack. "I'm not hungry." But he finally ate, and he kept looking sidewise at Baylor until he asked, "You've been here two nights?"

"Yeah."

"Any trouble?"

"Scared myself some," Baylor said. "Did you?"

"I didn't have to. Since the first night I spent here I've been jumping three feet every time a squirrel cut loose. I had a little fire on Hellion Creek that night, with a couple of hatfuls of wet sand, just in case."

Paxton had started with a defensive edge to his voice, but now it was gone and his bloodshot eyes were tight. "The stallion just naturally raised hell. He got snarled up on his picket rope and almost paunched himself on a snag. I got him out of that and then I doused the fire.

"From the way the horse moved and pointed, I knew something was prowling. It went all around the camp, and once I heard it brush a tree."

The hackles on Baylor's neck were up.

"You know how a lion will do that," Paxton said. He shook his head. "No lion. The next morning, in some fresh dirt where a squirrel had been digging under a tree, I saw a track"—Paxton put his hands side by side—"like that, Ken. No pads—just a big mess!" Paxton's hands were shaking.

"What was it, Baylor? The Thing that got Bill?"

The Thing. What else could a man call it? Baylor thought. He said, "There's an explanation to everything."

"Explain it then!"

"Take it easy, Pierce. We'll get it."

The thought of action always helped steady Paxton. "How?" he asked.

"First, we get this Moccasin Joe." Baylor thought of something so clear he wondered how he had missed it. "Did you stop in Battleground Park?"

"I didn't come down the Snake Hip."

"Old Moccasin Joe has trailed me once, and now I think I know why." The thought carried a chill. "Here's what we'll do, Paxton. . . ."

Later, Baylor divided the food. It would be parched corn now, and jerky, about enough for two days, if a man did not care how hungry he got. "Day after tomorrow," Baylor said.

They rode away in different directions, Baylor going back to Battleground Park. He found the tip-cluster that Baldray had stepped on, and dug it out of the earth and held it only a moment before dropping it again. Pine needles. Everything here was spruce. The fact had not registered the first time.

That tip cluster had come from a branch that Moccasin Joe had used to brush out sign. Probably he had carried the branch from across the creek. Moccasin Joe knew what the Thing was. He was covering up for it.

The dun whinnied. Baldray was riding into the lower end of the park. He veered over when he say Baylor's horse.

"You haven't moved!" Baldray grinned to show he was joking. He was clean-shaven. He appeared rested, calm. That came easier when a man slept in a cabin and ate his fill, Baylor thought.

"You look done in," Baldray said.

"I'm all right."

Baldray squinted at the fringes of his beaded shirt. His face began to redden. "It's no good sleeping out. Bumps and things, you know. I have a cabin near the Wall. Built it four years ago. Raven's there now. I wish you'd use it, Baylor. I'll tell you how to find it."

Paxton had taken care of that. "I know," Baylor said.

Baldray blinked. "Oh!" He raised pale brows. "Well, yes, I've been a little selfish. Reservation land, so-called. If the fact got around that someone had built here—"

Baylor picked up the tip cluster. "What kind of tree is that from?"

Baldray squinted. "Evergreen."

"Spruce or pine?"

The Englishman laughed. "You and Raven! I know evergreen from canoe birch, but that's about all."

Baldray was one Englishman who had not run for home after the big die-ups of the no-chinook years. He should know pine needles from spruce; but maybe he did not.

Baldray's face was stone-serious when he asked, "Any luck?"

Baylor shook his head.

"There are harsh thoughts about me." Baldray's voice was crisp. "Fifteen years here and I'm still not quite a resident, except with you and Crosby." Baldray looked around the park. "This won't be reservation always. Room for I.O.T. down here, as well as the rest —once the rustlers are dealt with, and the government sees the light."

Baldray slouched in the saddle, rolling a cigarette. "I have watched the breaks in the Wall from the rocks near my cabin. There is a sort of pattern to the way the scoundrels come and go. I would say, Baylor— it is a guess, but I would say—the next raid might be due to go out through Windy Trail."

His smoke rolled and lit, Baldray started away. "Windy Trail. I'm going to tell Crosby, some of the others. Good name, Crosby. English, you know."

He rode away.

It was not entirely hunger that made Baylor's stomach tighten as he rode across the burn the next afternoon. Like the others, the night before had been a bad one, with his mind and the deep, still forests speaking to him. He did not know now whether or not he was being trailed, but he had played the game all the way, and if Paxton had done his part, things might come off as planned.

Paxton was there, crouched in the rocks near the east side of the burn. They exchanged clothes behind the jumble of fire-chipped stone.

"I went out," Paxton said. "Sherry wants to see you tomorrow morning in Battleground Park."

"Why didn't you talk her out of it?"

"You know better." Paxton was stuffing paper under the sweatband of Baylor's hat.

"What does she want?"

"I don't know. She told me to go to hell when I ordered her not to come down here. Then she rode over to I.O.T. to see Baldray. I left a note in the bunkhouse for Gary Owen to come here with her."

They were dressed.

"Keep in plain sight on the burn," Baylor said. "And keep going."

"All right." Paxton took the reins. "Kullhem found out that Kreider was riding with the rustlers on the west prairie two weeks ago."

"Fine. Just right. Get going."

He watched Paxton ride away, past the black snags and leaning trees. The dun had gone into the rocks and the dun had gone out a few minutes later, and the rider was dressed exactly as he had been when going in. It might work, if Moccasin Joe was still trailing with his little pine-branch broom. The dirty bastard.

The sun died behind the red Wall. A wind came down across the rocks and stirred the tiny jackpines in the burn. Murk crept into basin.

The man came from sparse timber at the east edge of the burn.

Buckskins. Probably moccasins. Long yellow hair under a slouch hat. He paused and looked up where the dun had disappeared two hours before.

Baylor watched from a crack between the rocks. The man came clear, lifting his body easily over fallen trees. He walked straight at the rocks, then swung a little to the uphill side. Baylor drew his pistol and took a position behind a rock where the man would likely pass.

The steps were close, just around the rock. They stopped. With his stomach sucked in, breathing through a wide-open mouth, Baylor waited to fit the next soft scrape to the man's position. Silence pinched at nerve ends before the fellow moved again.

In two driving steps Baylor went around the rock. He was just a fraction late, almost on top of a beard-matted face, two startled eyes and that tangle of yellow hair. He swung the pistol.

Moccasin Joe went back like a cat, clutching a knife in his belt. Baylor's blow missed. The pistol rang on rock, and by then the knife was coming clear. Baylor drove in with his shoulder turned. The knife was coming down when the shoulder caught the man at the throat lacing of his shirt.

Baylor was on top when they went down. He got the knife arm then, and suddenly threw all his power into a side push. The man's hand went against the rock. Baylor began to grind it along the granite.

The rock was running red before Moccasin Joe dropped the knife. With the explosive strength of a deer, he arched his body, throwing Baylor sidewise against the rock. One of the man's knees doubled back like a trap spring, then the foot lashed out and knocked Baylor away.

Moccasin Joe leaped up. He did not run. He dived in. Baylor caught him with a heeled hand under the chin. The man's head snapped back but his weight came on. A knee struck Baylor in the groin.

Sick with the searing agony of it, Baylor grabbed the long hair with both hands. He kept swinging Moccasin Joe's head into the rock until there was no resistance but limp weight.

For several moments Baylor lay under the weight, grinding his teeth in pain; and then he pushed free, straightening up by degrees, stabbing his feet against the ground. The front sight of his pistol was smeared, the muzzle burred, and maybe the barrel was bent a little.

But he had the man who was going to tell him what was killing ranch scouts in Big Ghost Basin. Except for the knife, Moccasin Joe had carried no other weapon. Baylor cut the fellow's belt and tied his hands behind him. Blood was smeared in the tangled yellow hair.

Baylor had never seen him before.

Going down the burn, the prisoner was wobbly, but he was walking steadily enough before they reached the park, where Paxton was to come soon after dark. It was almost dark now. Just inside the timber Baylor made Joe lie down, then tied his ankles with Paxton's belt.

Firelight was a blessed relief after black, cold nights. "The first man killed here was one of yours, Joe," Baylor said. "You boys got on to something that makes it impossible for us to keep a man here. What is it?"

After a long silence Baylor removed one of his prisoner's moccasins. The man's eyes rolled as he stared at the fire. Baylor squatted by the flames, turning the knife slowly in the heat until the thin edge of the blade was showing dull red.

Where the hell was Pierce Paxton?

"Put out the fire," Moccasin Joe said.

"Talk some more." Baylor kept turning the blade. "That first man was one of yours, wasn't he?"

"Yeah." Moccasin Joe was beginning to sweat. The skin above his beard was turning dirty yellow.

Baylor lifted his knife to let him see it.

"Your Thing has got us stopped," Baylor said. "What is it?"

The firelight ran on a growing fear in the captive's eyes. He started to speak, and then he lay back.

"First, the flat of the blade against the bottom of your arch, then the point between the hock and the tendon. I'll reheat each time, of course." Even to Baylor his own words seemed to carry conviction.

"Put the fire out!"

Baylor lifted the knife again. The blade was bright red. "I saw Teton Sioux do this once," he lied calmly.

Moccasin Joe's breath was coming hard.

"You covered up something where Paxton was killed, didn't you? And then you checked back and wiped out a track of your own that you had overlooked."

"Yeah."

"Keep talking."

"I want a smoke. I won't tell you anything until I get a smoke!"

Baylor stared at the tangled face, at the terror in the man's eyes. For a customer as tough as this one had proved up in the rocks, he was softening pretty fast under a torture bluff.

Baylor laid the knife where the blade would stay hot. He rolled two smokes and lit them. He put one in Moccasin Joe's mouth.

"You got to untie my hands."

"You can smoke without that."

The cigarette stuck to the captive's lips. He tried to roll it free and it fell into his beard. He jerked his head back and the smoke fell on the ground. Baylor put it back in the man's mouth. He untied the fellow's hands.

Moccasin Joe sat up and puffed his cigarette, rolling his shoulders.

"Let's have it," Baylor said.

"The bunch that's been raiding here ain't the one from the west prairie, like you think. We been hanging out on the regular reservation. The agent is getting his cut."

It sounded like a quickly made-up lie. "Is Kreider one of the bunch?"

The captive hesitated. "Sure."

"Describe him."

Moccasin Joe did that well enough.

"What killed Paxton?"

"Which one was he?"

"The last one-in Battleground Park."

"I'll tell you." Moccasin Joe made sucking sounds, trying to get smoke from a dead cigarette.

Baylor took a twig from the fire. He leaned down. The captive's hands came up from his lap like springs. They clamped behind Baylor's neck and jerked. At the same time Moccasin Joe ducked his own head. Baylor came within an ace of getting his face smashed against hard bone.

He spread his hands between his face and the battering block just in time. Even so, he felt his nose crunch, and it seemed that every tooth in his mouth was loosened. He was in a crouch then, and Moccasin Joe's thumbs were digging at his throat. Baylor drove his right knee straight ahead.

Moccasin Joe's hands loosened. He fell back without a sound.

Baylor stood there rubbing his knee. He could not stand on the leg for a while. The sensitive ligaments above the cap had struck squarely on the point of Moccasin Joe's jaw.

Once more Baylor cinched the man's arms tight behind his back. Let him die for want of a smoke. Blood dripped into the fire as Baylor put on more wood. He stared at the red hot knife, wishing for just an instant that he was callous enough to use it.

Where in hell is Paxton? he thought.

Blood began to stream down his lips. He felt his way to the creek and washed his face and dipped cold water down the back of his neck. After a while the bleeding stopped. Both sides of his nose were swollen so tight he could not breathe through them. His lips were cut.

I'm lucky, he told himself, getting out with only a busted nose after falling for an old gag like that.

You're not out of it yet, Baylor. It's night again.

Once more the old voices of Big Ghost were running in his mind. Baylor dipped Paxton's hat full of water and went back to the fire and Moccasin Joe.

"Sit up if you want a drink."

It was a struggle for Moccasin Joe but he made it. His eyes were still a little hazy, but clear enough to look at Baylor with hatred.

Baylor took the knife from the fire and stood over his captive, tapping his boot against the man's bare foot. Moccasin Joe looked at the glowing steel, and then at Baylor. His eyes showed no fear.

"You ain't got the guts."

The bluff was no good. Baylor drove the knife into the ground near the fire. "I've got guts enough to help hang you," he said. "We know you're one of the rustlers, and we know you've been doing chores for the Thing in the basin that's killed our men. Better loosen up, Joe."

"My name ain't Joe."

"That won't make any difference when you swing."

"Talk away, cowboy."

He's not afraid of me, Baylor thought, but it's up in his neck because of what he knows is out there.

It's out there, the night said.

Paxton should be coming. He should have been here an hour ago.

He went to the edge of the park, listening for the hoof sounds of the dun. There was nothing on the park but ancient night and aching quiet. Grunting sounds and the cracking of twigs sent Baylor running back to the fire. Moccasin Joe was trying to get away, pushing himself by digging his heels into the ground. He had gone almost twenty feet.

Baylor hauled him back to the fire. The man's muscles were jerking. "They'll kill me," he said, "but that'll be the best way. Put out the fire. I'll tell you!"

"You've pulled a couple of fast ones already."

"Put it out!"

Brutal fear came like a bad odor from the man. Baylor's back was crawling. He turned toward the creek to get another hatful of water.

Twigs popped. Something thudded softly out in the forest.

"It's coming! Turn me loose!" Moccasin Joe's voice rose in a hoarse, quavering scream. "O Jesus . . ." And then he was silent.

Standing at the edge of firelight, with his bent-barrelled pistol in his hand, Baylor was in a cold sweat.

Paxton's voice came from the forest. "Baylor!"

"Here!" Baylor made two efforts before he got the pistol back in leather. By the time Paxton came in, leading the dun, Baylor's fear had turned to anger.

"Did you make another trip out to visit and have a shave!"

Paxton was in no light mood, either. His face was swelling from mosquito bites. He had clawed at them and smeared mud from his hairline to his throat. "I got bogged down in a stinking swamp! Lost your carbine there, too." He looked at Moccasin Joe. "I see you got—What ails him?"

Moccasin Joe's eyes were set, unseeing. His jaw was jerking and little strings of saliva were spilling into his beard.

Mice feet tracked on Baylor's spine. "Umm!" he said in a long breath. "He thought you were the Thing!"

"The Thing! Good God!" Paxton's eyes rolled white in his mud-smeared face. His voice dropped. "Your horse raised hell back there a minute ago."

The dun was shuddering now, its ears set toward the creek. It was ready to bolt. Paxton drew his pistol.

"Put that popgun away!" Baylor cried. "Help me get him on the horse!" He grabbed the knife and slashed the belt around Joe's ankles. "Stand up!"

The man rose obediently, numbly, his jaw still working. Paxton leaped to grab the dun's reins when the horse tried to bolt toward the park.

Baylor threw Moccasin Joe across the saddle of the plunging horse. "Lead the horse out of here!"

They crashed toward the park, with the horse fighting to get away, with Baylor fighting to keep Moccasin Joe across the saddle. The dun tried to bolt until they were in timber at the lower end of the park, and then it quieted.

"How far to the cabin where Raven is?" Baylor asked.

"Maybe four miles," Paxton answered. "I won't try no short cuts through a swamp this time." He laughed shakily.

They spoke but little as they moved through the deep night of Big Ghost Basin. Baylor walked behind now. Paxton broke off a limb and used it as a feeler overhead when they were in timber. Each time he said, "Limb!" they heard Moccasin Joe grunt a little as he ducked against the horn.

Baylor guessed it was well after midnight when Paxton stopped in the rocks and said, "It's close to here—some place. I'll go ahead and see."

Baylor was alone. He heard Paxton's footsteps fade into the rocks. The dun was droop-headed now. Moccasin Joe was a dark lump in the saddle.

Relief ran through Baylor when he heard the mumble of voices somewhere ahead, and presently Paxton came back. "The cabin is about a hundred yards from here. Raven's there."

Paxton took care of the dun. Raven and Baylor led the captive inside. Moccasin Joe was like a robot. Light from a brass Rivers lamp showed a four-bunk layout, with a large fireplace at one end. There was a shelf of books near the fireplace, and rock specimens scattered everywhere else.

Raven's hair was rumpled. He was in his undershirt and boots. His pink face was shining and his eyes were sharp. He looked at Moccasin Joe and said, "I thought *I* brought in specimens."

Moccasin Joe was staring.

Raven took the man's right hand and looked at the grated knuckles. He stood on tiptoe to peer at the marks where Baylor had banged Moccasin Joe's head against the rock.

"I roughed him up," Baylor said.

"You didn't hurt him." Raven passed his hand before the man's face. "Oregon! Oregon!" he said.

"Huh?" the man said dully.

"You know him?" Baylor asked.

"I saw him out on the west prairie a month ago, camped with a group of men. They called him that."

"Rustlers, huh?"

"Probably. I ride where I like. Nobody bothers me. I've doctored a man or two out that way, without asking his business."

"What's wrong with this one?" Baylor asked.

"Shock. His mind, roughly, is locked on something. Did you try to scare him to death?"

"Not me. Something scared the hell out of me, and Paxton, too. Maybe if we'd known what it was, we'd be like Mocc—Oregon"

Paxton came in. Raven glanced at his face. "Wash it off, and quit scratching the lumps, Paxton. Get some grease out of that jar there by the books." Raven motioned Oregon toward a chair. "Sit down there."

Doc Raven went to work. He cleansed and dressed Oregon's hand, and took care of the cuts on his head, shearing into the long hair with evident satisfaction. "Retire!" he muttered. "I've got so I don't go to an out-building without taking a medical kit along."

Raven was completely happy, Baylor thought.

"Help yourselves to the grub, boys," the doctor said.

Oregon ate mechanically, staring at Raven most of the time. When Raven was briskly directing him into a bunk afterward, the doctor asked casually, "Did Martin get over that dislocated shoulder all right?"

"Yeah," Oregon said. "Yeah, he's all right," and then his eyes slipped back to dullness once more.

Raven looked at Paxton and Baylor. "I think he'll be coming out of it after a night's rest. Go to bed. I'll just sit here and read."

"I don't want that man to get away," Baylor said. "He's going to tell me something in the morning."

Raven shook his head. "You won't get anything out of this one, Baylor. I probed two bullets out of his chest once, and he never made a peep."

Raven smiled at the suspicious stares of the two ranchers. "I'm a doctor," he said. "Retired." He laughed. "Now go to bed, both of you."

Raven was cooking when Baylor woke up. Paxton was still sound asleep. Oregon was lying in his bunk awake. There was complete awareness in his eyes when he looked at Baylor. Baylor said, "Ready to talk?"

"To hell with you," Oregon said.

Paxton woke up while Baylor was dressing. He took his pistol from under his blankets and walked across the room to Oregon. "That was my brother that was killed by your pet a few days ago."

"Too bad," Oregon said.

Paxton turned toward Baylor. "Let's stake this bastard out by a fire tonight—and leave him!"

"That's enough!" Raven's voice cut sharply. "Oregon is yours, but let's have no more of that kind of talk."

"What'll we do?" Paxton asked. "I want to go with you to meet Sherry this morning, and—" He glanced at Raven.

"You stay here," Baylor said. "I'll see Sherry. What the hell does she want?"

The first hot meal in several days was like water in a desert. After breakfast Baylor brought the dun from a barred enclosure where a spring made a green spot in the rocks.

Paxton grumped about being left to watch the prisoner. Sherry would take some of that out of him soon enough, after they were married, Baylor thought.

Baylor went inside for one last word with Oregon. "I know you lied about your bunch hanging out on the reservation. Oregon. How about Kreider?"

"You find out," Oregon said.

Baylor looked at Paxton.

"Don't fret," Paxton said. "I'll watch him, all right."

Raven walked outside with him. "I know how you boys feel, Baylor. Out here you try to make things all black or all white. There's shades between the two, Baylor. I don't defend Oregon. I don't condemn him. You understand?"

"I'm trying to."

"That helps. You want my rifle?"

"Carbine." Baylor shook his head. "Thanks, no."

Sherry and Gary Owen were waiting in Battleground Park when he reached there. It was close to where Bill Paxton had been killed.

"What happened to your nose?" Sherry asked.

"Froze it in the creek. Nice place you picked to meet me."

"Yeah." Owen looked toward the little mound that covered the fire site. "She picked it."

Sherry said, "Did you see anyone last night?"

"Pierce and me met a man, not socially, though. Who do you mean?"

"Any of the ranchers, tight-mouth. They came in last night, the crews from every outfit. Crosby and Baldray got them together. They're going to filter around and trap the rustlers tomorrow or the next day near the Wall."

"Baldray's idea?" Baylor asked.

Owen nodded. "Him and Kreider."

"Kreider!"

"He's a special agent of the Indian Department," Owen said. "He was sent here to investigate a rumor that the rustlers were operating from reservation land. For a while he was in solid with them. From what we gathered, he's got a chum still with the bunch on the west prairie, and that fellow tipped Kreider off about the next raid."

The rustlers must have caught on to Kreider, Baylor thought. That was why Oregon had been so willing to identify him as one of the gang. Tomorrow or the next day. . . . Plenty of time for what Baylor had to do. He looked at a .45-90 Winchester in Owen's saddle boot.

"I'd like to borrow your rifle, Gary."

"I brought one for you," Sherry said. She walked into the grass and returned with a double-barreled weapon.

Baylor hefted the piece. "One of Baldray's."

"Elephant gun," Sherry said. "A .577, whatever that is." She gave her brother, one by one, a half-dozen cartridges. "Pierce told me he saw the track of something down here that scared him. Where is Pierce?"

His sister was quite a woman, Baylor thought. He told her and

Owen about capturing Oregon. "I figure it will be easier to get a line on this Thing, now that Oregon is out of the way."

Owen stared at the timber edges of the park. "Thing," he muttered. "I'll stay with you, Ken."

"Take Sherry back to the benches—"

"I know the way," Sherry said. "You know something? Kreider says there's a bill going into the next Congress to make Big Ghost public land again."

"Owen's taking you back to the benches," Baylor said.

"You know who got action started on that bill?" Sherry asked. "Jim Baldray."

"Yeah," Owen said. "Even Kullhem admits now that he must have had the wrong idea about Baldray. I'll stay down here with you, Ken."

"The two of you work well together," Baylor said, "changing the subject, throwing me off. All right, get out of here, Sherry, and be sure you're good and out before night."

The girl got on her horse. Her face was pale under its tan. "Don't depend entirely on that elephant gun, Ken. Get up in a tree, or something."

"I figured on that," Baylor said. "So long, Red."

The two men watched until she disappeared into the timber at the upper end of Battleground Park.

"Fighting rustlers don't scare me no more than a man's got a right to be scared," Owen said abruptly. He dug out his short-stemmed pipe and lit it. "But after I saw Paxton—and them other two, I'll admit I didn't have the guts to come down here at night. Now I'm here, I'll stay."

Baylor was glad to have him—with that big-bored Winchester.

"I don't know what we're after," Baylor said. "But maybe in a couple of hours we'll know. Come on."

They went back in the timber, and stayed out of sight until they came to the park below the burn, the place where Baylor had built his fire the night before. The memory of the night began to work on Baylor.

He felt a chill when he saw that the fire he and Paxton had left burning in their quick retreat had been covered with a great heap of dirt and needles. There were long marks in the torn ground, but no sharp imprints. The story was there. The fire had kept on smoldering under the first weight of dirt and dry forest mat, and the Thing had continued to throw dirt in a savage frenzy until the smoke had ceased. Fire. That was the magnet.

Owen sucked nervously on his pipe, staring. "What done it?"

Baylor shook his head. "Let's try the soft ground by the creek." They stood on the east bank. Baylor stared at the choke of willows and trees on the other side. Last night he had dipped water from this very spot, and over there somewhere the Thing had been pacing, circling, working up to coming in. It must have been quite close when he threw Oregon at the dun and ran in terror.

Night will come again, the voices said.

Baylor and Owen stayed close together while they searched. Farther up the stream they found where the Thing had leaped the creek in one bound. Four imprints in the muddy bank.

"I'll be dipped in what!" There was a little fracture in Owen's voice. "That ain't no track of nothing I ever seen!"

The outlines were mushy. The mud was firm, but still there was no clear definition of form. The whole thing was a patchwork of bumps and ridges that would not fit any living creature Baylor had ever seen or heard of. "That's no bear," he said.

"Back in Ireland my grandmother used to scare us. . . ." Owen shook his head.

On a limb snag across the creek they found a small patch of short, brittle hair with a scab scale clinging to it.

"There ain't nothing in the world with hair like that!" Owen cried.

Here with the shroud moss motionless on gray limbs, in the ancient stillness of Big Ghost, Baylor was again prey to fear of the Unknown, and for a moment there was no civilization because nothing fitted previous experience.

"The rustlers have seen it," he said. "Oregon said it got one of their men. They wouldn't have covered up for it if they hadn't been afraid we might recognize the sign." He stared at Owen. "Fire, Gary. Fire is what brings it!"

"I been here at night—with fire." Owen hunched his shoulders.

"It's a big hole. A man might be lucky here for a long time, and then one night. . . . Where are the ranchers going to meet?"

"They'll camp out in little bunches on those timbered hogbacks that point toward the West Wall. When they see Crosby's smoke signal from the Wall—"

"We've got to warn them, Gary. Orahood never spent a night out in his life without building a fire. Get down there and pass the word—no fires!"

"That leaves you alone."

"I've been several nights alone. Take the dun with you. I don't want him hurt."

"Holy God, Ken! You don't want the dun hurt, but you—"

"Stick to the timber, Gary, so you won't mess up their trap."

Baylor took both ropes from the saddles. Ready to leave, Owen said, "Take my rifle. That elephant business only shoots twice."

"I'll do better than that, from where I'll be. Tonight you'll like the feel of that big barrel across your knees, Gary."

"Don't scare me. I already know I'm a damned coward. I *want* to leave here. I'll admit it." Owen rode away.

Baylor did not like to admit how alone he felt.

Big Ghost nights always seemed to settle as if they had special purpose in making the basin a black hole. From his platform of laced rope between two limbs of a spruce tree, Baylor peered down to where his pile of wood was ready for a match. He had pulled in other fuel close to the site, enough to keep a fairly large fire all night.

It was about time to light it. The sooner the better. The smoke would make a long trail through the forest, the flames a little bright spot in the murk, and this Thing that must kill fire might be attracted. It would be a cinch from here.

A cinch? Maybe the Thing climbs trees.

Baylor climbed down and lit the fire. He waited just long enough to know that it would burn, and then he climbed again to his rope perch.

The blackness laughed at his haste.

Smoke came up between the ropes and began to choke him. That was a point he had not thought of at all; but presently the fire took hold in earnest, light reached out to touch the gray holes of waiting trees, and a small wind began to drift the smoke at a lower level.

Baylor tried to settle comfortably against the ropes. The sling of the heavy double-barrel was over a limb above him, so the weapon could not fall. The four spare cartridges were buttoned in the breast pocket of his jumper. He felt the cold, big roundness of them when he took out the makings of a cigarette.

It was as dark as a pocket up in the tree. For a while the oddness of being where he was intrigued Baylor, and then he thought of a dozen flaws in his plan. But if it did not work tonight, he would stay with it until it did. He reached over to touch the .577. The four spare cartridges did not count. He had two shots coming. They should be enough.

Bill Paxton's forty-five was empty when Kreider found him.

The night lagged. Big Ghost gathered all its secrets to it, and the darkness whispered. Three times Baylor went down to put wood on the fire. Each time he took the heavy rifle, and each time his flesh crawled until he was back on the rope net once more.

He smoked all his tobacco. Thirst started. He listened to the creek. It was not very far.

Go get yourself a drink, Baylor.

He tried not to listen. His thirst grew out of all proportions, and he knew it was not real. He could not be thirsty; he had drunk just before dark.

Get yourself a drink. Don't be a fool.

He waited until the fire needed wood. After building it up, he stood a moment by the tree, with one hand on the rope that led to safety.

Go on, Baylor. Are you afraid to get a drink?

The water was icy cold against the sweat on his face. He drank from cupped hands, then wiped them on his jumper, staring at the blackness across the creek. Last night the Thing had been somewhere out there. It might be there now.

He took two steps toward the fire. Something splashed in the water behind him. He was cocking the gun and swinging around all the time he knew the splash had come from a muskrat.

For a few moments he stood drying his hands over the heat, a little gesture of striking back at the Unknown. But when he started up the tree he went all the way with a rush.

In the cold hours long after midnight he was on the ground tending the fire when he heard a soft sound beyond the limits of the light. He unslung the rifle and felt the thumping of his heart.

It's there. It's watching you.

He turned toward the tree. He heard the crush of dry pine needles. He cocked the gun and backed toward the tree, feeling behind him for the rope. Something moved on the edge of firelight. An enormous, shadowy form emerged from blackness. It rocked from side to side. A hoarse roar enveloped Baylor.

He fired the right barrel, and then the left. The Thing came in, bellowing. Straight across the fire it charged, scattering embers. Baylor had another cartridge out, but he dropped it and clubbed the rifle. He was completely stripped now of all the thinking of evolved and civilized man.

The bellowing became a strangled grunt. The Thing was down, its hind legs in the flames. It tried to crawl toward Baylor, and then it was still. Baylor rammed another cartridge in and fired a third shot. The great bulk took the fearful impact without stirring.

Cordite rankness was in Baylor's nostrils as he kicked embers back toward the fire and put on fuel with shaking hands. The stench of burning hair sickened him. He pulled the flames away from the hind legs of the beast.

He had known what he was up against from the moment the animal had stood higher than a horse there on the edge of firelight, then dropped to the ground to charge. He had killed a grizzly bear.

When the flames were high he examined it. The feet were huge, misshapen, lacking the divisions of pads. All four were tortured, scrambled flesh that had fused grotesquely after being cruelly burned. Along the back and on one side of the bear were scabby patches where the hair had come back crisp and short. Around the mouth the flesh was lumpy, hideous from scar tissue. The jaws had been seared so terribly that the fangs and front teeth had dropped out.

He lifted one of the forelegs with both hands. There were traces of claws, some ingrown, the others, brittle, undeveloped fragments.

The forest fire several years before! The bear had been a cub then, or perhaps half grown. The poor devil, caught by the flames, probably against the rocks, since only one side was scarred. He pictured it whimpering as it covered its face with its forepaws. And then, when it could no longer stand the pain and fear, it must have gone loping wildly across the burning forest mat.

Before it recovered it must have been a skinny, tortured brute. No wonder it had gone crazy afterward at the smell and sight of flames.

He found one of his bullet holes in the throat. That had to be the first shot, when the grizzly had been erect. The other must be in the shoulder that was underneath, and it would take a horse and rope to make sure. He cut into a lump on the shoulder that was up. Just a few inches below the tough hide, under the fat, he found a .45 bullet. One of Bill Paxton's, probably.

That was enough examination. The poor, damned thing.

He was asleep by a dead fire when the savage crackling of gunfire roused him shortly after dawn. He sat up quickly. The firing ran furiously, somewhere near the Wall. Then the sounds dwindled to single cracks, at intervals. A little later Big Ghost was quiet.

Baylor hoped there was truth in what Owen had said about the basin going back to range. For the first time in days he heard the wakening sounds of birds. Before, he had been listening for something else.

He was asleep in the sun out in the park when the clatter roused him. The ranchers were coming out. Kullhem, his left arm in a sling, was riding with Baldray in the lead. Farther back, a man was tarpaulin-draped across his saddle.

Owen and Paxton spurred ahead to Baylor, who pointed toward the tarpaulin.

"Orahood," Owen said. "The only man we lost."

Baylor was stabbed by the thought of Orahood's wife alone at Sky Hook, with a baby coming on.

Paxton said, "We caught 'em foul on Windy Trail! We broke their backs!"

"Oregon?" Baylor asked.

"He tried one of his little tricks."

Owen kept looking toward the forest.

"It's there," Baylor said wearily.

Men gathered around the grizzly.

"Good Lord!" Crosby kept saying. "Would you look at the size of that!"

"That must have been a spot of fun, eh, Baylor?" Baldray frowned, not satisfied with his words. "You know I mean a narrow place—a tight one."

Raven was all around the bear, like a fly. "Unusually fine condition," he mused. "How did he get food while he was recovering from those burns?"

"He healed himself in a swamp," Kullhem growled. "There's always cows and calves bogged down in the swamps."

"A remarkable specimen, nonetheless." Raven drew a sheath

knife. "I'll have a look at that stomach and a few other organs." He hesitated. "Your bear, of course, Baylor. You don't mind?"

"Yeah." Baylor shook his head slowly. "Leave him be, Raven. The poor devil suffered enough when he was alive."

Raven stood up reluctantly. He put his knife away. "I guess I understand."

Baldray's bony face showed that he understood. "Fire killer," he said. "The poor damned beast."

The Man at Gantt's Place

With the time at hand for the actual break, Lew Gantt was a little nervous. He did not return to the wild-horse corral after dinner to continue replacing posts that old Stump had chalked as unsound. Work was all there ever had been around this place–fix something before it busted, get ready for winter, get ready for summer, scatter grass seed from heck to breakfast, push yourself into old age by trying to look ahead so blamed far.

Lew was seventeen and one day. He had waited the one day so Stump could not say it was because of his birthday. He went down to where Stump was watching Railroad Costigan lead a big, wall-eyed bay gelding around the breaking corral.

Stump did not ask why Lew was loafing. He did not even look at his son, and that made Lew more uneasy. Old Stump just stood there watching Railroad and the bay, and after a while he said, "Try a blanket on him, Railroad."

The gelding did not like the blanket, and Costigan had a devil of a time. The way to break horses was to top 'em off and show 'em who was boss, and get things done without a lot of fooling around. But no, Lew's father would rather get six mounts half gentled in two weeks than break a whole corralful in a week; he did everything that way.

Old Stump had just been too long up here in the hills, looking down at Revelation Valley, where they did things with a bang. He was pretty old, all right—anyway past forty, Lew figured. He studied his father from the side. Not a very big man at all, but he was pretty tightly put together. He didn't care much what he wore, even a patch on the seat of his pants. His mouth was sort of tight, and he did not use it much.

He shaved every morning. He never leaned or sprawled all over things, like Lew was doing right now. He favored a bench to sit on, or a stool. Chairs with backs made men without backbones, Stump always said.

Lew knew plenty about his father, and none of it was very interesting. Lew put both feet on the ground.

"Work him until he'll carry the blanket," Stump said. "Don't rush him. There's going to be a good saddle horse."

Don't rush nothing! Stump had been here when he could have taken up the choice part of Revelation Valley, where the Mexican Spur had its home ranch now; but no, he had to settle up here in the dry hills where there was water one year and not much the next year. He let the cattlemen run over him, even let them range some of their stuff up here without saying boo about it. If he saw a critter that was loaded up on larkspur, down and bloated and dying, he took his knife and tried to save it. Generally he never even bothered to tell anyone.

"What is it, Lew?"

"Uh—I—" The old man was looking at him like he knew just what Lew was thinking. Aw, it was just that slow way of his when he threw a study on anything. "I'm leaving, Stump. I got to do something besides fix fences and make little dams and fool around with horses, and besides. . . ." Lew let it drift away like smoke.

Stump never let anything drift. "Besides what?"

You couldn't tell old Stump about things he had never felt, of the wishing rock in the pines where Lew sat sometimes at night, looking at the twinkling pinpoints in the valley, wondering what everybody was doing down there; about his clothes and the beat-up wagon when he went to Revelation for supplies, and saw the cowboys thundering down the street, yelling and shooting, plunging off their horses in front of the Valley Saloon; about the time the four fancy women from Arbor's Dance Hall passed Lew on the street, looking at him with the merest brush of interest that died before it really lived, telling him that they figured him in a class with the nesters from the range east of town. Stump wouldn't understand those things at all.

"I'm riding out," Lew said.

Stump put out his hand. "So long, son." They shook hands, and Stump turned back to the corral.

Lew spun away and went to the house. Lew's mother was sitting in the big rocker with brass-capped arms, looking out the bay window at Gantt Creek and the pines with sunlight on them. She wasn't much for sitting around. Nobody who stayed around old Stump did much sitting, Lew thought bitterly, except Odalie, and she was only a brat sister. He heard Marian in the kitchen.

"I'm leaving, Ma," Lew said.

Mrs. Gantt did not seem surprised, and that nettled Lew a little. "Where are you going?"

"Down in the valley for a spell. If I don't like it there, maybe I'll drift on west a few hundred miles." He had not intended to add the last, because his vague plans extended no farther than the valley, but now that it was out, it sounded pretty good. Some of the riders who brought horses up to Stump had told Lew of far places that old Stump didn't even know about. Why, out there on those distant ranges, where a man wasn't known just as Stump Gantt's boy. . . .

"We packed your things, son."

Lew blinked. Marian came on into the living room with a sort of scared smile on her face. Anyway, there was one person around here who thought it was bad that he was going so far away. Marian was a pretty girl, with her mother's slenderness and dark good looks, but she was just another sister.

"Well, I'm going," Lew said. He wanted to tell his mother how crazy it was for all of them to stay up here in the hills and work themselves old for Stump. But his mother did not look so old right then. In fact, she did not look a heck of a lot older than Marian. She sure was a healthy, strong woman, to look so good after putting up with old Stump all these years.

"I guess I'll get my stuff." Lew went upstairs to his room. Odalie was there, her face buried so deeply into his pillow that only her red pigtails showed. "What the devil are you—" She raised her head and he saw that she was crying, so instead of finishing by asking what she was doing in his room, he said "—bawling about, Odalie?"

"You're going away!" she wailed.

"Well, cut it out. I'm only going a couple thousand miles, and maybe in a few years I'll come back."

"A few years!" Odalie began to wail louder.

"I'll bring you back something."

Odalie rolled over and looked at him. She sniffed a little. "What?"

"A parasol."

"I want a saddle."

Lew considered. He probably would be in the chips when he returned. . . .

Odalie saw his hesitation, and began to screw up her face.

"All right!" he said. "A saddle."

"With silver trimmings?"

"I make no promises about that."

Odalie began to laugh. "You look just like Pa when he says that!" She wiped at her tears with the bends of her wrists, then laughed some more.

She sure was a pug-nosed, scheming little brat. Lew scowled at her, and then he grinned. "Where's my warbag?"

"It's in there." Odalie pointed at a flat leather bag lying on a chair. "So's your noisy old six-gun that Pa wouldn't let you wear."

Lew looked disgustedly at the bag. "That thing!"

"Ma says that folks who carry their belongings in warbags don't know where they're going. She says—"

"I know what she says. I know what everybody around here says! That's why I'm going away for keeps."

"You said you'd be back, with my saddle—with the silver trimming."

Lew shook his head. Sisters, parents—they gave you nothing but arguments. Odalie trailed him downstairs. Marian was standing by Mrs. Gantt, and Marian was getting ready to bawl. Lew gave them each an awkward hug. He would have hugged Odalie, but she made a face at him and ran out the back door.

Mrs. Gantt looked at Lew the way she had when he was a little boy. "Stay decent, stay clean, Lew." She looked at him a moment longer and then started toward the kitchen. "Come on, Marian. Let's finish the dishes."

Lew threw his sprung saddle on old, rough-coated, slow Ranger, the only horse he had ever owned. Stump did not even look away from the breaking corral when Lew rode past, but Railroad stared at the black bag behind the saddle, and then went over to the bars and asked Stump something.

"He's going out to try on a new pair of britches," Stump said. "Put the saddle on the gelding now, Railroad."

"Good luck, Lew!" Railroad called.

Lew waved. Over in the pines Odalie was jumping up and down on the wishing rock, yelling his name. He waved at her, then turned toward the valley.

Mrs. Gantt and Marian cleaned up the dishes in silence, then Mrs. Gantt went to the back door and called Odalie in from the wishing rock.

"Go down the trail after Lew, Odie. When you get near the gyp rock caves, watch Ranger's tracks carefully until—"

"I know, Ma! He'll stop and switch his plunder from that suitcase into his dirty old warbag, and hide the suitcase in one of the caves."

Mrs. Gantt smiled on the thin line between laughter and tears. "Bring the suitcase back, Odie."

Marian said, "At least, he didn't ride away looking like a saddle bum, even if nobody but us saw him."

Down at the corral, Stump's brown, clean-shaved face showed no change, except that his mouth was a little tighter. From the corner of his eye he saw Odalie running down the trail, but mainly he watched the bay gelding circling nervously with the saddle on its back.

"Ride him, Railroad."

Slim and wiry, Costigan stopped in mid-stride. "What?"

"I said ride him!"

Railroad's eyes went sidewise, toward the valley.

"You don't mean that, Stump."

"No, I guess I don't." Stump Gantt walked away toward the upper meadow.

Railroad called after him, "Never was a kid that was any good didn't pull his picket pin a few times!"

Gantt went on walking. Railroad resumed his patient circling of the corral, now and then speaking to the bay in a soothing voice, and all the time thinking of the days when he was seventeen down in Arizona Territory, many years before. He made a dozen trips around the big corral before he noticed the gelding was no longer humping or pulling sidewise in an effort to get from under leather.

Railroad stopped then, facing the emerald flatness of the distant valley, looking far beyond the purple ranges. He was glad that his guns had long ago been laid aside. Here was the only place he had ever been at home, at peace. If he were seventeen again . . . if he were seventeen and knew what he knew now . . . life would be awful dull.

Free with fifty dollars in his pocket, Lew strolled the main street of Revelation. Now that he was here, all the things he had longed to do when he was not free to do them did not have the same appeal. He would be a little cautious about what he did first, sort of get the feel of things. There was no rush.

He saw Mexican Spur horses in front of the Valley Saloon, and four or five Short Fork horses before the Green Grass Saloon. There was not a single nester wagon in town. It was time the danged nesters learned they couldn't move right in on cattle range. They claimed to have legal right, but Lew did not take much stock in that; in fact, he knew only the superficial facts about the trouble that was shaping up, but his sympathy was with the cowmen, so he did not need to have many facts.

Gaunt, blistered Custer Wigram, owner of the Spur, came from the Valley as Lew was passing for the third time. He bunched pale brows at Lew and said, "Howdy, kid. What's Stump doing in town in the middle of the week?"

"He ain't here, Mr. Wigram."

Wigram sized the youth up once more. Lew's levi's were new, but he had soaked them for a week in mild lye water to take away their giveaway blueness. He was wearing the long barreled .44, for which he had traded a month's work at Wigram's hay ranch the year before.

"Oh," Wigram said in a long breath. "You're out on your own now, huh?"

"Yeah."

Townspeople passed. Four cowboys drifted from the Green Grass to the Valley. They all spoke with deference to Wigram. Lew did not mind at all being seen talking on equal terms to the biggest rancher in the country.

"How does it look out there?" Lew nodded east.

Wigram shook his head. "We overlooked a thing or two when we settled here. Then we didn't work together." His eyes strayed toward the west hills. "A few days ago four farmers filed on the very ground Joe Hemphill's home ranch stands on."

Hemphill owned the Short Fork. Lew cursed to show concern. Not used to profanity, he overdid it. "That won't stand, will it?"

"I don't know." Wigram shook his head dubiously.

"You ought to run every nester out of the country right damn now!"

The Spur owner smiled vaguely. "That would be quite a drive—now. You want a job, Lew?"

Lew's heart leaped. Never be overanxious, Stump always said. "Well . . . my horse ain't too good with cows."

"All you'll need him for is to ride to Spur. I want some range stuff broke."

That was a wet slap. Break horses! There was no fun in that, not doing it Stump's slow way, which was the only method Lew understood.

"Your old man says you're about as good as Costigan."

"Huh!" Stump had never mentioned that to Lew.

"No thanks, Mr. Wigram. I don't much care for that kind of work."

The corners of Wigram's eyes crinkled. "Too much like home, huh?" Then he started up the walk. "Ride over if you change your mind."

The youth swung his gun belt around and went into the Valley. Spur and Short Fork riders at the bar were talking about the nesters. There was a pause until Shindy Lemons said, "Aw, that's only Stump Gantt's boy from the west hills. C'mon over, Lew, and have a drink."

Lew was awkward at the bar, not sure just what to do with his hands. He saw the others watching him closely, and knew they were guessing it was his first drink of whiskey. It was. No rush about it. He took his time.

"Hmm!" a cowboy said. "Old Stump must run a still up there."

They all laughed. Lew tossed a coin on the bar. "Have one around on me." It was the thing to do, but he sure didn't like to see the money go into the till. There were better ways to spend money, and while the whiskey was loosening social tightness inside him, he still didn't think it was worth good gold that he had been a long time saving. He had a drink on four others, and he could honestly say that, other than a sort of warm pushing behind his eyes, the whiskey did not seem to affect him.

Before it was his turn to buy again, he thanked the cowboys and strolled over to a poker game in the corner. Confidential Pete, the houseman, was having a bad time with Buck Hodel, the Spur foreman, and a slim stranger dressed in gray. Ivers, the liveryman, and two cowboys were in the game, too.

"Jump in, kid, and get your feet wet," Hodel said. He was a broad, black-browed man, about half drunk at the moment. He had a pretty bad temper, they said.

"No rush," Lew said. "I like to see where the power is before I jump."

"You sound just like your old man," Hodel said.

The stranger in gray smiled at Lew. It was hard to figure that one out. He was a handsome devil, gray eyes, curly brown hair and a clean grin. His face was brown and so were his hands, and he wasn't dressed quite like a gambler, not the kind old Railroad talked about, leastwise. But he was dressed just a little better than a range hand, too.

Lew watched the game. One of the cowboys won a small pot. The stranger won a big one when the houseman bucked into a full house with two pair. After a while Lew got things figured out. The man in gray was merely having a big lucky streak, and the others were letting him draw too cheap when they should have been raising the devil.

At least, that was the way Railroad Costigan would have figured it, and Lew had spent many an evening playing poker for fun with Railroad.

This beat drinking whiskey. Lew itched to get into the game, but he waited a while, watching how they played, before he bought forty dollars' worth of chips.

Confidential Pete hesitated before he shoved the stack across. "You sure you know how to play this, Gantt?

"I learn fast."

Pete grunted, "I don't want your old man on my neck after you lose your money." He was half afraid it was Stump's money.

Lew grinned. "Worry about the man who owns this dump getting on *your* neck after I take *his* money."

The stranger laughed. "You'll do, Gantt. Smoky Cameron." He put out his hand as Lew settled into a chair beside him.

"Lew Gantt." The name had a fair sound, at that. Cameron's hand was hard, with work bumps there, all right, but not the dry-raspy kind. He had not worked recently, Lew figured.

Lew drifted along for about a half hour, like someone who wanted to make his forty bucks last a long time. And then on a pot that Hodel opened for five dollars, five men stayed. Lew was the last one. He raised five. One of the cowboys dropped out. Everybody else stayed. They drew cards. Ivers took one. He cursed. Before he tossed in his hand he spread it to show how he had missed a flush. Nobody paid any attention. They were all watching Lew, who had not drawn any cards.

"Beginner's luck!" one of the cowboys muttered, and threw away his hand.

Hodel bet five dollars, scowling at Lew. The houseman stayed, and raised five more. When it came to Lew he met the raise and pushed in all the chips he had.

"Never try to bluff a dumb kid," Pete said. He tossed his hand away.

Cameron got out with a laugh, and that left it up to Hodel. He scowled and grunted and tried to read Lew's face, and at last threw his hand away with a curse. "What have you got you're so proud of?"

Lew pushed his hand into the discards. "You didn't pay to see, Hodel." Lew had been bluffing.

"I think he was pulling a whizzer," Cameron said goodhumoredly.

"He's too dumb for that!" Hodel growled. But still he was not sure. It showed in his eyes, and it would keep eating at him. The next time he would call anything, Lew figured. And that was just what happened an hour later. Hodel was still far ahead of the game, and Lew had made steady little winnings, so he now had about two hundred dollars.

He got a full house, queens over sixes, on the deal. When the smoke cleared there was about two hundred dollars in the pot, with only Lew and Hodel left. The Spur foreman had drawn one card, and Lew was sure he had filled something. Hodel pushed out chips to match everything Lew had. His face went splotchy red when he saw the full house. He slapped a Jack-high straight on the cloth and pushed his chair back savagely.

"You're just too damned lucky, Gantt, or else—"

"Else what?"

"—or you're too slick for this game. You'd better get out now."

Cameron said, "Don't push on the lines, Hodel. The kid's been lucky, and played good poker."

Hodel's face swung like a club at Cameron. "You keep that little thing under your nose quiet, tinhorn. I ain't just sure about you anyway."

"Is that a fact?" Cameron rose. "Just what is it you aren't sure about?"

Lew had his chance to get from under, but he wasn't letting anyone carry the load for him. "It's a free country, Hodel. Get out yourself if you don't like the way I play." An instant later he thought that maybe the whiskey had not been quite as harmless as it seemed.

"Why, you little west-hills pup!" Hodel kicked his chair away. He was a blocky, solid man, and it was his boast that he could lick any man in the valley.

Confidential Pete's voice was a lost squeal. "No trouble in here, boys! No trouble in here!"

Across the room a Spur rider said to the bartender, "No, Sammy. Just lay your little white mitts on the cherrywood and watch the fun."

"I guess," Hodel said, "I'd better slap some manners into you, Gantt." He flung aside a cowboy who was struggling to rise with his feet entangled in the baling wire braces of his chair. Hodel walked through the space toward Lew.

Lew went around the table. He was hot-scared, but he was not going to run.

"Stay back, Hodel," he said.

The Spur foreman made a lunge. Lew kicked a chair in front of him and went farther around the table. Hodel crashed over the chair and fell. He came up insane with anger.

"Stay back, Hodel." Lew kept the table between them. He saw it coming then. He could almost smell the brimstone scent of it.

Hodel went for his pistol.

He was not fast. No one in the Revelation country was fast with a gun. Lightning draws were merely something men like Railroad talked about. But Buck Hodel was faster than Lew Gantt, who had never drawn his .44 quickly, except in secret practice against old Railroad.

The explosion almost deafened Lew. He did not hear or feel the bullet, and he did not know where it went until someone told him afterward. He smelled the great bloom of dirty-gray powder smoke that obscured the middle of Hodel's body. Lew had drawn by then, and now he shot, trying to aim through the rising murk and hit Hodel in the right leg to knock him flat. Instead, he shot Hodel through the side. The man twisted back and fell into the check rack.

Lew had to step to one side to see through the acrid fumes. Hodel was lying there, his mouth open with shock. Lew Gantt stared. He was scared to death, and sick.

Smoky Cameron was against the wall, off to one side. His gun was in his hand and his eyes were on the Spur and Short Fork men. "Was it fair?" he asked.

After a moment grizzled Rip Goodwin said, "Yeah, it was fair." He sent a sullen, wicked look at Lew. The cowboys went over to Hodel.

With his gun still in his hand, Lew started to run. He would get Ranger. He would ride as fast as he could, clear out of the country. He had killed a man, and a deadly fear was riding him and urging him to get away quickly.

Cameron caught him at the door. Lew clubbed his gun and tried wildly to beat the man away, but Cameron caught his wrist and hurled him against the wall.

"Where you going, Gantt?"

After a while Lew stopped struggling. He stared at Cameron. The man was calm and friendly. "I know," Cameron said. "You want to run from here to the Pacific. I know how you feel. Put that gun away and sit down there in a chair."

Lew obeyed, gaining control from Cameron's quiet voice. The man in gray went back to the poker table. He scooped Lew's chips into his hat. He stood there a while looking steadily at Confidential Pete, and after a few moments Pete took his hand from his coat pocket and added a fistful of yellow chips to the hat. Cameron found two more in the pocket.

"Them are mine!" Pete protested. Cameron dropped the chips in the hat.

"Interest on a filthy trick," he said. Pete slunk away.

About then Lew heard Hodel curse weakly and say something to Goodwin. A breath of terror went out of Lew.

The sheriff came in with Plug Riddle, the druggist, who was also the doctor for men and horses. A lot of people streamed in, crowding close to Hodel, then turning to stare in surprise at the boy in the chair by the door.

Riddle said loudly. "If he don't get complications or something, he may be all right in a month or so."

Lew stood up, and his legs held him without shaking. He wanted to tell Hodel he was sorry, but just then Wigram came over, a savage, calculating look on his face. "For a punk button, you sure messed things up, didn't you?"

"He started it."

Wigram turned away and went to the bar. Cameron came up and handed Lew a canvas sack. "Five hundred and twenty-five."

Lew wanted to throw the gold through the window. He wished he had never left home. No matter whose fault this was, it made him sick again to see blood dripping as they carried Hodel out.

Sheriff Nate Springer was a big, slow-moving, chunky man who surveyed everything thoughtfully from green eyes almost buried under his brows. Stump said he got that way from figuring how to stay in office the rest of his life.

"I don't figure to make a fuss," the sheriff told Lew, "but you better come down to the office with me."

Wigram turned around at the bar. "Let's hear what you got to say right here, Springer."

"He said his office." Cameron took Lew's arm and hustled him outside, and a moment later Springer followed, relieved because he had not been forced to argue the matter.

They did not go inside. Springer kept his office neat, and he did not like dirt on the oiled floor or things moved out of place on his desk.

Springer said, "You'd best get on back home right away, Gantt—and stay clear of town for quite a spell."

"What for? I didn't start anything."

"I don't like trouble here."

"It wasn't my fault!" Lew said.

"Nobody said it was. Go on home."

"You want to run me out of town because I'm only a kid, but you don't say nothing about running the others out because Spur and Fork elect you."

Springer nodded slowly. "That's right as far as it goes. Also, I don't want to have more grief when some drunk cowboy sees you around and jumps you."

"I'll take care of myself."

"That's what I'm afraid of," Springer said quietly. "Stump Gantt's likely to have enough trouble on his hands, without his son trying to be a gun fighter."

"I don't want to be a gun fighter, and I didn't start anything, so I don't see what right you got to tell me to beat it."

The sheriff looked at Cameron. "It's still the best thing for you, kid."

That was what Lew was mainly tired of, someone telling him what he ought to do.

"You ordering me to go?" he asked.

"No, but I sure suggest it strong." Springer sighed. He turned away and went into his office.

"I wasn't figuring to stay anyway," Lew said to Cameron. "Now I might."

Cameron asked casually. "What are you planning to do with the money?" Lew was still holding the sack.

"Half of it is yours. If you hadn't picked the chips up, I wouldn't have any money at all. And I think you had me beat that first hand I won, when I shoved in everything I had."

"Yes," Cameron said, "I knew you were bluffing." He smiled briefly. "It would have saved a lot of trouble if I'd busted you right there."

"Yeah," Lew said, thinking of the way Hodel had looked on the dirty floor. "I don't much care about this money now."

"I'll be glad to ease half of your conscience."

They went behind the livery stable to divide the gold.

"You drifting out?" Lew asked. He'd go along with Cameron if Cameron asked him. "You won't stand much chance to get a job here now—after siding in with me today."

"You may be right," Cameron said vaguely. "But I thought I'd look the ranches over and see what I could stir up. I sort of like this country."

"Huh! It ain't much."

Cameron gave him a grave look. "Maybe you've lived too close to it to see its good points, Lew."

A short time later Lew watched Cameron ride away on a leggy claybank that was a jim-dandy. Lew thought of old Ranger there in the stable. He had enough money now to make a trade for a good horse, but he hated to part with Ranger. No need to rush things. Maybe later, when Cameron returned from looking for a job nobody would give him, the two of them could ride away together.

Lew put a hundred dollars in the bank. He did not know just why he did, unless it was because Stump was always saying a man ought to save something out of every chunk he made. The banker was glad to take the money. He asked a lot of questions about how Stump was, and you'd have thought old Stump was a big wheel around the valley.

In two days the draw game in the Green Grass took everything Lew had in his pockets. He walked past the bank several times before he went in to get his hundred dollars. The banker was just as polite as before.

When Lew went out the nesters were coming into town. There was quite a bunch of them. Judging from the rifles and shotguns on their wagon seats, a man could say they were ready for trouble if it came.

Lew studied the farmers pretty closely. They were clean, quiet, going about their business as if they figured to be in the country a long time. A few days in Revelation taught Lew that the town was not against the nesters. Maybe the farmers did have some right on their side.

A nester named Cranklow, a raw-boned, sun-blistered man with a square jaw, said hello to Lew, and the youth remembered him from the times Cranklow had been to the horse ranch to talk to Stump about grass seed and dams. Cranklow stopped to talk, but Lew just said hello curtly and went on toward the Green Grass.

Lew was pretty lonely right then, and it occurred to him how he would have felt if someone had been short with him for no reason. A lot of people had talked to Lew, but generally only to ask how he had become so fast with a pistol.

He was cleaned out in three hours, losing his last twenty dollars when he tried to run a busted flush past the houseman's two pairs. He was hungry when he reached the street. At noon he had eaten well, but now, knowing he was broke, he was hungry ahead of time. He stood there wondering what his mother would have for supper that night.

Three cowboys from two-bit outfits were lounging at the hitch rail, watching the farmers leaving town in a body.

The devil could take the whole works, he thought angrily. He did not want anything to do with nesters, and cattlemen wanted nothing to do with him since he shot Buck Hodel. The thing to do was get as far away as possible from this two-bit valley and find a good riding job where nobody knew he was Stump Gantt's kid from the west hills, or that he had shot a man. Something deep inside him warned him that he was not thinking straight, but he was too flushed with resentment to pay any attention.

To heck with Smoky Cameron, too. Cameron had taken half of the five hundred and not even asked Lew to ride out with him. Lew Gantt was on his own. He did not owe anyone anything. He could do as he pleased. He was. . . .

Pitching hay at a nester place two days later for a dollar a day and all he could eat. The whole deal had been Cameron's idea, after he returned from riding the ranches and reported no jobs available. Cameron was pitching hay right alongside Lew. The weather held good. For a month they moved from place to place. Lew kept his eyes open and learned a lot.

The last place was Jemmie Cranklow's, on Little Elk, smack in the middle of what had been Spur range. Cranklow had put in a pile of work. He was figuring on planting winter wheat, and building a canal to water his upper eighty.

"This is as good farmland as any in the valley." Cameron explained. "It's even more sheltered." He put up a shock of hay to Cranklow's youngest boy on the rack. "The thing is, these people have made legal filings. Some of the ranchers don't even own the land where their buildings are. Wigram got wise two years ago and protected himself, but Hemphill waited too long. Now he'll have to compromise or lose the very land he lives on."

Lew looked sidewise at Cameron's gray clothes. "You know quite a bit about this valley, don't you?"

"I do." Cameron hoisted a shock that made the fork handle creak.
"You favor law, don't you?"

"I guess I do. What happens, though, if there's a big fight?"

"There won't be," Cameron said. "Not on this side of the valley.
The farmers are too strong here now."

Lew couldn't seem to get his fork into shocks just right for a long
time. Stump had been throwing grass seed around in the west hills
since before Lew—or even Marian—was born. He owned rock
claims, timber claims, placers, five homesteads that had fizzled—just
about everything that was worth a dime over there. Come to think of
it, Stump had been building something slowly in the west hills. A man
could run cattle there now, not like it used to be on this side, of course,
but still the west hills would stand grazing. Spur and Short Fork were
already running stuff over there.

The cowmen were beat on this side, but over there—just one man
standing between them and all the range.

"My father has got legal claim to everything he holds!" Lew said.

"I know. So have the farmers over this way."

Sheriff Springer had it figured out. That's what he had meant when
he said Stump was going to have trouble. Wigram said he had overlooked something, and then he had glanced toward the west hills.

"I was at your father's place after I left Revelation," Cameron said
casually. "I never saw so much good solid craftsmanship in everything
around there."

"My father does things right!" Lew was darned sure of that now,
having seen plenty of work that wasn't done well.

In the shadowy bunkhouse at Stump Gantt's ranch the owner and
Railroad Costigan looked at each other past a dim lamp on the table
between two Walker Colts that were shiny-worn.

Costigan's face was as brown and wrinkled as a frost-rotted apple.
"They might be a little afraid of him, Stump. It wasn't luck when he
shot Hodel. They might want him out of the way."

"Cameron's with him."

"Cameron has to go prowling at times."

Gantt shook his head. "He's on his own. It's got to be that way.
We've got to let him make his own decisions, Railroad."

He shook his head sadly. "I never thought it would come down to
this again. I guess I've just been too blind to everything you've been

doing here, Stump, scattering seed, making those little rock dams. . . . Of course, it's been only the last year or two that the results began to show up."

Stump nodded somberly. "They still call 'em the 'dry hills,' but Wigram and Hemphill have seen, and Springer saw it long ago."

"Springer won't be no help."

Stump smiled. "When did we ever ask the law for help?"

"Maybe I'm getting old." Railroad said. "Maybe I've slipped since I been here, but it seems to me this is one time when the law ought to work. You've spent the best part of your life here, Stump, raising a family, building up a range that no one wanted, putting every dime into developing something. Now—"

"That makes it all the more worth fighting for. I didn't want the fight. I hoped they'd learn from what was happening over east, but now a fight is all that's left."

"Wigram is ordinarily a reasonable man." Railroad picked up the other gun. "Joe Hemphill isn't much on fighting."

"Wigram is desperate now. I offered to lease the west hills. I made him a good offer. Hodel was the one who made him stiffen when he was about to come around. Wigram knows he's been beat over east. He knows it too late, and it rankles all the more to think he let the west hills get away from him. He's carrying Hemphill, too. Joe don't want the fight. Joe was the one who stopped Wigram from burning out nesters years ago, when the cowmen might have made it stick.

"Now Wigram is working on Hemphill by telling him what a terrible mistake that was. They're both ruined unless they get the west hills, and Hemphill's ruined any way you figure it, because Wigram will ease him out later if they win. I've let them run a few cattle over here, Railroad. They let me take a beef whenever we needed meat. The hides have always been right there on the fence for anyone to see. I got the worst of it, of course, but I wanted to see just how well the west hills would stand up under grazing. They'll stand it, but we'll have to watch the dry years and cut herds—and there will never be a time when my range will stand one third of the cows Spur and Short Fork have."

Costigan picked up both guns. His eyes had a young look in his old, brown face. "A man never changes, Stump. I thought maybe you had, since the old days in Arizona, but you're just the same inside." He scowled. "How about Emily and the kids?"

"Emily got sore when I tried to edge around to sending her away. She knows what we both know, Railroad—nothing is any good to you unless you get it the hard way and hold it the same way against all comers."

Stump hesitated at the door, looking at the warm lights of the house. When Cameron, that young United States Marshal, had been here, he and Marian had looked at each other with the same expression springing in their eyes that Stump remembered from long ago, when he first saw Emily.

Stump looked toward the valley. It was overcast tonight, with a threat of rain, and the lights down there were not visible. Why didn't Lew come back? He must know by now how things were shaping up. But if he did not come back, he was still a boy that Stump Gantt was mighty proud of. Stump's mouth was sort of loose when he thought that perhaps he should have hinted that to Lew now and then, but such things came hard to Stump.

Stump's mouth was tight when he turned again toward the room. "You and me both know how easy it is to stop a fight before it gets started."

Railroad's eyes were wicked and narrow. Both Walkers were in holsters on his hips, and he was standing there with something on his mind that made him look as wound-up and dangerous as he had been in the old days. Stump and Railroad had ridden much of the West together as young men, and Railroad was the only man Stump had ever known who could actually use two guns with quick accuracy. There was a cold spot on Costigan's conscience; he had never worried about killing men who asked for it.

"Yeah," Railroad said. "Blast a rattler's head and all you got left is a lot of sickening twisting and humping. The trouble is all gone."

"Hodel is up and around," Stump said slowly. "He's been making talk about Lew, and about the west hills, too. It struck me that you might figure to go down and take Hodel and Wigram."

"Did it?" Railroad stood there, thin and wrinkled, wearing the tough, blank look Stump had almost forgotten.

"You wouldn't figure to come clear," Stump said. "You think you've lived a long time, but the older we get the better we like the thought of getting still older. We both want to live to see Lew running this place, see the girls married off to decent youngsters, with you and me having time to fool around with blooded horses, like we've always wanted."

"Sure," Railroad said. "I've thought of all that. I've also thought that we ain't got much chance, waiting for them to come after us."

Stump had never been one to try to make words change facts. He said, "That's right. But we've got to stay with the law all the way. That's the way this place was built, and that's the way I want to leave it. We've got the right to defend ourselves, but we can't go out and start killing before we're attacked."

After a while the tenseness went out of Railroad. He sat down on a bench and he was just an old man wearing two pistols that were out of date. "I wish Lew would come back," he muttered.

"Maybe he will." Stump peered again at dark mist over the valley. He shut the door quietly and went toward the house. Before he crossed the flagstone porch he straightened his shoulders and composed his face, so Odalie, at least, would not know what he was thinking. With him and Railroad gone, Emily would still be in legal possession of most of the west hills. Wigram knew that, and he also knew that women could not run a horse ranch. After doing half his work by violence, Wigram would do the other half legally, letting shock and necessity wear Emily to the point of selling everything at his price.

It was worry about Lew that made Stump feel scared and helpless. They would figure to take Lew first. He went inside. Emily read his face, and then glanced toward the bedroom where Marian was waging a battle to get Odalie down for the night.

"Has the rain start—" Emily asked.

"Pa! Lew's going to bring me a silver-mounted saddle, just my size, and a real Navajo bridle!" Odalie popped out of the bedroom.

"Is that a fact?"

"It ought to be. I've told you about ten times," Odalie said. "When's Lew coming back?"

"When he gets ready. Get to bed, Odie." Stump looked at his wife. "It's fixing to rain, all right."

Blocking the bedroom door, Marian turned her head to look at her parents. There was a starkness in the room as the first drops began to fall.

In the mow of Cranklow's barn Lew shook hay from his blankets and prepared to go to bed. "I'm going home tomorrow," he told Cameron.

Standing by the ladder, fully dressed, Cameron was silent as the rain hit the roof in a steady whisper. Then he said. "It's too far now, Lew, too far across the valley and up through the rocks to the west hills."

"I don't think I get you, Cameron."

"You wouldn't get there, Lew."

After a while Lew asked, "Wigram?"

"In a day or two I'll need your help. We can keep this thing from ever starting, maybe. Will you stay with me, Lew?"

"I don't know what you're going to do." Lew decided he did not know much about Cameron at all. The man had a habit of riding out almost every night, and never saying where he went.

"Believe me, you can help your father more by staying with ne and helping me than by getting waylaid on your way home."

"I'll stay two days."

"Wear your gun," Cameron said. He went down the ladc minutes later Lew heard him head the claybank toward Revelation.

The slender little man rode into the yard while Lew was still eating breakfast. The others had finished, but Lew was having one last stack of pancakes when he heard the man ask, "How do you get to Stump Gantt's place?"

Cameron's voice was casual. "How'd you happen to get so far north of the road, stranger?"

Lew took his gun belt off the peg by the wash bench and strapped it on before he went out. If the man looked at him at all it was merely a side flick of eyes like black chips. "I got off the track last night," the fellow said. "Where at is this Gantt place?"

"What do you want with Stump Gantt?" Cameron asked.

Whew! Cameron sure didn't mind asking personal questions.

The man didn't mind answering either. "That old cutthroat gave me a rasping on a horse I bought from him a few months back. I aim to get some satisfaction."

"You waited quite a while to squawk, didn't you?" Cameron glanced at the man's mount, a deep-barreled bay with a beautiful saddle. "That the horse?"

"Yeah."

Lew was walking forward stiffly, so mad he could hardly see. "You're a dirty liar, mister," he said. "My father never cheated nobody in his life, and you're another dirty liar when you say that horse ever came from his place."

"Easy, Lew!" Cameron said.

It was too late. The man swung his face toward Lew, and the boy got his first full glimpse of the stranger. There was a deadly sort of blankness in the face, a frozen look of concentration in the black eyes. Lew realized he had stepped full-on into something pretty stout. It did not make any difference. Nobody was lying about old Stump while he was around.

"You call me a liar?" the man asked.

"Twice," Lew said. "What do you want to do about it?"

The man stretched thin lips across rows of teeth that were small and brown and strong. "You know I can't take that kind of talk, sonny."

Lew was not angry now. The thing fell into place in his mind. If he had used his head at all a minute before, he would have seen how raw and direct the whole plant was. He ought to back out now. Native pride would not let him. He sensed that this little man would not make any of Buck Hodel's mistakes.

"Kid. . . ." the man said casually, and went for his pistol. It was all too fast for Lew. He saw the fellow's gun come clear. He heard the ear-stunning roar, and saw the man spin clear around and almost fall. And then the stranger was standing there, gray-faced, his gun on the ground, his right arm hanging heavily, with blood sopping all around the elbow.

Cameron's pistol was in his hand, and a cloud of stinking, acrid smoke was drifting away from it. Lew Gantt had not even got his pistol out of the holster.

"It had moss all over it, Martin," Cameron said.

The black eyes glittered in the cold-gray face. "Who are you?" Martin asked. "How do you know me?"

"I'm Smoky Cameron."

"Ah. . . ." the fellow said in a long breath. "I can feel a little better about this now." His eyes grew blank. Pain and shock dropped him. His cheek slashed along the hard earth. His hat came off and showed a bald spot at the back of his head. At the wrinkled crook of his right coat sleeve bits of bone from his shattered elbow showed in the bloody fabric.

Lew sensed some of it, just enough to know that he was far out of his class, that years of experience separated him from complete understanding. He knew that he was just a greenhorn who had tried to sit in a high-rolling game. The feeling was heightened when, after Cameron dressed Martin's wound and put him on his horse, Martin went away without another glance at Lew.

Lew heard him tell Cameron, "I sort of got sucked into something, didn't I?"

"You hired out once too often."

It took a good deal of self from Lew's thinking. Sure, they were afraid enough of him to send a killer to drop him and help clear the way to the west hills, but that did not make him feel important. It did not scare him, either. It made him more anxious to go home and ask Stump what he could do to help. Tomorrow his promise to Cameron would be up.

Worry ran the sharp points of restlessness through Lew as he waited for Cameron to return. He offered to start digging the canal for Cranklow.

"Too rainy, Lew," the farmer said. "You just lay low today, and trust your friend."

Cameron came back through the rain that night. He took care of the claybank and ate his supper. He did not have much to say, other than that he had taken Martin to Revelation and turned him over to Sheriff Springer.

"What's the charge?" Cranklow asked.

"No charge. Just holding him. He couldn't go anywhere with that arm, anyway."

Lew felt that a mighty wall of violence was building in the valley, with him not able to understand all the details. When he and Cameron were crossing the rain-greased yard on their way to the haymow, Lew said, "I've decided not to wait the other day. I'm going to start for home tonight."

Cameron did not answer until he was in the mow, struggling out of wet boots. "Tomorrow. We'll win or lose the whole deal tomorrow."

"Is that all you want to say?"

"Yeah."

Lew sat down on his blankets. "Who hired that Martin?"

"I don't know," Cameron said.

It was still raining when they rode out before daylight. Lew figured they would go toward Spur, but they went down-valley instead. Where the roads forked a mile from town, Sheriff Springer was waiting under the cottonwoods. He looked gloomily at water darkening the skirts of his rig, and he showed no enthusiasm for what lay ahead. His slicker rattled as he turned his horse toward Short Fork. There were tracks of five or six horses already in the muddy ruts.

"You were right, Cameron," Springer said. "I got the word that it starts from Short Fork."

"Wigram has got to push Hemphill all the way, but he's pushing a dead horse now. How's Martin?"

"Plug Riddle was taking his arm off when I left. You'd a done him a favor to kill him instead of that."

The Short Fork yard was full of horses. A poker game was going on in the bunkhouse. The four men lounging out of the rain on the wide front porch of the main building paid little attention to the riders drifting in through the misty drizzle until Lew and his companions were right at the gate. Then someone said, "Oh, oh!" and went quickly into the house.

Custer Wigram was on the porch by the time the three dismounted. The bleak planes of his face were white with anger. Hemphill came out and stood beside him. He was a stocky man with a big shoulder reach and a pugnacious face that said he was willing to tackle the devil and give him odds; but that only went as deep as his face, which right now was flushed, and more stubborn than determined.

Buck Hodel and Rip Goodwin, followed by nine or ten others, came from the bunkhouse. Hodel was a little pale, Lew observed, but otherwise he seemed all right.

There ought to have been some better way to get things stopped than this, Lew thought. His stomach felt like it was flat against his backbone.

Cameron went out in front of his horse. "You're not taking a gang to Stump Gantt's today, Wigram—or any other day."

Wigram looked at Springer. "How'd *you* get into this?"

"First, because the U. S. Marshal here asked me; second, because he's right." Springer unbuttoned his slicker. He removed it and let it drop in a stiff heap over a puddle of water. Under his corduroy coat he was wearing an old black sweater, with his gun belt buckled over it, and the trim, curving handle of his .45 right in handy reach.

He looked pretty solid and dangerous, Lew thought, and wished he could make some kind of gesture, too; but all Lew could do was gulp at dry cotton in his mouth and try to hold a poker face.

"You're licked, Wigram," Cameron said. "You know it. To start what you want to start you're going to have to kill us three, and you'll have to do it before Hemphill, a man who no longer owns a cow or piece of land in the valley."

Wigram swung his gaunt head toward Hemphill, who stared at the floor of the porch.

"So that's why you backed out!" Wigram said.

Hemphill raised his head. "By God, I've had about enough of your abuse, Wigram! Sure, I sold out! What right I had from use of the land here I relinquished to four farmers. I told you two years ago we couldn't beat this thing."

"You chicken-livered, gutless—"

"Shut up, Wigram, or I'll knock the blisters off that skinny face of yours!" This was a personal affair now.

Even in his rage Wigram realized that. "What'd you do with your cattle?"

"That's none of your business," Hemphill said.

"Buck Hodel, your own foreman, took an option on them, Wigram." Cameron said. "Does that give you an idea of what might have happened to you, if you'd been lucky enough to grab the west hills?"

All Wigram's rage seemed to evaporate, but it was worse than ever inside him, Lew figured, as he watched the Spur owner pace deliberately from the porch and start toward Hodel.

"Is that the truth, Buck?" Wigram asked.

"Just a minute!" Cameron's voice was a hard crack in the tension as men moved away from Hodel, as Spur and Short Fork began to separate. "Lew here has a little business with Hodel first. Hodel is the one who sent for Trey Martin to come in here and kill Gantt."

Hodel was set like a spring. "That's a dirty lie."

"It all came out of Martin—this morning while Plug Riddle was taking his arm off without chloroform."

Lew saw on Hodel's face that Cameron had bluffed through to the truth. The Spur foreman's mouth loosened. His eyes flicked from side to side. He was alone with hostile men.

"What do you want to do with him, Lew?" Cameron asked in a flat tone.

For a moment Lew did not want to do anything, and then he gathered thoughts about Hodel from here and there, and the feel of watching men helped, and he brought everything into a great cold lump that resembled reason, which said that he must kill Buck Hodel in the name of justice.

He started slowly toward Hodel. This second time would be easy. Hodel was scared tight, so desperate that he would try to do everything at one time—and be wild and helpless. Lew Gantt was cold and sure. For the first time he understood the intangible factors that old Railroad Costigan always claimed were the real weights in a pistol scrap—complete disregard for life; don't think, just shoot.

For three slow steps Lew Gantt was as impersonal as death, a stocky youth with a tight mouth and blue eyes knife-cold with blankness. He was geared to kill, and the rest was nothing but obedience. Then he stopped. The reasons he had summoned fell apart before the trapped look in Hodel's eyes. Habit and training made Lew weigh the forces that pushed him. He remembered the fine green lines of evil in Trey Martin's face. A man could become another Martin too easily.

"I think," he said slowly, "you better get clean out of this country for good, Hodel."

"I'll go," Hodel said.

Cameron made a little nod and something quick ran across his face. He was saying that Lew had done the right thing.

Springer's eyes were pale points under the cliffs of his brows. He did not look at Lew. The tension of a waiting mountain sat in Springer, and Lew wondered why the sheriff did not realize that the backbone of the fight was broken.

Wigram said, "The kid is soft, Buck. But I can't let you go."

"Yes, you will," Springer said suddenly. "It's time I got my spoon into this mess. Hodel is drifting. I'm arresting you, Wigram."

Wigram thought a moment. "What for?" he challenged.

The cone of interest now ran its point between the bulky sheriff and gaunt Wigram, but Lew observed that Springer was only half watching Wigram. And then, standing there in the rain beside the tepee of his yellow slicker, Springer drew his gun. The thick fumes of black powder smoke hung in the damp air.

Across the yard Hodel's mouth dropped open. The pistol bearing on Lew fell into a puddle, and then Hodel went down in the mud like a head-shot beef.

Springer looked angrily at Lew. "You can't turn your back on a man like that. Don't you ever learn nothing?"

"I slipped, too," Cameron said.

Wigram only glanced at Hodel. "You can't arrest me, Springer."

"I know it," the sheriff said. "You're bad beat, though. You got your choice of clearing out or going to Stump Gantt on his own terms if you figure to run cows in the west hills."

"Dead as hell," a Short Fork rider said, turning Hodel over.

"I get paid for it," Springer said bitterly. "Let's get out of here."

The sheriff did not like the mud on his floor, or the way Cameron pushed things aside to sit on a corner of the desk. But he did his best to cover up his feelings. "You put me in for another term, Cameron. Considering the farmer vote that's come in the last two years, I wouldn't have made it this fall."

"Nobody *dragged* you out to Short Fork this morning," Cameron answered.

"Uh-huh." Springer looked at Lew. "I guess I earned my votes all right." In a curiously somber voice he asked Lew: "Do you know what it might have meant if you'd gone over the hump and killed Hodel when you started to?"

"I guessed. It wouldn't have been so good for me."

"Maybe you did learn something down here," Springer said. "Maybe you crossed the line between being a kid and a man. You can go back to Stump now and see how much he's changed."

Cameron's face was dead sober. "You may find that your old man has learned a lot since you been gone."

Springer knew Mark Twain, too, but he had never heard him so aptly quoted. The sheriff forgot the muddy tracks. He made little noise but he was laughing all the way down when Cameron and Lew stepped outside.

"Tell your sis—tell your father—I'll be up in a few days," Cameron said. "Don't forget the rig for that pigtailed demon. She told me about it when I was up there. I see just the answer in Bixler's saddle shop every time I go past."

"Yeah. That's where Odalie saw it. I couldn't buy a secondhand saddle blanket now, let alone a silver-trimmed rig."

"Try the bank," Cameron said. "When I start splitting with a man in a poker game I'll know I'm not fit to make an honest living. You must have about two hundred and fifty bucks left." He gave Lew a little shove, and then went back into Springer's office.

For a while Lew stood on the walk with his hat brim drooping lower in the rain. From the corners of his eyes he saw them watching him from inside. It would take a little time to straighten out and sort some of the things which he had learned. But there was no rush.

This rain was going to be mighty good for the grass in the west hills. Lew Gantt went slowly up the street toward Bixler's saddlery.

Learn the Hard Way

They were going to hang Danny Ensign down there near the train. He would swing from the raw yellow bridge timber the cowmen had laid from the top of the engine cab to the roof of the Sand Creek depot.

Bert Ullman was not doing anything about it; he was just lying here like a faded blue lizard, staring down through the dusty leaves of the scrub oak. Just lying here—and he had ridden with Danny for years.

It was too much for Billy Hafen—and he had been with Danny only four months. He cursed as he grabbed Ullman's arm. "They're going to lynch him, Bert!"

Ullman turned his head slowly. The flow of time had scalded gullies in his gaunt face. His thoughts came to this baking, brush-clotted hill from a long way off; and then his eyes were black chips again, and his lips took their twisted set against his teeth.

He said, "Sure, kid. The sheriff got him, but you never figured the sheriff intended to put him on that train?"

Billy Hafen stared at the scene a hundred and fifty yards away, at the spectators who had drained out of the fifteen or twenty buildings of the town, at the cowmen who were the hard core in command down there.

The engine stack coughed heat above the raw timber. Saddle horses grazed along the green-edged brightness of Sand Creek, a glittering knife slicing off toward the rabbit-brush mesas below purple mountains. The sky was calm, insulting blue. There was freedom everywhere, except where tall Danny Ensign stood, hatless, roped, on the depot platform.

Two cowboys dumped the water barrel at the corner of the red building and rolled it toward the open space under the beam.

"Bert! We got to—"

"Never seen a hanging, huh?" Ullman looked at Billy with savage contempt. "That barrel won't be enough, kid. Danny's got a strong neck. He'll choke there, pulling his feet up to his chest, slobbering." Ullman nodded.

"Stay down, kid!"

"If *you* won't do anything—"

"Get down." Ullman's rifle barrel wagged.

Billy Hafen's cursing broke on a sob.

The two cowboys set the barrel under the beam, upside down. Morgan Campion got up on it, yelling, waving his Scotch tam. He was the one, the old hellion. He had bullied and led the other cowmen until they had brought Danny to this day.

Billy tried to grab Ullman's rifle.

"You'll get it across the side of the neck if you don't behave, kid." Ullman's eyes were dead points until Hafen rolled away.

"Why kill old Morg?" Ullman asked. "A man's got reason to be sore when his cows are stole."

I should have got him that night! Billy Hafen thought. With the same rifle Ullman was now holding. The door of the Stirrup ranch house had opened to the call, and Campion had been squat and bulky in the light. In the willows at the edge of the yard the twist of cotton on the front sight had moved up to cover his chest.

And then Billy Hafen had lost his guts. After a while Campion had gone back inside. Danny had been shouting—angry when Billy told him afterward—and now Danny was going to hang because of Billy's failure.

"Follow it all the way and this is where it generally ends," Ullman said.

"Your same old talk! Shut up!" It seemed to Billy that Ullman was watching something he had hoped to see for a long time; watching, and afraid.

Campion was talking loudly. Train passengers leaned from the windows. Two women got out of the second coach, holding their skirts as they trotted around the caboose to get closer to the crowd. The conductor came over to the barrel and tried to say something, pointing up at the beam. Campion waved him off angrily.

"He'll jaw for a spell," Ullman said. "Maybe long enough for you to figure out what Danny done for you."

That didn't need figuring. Ullman was stalling because he had no guts to do anything. The sun was a hot iron on Billy's ragged jumper, pressing down like the weight of the situation below.

"He took you out of that livery stable, the only place you could get a job after the trouble your old man was in. Why'd he do that, kid?"

Sweat jerked down through the dust on Billy's cheeks as he stared at Campion, who had led the fight against Billy's father, one of the first ranchers in the San Isabel. Frank Hafen had said there was room for both ranchers and farmers.

"I should have killed him that night," Billy said. He glanced at Ullman's rifle. Bert was watching him.

"Why'd Danny pick you to join the bunch, kid?"

Ullman had always hinted it was because Danny wanted someone to get rid of Campion the easy way. That wasn't so. Danny had been sorry for a youngster no one would have anything to do with. Danny was a square shooter.

Old Bert knew that, but he had always been jealous of Danny, always trying to hold him down. And now the fear of going against those men below was clear up in Ullman's neck, and he would not do anything but talk.

"Look at that!" Billy said.

The sheriff was walking across the bridge toward town. He beat dust from his sleeves, and then he slapped his hands together to knock dust from them. He went all the way to his office without glancing back, and the dust of his going still hung in the deserted street after he disappeared inside.

Ullman merely glanced at the incident. "I don't know whether it's worth the effort to talk to you, Billy. I've talked to a lot of them that Danny—"

"You sure did! Your mouth was always going behind Danny's back. I don't know how he stood for the things you tried to pull!" Always telling the younger ones they ought to get out of the bunch, to get on the other side of the fence before they were in so deep they couldn't change.

Ullman started to say something, and then he looked down the hill again. His breath went out in a long sigh. Scared to death, Billy thought.

Campion's voice came up. "We're the law, boys, but we're going to act right. We got to consider the evidence against Ensign before we hoist him."

Laughter rolling up the hill smashed against Billy Hafen in an obscene, sickening wave.

The coils of manila rope around Danny's middle made bright streaks against his black coat as he turned his head slowly, watching the oak thickets on the hill.

"What did you get out of your months with Danny?" Ullman asked.

Not money. That was the only way Ullman would know how to figure it. Once, after the big haul of Campion stuff on Sad Squaw, Danny had given Billy Hafen a six-gun, and promised him other things later on. It was not always so easy to collect from those mining-camp butcher shops all at once, Danny had said.

Danny Ensign, a bold-nosed man with a white-streaking smile, had given Billy Hafen freedom from insults about his father; a chance to do something besides use a pitchfork in a stable; a chance to strike back at the men who had pushed his father into the grave.

To hell with even trying to talk to Bert Ullman about it.

"We'll testify one at a time, boys!" Campion said. "Speak up loud and don't lie about nothing."

Billy and Ullman heard the horse somewhere back in the deep part of the gulch where they lay. The sounds said it was tired. Hafen pictured the roaching back, the lather, the belly-pinching of exhaustion.

Ullman said "Stay here" by looking at Billy and pointing at the ground. Crouched low, Ullman took his rifle and went up the gulch like a prowling lobo.

With one eye on the red depot, Billy heard the murmur of voices a few moments later. A stirrup clanked when a saddle was thrown on the ground, and there came the gusty breathing of a horse too nearly dead to shake itself.

Below, Fred Clayborne, the Window Sash owner, walked over to the barrel and began to talk, pointing at Danny.

Ullman came back with Ace Strohmeyer crouching behind him. For just a moment Billy Hafen forgot Danny.

"Ace! We heard you was dead!"

Strohmeyer pivoted with one hand reaching for the bank. He sat down heavily and leaned his head back against the forks of a branch.

He said, "Everybody that got clear of the Fossil Basin mess is here now."

But Danny was down below; and he did not look so tall now against the red boards.

"We heard they killed you at the Dutchman's—after you and Danny got clear of the basin," Billy said.

"Great country for rumor." Strohmeyer closed his eyes. The backs of his long hands glistened with a dry sheen on the rifle across his legs. "How much time?"

"A few minutes." Ullman shook sweat off his forehead. "Campion likes a big show." Ullman turned his head. "Still want to sight down on Campion, kid?"

"Yeah. Give me your rifle."

"You had it that night at the Stirrup. I rode into the yard and hailed him out. You didn't shoot. Why not?"

"You know I lost my sand!"

"I hoped it was because of something else." Ullman shook his head. "No, Billy, shooting old Morg now won't help Danny none. Danny won't hang, don't worry."

Suddenly there was a solid island in the flood of despair around Billy Hafen. Sure! Ullman was all right. He had pulled Danny out of scrapes before.

Back in the gulch Strohmeyer's horse went down with a thump. Its feet made scrabbling sounds in the rocks for a while, and then the gulch was still again. Engine smoke went up toward a sky that was bright with the blue of hope for Billy Hafen.

"How do we go about it, Bert?" he asked.

"I'll show you—when it's time."

Someone passed a parasol from a coach window to one of the waiting women. The engineer leaned from his cab. White vapor plumed from the whistle, and then the sound made Billy Hafen jump. Campion shouted angrily at the engineer.

Danny Ensign was leaning against the depot now, sort of slumped.

"What they doing now?" Strohmeyer asked. He had not opened his eyes since sitting down.

"Getting close," Ullman said. "That whistle set 'em on edge."

The whistle came again. Campion's face was red as he waved his arm at the engineer. There was a shifting and a stirring in the crowd. The woman with the parasol began to edge forward.

"We got to do it fast!" Billy said.

"Just the three of us left, huh? I'll bet we make a pretty sight." Strohmeyer cleared his throat carefully. "They put the rope up yet?"

"Not yet." The bones were pushing hard at Ullman's tight, leathery face. "Danny couldn't get none of the rest of us to take Campion from the dark, kid. He knew you hated old Morg, besides wanting to show you was really one of the bunch."

Billy Hafen only half heard. Campion was getting off the barrel. Two men were bringing Danny forward, holding him under the arms. He was wounded! They were going to hang a wounded man!

"From the time he was fourteen," Ullman muttered. His face was the color of the rabbit-brush mesas. "She knew it. I promised her to keep him out of hanging trouble."

"He's been shot!" Billy said.

"No he ain't," Strohmeyer said. "What they doing now?"

"Starting." Ullman stood up. "Cover me from here, Billy." He looked like a dead man as he went out of the scrub oak and started along the open slope.

"Wait a second!" Billy cried. "Let me—"

"You stay here, kid." Strohmeyer's eyes were wide open now, the yellowish, stary eyes that had made some of the bunch say he was a little crazy, one to walk wide around. His rifle was tilted across his legs at Billy Hafen. "Bert will handle it."

"He can't—alone!"

"Stay here."

They had to lift Danny Ensign up on the barrel. The rope flashed over the timber above him. He yelled then and began to struggle. Riders held him where he was, with his feet drumming against the barrel.

A gush of sickness was thin and vile in Billy Hafen's mouth, but he could not look away. Old Bert was standing on the slope now, not moving, his rifle in both hands across his thighs.

"They putting it around his neck yet?" Strohmeyer asked.

"Bert ain't doing nothing!"

"He will."

"He don't care!" Billy retched. "You don't either."

"Bert does. Danny's his boy."

It did not sink in for a while. Billy Hafen wiped his lips and stared at Strohmeyer. One thing Ace never did was lie.

"Some men do what they can for their own blood," Strohmeyer said. "Bert tried mighty hard. He give up his ranch after Danny took to rustling, and he went along with the bunch and still kept trying." Strohmeyer's teeth made a wolf sneer in his dirty beard.

"Danny was no good, born that way. Bert was admitting that when he shifted over to working on wet-eared brats like you—and them two he got to quit the bunch."

Strohmeyer grunted as he held down a cough. "I never figured telling a man anything was worth the trouble. Stay down, kid. I promised Bert I'd do this much."

The yellow eyes were crazy all right. Billy looked down the hill again.

"They putting the noose on him?"

"Yes!" Campion was doing it, from a white horse that shone like wet satin. "Why'd you come here?"

Strohmeyer said, "To see him swing."

Campion snugged the knot against the side of Danny's neck. Billy groaned. "I should have killed Campion."

"You couldn't, kid. Bert pulled the powder in the shells that night. If you'd popped a primer you'd be out there going to hell with Bert right this minute." A sodden cough came up in Strohmeyer, and it was several moments before he spoke again. "They got men on the rope now?"

Strohmeyer was enjoying this. There was no loyalty, no decency, in all the world.

The crowd was silent now. It seemed to Hafen that no one wanted to touch the free end of the rope. Then a cowboy turned it twice around his saddle horn and backed his horse away until Danny was forced to stand by himself.

The inner rim of men pressed back, clearing the space around the barrel. Danny was alone, with the hot sun striking from the clean rope that bound his arms. A mottled green and yellow parasol, clear to the front now, made a vivid mark against the drab clothes of the cowmen.

No one saw Bert Ullman standing on the slope, and Billy Hafen refused to look at him any longer.

Strohmeyer saw Billy's head go down and watched his fingers dig like talons at the hot earth. "They're all set, huh? He's standing in the clear, is he?"

Billy had to look. Danny was on his tiptoes now. A hard line ran up from him to the yellow timber, and then slanted away to the saddle of a nervous horse.

"Kick the damned barrel out!" Campion yelled.

Three men edged forward, reaching hesitantly; and then they looked around for more support.

"Kick it over! Kick it over!" Campion roared.

Danny's cry sliced into Billy Hafen where a man holds thoughts he cannot talk about. It sent ice worms twisting through the sweat on his back. It carried despair, the squeal of cowardice, and the terror of a frightened child.

"Dad!" Danny screamed. "Dad!"

Even then no one down there but Danny knew that Ullman was standing on the hill.

"Dad!" Strohmeyer said. He laughed.

Bert Ullman raised his rifle swiftly. Its roar broke on the rocks and its sounds raced off toward the mountains. Danny's weight went dead against the rope. His knees unhinged and his body twisted sidewise until it made a true plumb line of the rope to the timber.

Except for the nervous horse, there was a frozen picture at the depot for just an instant; and then there was wildness as men knocked each other down in their confusion. The parasol disappeared. Its owner's angry scream was clear, above the shouts and yells.

The first rifle shots up the hill came from startled anger; and then they were aimed with care. Ullman stood where he was. Dust jumped on his shirt. He staggered back against a sloping rock, bracing his legs against it, still holding his lowered rifle.

Bullets ground spray from the rock. Some of them were taking chips from stone directly behind Ullman's back. He stood until he fell, and that was only seconds.

Stupid with shock, Billy Hafen lay where he was.

"Get out of here, kid," Strohmeyer said.

The cowboy below had thrown off the turns around his saddle horn and was fighting to get his horse under control. Danny Ensign was lying on the ground, with men stumbling over him.

"Get out of here!" Strohmeyer said.

There was blood at the corners of his lips. He had not tried to move since sitting down.

Campion bellowed orders for men to flank the hill. Animal panic sent Billy Hafen up the gulch on his hands and knees. He went past Strohmeyer; and then he came back and grabbed his arm.

"Come on! I'll help you."

The evil on Strohmeyer's face was tempered with a strange expression, as if he thought it odd that any man would try to help another.

"Huh-uh, Billy. I was dead back there at the Dutchman's. Danny. His horse was limping when they started to catch up with us."

Billy Hafen tried to pull him to his feet.

"Stop it, damn it! That hurts."

"Where you hit?"

"If you'd knowed Danny at all, you wouldn't ask. In the back, kid. Get out of here. You been chewing on meat too strong for you."

Billy Hafen started away.

"If that sorrel ain't dead shoot the poor devil." Strohmeyer closed his eyes and let the rifle slide from his legs, muzzle-first into the dust. "You got two good horses. Ride a long ways, kid, and remember what you seen today."

Billy Hafen ran up the gulch.

Great Medicine

Deep in the country of the Crows, Little Belly squatted in the alders, waiting for his scouts. The Crows were many and angry in the hills this summer, and there was time to think of that; but since Little Belly was a Blackfoot who had counted five coups he could not allow his fear, even to himself.

He waited in the dappled shadows for more important news than word of Indians who did not love the Blackfeet.

Wild and long before him, the ridges whispered a soft, cool song. In shining steps, beaver ponds dropped to the great river flowing east toward the land of those with the mighty medicine. Dark and motionless, Little Belly waited.

He saw at last brief movement on a far hill, a touch of sun on the neck of a pony, the merest flash of a rider who had come too close to the edge of the trees.

That was No Horns and his appaloosa. No Horns, as ever, was riding without care. He was a Piegan and Little Belly was a Blood, both Blackfeet; but Blackfeet loved no one, sometimes not even each other. So Little Belly fingered his English knife and thought how easily small things caused one to die.

He saw no more of No Horns until the scout was quite close, and by then Whirlwind, the other scout, was also on the ridge. They came to Little Belly, not obliged to obey him, still doubtful of his mission.

Little Belly said to No Horns, "From a great distance I saw you."

"Let the Crows see me also." No Horns stretched on the ground with a grunt. Soon his chest was covered with mosquitoes.

Whirlwind looked to the east. Where the river broke the fierce

sweep of ridges there was a wide, grassy route that marked the going
and coming of Crows to the plains. Whirlwind pointed. "Two days."

"How many come?" Little Belly asked.

Whirlwind signalled fifty. "The Broken Face leads."

No white man in the mountains was greater than the trapper chief,
Broken Face, whom the white men knew as Yancey. He took beaver
from the country of the Blackfeet, and he killed Blackfeet. The Crows
who put their arms about him in his camps thought long before trying
to steal the horses of his company. If there was any weakness in
Broken Face it was a weakness of mercy.

So considering, Little Belly formed the last part of his plan.

Half dozing in the deep shade where the mosquitoes whined their
hunting songs, No Horns asked, "What is this medicine you will steal
from the white trappers?"

It was not muskets. The Blackfeet had killed Crows with English
guns long before other white men came from the east to the mountains. It was not ponies. The Blackfeet traded with the Nez Perces for
better horses than any white trapper owned. It was not in the pouches
of the white men, for Little Belly had ripped into the pouches carried
on the belts of dead trappers, finding no great medicine.

But there was a power in white men that the Blackfeet feared.
Twice now they had tried to wipe the trappers from the mountains
forever, and twice the blood cost had been heavy; and the white men
were still here. Little Belly felt a chill, born of the heavy shade and the
long waiting, but coming mostly from the thought that what he must
steal might be something that could not be carried in pouches.

He stood up. "I do not know what it is, but I will know it when I see
it."

"It is their talk to the sky," Whirlwind said. "How can you steal
that?"

"I will learn it."

No Horns grunted. "They will not let you hear."

"I will travel with them, and I will hear it."

"It is their Man Above," Whirlwind said. "He will know you are
not a white man talking."

"No," Little Belly said. "It is something they carry with them."

"I did not find it," No Horns said, "and I have killed three white
men."

"You did not kill them soon enough," Little Belly said. "They hid their power before they died."

"If their medicine had been strong, I could not have killed them at all." No Horns sat up. He left streaks of blood on the heavy muscles of his chest when he brushed mosquitoes away. "Their medicine is in their sky talk."

Whirlwind said, "The Nez Perces sent chiefs to the white man's biggest town on the muddy river. They asked for a white man to teach them of the Man Above, so that they could be strong like the white men. There were promises from the one who went across these mountains long ago. The chiefs died. No white man came to teach the Nez Perces about the sky talk to make them strong."

"The Nez Perces were fools," Little Belly said. "Does one go in peace asking for the ponies of the Crows? It is not the sky talk of the trappers that makes them strong. It is something else. I will find it and steal it."

Whirlwind and No Horns followed him to the horses. Staying in the trees, they rode close to the river, close to a place where the trappers going to their summer meeting place must pass.

Little Belly took a Crow arrow from his quiver. He gave it to Whirlwind, and then Little Belly touched his own shoulder. Whirlwind understood but hesitated.

He said, "There are two days yet."

"If the wound is fresh when the trappers come, they will wonder why no Crows are close," Little Belly said.

No Horns grinned like a buffalo wolf, showing his dislike of Little Belly. He snatched the arrow from Whirlwind, fitted it to his bow and drove it with a solid chop into Little Belly's shoulder.

With his face set to hide his pain, Little Belly turned his pony and rode into the rocks close by the grassy place to wait for the coming of the trappers. The feathered end of the shaft rose and fell to his motion, sawing the head against bone and muscle.

He did not try to pull the arrow free while his companions were close. When he heard them ride away on the long trip back to Blackfoot country he tried to wrench the arrow from his shoulder. The barbs were locked against bone. They ground on it. The pain made Little Belly weak and savage, bringing water to his face and arms.

He sat down in the rocks and hacked the tough shaft off a few inches from his shoulder. He clamped his teeth close to the bleeding flesh, trying with strong movements of his neck to draw the iron head. Like a dog stripping flesh from a bone he tugged. The arrow seemed to loosen, dragging flesh and sinew with it; but the pain was great. All at once the sky turned black.

Little Belly's pony pulled away from the unconscious man and trotted to join the other two.

When Little Belly came back to the land of sky and grass he was willing to let the arrow stay where it was. It was better, too, that the white men would find him thus. But that night he was savage again with pain. He probed and twisted with the dull point of his knife until blood ran down and gathered in his breech clout. He could not get the arrow out. He thought then that he might die, and so he sang a death song, which meant that he was not afraid to die, and therefore, could not.

He dozed. The night was long, but it passed in time and the sun spread brightness on the land of the Crows. Hot and thirsty, Little Belly listened to the river, but he would not go to it in daylight. It was well he did not, for seven long-haired Crows came by when the sun was high. Three of them saw his pony tracks and came toward the rocks. Others, riding higher on the slope, found the tracks of all three horses. They called out excitedly.

A few seconds more and the three Crows coming toward Little Belly would have found him and chopped him up, but now they raced away to join the main hunt.

All day the wounded Blackfoot burned with thirst. The sun was hotter than he had ever remembered; it heaped coals on him and tortured his eyes with mist. When night came he waded into the tugging current of the river, going deep, bathing his wound and drinking. By the time he crept into the rocks again he was as hot as before. Many visions came to him that night but they ran so fast upon each other afterward he could not remember one of them clearly enough to make significance from it.

Old voices talked to him and old ghosts walked before him in the long black night. He was compressed by loneliness. The will to carry out his plan wavered. Sometimes he thought he would rise and run away, but he did not go.

From afar he heard the trappers the next day. He crawled to the edge of the rocks. The Delaware scouts found him, grim, incurious men who were not truly Indians but brothers of the white trappers. Little Belly hated them.

Without dismounting, they watched him, laughing. One of them tipped his rifle down.

Little Belly found strength to rise then, facing the Delawares without fear. The dark, ghost-ridden hours were gone. These were but men. All they could do to Little Belly was to kill him. He looked at them and spat.

Now their rifles pointed at the chest, but when the Delawares saw they could not make him afraid, they dismounted and flung him on the ground. They took his weapons. They grunted over his strong Nez Perce shield, thumping it with their hands. Then they threw it into the river. They broke his arrows and threw away his bow. One of them kept his knife.

When they took his medicine pouch and scattered the contents on the ground, Little Belly would have fought them, and died, but he remembered that he had a mission.

The big white man who came galloping on a powerful horse was not Broken Face. This white man's beard grew only on his upper lip, like a long streak of sunset sky. His eyes were the color of deep ice upon a river. Strong and white his teeth flashed when he spoke to the Delawares. Little Belly saw at once that the Delawares stood in awe of this one, which was much to know.

The white man leaped from his horse. His rifle was strange, two barrels lying one upon the other.

"Blackfoot," one of the Delawares said.

Curiously, the white man looked at Little Belly.

A Delaware took his tomahawk from his belt and leaned over the Blackfoot.

"No," the white man said, without haste. He laughed. From his pocket he took a dark bone. A slender blade grew from it quickly. With this he cut the arrow from Little Belly's shoulder. He lifted Little Belly to his feet, looking deep into the Blackfoot's eyes.

Little Belly tried to hide his pain.

"Tough one," the white man said.

The Delaware with the tomahawk spoke in Blackfoot. "We should kill him now." He looked at the white man's face, and then, reluctantly, put away his tomahawk.

Broken Face came then. Not far behind him were the mules packed with trade goods for the summer meeting. Long ago a Cheyenne lance had struck Broken Face in the corner of his mouth, crashing through below his ear. Now he never spoke directly before him but always to one side, half whispering. His eyes were the color of smoke from a lodge on a rainy day, wise from having seen many things in the mountains. He put tobacco in his mouth. He looked at Little Belly coldly.

"One of old Thunder's Bloods," he said. "Why didn't you let the Delawares have him, Stearns?"

"I intended to, until I saw how tough he was."

"All Blackfeet are tough." Broken Face spat.

Little Belly studied the two men. The Broken Face was wise and strong, and the Blackfeet had not killed him yet; but already there were signs that the weakness of mercy was stirring in his mind. It was said that Broken Face did not kill unless attacked. Looking into Stearns' pale eyes, Little Belly knew that Stearns would kill any time.

"Couldn't you use him?" Stearns asked.

Broken Face shook his head.

Stearns held up the bloody stub of arrow. He smiled. "No gratitude?"

"Hell!" Broken Face said. "He'd pay you by slicing your liver. He's Blackfoot. Leave him to the Delawares."

"What will they do?"

"Throw him on a fire, maybe. Kill him by inches. Cut the meat off his bones and throw the bones in the river. The Bloods did that to one of them last summer." Broken Face walked to his horse.

"Couldn't you use him to get into Blackfoot country peacefully?" Stearns asked. "Sort of a hostage?"

"No. Any way you try to use a Blackfoot he don't shine at all." Broken Face got on his horse, studying the long ridges ahead. "Likely one of the Crows that was with us put the arrow into him. Too bad they didn't do better. He's no good to us. Blackfeet don't make treaties, and if they did, they wouldn't hold to 'em. They just don't shine no way, Stearns. Come on."

Not by the words, but by the darkening of the Delawares' eyes, Little Belly knew it was death. He thought of words to taunt the

Delawares while they killed him, and then he remembered he had a mission. To die bravely was easy; but to steal powerful medicine was greatness.

Little Belly looked to Stearns for mercy. The white man had saved him from the Delawares, and had cut the arrow from his shoulder; but those two deeds must have been matters of curiosity only. Now there was no mercy in the white man's eyes. In one quick instant Little Belly and Stearns saw the utter ruthlessness of each other's natures.

Stearns was greater than Broken Face, Little Belly saw, for Stearns made no talk. He merely walked away.

The Delawares freed their knives. "Is the Blackfoot a great runner?" one asked.

In his own tongue Little Belly spoke directly to Broken Face. "I would travel with you to my home."

"The Crows would not thank me." Broken Face began to ride away, with Stearns beside him.

"Is the Blackfoot cold?" A Delaware began to kick apart a rotten log to build a fire.

"I am one," Little Belly said. "Give me back my knife and I will fight all of Broken Face's Indians! Among my people Broken Face would be treated so."

"What did he say?" Stearns asked Broken Face.

Broken Face told him. He let his horse go a few more paces and then he stopped. For an instant an anger of indecision twisted the good side of Broken Face's mouth. "Let him go. Let him travel with us."

The ring of Delawares was angry, but they obeyed.

It had been so close that Little Belly felt his limbs trembling; but it had worked: deep in Broken Face was softness that had grown since his early days in the mountains because he now loved beaver hides more than strength. Now he was a warrior with too many ponies.

Little Belly pushed between the Delawares and began to gather up the items from his medicine pouch. It shamed him, but if he did not do so, he thought they might wonder too much and guess the nature of his cunning.

Jarv Yancey—Broken Face—said to Stearns, "You saved his hide in the first place. Now you can try to watch him while he's with us. It'll teach you something."

Stearns grinned. "I didn't know him from a Crow, until the Delawares told me. You know Blackfeet. Why'd *you* let him go?"

Broken Face's scowl showed that he was searching for an answer to satisfy himself. "Someday the Blackfeet may catch me. If they give me a running chance, that's all I'll want. Maybe this will help me get it."

"They'll break your legs with a club before they give you that running chance." Stearns laughed.

There was startled shrewdness in the look the Mountain Man gave the greenhorn making his first trip to the Rockies. "You learn fast, Stearns."

"The Scots are savages at heart, Yancey. They know another savage when they see him. Our wounded friend back there has a heart blacker than a beaten Macdonald trapped in a marsh. I took several glances to learn it, but I saw it."

The Delawares rode by at the trot, scattering to go on ahead and on the flanks as scouts. Neither Stearns nor Yancey looked back to see what was happening to Little Belly.

Ahead, the whispering blue of the mountains rose above the clear green of the ridges. There were parks and rushing rivers yet to cross, a world to ride forever. Behind, the mules with heavy packs, the *engagées* cursing duty, the wool-clad trappers riding with rifles aslant gave reason for Jarv Yancey's presence. As Stearns looked through the suntangled air to long reaches of freshness, a joyous, challenging expression was his reason for being here.

Just for a while Yancey thought back to a time when he, too, looked with new eyes on a new world every morning; but now the ownership of goods, and the employment of trappers and flunkies, gave caution to his looks ahead. And he had given refuge to a Blackfoot, which would be an insult to the friendly Crows, an error to be mended with gifts.

Stearns spoke lazily. "When he said, 'I am one,' it touched you, didn't it, Yancey? That's why you didn't let the Delawares have him."

Jarv Yancey grunted.

The Blackfoot walked with hunger in his belly and a great weakness in his legs, but he walked. The horses of the trappers kicked dust upon him. The *engagées* cursed him, but he did not understand the words. He could not be humble, but he was patient.

And now he changed his plan. The Broken Face was not as great as the other white man who rode ahead, although the other was a stranger in the mountains. The cruel calmness of the second white man's eyes showed that he was protected by mighty medicine. Little Belly would steal greatness from him, instead of from Broken Face.

There would be time; it was far to the edge of Blackfoot country.

The one called Stearns took interest in Little Belly, learning from him some Blackfoot speech through talking slowly with the signs. Little Belly saw that it was the same interest Stearns took in plants that were strange to him, in birds, in the rocks of the land. It was good, for Little Belly was studying Stearns also.

It was Stearns who saw that Little Belly got a mule to ride. Also, because of Stearns the Delawares quit stepping on Little Belly's healing shoulder and stopped stripping the blanket from him when they walked by his sleeping place at night.

There was much to pay the Delawares, and there was much to pay all the white men, too, but Little Belly buried insults deep and drew within himself, living only to discover the medicine that made Stearns strong.

By long marches the trappers came closer to the mountains. One day the Crows who had ridden near Little Belly when he lay in the rocks came excitedly into the camp at nooning, waving scalps. The scalps were those of No Horns and Whirlwind. Little Belly showed a blank face when the Crows taunted him with the trophies. They rode around him, shouting insults, until they had worked up rage to kill him.

The Broken Face spoke to them sharply, and their pride was wounded. They demanded why this ancient enemy of all their people rode with the friends of the Crows. They were howlers then, like old women, moaning of their hurts, telling of their love for Broken Face and all white trappers.

Broken Face must make the nooning longer then, to sit in council with the Crows. He told how this Blackfoot with him had once let him go in peace. The Crows did not understand, even if they believed. He said that Little Belly would speak to his people about letting Broken

Face come into their lands to trap. The Crows did not understand, and it was certain they did not believe.

Then Broken Face gave presents. The Crows understood, demanding more presents.

Dark was the look the white trapper chief gave Little Belly when the Crows at last rode away. But Stearns laughed and struck Broken Face upon the shoulder. Later, the Blackfoot heard the Delawares say that Stearns had said he would pay for the presents.

That was nothing, Little Belly knew; Stearns gave the Delawares small gifts, also, when they brought him plants or flowers he had not seen before, or birds they killed silently with arrows. It might be that Stearns was keeping Little Belly alive to learn about his medicine. The thought startled him.

Now the mountains were losing their blue haze. At night the air was like a keen blade. Soon the last of the buffalo land would lie behind. There was a tightening of spirit. There were more guards at night, for the land of the Blackfeet was not far ahead. With pride, Little Belly saw how the camp closed in upon itself by night because his people were not far away.

And still he did not know about the medicine.

Once he had thought it was hidden in a pouch from which Stearns took every day thin, glittering knives to cut the hair from his face, leaving only the heavy streak across his upper lip. On a broad piece of leather Stearns sharpened the knives, and he was very careful with them.

But he did not care who saw them or who saw how he used them; so it was not the knives, Little Belly decided. All day Stearns' gun was busy. He brought in more game than any of the hunters, and since he never made sky talk before a hunt, the Blackfoot became convinced that his powerful medicine was carried on his body.

At last Little Belly settled on a shining piece of metal which Stearns carried always in his pocket. It was like a ball that had been flattened. There were lids upon it, thin and gleaming, with talking signs marked on them. They opened like the wings of a bird.

On top of it was a small stem. Every night before he slept Stearns took the round metal from his pocket. With his fingers he twisted the small stem, looking solemn. His actions caused the flattened ball to talk with a slow grasshopper song. And then Stearns would look at the stars, and immediately push the lids down on the object and put it back into his pocket, where it was fastened by a tiny yellow rope of metal.

This medicine was never farther from Stearns' body than the shining rope that held it. He was very careful when the object lay in his hand. No man asked him what it was, but often when Stearns looked at his medicine, the trappers glanced at the sky.

Little Belly was almost satisfied; but still, he must be sure.

One of the *engagées* was a Frenchman who had worked for the English fathers west of Blackfoot country. Little Belly began to help him with the horses in the daytime. The Broken Face scowled at this, not caring for any kind of Indians near his horses. But the company was still in Crow country, and Little Belly hated Crows, and it was doubtful that the Blackfoot could steal the horses by himself, so Broken Face, watchful, wondering, allowed Little Belly to help the Frenchman.

After a time Little Belly inquired carefully of the *engagée* about the metal ball that Stearns carried. The Frenchman named it, but the word was strange, so Little Belly soon forgot it. The *engagée* explained that the moon and stars and the sun and the day and night were all carried in the metal.

There were small arrows in the medicine. They moved and the medicine was alive, singing a tiny song. The *engagée* said one glance was all Stearns needed to know when the moon would rise, when the sun would set, when the day would become night and the night would turn to day.

These things Little Belly could tell without looking at a metal ball. Either the Frenchman was a liar or the object Stearns carried was worthless. Little Belly grew angry with himself, and desperate; perhaps Stearns' medicine was not in the silvery object after all.

All through the last of the buffalo lands bands of Crows came to the company, professing love for the Broken Face, asking why a Blackfoot traveled with him. The trapper chief gave them awls and bells and trinkets and small amounts of poor powder.

He complained to Stearns, "That stinking Blood has cost me twenty dollars in goods, St Louis!"

Stearns laughed. "I'll stand it."

"Why?"

"He wants to kill me. I'd like to know why. I've never seen a man who wanted so badly to kill me. It pleases me to have an enemy like that."

Broken Face shook his head.

"Great friends and great enemies, Yancey. They make life worth living; and the enemies make it more interesting by far."

The Mountain Man's gray eyes swept the wild land ahead. "I agree on that last." After a while he said, "Besides wanting to kill you, like he said, which he would like to do to any white man, what does he want? There was three of them back there where the Delawares found him. He didn't have no cause to be left behind, not over one little arrow dabbed into him. He joined us, Stearns."

"I don't know why, but I know what he wants now." Stearns showed his teeth in a great streaking grin. "I love an enemy that can hate all the way, Yancey."

"If that makes you happy, you can have the whole damned Blackfoot nation to love, lock, stock and barrel." After a time Yancey began to laugh at his own remark.

Little Belly was close to Stearns the evening the grizzly bear disrupted the company, at a bad time, when camp was being made. There was a crashing on the hill where the *engagées* were gathering wood. One of them shouted. The other fired his rifle.

The coughing of an enraged bear came loudly from the bushes. The *engagées* leaped down the hill, throwing away their rifles. Little Belly looked at Stearns. The big white man was holding his medicine. He had only time to snap the lids before grabbing his rifle from where it leaned against a pack. The medicine swung on its golden rope against his thigh as he cocked his rifle.

Confusion ran ahead of the enormous silver bear that charged the camp. The mules wheeled away, kicking, dragging loosened packs. The horses screamed and ran. Men fell over the scattered gear, cursing and yelling as they scrambled for their guns. There were shots and some of them struck the bear without effect.

Thundering low, terrible with power, the grizzly came. Now only Stearns and Little Belly stood in its path, and the Blackfoot was without weapons. Little Belly fought with terror but he stayed because Stearns stayed. The white man's lips smiled but his eyes were like the ice upon the winter mountains.

Wide on his feet he stood, with his rifle not all the way to his shoulder. Tall and strong he stood, as if to stop the great bear with his body. Little Belly covered his mouth.

When Stearns fired, the bear was so close Little Belly could see the surging of its muscles on the shoulder hump and the stains of berries on its muzzle. It did not stop at the sound of Stearns' rifle, but it was dead, for its legs fell under it, no longer driving. It slid almost to Stearns's feet, bruising the grass, jarring rocks.

For a moment there was silence. Stearns poured his laugh into the quiet, a huge deep laugh that was happy, wild and savage as the mountains. He looked at his medicine then, solemnly. He held it to his ear, and then he smiled and put it back into his pocket. He stooped to see how his bullet had torn into the bear's brain through the eye.

There was still confusion, for the mules and horses did not like the bear smell, but Stearns paid no attention. He looked at Little Belly standing there with nothing in his hands. Stearns did not say the Blackfoot was brave, but his eyes said so. Once more he laughed, and then he turned to speak to Broken Face, who had been at the far end of camp when the bear came.

One of the *engagées* shot the bear in the neck. Broken Face knocked the man down for wasting powder and causing the animals more fright.

Quickly Little Belly left to help with the horses, hiding all his thoughts. Truly, this medicine of Stearns' was powerful. Little Belly could say that Stearns was brave, that he shot true, standing without fear, and laughing afterward. All this was true, but still there was the element of medicine which protected a brave warrior against all enemies.

Without it, bravery was not enough. Without it, the most courageous warrior might die from a shot not even aimed at him. In the round thing Stearns carried was trapped all movement of the days and nights and a guiding of the owner in war and hunting.

Now Little Belly was sure about the object, but as he pondered deep into the night, his sureness wore to caution. He could not remember whether Stearns listened to the talk of his medicine before the bear made sounds upon the hill or after the shouts and crashing began.

So Little Belly did not push his plan hard yet. He watched Stearns, wondering, waiting for more evidence. Sometimes the white man saw the hard brown eyes upon him as he moved about the camp, and when he did he showed his huge grin.

Three days from the vague boundary of ridges and rivers that marked the beginning of Blackfoot lands, the Delaware scouts reported buffalo ahead. At once the camp was excited. Broken Face looked at the hills around him, and would not let more than a few ride ahead to hunt.

Stearns borrowed a Sioux bow and arrows from one of the Delawares. He signalled to Little Belly. Riding beside Stearns, the Blackfoot went out to hunt. With them were the Delawares, Broken Face, and a few of the trappers. When Broken Face first saw the weapons Little Belly carried he spoke sharply to Stearns, who laughed.

Little Belly's mule was not for hunting buffalo, so the Blackfoot did not go with the others to the head of the valley where the animals were. He went, instead, to the lower end, where he would have a chance to get among the buffalo when the other hunters drove them. The plan was good. When the buffalo came streaming down the valley, the startled mule was caught among them and had to run with them, or be crushed.

In the excitement Little Belly forgot everything but that he was a hunter. He rode and shouted, driving his arrows through the lungs of fat cows. He could not guide his mount, for it was terror-stricken by the dust and noise and shock of huge brown bodies all around it. When there was a chance the mule ran straight up a hill and into the trees in spite of all that Little Belly could do to turn it.

He saw Stearns still riding, on through the valley and to a plain beyond where the buffalo still ran. Little Belly had one arrow left. He tried to ride after Stearns, but the mule did not like the valley and was stubborn about going into it. By the time the Blackfoot got steady movement from his mount, Stearns was coming back to where Broken Face and some of the other hunters were riding around a wounded bull that charged them in short rushes.

Down in the valley, Stearns said to Yancey, "That bull has a dozen bullets in him!"

"He can take three dozen." Yancey looked up the hill toward Little Belly. "Your Blackfoot missed a good chance to light out."

Stearns was more interested in the wounded buffalo at the moment.

The hunters were having sport with it, running their horses at it. Occasionally a man put another shot into it. With purple blood streaming from its mouth and nostrils, rolling its woolly head, the bull defied them to kill it. Dust spouted from its sides when bullets struck. The buffalo bellowed, more in anger than in pain.

"How long can it last?" Stearns asked, amazed.

"A long time," Yancey said. "I've seen 'em walk away with a month's supply of good galena."

"I can kill it in one minute."

Yancey shook his head. "Not even that gun of yours."

"One shot."

"Don't get off your horse, you damned fool!"

Stearns was already on the ground. "One minute, Yancey." He looked at his watch. He walked toward the bull.

Red-eyed, with lowered head, the buffalo watched him. It charged. Stearns fired one barrel. It was nothing. The bull came on. Stearns fired again. The buffalo went down, and like the bear, it died almost at Stearns' feet.

"You damned fool!" Yancey said. "You shot it head-on!"

Stearns laughed. "Twice. For a flash, I didn't think that second one would do the work."

Little Belly had seen. There was no doubt now: Stearns had made medicine with the round thing and it had given him power to do the impossible.

The hunters began to butcher cows. Fleet horses stood without riders. Little Belly had one arrow left, and Stearns was now apart from the others, examining the dead bull. But when the Blackfoot reached the valley Broken Face was once more near Stearns, with his rifle slanting toward Little Belly.

"Take that arrow he's got left," Yancey said.

Stearns did so. "I was going to give him his chance."

"You don't give a Blackfoot any chance!" Yancey started away. "There's other arrows sticking in some of the cows he shot. Remember that, Stearns."

Little Belly did not understand the words, but the happy challenge of Stearns' smile was clear enough.

They went together to one of the cows Little Belly had killed. The white man cut the arrow from its lungs. He put the arrow on the ground and then he walked a few paces and laid his rifle on the grass. He looked at Little Belly, waiting.

The white man still had his medicine. It was too strong for Little Belly; but otherwise, he would not have been afraid to take the opportunity offered him. He tossed his bow toward the mule. The white man was disappointed.

They ate of the steaming hot liver of the cow, looking at each other while they chewed.

That night the company of Broken Face feasted well, ripping with their teeth, the great, rich pieces of dripping hump rib as they squatted at the fires. Little Belly ate with the rest, filling his belly, filling his mind with the last details of his plan.

When the stars were cold above, he rose from his blanket and went to the fire. He roasted meat, looking toward the outer rim of darkness where Stearns slept near Broken Face. Then, without stealth, Little Belly went through the night to where the French *engagée* guarded one side of the horse corral.

The Frenchman saw him coming from the fire and was not alarmed. Little Belly held out the meat. The man took it with one hand, still holding to his rifle. After a time the guard squatted down, using both hands to hold the rib while he ate. Little Belly's hand trailed through the dark, touching the stock of the gun that leaned against the man's leg.

The *engagée* smacked his lips. The meat was still against his beard when Little Belly snatched the gun and swung it. Quite happy the Frenchman died, eating good fat cow. Little Belly took his knife at once. He crouched, listening. The rifle barrel had made sound. Moments later, the horses shifting inside their rope enclosure made sound also.

Little Belly started back to the fire, and then he saw that two trappers had risen and were roasting meat. He put the knife at the back of his belt and went forward boldly. He picked up his blanket and threw it around him. He lay down near Stearns and Broken Face.

One of the trappers said, "Was that Blackfoot sleeping there before?"

Grease dripped from the other trapper's chin as he looked across the fire. "Don't recall. I know I don't want him sleeping near me. I been uneasy ever since that Blood took up with us."

After the white men had eaten they went back to their blankets. The camp became quiet. For a long time Little Belly watched the cold star-fires in the sky, and listened to the breathing of Stearns.

Then, silent as the shadows closing on the dying fire, the Blackfoot moved. At last, on his knees beside Stearns, with the knife in one hand, Little Belly's fingers walked beneath the blanket until he touched and gripped the metal rope of Stearns' great medicine. To kill the owner before taking his medicine would mean the power of it would go with his spirit to another place.

Little Belly's fingers clutched the chain. The other hand swung the knife high.

Out of the dark came a great fist. It smashed against Little Belly's forehead. It flung him back upon the ground. The white stars flashed in his brain, and he did not know that he held the medicine in his hand.

Stearns was surging up. Broken Face was out of his blanket in an instant. The hammer of his rifle clicked. Little Belly rolled away, bumping into packs of trade goods. He leaped up and ran. A rifle gushed. The bullet sought him. He heard it tear a tree. He ran. The medicine bumped his wrist. Great was Little Belly's exultation.

Stearns' rifle boomed twice, the bullets growling close to Little Belly; but now nothing could harm him. The great medicine was in his hand, and his legs were fleet.

The camp roared. Above it all, Little Belly heard Stearns' mighty laugh. The white man had not yet discovered his terrible loss, Little Belly thought. Stearns and maybe others would follow him now, deep into the lands of his own people.

When day came Little Belly saw no signs that Stearns or any of the white men were pursuing him. It occurred to him that they were afraid to do so, now that he had stolen their greatest power.

The medicine was warm. All night he had carried it in his hand, sometimes listening with awe to the tiny talk it made. It frightened him to think of opening the lids, but he knew he must do so; this medicine that lived must look into his face and know who owned it now. He pried one lid open. There was another with a carved picture of a running horse and talking signs that curved like grass in the wind.

Now Little Belly knew why Stearns' horse had been more powerful and fleeter than any owned by other members of Broken Face's
company.

Little Belly opened the second lid. His muscles jerked. He grunted.
Golden talking signs looked at him from a white face. There were two
long pointing arrows, and a tiny one that moved about a small circle.
The song of the medicine was strong and steady, talking of the winds
that blew across the mountains, telling of the stars that flowed in the
summer sky, telling of the coming and going of the moon and sun.

Here was captured the power of strong deeds, held in the mysteri-
ous whispering of the medicine. Now Little Belly would be great
forever among the Blackfeet, and his people would be great.

The age-old longing of all men to control events that marched
against them was satisfied in Little Belly. He pushed the lids together.
He held the medicine in both hands, looking at the sky.

In his pouch was his old medicine that sometimes failed, the dried
eye of a mountain lion, a blue feather that had fallen in the forest when
Little Belly had seen no bird near, a bright green rock shaped like the
head of a pony, the claw of an eagle, and other things.

When the sun was straight above, the Crows were on his trail. He
saw all three of them when they rode across a park. His first thought
was to run hard, staying in the heavy timber where their ponies could
not go. He had learned that on his first war party against the Crows
long ago.

One of the enemies would stay on Little Belly's trail. The others
would circle around to keep him from reaching the next ridge. It was a
matter of running fast. Little Belly started. He stopped, remembering that he had powerful medicine.

He took it from his pouch and looked at it, as Stearns had done
before he killed the bear, before he killed the great buffalo. The
medicine made its steady whisper in the silent forest. It told Little
Belly that he was greater than all enemies.

So he did not run. He went back on his own trail and hid behind a
log. No jay warned of his presence. No squirrel shouted at him. His
medicine kept them silent. And his medicine brought the Crow, leading his pony, straight to Little Belly.

While the Crow was turning, Little Belly was over the log with his knife. Quickly, savagely, he struck. A few minutes later he had a scalp, a heavy musket, another knife, and a pony. He gave fierce thanks to his medicine.

Little Belly rode into the open below one end of the ridge. The Crow circling there saw him and came to the edge of the trees. Little Belly knew him at once, Thunder Coming, a young war chief of the Crows. They taunted each other. Little Belly waved the fresh scalp. Thunder Coming rode into the open to meet his enemy. Out of rifleshot, they ran their ponies around each other, yelling more insults.

At last they rode toward each other. Both fired their rifles and missed. At once Thunder Coming turned his horse and rode away to reload.

Little Belly would have done the same, except that he knew how strong his medicine was. He raced after Thunder Coming. The Crow was startled by this breach of custom, but when he realized that he was running from one who chased him, he started to swing his pony in a great circle to come back.

The Blackfoot knew what was in Thunder Coming's mind then. The Crow expected them to try to ride close to each other, striking coup, not to kill but to gain glory.

Little Belly allowed it to start that way. Then he swerved his pony, and instead of striking lightly and flashing past, he crashed into Thunder Coming, and swung the musket like a war club.

Thunder Coming died because he believed in the customs of war between Blackfeet and Crows; but Little Belly knew he died because of medicine he could not stand against. There was meat in Thunder Coming's pouch. That, along with his scalp, was welcome.

For a while Little Belly stayed in the open, waiting for the third Crow to appear. The last enemy did not come. Although the Blackfoot's medicine was great this day, he did not care to wait too long in Crow country. He went home with two Crow scalps and two Crow ponies.

The young men called him brave. The old chiefs were pleased. Little Belly boasted of his medicine. With it, he sang, the white men could be swept from the hills. The Blackfeet became excited, ready for battle. The women wailed against the coming bloodshed.

Each night when the first stars came Little Belly talked to his medicine, just as he had seen Stearns do; but the Blackfoot did not let others see him when he twisted the small stalk that protruded from the flattened ball. The medicine made a tiny whirring noise to show that it was pleased.

While the Blackfeet made ready for war, sending scouts to report each day on the progress of Broken Face and his company, Little Belly guarded his medicine jealously. It was living medicine. It was what the white men would not reveal to the Nez Perces who had sent chiefs down the muddy river. Little Belly had not gone begging white men to tell what made them powerful; he had stolen the secret honorably.

Now he had the strength of a bear and the wisdom of a beaver. His fight against the Crows had proved how mighty was his medicine. With it he would be great, and the Blackfeet would be great because he could lead them to victory against all enemies.

It was right that he should begin by leading them against the trappers. Let the old chiefs sit upon a hill. Every day the scouts returned, telling how carefully the white men held their camps. The scouts named men they had seen in the company, strong warriors who had fought the Blackfeet before.

Thunder and the old chiefs were thoughtful. They agreed it was right for Little Belly to lead the fight.

At last the Blackfeet rode to war.

For several days Jarv Yancey had been worried. The Delaware outriders were not holding far from the line of travel now; they had seen too much spying from the hills, and this was Blackfoot country.

"How do they usually come at you?" Stearns asked.

"When you're not looking for 'em," Yancey said.

"Would they hit a company this big?"

"We'll find out."

Stearns laughed. "Maybe I'll get my watch back."

"Be more concerned with holding onto your hair."

The trappers camped that night in a clump of timber with open space all around it. Yancey sent the guards out into the open, and they lay there in the moonlight, peering across the wet grass, watching for movement from the black masses of the hills. The silence of the mountains rested hard upon them that night.

Cramped and wet, those who stood the early morning watch

breathed more easily when dawn came sliding from the sky and brought no stealthy rustling of the grass, no shrieks of bullets.

All that day, the Delawares, on the flanks and out ahead and on the backtrail, seemed to be crowding closer and closer to the caravan. They knew; they smelled it. And Yancey and the other trappers could smell it too. Stearns was quieter than usual, but not subdued. His light blue eyes smiled into the fire that night before he went out to take his turn at guard.

The trappers watched him keenly. They knew how joyfully he risked his neck against big game, doing foolish things. The Bloods were something else.

Mandan Ingalls was satisfied. He said to Sam Williams, "He don't scare for nothing. He's plumb anxious to tackle the Bloods. He'd rather fight than anything."

"He come to the right country for it," Williams said.

That night a nervous *engagée* fired his rifle at a shadow. Without shouting or confusion, the camp was up and ready in a moment. Then men cursed and went back to bed, waiting for the next disturbance. The old heads remembered the war cries of the Blackfeet, the ambushes of the past, and friends long dead. Remembering, the veterans slept well while they could.

When the moon was gone Little Belly led four young men in to stampede the white men's horses. They came out of a spit of timber and crawled to a winding stream. Close to the bank, overhung with grass, they floated down the creek as silently as drifting logs.

They rose above the bank and peered fiercely through the darkness. The smell of animals close by told Little Belly how well his medicine had directed him. A guard's rifle crashed before they were among the horses. After that there was no more shooting, for Broken Face himself was at the corral, shouting orders.

In addition to the rope enclosure around the animals, they were tied together, and then picketed to logs buried in the earth. So while there was a great kicking and thumping and snorting, Little Belly and his companions were able to run with only the horses they cut loose.

But still, it was good. The raiders returned to the main war party with ten animals.

Remembering the uproar and stumbling about when the bear

charged the trappers as they prepared to rest, Little Belly set the attack for evening, when Broken Face would be making camp. Two hundred warriors were ready to follow the Blackfoot war chief.

The scouts watched the trappers. The Blackfeet moved with them, staying in the trees on the hills. A few young men tried to surprise the Delawares, but the white men's scouts were wary. In the afternoon Little Belly thought he knew where the trappers would stop, in an open place near a small stand of trees. They did not trust the dark forest, now that they knew the Blackfoot were watching.

Little Belly went to make his medicine.

He opened the lids to look upon the white face with the shining talking signs. Upon the mirror of the medicine was a drop of water, left from last night's swimming in the creek. Little Belly blew it away. His face was close to the medicine. The tiny arrow was not moving. Quickly, he put the round thing to his ear.

There was no whispering. The medicine had died.

Little Belly was frightened. He remembered how Stearns had laughed through the darkness when Little Belly was running away with the round thing. There was trickery in the medicine, for it had died as soon as Little Belly sought its strength to use against white men.

The Blackfoot let the medicine fall. It struck the earth with a solid thump. He stared at it, half expecting to see it run away. And then he saw the tiny arrow was moving again.

Little Belly knelt and held the round thing in his hands. It was alive once more. He heard the talking of the power inside, the power of white men who smiled when they fought. Once more that strength was his. Now he was warm again and his courage was sound.

Even as he watched, the arrow died.

In desperation, with all the memories of Blackfoot sorrows running in his mind, Little Belly tried to make the medicine live. He talked to it by twisting the stalk. For a time the medicine was happy. It sang. The tiny arrow moved. But it died soon afterward. Little Belly twisted the stalk until the round thing choked, and the stalk would not turn any more.

He warmed the medicine, cupping it in his hands against his breast. Surely warmth would bring it back to life; but when he looked again there was no life.

He was savage then. This was white man's medicine, full of trickery and deceit. Little Belly hurled it away.

He went back to the Blackfoot warriors, who watched him with sharp eyes. Wind Eater said, "We are ready."

Looking through a haze of hate and fear, Little Belly looked below and saw that Stearns was riding with the lead scouts. "It is not time yet." The spirit of the medicine had fled back to Stearns.

"We are ready," Wind Eater said.

Little Belly went away to make medicine, this time with the items in his pouch. He did many things. He burned a pinch of tobacco. It made a curl of white smoke in the shape of death.

Yesterday, it would have been death for Blackfoot enemies. Now, Little Belly could not read his medicine and be sure. After a while he went back to the others again. They were restless.

"The white men will camp soon."

"Is not Little Belly's medicine strong?"

"The Broken Face will not be caught easily once he is camped."

"Is not Little Belly's medicine good?" Wind Eater asked.

"It is strong." Little Belly boasted, and they believed him. But his words struck from an emptiness inside. It seemed that he had thrown away his strength with the round thing. In desperation he considered going back to look for it. Maybe it had changed and was talking once more.

"We wait," Wind Eater said. "If Little Belly does not wish to lead us—"

"We go," Little Belly said.

He led the warriors down the hill.

The length of Little Belly's waiting on the hill while dark doubts chilled him was the margin by which the Blackfoot charge missed catching the trappers as the bear had caught them. Little Belly saw that it was so. The thought gave fury to his movements, and if he had been followed to where he rode, the Blackfeet could have overrun the camp in one burst.

They knocked the Delawares back upon the main company. Straight at the camp the Blackfeet thundered, shrieking, firing muskets and arrows. The first shock of surprise was their advantage. The *engagées* leaped for the clump of timber, forgetting all else. The trappers fired. While they were reloading Little Belly urged his followers to carry over them.

He himself got into the camp and fired his musket into the bearded face of a trapper standing behind a mule to reload his rifle. But there was no Blackfoot then at Little Belly's back. All the rest had swerved and were screaming past the camp.

Little Belly had to run away, and he carried the picture of Stearns, who had stood and watched him without firing his two-barrelled rifle when he might have.

The Broken Face gave orders. His men ran the mules and horses into the little stand of trees. They piled packs to lie behind. Broken Face rallied the *engagées*.

It was a fort the Blackfeet tried to ride close to the second time. The rifles of the trappers slammed warriors from the backs of racing ponies.

There would never be a rush directly into the trees, and Little Belly knew it. The fight might last for days now, but in the end, the white men, who could look calmly on the faces of their dead and still keep fighting, would win. They would not lose interest. The power of their medicine would keep them as dangerous four days from now as they were at the moment.

The Blackfeet were not unhappy. They had seen two dead white men carried into the trees, and another crawling there with wounds. There were four dead warriors; but the rest could ride around the trees for a long time, shooting, yelling, killing a few more trappers. And when the Indians tired and went away, it would take them some time to remember that they had not won.

All this Little Belly realized, and he was not happy. True, his medicine had saved him from harm even when he was among the mules and packs; but if the white man's medicine had not betrayed him before the fight, then all the other warriors would have followed close upon him and the battle would be over.

He rode out and stopped all the young men who were racing around the trees, just out of rifleshot. He made them return to the main body of warriors.

"I will kill the Broken Face," Little Belly said.

Wind Eater smiled. "By night?"

"Now. When it is done the others will be frightened with no one to lead them. They will be caught among the trees and we will kill them all." His words were not quite true, Little Belly realized. The men who rode with Broken Face would not fall apart over his death, but an individual victory would prove how strong the Blackfeet were; and then they might go all the way in, as Little Belly had fought Thunder Coming, the Crow war chief.

Cold-seated in Little Belly's reason was the knowledge that one determined charge into the trees would end everything; but a voice whispered, *If the medicine is good.*

Signalling peace, Little Belly rode alone toward the trees. The Broken Face came alone to meet him.

"Before the sun dies I will fight Broken Face here." Little Belly made a sweeping motion with his hand. He saw blood on the sleeve of the white man's shirt, but Broken Face held the arm as if it were not wounded. Little Belly knew that fear had never lived behind the maimed features of the man who watched him coldly.

"When you are dead the Blackfeet will go away?" Broken Face asked.

"If the white men go away when you are dead."

Broken Face's mouth was solemn but a smile touched his eyes briefly. "There will be a fight between us." He went back to the trees.

When Stearns knew what had been said, he grinned. "High diplomacy with no truth involved."

"That's right," Yancey said. "But killing Little Belly will take a heap of steam out of the rest."

"If you can do it."

Yancey was surprised. "I intend to."

"Your arm is hurt. Let me fight him," Stearns said.

Yancey bent his arm. The heavy muscles had been torn by a hunting arrow, but that was not enough to stop him. He looked at his packs, at mules and horses that would be fewer when the Bloods swept past again. Something in him dragged at the thought of going out. It was foolish; it was not sound business.

Casually he looked at his trappers. No matter what he did, they would not doubt his guts. Jarv Yancey's courage was a legend in the mountains and needed no proving against a miserable riled-up Blackfoot war chief. The decision balanced delicately in Yancey's mind. A man died with his partner, if the time came; and a man in command fought for those he hired, or he should not hire good men.

Yancey shook his head. "I'll do it."

"I thought so." Stearns put his arm around Yancey's shoulder in friendly fashion, and then he drove his right fist up with a twist of his body. Yancey's head snapped back. He was unconscious as Stearns lowered him to the ground.

"It's my fault that Little Belly is still alive," Stearns said. He looked at Mandan Ingalls. "You might take a look at Yancey's arm while things are quiet."

Ingalls spat. "For a while after he comes to, you're going to be lucky to be somewhere with only a Blood to pester you. If you don't handle that Blackfoot, Stearns, you'd just as well stay out there."

Stearns laughed. He took his horse from the timber with a rush. Once in the open, looking at the solid rank of Blackfoot cavalry across the grass, he leaped down and adjusted his cinch. He waved his rifle at them, beckoning. He vaulted into the saddle and waited.

The song of the dead medicine was in Little Belly's ears. It mocked him. Once more he had been tricked. Stearns, not Broken Face, was down there waiting. The power of the stolen medicine had gone through the air back to the man who owned it, and that was why the great one who laughed was waiting there, instead of Broken Face.

Silent were the ranks of Blackfeet and silent were the rifles of the trappers. Little Belly hesitated. The fierce eyes of his people turned toward him. In that instant Little Belly wondered how great he might have been without the drag of mystic thinking to temper his actions, for solid in him was a furious courage that could carry him at times without the blessing of strong medicine.

He sent his pony rushing across the grass. He knew Stearns would wait until he was very close, as he had waited for the bear, as he had faced the wounded buffalo. Riding until he estimated that moment at hand, Little Belly fired his musket.

He saw Stearns' head jerk back. He saw the streak of blood that became a running mass on the side of the white man's face. But Stearns did not tumble from his horse. He shook his head like a cornered buffalo. He raised the rifle.

Stearns shot the pony under Little Belly. The Blackfoot felt it going down in full stride. He leaped, rolling over and over in the grass, coming to his feet unharmed. The empty musket was gone then. Little Belly had only his knife.

There was a second voice to the white man's rifle. The silent mouth of it looked down at Little Belly, but the rifle did not speak. Stearns thrust it into the saddle scabbard. He leaped from his horse and walked forward, drawing his own knife. The shining mass of blood ran down his cheek and to his neck. His lips made their thin smile and his eyes were like the ice upon the mountains.

It was then that Little Belly knew that nothing could kill the white man. It was then that Little Belly remembered that his own medicine had not been sure and strong. But still the Blackfoot tried. The two men came together with a shock, striking with the knives, trying with their free hands to seize the other's wrist.

Great was Stearns' strength. When he dropped his knife and grabbed Little Belly's arm with both hands, the Blackfoot could do nothing but twist and strain. The white man bent the arm. He shifted his weight suddenly, throwing his body against Little Belly, who went spinning on the ground with the knife gone from his hand and his shoulder nearly wrenched from its socket.

A roar came from the trees. The Blackfeet were silent. Stearns picked up Little Belly's knife.

Then, like the passing of a cloud, the cold deadliness was gone from Stearns. He held the knife, and Little Belly was sitting on the ground with one arm useless; but the white man did not know what to do with the knife. He threw it away suddenly. He reached out his hand, as if to draw Little Belly to his feet.

The trappers roared angrily. Stearns drew his hand back. Little Belly was no wounded buffalo, no charging bear; there was no danger in him now. Stearns did not know what to do with him. Seeing this, the Blackfoot knew that the greatest of white men were weak with mercy; but their medicine was so strong that their weakness was also strength.

Stearns went back to his horse.

"Shoot the stinking Blood!" a trapper yelled.

Stearns did nothing at all for a moment after he got on his horse. He had forgotten Little Belly. Then a joyful light came to the white man's eyes. He laughed. The white teeth gleamed under the streak of red beard. He drew his rifle and held it high. Straight at the Blackfeet ranks he charged.

For an instant the Bloods were astounded; and then they shouted savagely. Their ponies came sweeping across the trampled grass.

Stearns shot the foremost rider. Then the white man spun his horse and went flying back toward the trees, laughing all the way.

Wild with anger, the Blackfeet followed too far.

They raced past Little Belly and on against the rifle fire coming from the island of trees. They would crush into the camp, fling themselves from their ponies, and smash the white men down! But too many Blackfeet rolled from their ponies. The charge broke at the very instant it should have been pressed all the way.

Little Belly saw this clearly. He knew that if he had been leading there would have been no difference.

His people were brave. They took their dead and wounded with them when they rode away from the steady fire of the trappers' rifles. They were brave, but they had wavered, and they had lost just when they should have won.

For one deep, clear moment Little Belly knew that medicine was nothing; but when he was running away with the rest of the warriors old heritage asserted itself; medicine was all. If the power of Stearns' round object, which could not be stolen for use against white men, had not turned Little Belly's bullet just enough to cause it to strike Stearns' cheek instead of his brain, the fight would have been much different.

Little Belly knew a great deal about white men now. They laughed because their medicine was so strong, so powerful they could spare a fallen enemy. But he would never be able to make his people understand, because they would remember Little Belly was the one who had been spared.

As he ran from the field he knew it would have been better for him if Stearns had not been strong with mercy, which was medicine too.

The Bretnall Feud

When old Stivers Bretnall and his wife and Preacher Yont returned from church, they saw the boys trying to beat each other's brains out with oak singletrees. It appeared that they had a fair chance of doing so. Their faces were raw. They were circling each other like wolves.

The Bretnalls still called them boys. Cairns was chunky and dark, a reckless, self-centered man who weighed one hundred and eighty-five pounds. Hornsby was tall and fair, a heller at a dance, a rough man to buck in a card game. They were both wicked in a fight, particularly against each other, for they had practiced their hatred since they first learned to waddle.

They sparred with their iron-tipped clubs. They had not heard the buggy and they could not see anything but each other.

"Boys!" Mrs. Bretnall tried to scramble from the buggy. Her husband held her back.

"On the Lord's day, too," Preacher Yont murmured. He was a tremendous man with a great brown bush of a beard and a booming voice.

"I've always said they'd kill each other some day." Old Stivers' face was stony. "Now we'll find out."

"Boys!" Mrs. Bretnall cried.

"Set still and let them go their best." Stivers' back was as straight as the blade of a knife. His nose was a thin, fierce jut above his gray mustache. The bright points of his cold blue eyes moved with the feinting clubs. "This has been going on for years, and now I'm done with it. If they don't settle it themselves right now, I will."

Hornsby's bright hair bounced on his head as he started a swing. Cairns brought his singletree around with full force to meet the blow. Hornsby checked his swing and let his brother's club go by until Cairns' right arm lay across his chest. Then Hornsby drove the end of his singletree at his brother's face. Cairns tried to twist away. The iron ring on the end of the singletree raked down his jaw, driving him back. He gained his balance as Hornsby hauled his weapon back for another overhand thrust.

Half crouching, Cairns swung his singletree against Hornsby's right arm. The arm dropped limp. Hornsby took a new grip on his club with his left hand. He struck down at Cairns' head. Cairns dodged, taking the blow on the sloping muscles beside his neck. And now his own right arm was powerless.

"They'll cripple each other," Preacher Yont said.

Old Stivers grunted. "Let it be so."

Mrs. Bretnall's eyes were closed. Her head rocked back and forth gently as she whispered a prayer.

Cairns and Hornsby did not taunt or curse or laugh. They tried to kill each other. They ground their boots against the earth, panting. Their parried blows crashed and the rings on the singletrees rattled. Each tried to smash the other's hand, his head, his body.

Preacher Yont licked his lips. "Isn't it about time we—"

"No," Stivers said.

Cairns and Hornsby beat each other down. There was bright blood on Hornsby's yellow hair and dark blood on Cairns' close-cropped head. They lost their weapons and rolled on the ground, trying to strangle each other.

Mrs. Bretnall opened her eyes when her husband put the lines in her hand. The buggy seat bounced when Preacher Yont leaped out.

Set and terrible in their determination, Cairns and Hornsby had rolled against a watering trough and were still working on each other. When Stivers threw a hatful of water the fighters increased their efforts. "Like dogs," Stivers growled. He dipped more water and poured it slowly, swinging the stream across their faces, pouring it into their mouths until Cairns and Hornsby were choking.

"Get 'em up!" Stivers said.

Preacher Yont kicked them to their feet. Spitting blood and water, they swayed toward each other. Preacher Yont scissored them apart with arms that could hold two sacks of flour at full length without trembling. "You've got a mighty problem here, Bretnall."

"It's them that have a mighty problem," Stivers said. "And we ain't going to pray about it none at all." To his sons he said, "You've fought your last time on this ranch. March inside now."

The beams of the living room in the great adobe house were gray with smoke and age. The fireplace was enormous, and the room was dark with furniture that had tossed in the holds of galleons two centuries before. From here, Bretnall land ran in four directions.

Cairns sat in a high-backed chair that once held a Spanish governor. Hornsby sat on a chest that was full of silver plate which Mrs. Bretnall considered too sinful to use upon a dining table. Stivers stood in the middle of the room, his mouth tight.

The hallway to the kitchen was wide. The middle part of it held soft gloom, and it was there Mrs. Bretnall waited, while in the kitchen at her back women worked on a dinner that would bring no joy to anyone except, perhaps, Preacher Yont.

Bruised and wet, with the blood still seeping from their hurts, Cairns and Hornsby watched their father. The old man's expression was hard and knotted. He looked at his sons from eyes that had seen more violence than they would ever look upon. For the first time there came to Cairns a realization of how hard and dangerous the early years of Stivers' life must have been.

"Men should fight when there is reason for it," Stivers said. "You two have been fighting only because you've hated each other since you were two years old. That's when you came to us."

Cairns and Hornsby stared. Preacher Yont was startled, too. From the shadowy hall, with her heart in her eyes, Mrs. Bretnall watched the shock break across the faces of two men she had raised from nameless whelps.

Hornsby said, "Then we're not—"

"No, you're not!" Stivers said. "Soldiers found you in a camp that had been wiped out by cholera." His voice was harsh and there was granite in his face. "Since then you've learned nothing but to hate each other."

"No, Stivers," Mrs. Bretnall said. And Preacher Yont murmured from his heavy beard, "Hate is a terrible word."

To them both Stivers Bretnall said, "Shut up."

"You'll never get along together," Stivers told Cairns and Hornsby, "and my holdings will not be split to suit the hatreds of two childish men." He looked from one to the other of them slowly. "One of you will own everything some day." His arm was like an arrow as he pointed in turn at them. "You will leave as I first came here, with everything I owned upon a horse. I had an Apache arrow in my shoulder, but you two would not know about such things. In fifteen minutes I want you gone. Come back, both of you, when you feel you're ready to do so, and I'll judge then which one of you can stay."

"Suppose neither of them returns?" Preacher Yont asked.

Stivers looked at him bleakly. "That might be a blessing."

Cairns asked, "How will you judge?"

"You've learned nothing here," Stivers asked. "I'll judge by what you've learned and what you've become by going away. Now, get out."

He strode across his room and went into his office. A bolt on the heavy door went into the jamb with a thump, and that was the only weakness he showed, for the sound of the lock stopped Mrs. Bretnall when she started swiftly for the door to go in and talk to him in private.

She turned away, looking at Cairns and Hornsby. She was a tall woman who had seen her brothers die by Apache lances. The frontier had taken her beauty and turned her hair gray, but it had given her the calm strength that lay in her face. "You have brought this on yourselves," she said. She went toward the kitchen.

Slumped deep in his chair, Preacher Yont watched Cairns and Hornsby.

When they were ready to go, they led their horses across the yard, not looking at each other.

Hornsby took from his saddlebags a pistol Cairns had coveted for a long time. "Here, Cairns, you've always wanted this. Maybe it will bring you luck." He was wistful and boyish as he smiled and held the pistol out.

It was hard then for Cairns to remember that they had hated each other for so long. Still, it was Hornsby offering a gift, Hornsby to be trusted least when he was most pleasant. "Keep your damned pistol."

"He offered it, Cairns," Mrs. Bretnall was standing in the doorway, and behind her the massive form of Preacher Yont. "He made the offer, Cairns."

The soft rebuke hit Cairns harder than any blow from Stivers ever had. He took from his saddle a hand-plaited rope of the best bullhide. He had spent weeks in making it. "Here, Hornsby take this."

They exchanged the gifts. When they kissed their mother, Hornsby swallowed hard and blinked tears down into the bruises on his clear skin. Cairns could not speak, but neither did he weep, and so he was distrustful of the tears that Hornsby shed.

"Say a prayer for them, Reverend."

"O Lord, these two young men are going forth from their rooftree, leaving the influence of a Christian woman. Give them strength to overcome the terrible passions in them. Direct them in the way of righteousness. . . ."

Preacher Yont asked for more things than Cairns thought the Lord would care to give to two wayward men. This Yont was a man of fearful strength, furiously alive. He had fought in the last of the Apache troubles, praying for the Indians before and after the fighting. He was without formal religion. Both Cairns and Hornsby had laughed at him at times, but now Cairns recognized a deep sincerity in the man, and it did not please him to see Hornsby smiling faintly.

Mrs. Bretnall's eyes were closed as if she were pressing tight against her brain a vision of her sons to serve in the future.

Preacher Yont was not too long in praying, mindful perhaps of the time limit set. When he wavered near the end he rallied by saying ". . . and may the best man win. Amen!" Whereupon he gave Mrs. Bretnall a startled look of apology, but she was going inside.

There might have been a grim, mustached face peering from the deep embrasure behind the mat of vines that almost hid the east window of Stivers' office, but Cairns could not be sure.

On the first knoll north of the house Cairns stopped to look back. The cottonwoods around the adobe were green clouds obscuring the heart of tremendous holdings that either he or Hornsby would lose. The thickly grassed bottom all around the grove, the distant timbered hills—they could never be thrown away because no man could really own them. For him these were strange thoughts, Cairns realized; but he had been uprooted and cast out this day.

He saw Hornsby riding south on his gleaming sorrel.

Cairns hurried. When the dips of the grassy hills concealed him, he turned east and headed for Fitz John Driscoll's place on the edge of the desert. His was the easy, direct route; by making his feint south Hornsby had injured himself and now, even if he rode the shoes off the sorrel, he would still be a half hour later than Cairns in reaching Elizabeth Driscoll.

Cairns would tell her the truth. Cairns would get her promise to wait for him until he returned. She had wavered long enough between the two of them, so now it was doubly important to be first to her with the news.

The claybank went lame before five miles had passed. Deerflies raked past Cairns' head and slashed at the flanks of the horse as the man looked at the leg. There was nothing jammed in the frog of the foot, but where hair lapped the burnished hoof a thin trail of blood led upward to a slit in the hock.

The quick jab of a knife deep into the vital joint. Hornsby had not been smiling at the words of Preacher Yont.

It was dusk when Cairns led his horse off the hills to the big springs near the Driscoll place. Heat was still rolling off the desert but it was cool here in the trees.

Cairns hailed the house.

Old Fitz John's wiry form blocked the doorway instantly. Light winked on his belt buckle and the glow from inside flowed past the edges of his hard-shaved red face.

"She won't be talking to you, Cairns. Go home."

"I came to see Elizabeth, not you."

"Go back to your own land, Cairns Bretnall." Fitz John's hostility came from him like a stinging winter wind.

"I came to see Elizabeth, Fitz John."

She pushed past her father then and came across the stony yard, a tall woman striding swiftly. Her full skirts rustled. Now that he could not see her face, Cairns knew that it was the liveness of her voice, her every movement that was most beautiful about her.

He dropped the reins on the ground. Elizabeth walked with him to where the big springs burst endlessly from the hill.

"Hornsby was here, Elizabeth?"

"Yes."

"I don't know what he said, but we were both thrown out and one of us will be judged a man by Stivers Bretnall—how, I can't say—when we return."

"Both of you, Cairns?"

"Yes."

"Stivers Bretnall—that's an odd way to speak of your father."

"He is not our father. He told us so."

Cairns heard her quick breath.

"Hornsby didn't tell you that, did he?"

The warm nearness of her was a power that swarmed at Cairns' emotions. It was difficult for him to stand and merely talk to her. She did not answer his question.

"Then he didn't tell you," Cairns said. "I don't care now what his story was." But he did, for Hornsby could use the quick knives of words as deftly as he had used a blade to cripple the claybank while Cairns was getting his saddle. "When I come back, Elizabeth, whether Stivers Bretnall points me away again or not, I want you."

The springs growled in their rocky depths. The woman said, "You're blunt."

"I should have been that way long ago. I've wasted my time, thinking it would run forever. When I come back—"

"You want a promise now, Cairns?" There was dignity in her words, and a slow undercurrent of sadness that warned Cairns.

"Yes," he said.

"I can't give it. We're dealing with time. Things can change so that what is said today lacks sense tomorrow."

"Promises between us can't change. I won't change."

"You have already." Elizabeth said. "You've never spoken bluntly to me before. You're grim and hurrying now, Cairns. And I can change, too, because I thought one thing when Hornsby was here this afternoon, and now I'm not sure."

"Do I get your promise, Elizabeth?"

"No."

"What did you promise him?"

Her silence made him afraid. Her continued silence brought his hatred of Hornsby to an intensity that made his voice tremble when he said, "Expect me back for a straight answer. I don't know when, but I'll be here again."

Fitz John stood in the shadows of the porch when Cairns led the limping claybank across the yard. Fitz John offered nothing, which served to increase Cairns' rage against Hornsby. "Which way did he go, Fitz John?"

There was no answer.

The desert was stony. In time the heat washed away. The stars were bright and cold. Cairns walked. At a water hole at dawn he saw the tracks of Hornsby's sorrel.

When the stars were fading the next day Cairns limped into Capulin, the crossroads of nothing. Dim trails crawled in from the desert and a wagon road faded away toward the scalded hills north where men mined gold.

In the doorway of a livery stable a hostler lay in drunken slumber. Cairns led the claybank across him. Hornsby's sorrel was not inside.

When he had taken care of his horse, Cairns rummaged in the empty mangers until he found a bottle with an inch of oily-looking whiskey in it. With that he bathed the wound in the claybank's leg, and then he forked hay on the floor of a stall and sprawled out. Sometime in the afternoon the pressure of heat drove him out. He hobbled to the watering trough and he splashed and blew until his hair was wet and spiky.

Bleary-eyed and listless, the hostler sat in the doorway of the harness room.

"There was an SB sorrel here," Cairns said. "When?"

The hostler yawned. "Night before last." He scratched his head. "You work for old Stivers Bretnall, mister?"

"Used to. What have you got for a bad rock cut in the hock?"

"Green salve," the hostler replied.

"Use plenty of it," Cairns tipped his hat against the hard strike of the sun. He started away.

"Maybe you'd better pay me now," the hostler said, "before you go into Boney Siddon's place." He shrugged when Cairns strode away without answering.

One fourth of Siddon's place was store, the rest saloon. The dirt floor had been sprinkled but there was still a litter of cigar stubs, cigarette butts and torn playing cards in a circle around a poker table. Siddon was a gaunt man with droopy eyelids and jowl flesh that sagged as if it had been disillusioned. He came from a gloomy doorway in the back of the room and stood behind the bar.

"Something to eat," Cairns said.

Siddon yelled in Spanish. After a while a Mexican woman shuffled out with a bowl of peppery goat stew. Cairns ate standing at the bar. When the stew was gone, Siddon hacked open a can of peaches and dumped the contents into the bowl. He shoved it toward Cairns.

Cairns ate the peaches. Siddon gave him a cigar. "No extra charge."

"Big game night before last?"

"Big enough for me," Siddon said.

"There was a yellow-haired fellow?"

Siddon nodded. "Him and a couple of fellows that wandered off the desert."

"He won?"

"Yeah, he did." Siddon studied Cairns from under the drooping lids. He put three dollars on the bar, change from a five-dollar gold piece, which was all the money Cairns had had when he left home. "You could invest the three."

"Which way did this yellow-headed man go?"

"He mentioned Quartzite." Siddon inclined his head to the north. "You could make the three increase."

"Twenty-one?"

"I play that, too."

"Let's find out."

The three dollars lasted one hand. Siddon looked at the gun in Cairns' belt. "Not that one," Cairns said. "Forty for the one in my holster?"

"Twenty."

They settled on thirty. The gun lasted six hands. "Two pistols make a man look foolish anyway," Cairns said.

"A hundred for your horse."

"You haven't seen him," Cairns said, shaking his head.

"One twenty-five then."

The claybank lasted a half hour.

"You won't need the rig now, will you?" Siddon asked.

When the saddle and bridle were gone, Cairns said, "That was a mighty poor run of luck."

"It sure was. Fifty for that other pistol?"

Cairns shook his head. He rose. "How far to Quartzite?"

"Thirty miles or so." Siddon glanced at Cairns' boots. He flipped a ten-dollar gold piece across the table. "No man ever leaves here broke."

"Here's one that will."

The hostler was still sitting in the doorway of the harness room when Cairns went after his bedroll.

"Did you dope the claybank's hock?"

"You still own him?"

"No."

"Then there's no hurry." The hostler grinned. "I thought you had a gambling look."

Maybe there was such a look, but the hostler had been too sure of certain facts in advance. Cairns pushed all the cartridges from his pistol. He held them in his palm and showed them to the hostler. He put one cartridge back into the pistol and spun the cylinder. The hostler watched uneasily. Cairns spun the cylinder a second time, and then again, until he saw the brass rim of the cartridge high on the right side of the frame.

"What's the idea?"

"A counting game. I count until you tell me what the man who owned the SB sorrel worked out with Boney Siddon concerning me."

"I was drunk that night. I wouldn't know."

Cairns pointed the pistol at the man's chest and snapped it. "One."

"I don't know what he said!"

Cairns snapped the pistol again. "Two."

"My God! That can go off, mister!"

Cairns knew he had three counts left. He used one. "Three."

"He told Boney you were a sucker for gambling. He said you couldn't tell when a man was cheating or not. He said you'd most likely be along and that he'd give fifty dollars more for your horse than it cost Boney to—"

"You've got a loose mouth, Sam." There was patience in Boney Siddon's voice. He was standing behind Cairns with a shotgun. "Drop the pistol, Bretnall."

Cairns obeyed. The pistol was beautiful. It hurt him to see it lying in the filth at his feet. He looked at Siddon. The man's eyelids were all the way up now. There was no bluff in him.

"Took me, huh?" Cairns said.

"I did. Your brother took me. A man has to stay at least even. Get your plunder."

When Cairns stood with his bedroll on his shoulder, Siddon held the pistol up. "A hundred dollars?"

The pistol was not worth that. It could be, Cairns thought, the man's way of trying to give him back some of his loss. Cairns shook his head.

Siddon tossed the pistol to him. "I never rob anyone."

By his own lights, maybe Siddon was right. Cairns was learning that different men have different codes.

The wagon road to Quartzite was little used. It did not follow the creek and there was no other water on the long lift to the tinted hills. That night when he slept in the sand, Cairns wondered if he would ever get his boots off without taking part of his feet with them. That, too, was Hornsby's fault.

Cairns threw his bedroll away the next afternoon. He was sweated dry, and staggering. Panic struck him, not that he would die of thirst after wandering off the dim road, but that he would not live long enough to find Hornsby. The pounding of his hatred of Hornsby and of the desert became almost equal.

It took another day before he reached a notch in the hills. The maroon dumps of Quartzite lay in a gulch, between buildings and almost on top of buildings. He saw the main roads to and from the town rising east and north through the burning hills. The lusty roar of the place came up to him. He stopped at a discolored creek to drink and to wash some of the hotness from his eyes. He checked his pistol.

And then he went up the street to find Hornsby. That proved quite simple. Hornsby was under the shaded front of the Arrow Saloon, talking to three gamblers. He saw Cairns as soon as Cairns saw him. Sensitive to changes in the expressions of men, the gamblers moved away from Hornsby at once.

Cairns came up the middle of the street.

"You're sore about a little joke, Cairns." Hornsby smiled as he peered at the grips of the pistol in Cairns' holster. "But if your mind is made up. . . ."

Hornsby went for his pistol.

Cairns was sure he was no worse than even on the draw, and he knew he was a steadier shot that Hornsby. Cairns' pistol made a splitting roar. His arm was shocked back and the pistol fell. He clutched his face with his left hand. Hornsby laughed. Cairns stumbled toward him and ran into the hitch rail.

"Crazy from the desert," Hornsby said. "His gun must have been choked with sand."

Cairns felt his way around the hitch rail and rushed at the sound of Hornsby's voice. He smashed headlong into the building. "Over here," Hornsby said.

Cairns made another rush and struck the heavy post of the wooden awning.

"Crazy from the desert," Hornsby said.

Again Cairns staggered toward the sound. Hornsby tripped him. He fell against the building and slid down it until his hands clutched rocks and hot sand. He was never unconscious. He knew that he was blind.

His name was Panamint Cooper. At times his voice was old, running vaguely on lost days and faraway things of the desert. He was a gray, stooped man with a ragged beard, Cairns thought. There were many days when Cairns did not care about Panamint or anything else. He lay in a cool cabin where the sound of falling water never ended.

Hornsby's laugh kept coming from sunlight that Cairns could not see. He heard it when he dozed. He saw Hornsby's handsome, tawny face smiling at him from under the awning of the Arrow Saloon.

One day he asked about his eyes.

"Nobody knows," Panamint said. "There ain't nobody here that *could* know. There's nothing right *in* them. There was a piece of the barrel between them, but I dug that out with my knife. You're splattered bad, but there don't seem to be nothing right in the eyes."

"I'm blind."

"There's folks worse off. Where'd you get that pistol?"

"From a fellow." Cairns' face began to pulse and hurt.

"You take it slow," Panamint said. "You unclinch your hands and just lay there. Maybe it's only powder in your eyes. Who knows?"

"I'm blind."

"That pistol—it had a spidery little crack along the underside of the barrel and someone had rubbed it full of lead. It blew out like a clinched rivet, but there was enough left near the frame for me to tell a thing or two. It was a poor pistol for a man to be carrying."

Cairns had been carrying something worse than a defective pistol: a hatred that had ruined his life. The thought was slow in taking root but it grew in the long, restless days and nights in Panamint's cabin.

The walls were made of rock, the furniture of rough lumber, and in one corner water fell from a pipe in the roof to a circular pile of stones, then ran away through a drain in the floor.

"Pure luxury," Panamint said. "When I sold the claims that started this camp, I held out right to have water splashing in my shack. You ever been on the desert?"

"Very little."

"Even that much is enough, I dreamed for years of having water always near me, and now I've got it."

There was a voice that came to the door several times and it seemed to be losing patience with Panamint, who always went outside to talk. Each time Panamint returned he said the same thing. "Always wanting me to invest my money in a mine! I'm through with mining but they won't quit pestering me."

There were degrees of darkness now before Cairns, but he did not mention that to Panamint. One night Panamint said, "Let's play poker. You set down here and let me show you a few things."

Cairns learned how easy it was to mark cards with fingernails. His sharpening sense of touch soon showed him how easy it was to read the marks.

"When I first got rich I paid a gambler to show me the tricks," Panamint said.

"Did you ever use them—for money?"

"That's a funny thing. Not once. I don't need the money, and— well, I just never cared to do it."

Day after day and sometimes long into the night, Cairns played cards with Panamint. The old man chattered. Sometime during the period when the blood lust was burning out of him, Cairns accepted the fact that he might be blind for life.

It struck him one day that the food was not what it had been when Panamint first led him off the street. That afternoon Panamint went out and returned with a gunny sack of grub which he thumped on the table. He spent some time banging stores into the cupboard. "A man grows forgetful," he said. "We were danged near out of grub, did you know it?"

"I hadn't noticed." That evening the water ceased all at once. A half hour later the cabin was stifling hot.

"Pipe busted again! I'll see about it tomorrow."

Cairns paced around the room. Blindness had taught him things he might have missed by having eyes. But he did not question Panamint. There was a pride in the old man that should not be humbled while Cairns needed help.

The day came when Cairns could see almost as well as he had ever seen, but only for short periods; and he could not yet face sunlight. Panamint was a bald, birdlike little man, clean-shaved, with sharp blue eyes.

They were out of food again. Panamint bustled around and went out. From the window Cairns watched him going up the street, walking slower and slower until he was a faded little figure that did not know where to go. Cairns lay down and put a damp cloth over his eyes when his vision filled with red flashes.

Panamint returned an hour later.

"Who came in with you?" Cairns asked.

"I came in!" It was the booming voice of Preacher Yont. "What have you got to say about it?"

Cairns took the cloth from his eyes, "You!"

Preacher Yont stood on massive spraddled legs, his arms behind his back, his yellow-flaked eyes twinkling above the brown cloud of his beard.

Cairns asked, "How is my mother?"

"Well."

"Stivers?"

"Unchanged."

"Who sent you?"

"The Lord!"

"I don't doubt that, but He didn't pay for the grub."

"I happened to have a small sum." Preacher Yont said. "Two weeks ago I stopped at a place east of the desert, a place called Bondad where there was a pock-marked man who tried to cheat me in a friendly game of cards. My anger overpowered me. While I was chiding the man, some gold accidentally fell from his pockets. I gave half of it to a young priest whose church was in need of an altar cloth, or some such outlandish thing. . . . Who are you to be questioning me, Cairns Bretnall?"

"Where's Hornsby?"

"I saw him three weeks ago, far away." Preacher Yont rocked forward on his feet. "Do you seek him?"

"No."

"You did, though."

"Yes, but not now."

"You're sure of that, Cairns?"

"I'm sure."

"Then you have gained more than Hornsby." Preacher Yont turned sidewise to go through the doorway. "I must be about the Lord's work now."

There was preaching that night in a saloon. Later, there were two shootings. The next night there was more preaching on the hill above the Apache shaft.

"That Yont," Panamint said, "he got a bet out of fifty men he couldn't lift Joe Pleasman's anvil with one hand on the horn. He did it. They had to pay off by going to hear him preach."

"Panamint, you sold your water to buy us grub the first time we ran out."

"You could say that, I suppose. In a way. The Apache mill would have got it anyway. I held out right to that water when I sold this camp, but I took payments on it now and then—and finally I took a last one, you might say, just to keep from being pestered."

"How much did you get for making this camp?"

"Three years ago? Thirty-five thousand."

"Gambled it?"

"I guess you could say some of it went that way. Maybe quite a chunk of it." Panamint dismissed the whole thing with a wave of his hands. "I can find another camp like this any old time."

"How long did it take you to find this one?"

"Fifty-two years." Panamint held up his palm quickly. "But I spent a lot of that time learning the business. Now I know how to prospect."

He was an old man, healthy-looking and dried down to the tough, lasting fibers, but the frailty was beginning to show, and Cairns knew he would never last to find another camp like Quartzite. But he was a prideful old man, so Cairns knew he must be careful with his words.

"You like running water, Panamint."

"Sure."

"Water running down to irrigate a valley."

"To hell with the irrigating. I like water, but only to have it around, not to irrigate nothing with."

"You know the SB ranch?"

"I've heard of it."

"Go there," Cairns said. "Tell Stivers Bretnall I sent you to show him how to build tunnels and canals to bring water through the hills to his western valleys."

"Huh-uh. I ain't looking for charity."

"You'll hop like a flea in a frying pan around Stivers Bretnall. When you've built one tunnel he'll want ten more and wonder why you haven't finished them. He'll give you fifty men and expect you to get the work of a hundred out of them. He'll plant wheat and oats in one of those valleys when the water is still ten miles away, and tell you to get the canals there before things dry up. Charity? After a week with him you'll want to go back to the desert for a rest."

"I can make water run anywhere," Panamint said.

"You won't get any rest around Stivers Bretnall."

"Maybe I've rested long enough."

"He's got a silver vein on his land. He might ask you to prospect that a little."

"Silver ain't much of a metal," Panamint said. "But I suppose I could do it."

"You may like Stivers Bretnall if you ever get used to him."

"You ought to know. He's your father."

"What else did Yont tell you?"

"That's about all."

"You'll go?"

"I suppose I could. If I had all my business cleared up here. . . ." Panamint frowned. "I'll have to get a burro."

Three days later Panamint left the camp he had founded. A half-million dollars' worth of gold was coming from the earth each month. He walked away with a lift to his shoulders, beside a mouse-colored burro with one droopy ear.

The owners of the Apache mill gave Cairns the use of the cabin for another week, and it was then he learned that Panamint had not owned the place for more than a year. When Cairns blew out the candle one evening and went away he took with him only one thing he had not brought: a Colt pistol that Panamint had given him. In the Arrow Saloon a few miners watched Cairns curiously.

The pallor of his face in the back-bar mirror was a shock, but the red scars would fade and the sun would darken his skin again. Cairns walked out as deliberately as he had entered.

Near the edge of town he heard the sharp click in the dark slot between two buildings. Someone grunted. Cloth ripped. There was a thump. Cairns was kneeling then with his pistol trained on the sounds. Preacher Yont came into the street, dragging a man by one foot. It was Sam, the hostler from Capulin.

"He figured to shoot you," Preacher Yont said.

"He was sent."

"You didn't hear me say that, Cairns."

"He was sent. Siddon wouldn't do it, and Sam is too shiftless to want to kill me because I scared him with a pistol long ago."

"We won't speculate," Preacher Yont said. "I've done one thing for each of you. There was a gambler who might have killed Hornsby because he didn't like the way your brother played cards. He would have killed him, I do believe, except that I turned suddenly and a bottle which happened to be in my hand accidentally struck the fellow in the head. Expect no more of me, by accident or otherwise."

Sam showed no signs of stirring. "What did you hit him with, your fist?" Cairns asked.

"Luckily, it was a rock. Go on, Cairns, and leave me to soak this sinner in the creek so that he and I can pray when he comes to." Preacher Yont started dragging Sam toward the creek by one leg. "I couldn't creep into the narrow place where he was lurking, after by sheer chance I saw him skulking through the gloom with a shotgun. Of course, I used a stone—may the Lord forgive me. Good-bye, Cairns."

Cairns went up the street, crossed the creek on a flume and came back toward town until he was close to splashing sounds.

"You're drowning me!" Sam protested.

"I'm washing your sins away," Preacher Yont said. "Who hired you?"

"Nobody. I was sore because—"

There was a sputtering and a gurgling and a mighty threshing. Sam choked. Finally he gasped. "Hornsby was his name. He rode a Bretnall sorrel. He gave me money to cripple this other fellow's legs in case he got over being blind. I wasn't going to kill him, honest!"

"You need more washing," Preacher Yont said. He thrust Sam under and held him. "And then we'll pray."

Cairns walked away quietly.

Domingo was another camp in the scorching rocks. Cairns worked there for a month at the Huderspahl mill. He wore gloves, which caused him to be regarded with suspicion by his fellow workers. Every night in his room at the boarding house he practiced with the cards; but he never took his skill into the gambling halls.

Ibex was a different sort of place, in the cool, blue timber high above the desert heat. Cairns mucked in the Overland tunnel. He was the only man who wore gloves and he had earned the right the hard way. The first day he went to work, Big Jack Delavern, the shift boss, asked to see the gloves. When Cairns gave them to him Delavern spiked them to a post at the portal, saying, "I want tough men. You work bare-handed here or else you lick me first."

"All right."

"All right what?" Delavern asked.

Cairns knocked him down. Delavern got up, blinking. "It's been a long time since that happened."

The fought all over the dump, scraping their boots through the yellow waste, tripping over the track, rolling through the chips of the timber yard. They got up and fought on their feet until Big Jack went down and could not rise. "You can wear gloves," he said.

Cairns thought how different it had been between him and Hornsby. He guessed it was a good thing, after all, that they were not brothers.

Every afternoon when Cairns came from the cool darkness of the tunnel into dying sunlight his first glance was far across the wild colors of the desert to where the Driscoll ranch lay somewhere on the rim of the long horizon. If Elizabeth had promised Hornsby unconditionally, then she must be made to change her mind.

He had learned much from Hornsby, from Panamint, and from Preacher Yont, but he had not learned anything about making a woman change her mind. Nor did he know what Stivers expected of him and Hornsby when they returned.

In the evenings before he practiced with cards on his cot in the Ouray boarding house, Cairns spent an hour or two talking to Brule Langley at the Ibex livery stable. Brule had stomped broncs for outfits all over the West until a crushed hip slowed him down. He was a wide-mouthed man who used his flexible lips as the basis of most of his facial expressions. The deeds of horsemen ran in all of Brule's speech. He was saving his money to go prospecting.

Like any man, Brule had a lament. "Only for a few two-bit outfits did I ever get to bust horses the way they should be gentled. The big outfits never had no time. Break a hundred head and do it in two weeks. Break 'em? Just ride them till you broke their hearts. You got a lot of mean broncs that way that could have been good horses. When I get rich mining, I'll buy fifty head and take my time gentling them just like I want to, and then I'll sell them to men that want good horses. I'll make money at it, too."

Cairns laughed. "What will be the use of fooling with bronc busting when you're rich?"

When the first snow came, running lightly on the tinted edges of the desert, bringing creaking cold in the timber around Ibex, Cairns remembered well the wide, warm lands where Stivers Bretnall ran his cattle. Ragged men who had not yet made a million began to leave Ibex.

"For a hundred bucks we can buy the Golden Wonder claim," Brule told Cairns. "Cabin, tools and all. I got the money, but one man can't work a shaft."

"I may as well get rich with you."

They bought the Golden Wonder. The shaft was in tight granite that showed wandering streaks of iron stain, but the gold could be two feet below. Wind blew snow through the cabin walls but they pooled their blankets in one bunk.

They both drilled in the bottom of the shaft. Cairns did the shooting and the mucking and Brule the hoisting. Brule had the strength of a bear in his arms and shoulders. When his feet were set right his bad hip was no problem. The shaft went deeper. Iron-streaked granite. The gold was always one more round below. They ate beans and salt-side and sourdough biscuits, saving their money for important items like dynamite.

"The Golden Wonder," Cairns said. "In the spring maybe we can sell it to two other suckers."

"I'll never get my horses that way," Brule said.

The next round was not a winner, nor many later rounds. Ready to shoot one afternoon, Cairns sent up the tools and the ten-foot ladder which bridged the gap between the bottom and the permanent ladders on the cribbing. The bucket came back. Cairns yelled up that he was ready to fire and Brule replied that he was ready to hoist. The split ends of the fuses gaped like the mouths of tiny snakes as Cairns spit them with his candle. He stepped on the rim of the bucket and yelled for Brule to hoist.

The bucket went about eight feet and stopped.

"Hey!" Cairns yelled. "Get me out of here!"

The bucket did not move. The fuses sizzled and bitter fumes drifted around Cairns. He stared at the rectangle of light above him that was split by the windlass beam. Brule's legs were there and Cairns could see the slant of his arms going down to the crank.

"What's the matter, Brule?"

"Nothing," Hornsby Bretnall answered. "Everything is just right, Cairns."

Brule started to turn the windlass. A pistol shot rocked across the collar of the shaft. The bucket stopped.

Hornsby said, "The next time, Langley, I'll smash that crippled leg and then you'll drop him on top of the shots." He yelled down the shaft, "Put your arms over your head! I don't want you killed, only mangled!"

The fuses were burning a foot a minute, and Cairns had cut them short to save expenses. Cairns shoved against the wall with his foot, swinging himself over to the ladder. Brule could not see but he knew what was going on. He diverted Hornsby's attention by shouting at him. "You'll kill a man!"

Hornsby laughed. "The bucket will protect him."

Cairns pulled a piece of rock from between the cribbing. Fumes from the burning fuses were thick and stinking. When he was close to the top, Brule saw him, and then Brule pointed with his eyes to where Hornsby was. Cairns went up the last few rungs with a surge. When his head was clear, he saw Hornsby standing across the windlass beam from Brule.

Cairns swung out on the ladder, holding with one hand. He hurled the rock with the other. Hornsby's eyes widened. He shifted the pistol, and then the rock took him solidly in the stomach. Brule dropped the windlass crank. He went around it in two hobbling steps and then he leaped the rest of the way. He bore Hornsby down by the throat and was choking the life out of him when Cairns got there. Cairns tried to tear Brule loose but he might as well have tugged at a tree. The holes went off in the shaft but no one was aware of that.

Cairns broke Brule's grip by beating him on the arm muscles with the pistol. Hornsby's breath came in hoarse gasps. The dark blood went out of his face and he rose, rubbing his throat.

The terrible thing in Hornsby that frightened Cairns was not there to see. Cairns looked for it, but all he saw was a cunning, defiant man whose mind was already racing on from this temporary defeat.

Hornsby picked up his hat and brushed snow from his sheepskin coat. "You're a damned fool, Cairns," he said. He held out his hand for his pistol.

Cairns punched the cartridges out. He stepped toward Hornsby, holding the weapon by the barrel, extending it. Hornsby's reach was casual until he had his hand on the pistol, and then he tried to jerk it away so that the sight would rip through Cairns' palm. At the same time he kicked at Cairns' groin.

Gripping the pistol hard, Cairns swung Hornsby sidewise and went around the kick. He pulled the pistol away from Hornsby with a twist and tossed it toward Brule. He smashed Hornsby in the face and sent him reeling.

They fought as they had fought before, silently and savagely, but this time the blinding rage was gone from Cairns. He smashed away at Hornsby for the same reason he had fought Big Jack Delavern: to put him down because it had to be done, and not because of madness that ran blood-red from anger.

When Hornsby went down at last, with blood dribbling from the corners of his mouth into the snow, Cairns felt only lostness and not a sharp thrill of victory. He hauled Hornsby to his feet and shoved him toward a sorrel horse standing cold and hipshot in the trail beyond the cabin.

"You're a fool, Cairns," Hornsby said with some bewilderment. "You'll lose when we go back, or long before we go back. You're a poor, weak fool."

Cairns took a rifle from a saddle scabbard. "For a pistol with a cracked barrel." The plaited rope that he had given Hornsby was on the saddle. Cairns looked at it a moment and turned away.

With the blood freezing on his cheeks and mouth, Hornsby laughed at him. He swung up after two tries, jerked the sorrel around and rode away.

Brule shook his head. Hornsby's bullet had mangled the lobe of his ear. "You should have let me kill him. Who is he, Cairns?"

"We have something between us. I'll tell you about it some day."

There was granite with streaks of iron, but no gold. One day there was no food or dynamite or coal for the forge. The snow was six feet deep.

"We'll work somewhere until spring and try again," Brule said. "I'll get those fifty horses yet."

"I'll give you two hundred head now, at least as much ownership as you really want. Go to the SB ranch, Brule. Tell Stivers Bretnall that I sent you. He's never broken horses properly. He's got bronc stompers that use Spanish bits and filed spurs and quirts that will snap the trunk of a scrub oak. Go there and break horses right for him."

"Suppose he won't hire me?"

"You tell him what you know of breaking horses."

"It would be warm there, wouldn't it?"

"Warm, with corrals full of horses—"

"We can both go," Brule said.

"Not me, for a while. You may run into the man who was here last month, Brule."

Brule nodded. "I can handle that, too."

They sold the Golden Wonder for fifty dollars to Frenchy Riddell, who ran the Golden Palace. Brule went toward the desert on the wagon of a six-horse freighter. Cairns went back to mucking in the Overland tunnel. He was behind with his cards, so he practiced, wondering idly what he would ever do with the skill after he had used it at the one place he had in mind.

On a day when the frozen teeth of winter were being softened by winds blowing from the desert, Cairns came from the tunnel and saw a group of miners around a loaded tram car derailed near the switch to the ore bins. Two men towered over the rest. Big Jack said, "No man can do it. I wouldn't even try it myself."

"The bets are made!" Preacher Yont said. He set his legs and with one hand lifted the rear wheels of the car back on the rails. He kicked waste from under the rails until he could hook the toes of his boots under the track. Then, with the great bloom of his beard tight against his chest, he rocked the car and tipped it with one hand on the dump bar, and swung it gently until he lowered the front wheels to the track.

"Good God!" a miner said.

"Amen!" said Preacher Yont. "And now you'll all pay your bets by being at the Masonic Hall for the Lord's word at seven o'clock tonight."

He strode across the dump and thumped Cairns on the back. "Your body is looking strong, Cairns Bretnall. How is your soul?"

"You just knocked it loose."

Preacher Yont lowered his voice. "They are odd people who have come to your father's place in your name."

"Panamint and Brule Langley?"

Preacher Yont looked across the desert. "It was spring when I left the SB."

"What do you mean by that?"

"I meant it was spring, that's all."

That evening Preacher Yont filled a cold hall with energy and the fear of the Lord, and took up a collection for the family of a miner killed in the Ibex Extension. Then almost everyone went downstairs to Frenchy Riddell's bar.

"Is Hornsby ready to go back?" Cairns asked.

"I don't know. Are you? Can you face failure?"

"I think so." In some things, perhaps, but Cairns doubted that he could face failure with Elizabeth Driscoll.

"Nine-tenths of my work is failure," Preacher Yont said. "So long, Cairns. I have tasks before me."

Late that night Cairns heard Preacher Yont leaving town with a rescue party of miners who were going to a high camp with food for prospectors trapped by late spring snows.

Cairns started home the next day, walking. When he went through Quartzite no one recognized him as the man who had lain blind in Panamint Cooper's cabin. He was bearded now and the winds and suns of long distances had darkened his face.

Two nights later the light of Boney Siddon's place rose in the warm dusk. Through the window Cairns saw Siddon behind the bar. Two dark-faced men sat idly at a poker table, with the marks of waiting on them. Cairns backed off and went to the stable.

Sam was nursing a bottle by lantern light in the harness room where he slept. "Put your horse in any empty stall you find," he mumbled.

Cairns looked at the brands of two wiry horses that showed evidence of resting and feeding for some time. He went back to Sam and stood smiling down at him, and all at once Sam's bleary eyes widened.

"It's him!" Sam put his bottle under his cot. "Now look! That preacher nearly drownded me, and every time he's been here since, he puts the fear of God into me. So there's no use of you—"

"Shut up, Sam. Now tell me, did Hornsby know the two men that are at Boney's right now?"

Sam nodded. "The three of them came here last week. Hornsby went on. They stayed. They keep looking north."

At the doorway of Siddon's place Cairns put his rifle on the ground. He went inside. The two men at the table were interested at once. They studied him, looked at each other. They were not sure—yet. Siddon knew in one instant. Without seeming to move, the eyes in his gaunt face warned Cairns.

"How's things at the Apache, Maguire?" Siddon asked. "I haven't seen you for a long time."

It was a relief to Cairns to know that he had guessed right about Siddon long ago. "It's all right, Boney. I know." Cairns walked toward the table and faced them. "I'm Cairns Bretnall, boys."

They tightened down, staring.

"You've been paid or you wouldn't have waited so long. Do you want to earn your money?"

One of the men shook his head. "We don't know what you're talking about."

Cairns moved slowly to the side of them, so if they tried to rise and draw, they would bump into each other, and one would block the other. "Try to earn your pay, or get out," he said.

They spread their hands on the table when they rose. They looked at Siddon. His hands were both below the bar now. They had guts and some to spare, Cairns thought, but they had been thrown off balance by the unexpected. He backed them across the room without touching his pistol. He sent them through the door and leaped out quickly behind them, kneeling where his rifle lay.

They walked out on the hard packed ground and then they stopped. "Get your horses," Cairns said, and then he moved swiftly to the corner of the building. The two men fired while he was still moving, chunking their lead into the adobes and against the ground where they had last heard his voice. He let them shoot six times and then he began to drill a raking fire low across the ground.

One of the men screamed. The other fired twice more and then he yelled, "That's enough! We quit!"

Cairns shifted ground and stayed silent.

Siddon brought a lantern out. One of the pair had a bad leg wound. The other had suffered only a collapse of purpose. Siddon wrapped the leg up. Sam brought two saddled horses from the stable and the men took one of the dim trails that led east across the desert.

Boney sighed. "Sometimes I think my place ain't located just right to draw a high-class trade."

This time he gave Cairns steak and potatoes and strong coffee, and afterward, a cigar. "No extra charge."

"I remember"—Cairns clicked the three silver dollars he had received in change for a five-dollar gold piece—"you charged me the same for goat stew."

"All meals are the same price."

Cairns clicked the dollars. "I could invest this."

Siddon began taking off his apron. "You had a bad run of luck before. Maybe it's changed."

Fifteen minutes later Siddon eyed Cairns speculatively and changed the deck. Before the new deck was well marked Cairns cut his bets against Siddon's winning streak. The decks were changed several times, but at the end of two hours Siddon looked at Cairns and shook his head. "That's all for me, Bretnall."

Cairns counted his chips into stacks. "One hundred twenty-five for the claybank."

"Your brother won him from me last week."

"Thirty for the pistol."

"Worth more, but you can have it back for that."

"I'm short five bucks on the rig," Cairns said. "One more hand."

Siddon tossed a chip across the table. He pulled the thirty-dollar stack toward him. "I'll get the pistol."

"I'll leave it for a while. I may be back. An extra pistol is too much weight for a man on foot anyway."

"You're walking? Hell, I've got a horse you can take."

"No, thanks." Cairns had walked all but a few miles after leaving home, and that was the way he was going back.

They had a drink at the bar. Siddon said, "Those two tonight were maybe tougher than you thought. I hear there's four or five like them hired on at the SB in the last few months. One of them is Darby Culwell. You'll know by his little eyes and his big-toother grin. Only it ain't no grin."

"Thanks."

"No thanks at all. I'd appreciate it if you happened to forget about Sam and the shot gun he stole from me when he went to Quartzite for a few days. He ain't much but he used to be halfway decent—and besides, he's my brother."

"Let's say Sam has been converted. I have no quarrel with him. Leave that to Preacher Yont."

"Amen! That Yont—he bet me he could tip my bar up from one end with three fingers. He done it. It ain't possible. I almost busted my hand trying it afterward. I had to sit here with my wife and Sam and her two sisters and listen to him preach for one hour. The women don't understand American, so I thought I had Yont three-fifths beat when he started, but he preached in Spanish. For a week the cooking was terrible while they fought about religion."

Fitz John Driscoll, working on a corral gate, had seen Cairns coming a long way out on the stony flats. Fitz John drove his hatchet into a post and said, "Howdy, Cairns. You look like you could stand a drink."

Cairns looked at him quietly.

Fitz John grew red and angry. "A big smooth lie can take in any man! Hornsby said you'd got him kicked out and that you were the fair-haired boy. I always favor the underdog."

Cairns grinned. "I'll take your offer." He looked casually at the house.

"She seen you," Fitz John said. "She's wandering around at the springs in a dress she ain't never worn before—but let her wait. Don't rush a woman, Cairns. Sort of sidle up." Fitz John slapped a corral rail and pointed at three buckskin geldings. "There's a good example of what I mean. I've tried to bust that strain head-on for years, and sometimes half of them was never really what you'd call gentled. Last winter a hobbling fellow name of Brule something or another talked me into giving him one horse out of five broncs I had if he could gentle the whole five so's a man could crawl between their feet or ride them without a bridle.

"He did it, too, and these four ain't lost one bit of their fire. They ain't pets by no means, but you can still trust them like a pet. Now that's what I mean about a woman. Let's get the drink."

They sat in Mrs. Driscoll's kitchen for an hour. She was a stocky, serene-faced woman, who asked Cairns quiet questions about where he had been and what he had done. At last she said, "I wouldn't sit here too long, no matter what offhand advice Fitz John gave you."

Elizabeth was waiting where the big springs boiled from the hill. She was vexed by the delay and eyed Cairns coolly.

"It's a beautiful dress, Elizabeth."

That pleased her for a moment.

"I've come back," Cairns said.

"It appears so, doesn't it?"

Damnation, Cairns thought. He looked at the trees. "Spring already."

"Is that what you call sidling up? I heard you and my father talking."

"What did you tell Hornsby when he came back?"

"That would be none of your business."

"The hell it isn't! No matter what you told him, I won't let you—" he checked himself.

"You won't let me what?"

"I need you, Elizabeth."

Some of the stiffness went from her. "The last time you said you wanted me."

They looked at each other for a long moment and then they closed the space between them and Cairns could not remember then that they had almost quarreled violently. After a time he was again aware of the rumbling springs.

"You said you wanted a straight answer, Cairns."

"Not now."

"Why not?"

"I have to go home first."

"What difference will it make what Stivers does?"

For them perhaps it did not matter greatly, or at least Cairns could think so at the moment. But there were Brule and old Panamint and the Driscolls themselves. No friend of Cairns would ever be in peace near the SB if Hornsby won at home but lost here.

"Not now," he said. "I'll go home and then I'll come back."

The long grasslands running west to the blue hills that shut the Dolores from Stivers Bretnall's western valleys were a mixture of green and brown. Far ahead a rider on a claybank was going toward a timbered crest.

Being afoot among longhorns that were ringy from the spring roundup did not appeal to Cairns. He kept thinking about the rider he had seen. He tried to set his course from one timbered hill to another. Avoiding a scattered bunch of cattle he had seen ahead, he was in a swale when a man on a buckskin, towing a saddled horse, rode from a grove of cottonwoods and came toward him.

It was Brule, saddle-brown, with a happy look in his eyes that Cairns had never seen when he and Brule were sinking the Golden Wonder. They shook hands, grinning.

"You're no better-looking," Cairns said.

"You don't look so good yourself, on foot." Brule came back.

Cairns swung up. Brule led him to the grove, around a hill and to the top of another hill. A half mile beyond, the rider on the claybank and four others were holding a large herd.

"Hornsby on my claybank?" Cairns asked.

Brule nodded.

"How'd he know I was afoot?"

"He had men out, all the way from Quartzite."

"I met two of them."

Brule fingered his disfigured ear. "I've been snooping. You made a mistake when you didn't let me kill him, Cairns."

"Has he given you any trouble here?"

"Not yet. He hasn't been here long."

They rode into the open. Hornsby saw them at once. A few moments later the riders with him let the herd go and gathered around him. Brule and Cairns rode toward the group. Twice they had to wheel away from angry cows that charged.

Tawny as fall sunlight, smiling, Hornsby hooked one leg around the horn. "Welcome home, brother."

Three of the riders were of the stripe Cairns had met at Siddon's place. The other was a pigeon-chested man whose head was over-big. His tiny eyes were sunk in moist puckers as he kept watching Brule. Cairns might have mistaken his expression for a toothy grin, except that Boney Siddon had spoken of this man—Darby Culwell.

"Shall we ride in together now, a triumphal procession for the prodigal son?" Hornsby smiled. A few minutes before he would have run excited cattle into a man on foot, but now neither he nor Cairns could afford bloodshed by pistols on SB land.

Cairns said, "Just keep Beaver Face there ahead of me all the way."

"I'd like to have this Langley," Culwell said. "He ruined it, Hornsby."

"He hasn't hurt anything," Hornsby said.

Culwell looked at Cairns then. "Beaver Face, huh?"

When they started, Hornsby drew blood on the claybank's shoulders with a vicious raking of his spurs. The horse began to buck. It almost unseated Hornsby. When he got its head up hard he raked the animal again. He looked at Cairns and laughed. "I like to see him jump."

Cairns glanced at the blood-streaked hide. "You hurt only the horse, not me."

"You didn't used to squint, Cairns," Hornsby said. "Does the sun bother your eyes?"

The wickedness in Darby Culwell was a simple quality, Cairns thought, a willingness toward murder that rode on the surface of his expression; but the foulness in Hornsby was without code or understanding.

They rode into the yard. Cairns looked at the ancient cottonwoods in full leaf. Home. It seemed that he had been gone for years.

He walked across the yard slowly. Mrs. Bretnall came out and stood with her hands behind her. When Cairns went up the steps he saw the smile trembling on her lips and the tears in her eyes. "Cairns," she said, and held out her arms.

Hornsby stood at the bottom of the steps, smiling as if the homecoming pleased him greatly.

Old Stivers came out, his back like a sword, long mustaches droop-

ing below the fierce thrust of his nose. He shook hands with Cairns.
"Well, you're both back now."

He looked from Cairns to Hornsby and something in his eyes said
that he was just realizing that he had bitten off a mighty chunk.

Late that night, Preacher Yont came riding from the north. His
voice was a rumble when he tried to talk quietly to Brule at the corrals.
He sat with Stivers in the office. After a while old Stivers was staring
angrily at him.

"You were everywhere they went! You know what they did and how
they lived. You never would talk about them, and now you still
won't."

"No."

"Maybe I was hot-headed the day I ran them off," Stivers said. "I
still think I had the right idea, but if you'd tell me what you know, I'd
have more than my own judgment to go on."

"You'd have my judgment, which might be faulty," Preacher Yont
said.

"I'll trust it."

Preacher Yont shook his head.

"Some of these wild stories that have come back—they had a pistol
fight in Quartzite. Panamint won't talk about it. They had some
trouble at another mining camp where Brule Langley was. He won't
talk about it."

"I asked Brule and Panamint not to."

"You meddled in my affairs, Yont."

"No. You meddled in God's affairs when you set yourself up to
judge two men. Now it's done and you have got to make a decision."

"You could help me."

Preacher Yont rose. "It's your land, your boys, your decision." He
opened the door and went out.

And then Stivers sat in a silent house. He must be getting old, he
thought, for no decision had ever weighed on him so heavily before.
He had come here when he was twenty-six years old. He had fought
Apaches, and then starvation and loneliness, and later, his neighbors,
to make the SB what it was today. His decisions had been quick. He
had never doubted the necessity of anything that he had done, and he
would not doubt now. But he must make up his mind.

He rose after a while and went through the wide west wing of the house to his bedroom. Mrs. Bretnall was sitting at the window.

"What do you think about them?" Stivers asked.

Her face turned slowly toward him in the gloom. "You have made up your mind, haven't you?"

"I have."

"They're both our boys. I keep remembering them when they were little."

"That don't help now. They're grown."

"I'm not trying to think of anything to help you, Stivers. I know them better than you. Hornsby has cheated and lied since he was little. Cairns has thought of no one but himself. But both of them are still our sons."

"One of them will fit here better than the other." Stivers took off his boots. "They can't get along and I will not split my land. Do you want to kow what I've decided?"

"No."

"Why not?"

"If I don't know I'll have them both here for one more night. Go to bed, Stivers, and may your decision let you sleep well."

Stivers grunted. "It will, don't worry." He had not needed Yont's help. The very act of making up his mind had cleared all doubt from it.

The next morning he walked with Cairns and Hornsby to the edge of the cottonwoods, near a corral where Brule was gentling a steeldust mare. Preacher Yont was on the porch, staring at the hills. Darby Culwell and Hornsby's other friends were rebuilding a wood trough that carried water from the spring to the house.

"How'd you lose the claybank, Cairns?" Stivers asked.

"Gambled him away."

"That was a hell of a thing. You couldn't run to me for money to get him back, could you? What did you do, walk until Hornsby took out one of my horses to meet you?"

"Hornsby brought a horse out to me?" Cairns let it go. "Yes, I walked."

"How much money did you bring back?"

"Very little."

"That doesn't matter so much, but a man who can't even hang onto his horse or raise the price of another one makes me wonder. You spent your time in mining camps. What could you learn there that would do you any good here?"

"I sent you two men from mining camps, Panamint and Brule," Cairns said.

"You also sent some others that I don't care about one bit," Stivers pointed toward the house. "That gang right there. Your judgment wasn't good in that case."

"Hornsby's men, not mine."

Stivers eyed Cairns bleakly. "They said you sent them. I let them stay this long only because of that."

A rage that he had not felt since he walked into Quartzite to kill Hornsby began to choke Cairns' reason. He steadied only when he saw Hornsby smiling. Anger and denial had never served to match Hornsby's lies before Stivers in the past. Cairns shook his head.

"Hornsby, did you send those men here?" Stivers asked.

His eyes clear and frank, his face boyishly solemn, Hornsby shook his head. And then he gave Cairns a puzzled look.

"Get rid of that bunch right now, Cairns," Stivers said.

"I didn't send them. Make Hornsby."

The bony expression of Stivers' face increased. "Fire them, Hornsby. There's money in my desk."

Hornsby walked away. He had a brief, low-voiced argument with Darby Culwell, and then Culwell went with the others to get his pay.

Cairns studied the man he had called father. There was a built-in rigidity in Stivers that Cairns had not understood before. Now he knew it came from never allowing the chance of serious error in dealing with human beings; from long devotion to the SB; from an exercise of power over an area that constituted the whole world to Stivers.

He had lived too long with no one to countermand his decisions. And now, if his belief in himself was broken—although Cairns doubted that it could be—the blow would shatter something vital in him.

Cairns looked out on the land. The SB was enormous. Until a few months ago it had been Cairns' world, also. In time it could become a crushing burden, blinding a man as Stivers was blinded.

I wonder if that comes to me because I know I have lost or because the belief springs honestly in me? The test would come when the words fell from Stivers' lips, when Cairns could measure their final force.

He said, "Let's not drag it out, Stivers. Tell me now."

"Hold your tongue." Stivers waited until Hornsby returned. "I'll rake up two thousand dollars for the one who leaves. That will be all he gets, and I'll have a lawyer—"

"I don't need it," Cairns said. "I don't want it."

"By God! Will you let me finish?" Stivers glared at them both. "Hornsby can get on better here. Cairns, I'll give you the money tomorrow to make a start somewhere else."

Cairns looked out on the land again. He had known that he could lose, and he had known, also, that he could win. He waited for the impact of Stivers' words to stir wicked anger against Hornsby. But no anger came.

If this was failure, Cairns could not feel the smash of it; and it could not be loss because no part of himself was compromised or lost. He remembered Panamint leaving Quartzite without a backward look; and Boney Siddon accepting blandly the same kind of defeat he had dished out, living by a code that was queerly twisted but clear in its application. A crushing blow? Cairns had feared it would be, but now he knew it was not so.

He took it further, running defeat to the limit to see what kind of man he was. If, on top of Stivers' words, Elizabeth Driscoll veered away from the answer she had been ready to give Cairns, he knew it could not ruin him, for he was a man who had won over himself when he once accepted the fact that he might be blind for life.

Stivers cleared his throat. "There's no rush, after all. It might take me more than a day or two to get the money."

Cairns smiled. "I don't want it."

Stivers jerked his shoulders irritably. "There's no use to sulk about the thing. The money is yours."

"I'll take a good horse and a rig instead."

Hornsby was watching with an odd expression. His smile was gone, his eyes narrowed. "You can have the claybank. The only reason I brought him back here was you."

"You keep him, Hornsby."

Something frightened showed on Hornsby's face. He said tensely, "You really don't want him, do you?"

Cairns walked toward the breaking corral and called to Brule, "I'm leaving. Do you want to go with me?"

"Now?"

"Right away."

Talking quietly to the steeldust he had been leading, Brule hobbled alongside her and removed the blanket and the pair of old stirrups she was carrying. He took the hackamore off the mare and put everything on a rail of the corral.

"Pick me a good horse," Cairns said.

Stivers strode toward the house. Preacher Yont watched him walk up the steps and through the doorway, and said nothing.

Hornsby grabbed Cairns' arm. "You'd even let another man pick out your horse? That's only part of the big bluff you're making. You're dying inside and you won't admit it!" Hornsby smiled and then the smile slid away as Cairns looked at him calmly.

Cairns recognized a simple fact: only in body was Hornsby any different from the malicious child of fifteen years ago who had tried to hurt others by stealing or destroying the things they loved. He looked at Hornsby, then walked away.

Hornsby stayed beside him. "I've won. You're leaving. How do you like it, Cairns?"

Preacher Yont met them at the top of the steps. He read their faces. He stared hell's fire at Hornsby. "I've held my peace so far, but now—"

"No." Cairns shook his head. "You and Stivers have been friends for thirty years. Keep it so. And anyway, no matter what you tried to tell him, you couldn't change his mind."

"I should have spoken up before," Preacher Yont said, "but I bet on Stivers to see with his own eyes. If I give an opinion now, having been silent when he asked my advice—"

"Just let it go," Cairns said. "I've gained more than I've lost."

"Elizabeth, you mean," Hornsby said viciously. "A woman! Can you balance her against what I'll have?"

Cairns and Preacher Yont knew each other now. They understood Hornsby and so they could afford him sympathy, in the look they exchanged.

Again, Hornsby misunderstood. He cursed them both and flung away from them. He watched them from the doorway. There was something here that was beyond him, and so it must be ridicule or injury aimed at him.

Preacher Yont almost crushed Cairns' hand in his grip. "I knew you were growing into a man when I saw you coming from blindness in Quartzite. Keep growing, keep understanding and no failure can touch you. May the Lord be with you wherever you go." He dropped Cairns' hand. There was a sadness in Yont's eyes when he glanced at Hornsby.

"It's a pretty bluff," Hornsby said. "Swallow that guff about religion if you can, Cairns, but I know you're bleeding inside. I told you you'd lose."

Cairns smiled. He saw the depths of Hornsby's defeat, for he knew now that Hornsby had not wanted what he had been given, no more than he had actually desired the claybank. Possession in both cases had been only an instrument with which Hornsby had thought he could scourge a man he hated.

Now Hornsby knew he had lost his power to hurt, and the knowledge brought to his face a terrible willfulness to destroy, a sickening sight because it was a child's quality housed within the framework of a man. When Cairns shook his head in pity, Hornsby's face turned white. He started to lash out with his fists, but Cairns threw him aside and walked into the house to say goodbye to his mother.

Cairns and Brule rode toward the western hills where Panamint was supervising a crew building tunnels. Brule kept looking over his shoulder.

"That Culwell—he didn't ride away in the same direction with them others. I don't trust your brother, either."

They rode past bunches of cattle that held their heads high to watch them pass.

"You didn't want to leave, did you, Brule?"

"It was the best job I ever had. I got along all right with your old man, but I couldn't stay and you know it. Don't think Hornsby ever forgot how I almost choked him to death. When I was saddling the horses, he told me I wasn't leaving quite soon enough." Brule looked again at the backtrail.

"Maybe Panamint won't want to go," Cairns said.

"He'd better. Is Hornsby your half brother?"

"We're no relation. The Bretnalls took us in."

"That's a relief."

It was not long afterward that Brule spotted the two riders coming behind them. He and Cairns stopped and turned their horses. Longhorns they had run from the edge of a bog gathered on a knoll and watched them with suspicion.

"Hornsby on the claybank," Cairns said.

"And that other one is Culwell. There's a third man a half-mile behind them. Showdown, Cairns."

"I didn't think he'd start anything on SB land." But Cairns knew that had been hope only. His last look at Hornsby had told him how bitterly the man realized how little damage he had done. Trickery and lies having failed him, Hornsby had only violence left.

"I don't want to kill him," Cairns said. There were the Bretnalls to consider. There was his own pride in what he had achieved when he was blind.

Brule loosened the rifle in his scabbard. "I'll take care of Culwell."

The claybank was a hundred yards away when Hornsby raised his hand and shouted, "Hold up a minute! Ma Bretnall sent me out with something you've got to take."

Deceit to the last! And then Cairns thought that it *could* be possible that Mrs. Bretnall had insisted he take some gift. But he put his hand on his pistol.

Hornsby and Culwell came on. Hornsby was smiling. Culwell's big head was bobbing, his teeth a white blotch in his face. He jerked a carbine from a boot when he was fifty yards away. He was slow. Brule shot him from the saddle with a rifle bullet while he was still aiming. It was doubtful that Hornsby ever knew it, for he came straight on, his face insane. There was a pistol in his holster, but he drew another from under his shirt. He spurred the claybank savagely to close the gap.

Cairns' pistol was aimed at Hornsby when the claybank began to buck. Hornsby tried a shot even as he was slipping. The horse got its head down and went toward the knoll in explosive jumps. It ran wild, still pitching after Hornsby was thrown. It burst through the ring of cattle on the hill and knocked a calf sprawling. Enraged cows bawled and lunged at the horse.

On hands and knees, Hornsby scrabbled for his pistol in the grass. He saw it lying ahead of him and ran toward it. He must have seen the two thin-rumped cows hurtling down the hill at him but he whirled to fire wildly at Cairns. Brule's rifle rocked back. One of the cows went down.

Cairns took a snap shot at the other. He heard the bullet smack solidly but it might as well have been a whack from a rope. The angry cow swept into Hornsby while he was running to get closer to Cairns. She twisted her head and drove into him. There was a swirling in the grass as she gored and bellowed, and then she raised her head and tried to stagger back up the hill toward her calf. She fell under the strike of Brule's bullet, with her stained horn uppermost.

Brule charged the herd, yelling, firing his rifle. He broke their stubborn front. They swung away and ran with their tails high, and then some of the cows swirled into another circle and faced him.

Hornsby's face was gray. He looked up at Cairns with the crumpled expression of a child about to cry. "It was all bluff, wasn't it? I licked you, didn't I?"

It was against the unformed block of Hornsby's character that Cairns' own character had been hammered into maturity. He could remember, too, that there had been times when the two of them had played together as brothers.

He gave Hornsby his victory. "Yes, I was bluffing. You'll never know how hard it hit me when Stivers picked you instead of me."

Hornsby smiled. "I thought so!"

Preacher Yont rode up on a lathered horse. He knelt beside Hornsby. Brule broke the defiance of the cows a second time and then he rode over to look briefly at Culwell, and then went to catch the claybank. He took the advantage of motion of doing things; he did not have to watch Hornsby die.

Hornsby went as Cairns had thought he would—looking pleasantly on the world as the life bubbled out of him. The tears Cairns shed, he told himself, were for Mrs. Bretnall and an unyielding old man who would have truth forced on him now.

Preacher Yont rose. "Will you go back?"

"Not now. Some day, maybe."

"That might be best."

Yont and Brule led two slow-moving horses toward the house. Cairns rode alone toward the Driscoll place.

Luck of Riley

With a dab of dust in a buckskin poke Riley Winslow waited for the usual lecture before hitting the trail to Baker City.

Boone Adams wasn't old, but he was settled in his ways. He hunched his neck against his shoulder to squash a mosquito. He cleared his throat and said: "Luck is a grasshopper, Riley. A man jumps where it was while it's hopping somewhere else. Wait for it in one place, I say."

"I always come back in the fall, don't I? This time I got a feeling, Boone, an awful lucky feeling. No telling what might happen." Riley grinned. "Anything special you want?"

Boone Adams gave the question deep consideration, looking toward the Poor Boy tunnel where a rickety wheelbarrow was ready to fall sidewise. He looked at a patched bellows hung under a tree near the portal of the tunnel. It leaked, it whistled, and sometimes it did not deliver enough air to the forge to keep a fire going.

"Nothing special, I guess," Boone said. "Just remember what I said about luck."

"I might even get back before fall."

Riley swung away, a slender man with bright blue eyes and a hunch that this summer luck was with him. Last year's dead leaves were floating away on the rise of Spikebuck Creek. The aspen leaves were small, pale green. There was a feeling of a newness in the world.

In the Gulch Saloon Sam Tully hefted the dust with an expert's touch. "Seventy bucks, Riley. Considering you boys got only a knife-edge streak and have to grind your ore like an Indian making meal on a flat rock, and then pan it, I'd say you was doing fair. Streak ever going to widen out?"

"Boone says it will." Riley kept eyeing the poker game. It didn't look very tough.

"Boone's the hopeful kind, sure enough," Tully said. "How much do you want to leave behind the bar this time?"

"All but ten bucks."

Tully stacked ten silver dollars on the bar. "I hear there's a freighter over in Sweetwater that wants to sell a tramcar, some track, and a lot of stuff he hauled out from Denver for a fly-by-night mining outfit that flew. That stuff would be real handy at the Poor Boy."

"Awful handy," Riley said, "if a man had a thousand dollars to buy it."

He headed toward the poker table. In no time he knew that he and luck had jumped into the same chair. At dawn he had five hundred dollars and three placer claims in Lincoln Camp, the latter won on a beautiful little straight that beat three aces. The claims didn't count because anybody knew that Lincoln Camp, on the Little Beaver, was only a flash in the pan that wouldn't last till winter. But of course it wouldn't hurt to have a look at the property on the way to Sweetwater. It was just possible that a man with five hundred dollars might be able to make a deal with the freighter who had all that mining equipment to sell.

By the time he had walked to Lincoln Camp, Riley was wondering how one sky could have held so much water. He found the miners of the camp probing three feet of wash for tents and other belongings. He stopped beside a man who was trying to unwind a suit of red underwear from a willow thicket.

"Can you tell me where the Jim Dandy claims are?"

"You own 'em?"

"Yep."

The miner scowled. "Then you should have been here last night to get drowned with the rest of us. Your claims are up on that hill to the west. They ain't no good, but neither is anything else here. However, in case you was damn' fool enough to stick around, you'd be where you wouldn't get washed out of bed every time it rains."

Riley was not figuring to stick around, and he could see that no one else was either. He didn't go near his claims. By the time he had boiled a pot of coffee the few dozen miners of the gulch were stringing out toward Baker City. Riley would have thrown away his quitclaim deed to the Jim Dandy ground, but the paper was in the bottom of his pack. He headed for Sweetwater.

Where the trail broke over the wind-cold spine of Jingling Mountain he met three Englishmen shivering beside a cairn. Their faces were gray and clammy from the altitude. Their pack horse had a list like the wheelbarrow at the Poor Boy mine.

"Lincoln Camp? Sure. I just came from there. Night before last a gully-buster—" Riley looked at the odd clothes of the Britons, at the ancient pack horse which somebody had unloaded on them.

The tallest man raised pale brows in a pained expression. "A gully-buster? What in the world—"

"That means a rich strike," Riley said. "Yes sir, things were really roaring in Lincoln Camp night before last."

"Ah, yes," one of the men said. "A reliable man in St. Missouri, Louis, told us Lincoln Camp was one of the most prosperous—ah—diggings?—in America. I hope we're not too late."

"I'm afraid you are," Riley said. He saw disappointment shadow the faces of the Englishmen.

"You mean everything is taken?"

"The gulch was pretty well covered when I last saw it." Riley began to dig into his pack. "But it so happens that I own three claims down there. If it wasn't that my mother is very sick back in Maine. . . ."

He sold his claims for six hundred dollars. He went down the mountain singing, shying rocks at curious whistle-pigs.

The freighter in Sweetwater had the prettiest pile of mining equipment Riley had ever seen. Boone Adams would sit up all night talking when he saw all that stuff at the Poor Boy mine.

"Nine hundred for the works," the freighter said, "including the forge and ten sacks of blacksmith's coal. That just covers my expenses from Denver. All I want to do is get even."

"Four hundred," Riley said. "And fifty for your expenses from Denver. I'd like to keep you even too."

The freighter spat against the pastern of a gray wheeler. "I can get a thousand any day by hauling the stuff over the hill to Lincoln Camp. Seven hundred where she lays. If I don't get that I'll go to Lincoln with the whole works."

"On second thought, four hundred is all I can stand," Riley said. "I have to work for my money. I don't own a rich claim like those fellows in Lincoln Camp."

"Six-fifty?" the freighter asked.

Riley shook his head.

"Hell, I'm not giving things away. I'll head for Lincoln in the morning."

And that was what the freighter did. Sometimes, Riley thought, you have to make the grasshopper jump and then be waiting where he lands. The freighter could get over Jingling Mountain with his six-horse team, but it would take all his horses had to bring an empty wagon up the west side, so there was going to be a fine bargain in mining equipment at Lincoln Camp.

Like any mushroom settlement, Sweetwater straddled the creek, spurning a fine level mesa fed by big springs just a quarter of a mile toward the southern spur of the main range. *There* was the place for the town that would spring here in earnest when someone got around to bringing in a railroad. The man who lived in a little cottonwood cabin on the mesa spent his time in Sweetwater, unloading wagons for two dollars a day.

"Sure I own the mesa," he told Riley. "Proved up on it last year." Three hundred dollars wasn't enough, he said. He ought to have fifteen hundred anyway.

Riley finally gave him five hundred, and within the hour had a surveyor laying out a townsite. That night as he was automatically winning a few hundred bucks in a poker game, riders came down Puerta Pass with news that the Utes were cutting up again in the San Luis Valley on the other side of the main range. The riders said things were really fierce this time.

The poker players agreed that it was hard to make an honest living, what with the Indians always raising hell. A bushy-bearded little man said, "The army ought to show them Utes how the boar et the cabbage."

"Them soldiers!" another man said. "In the first place, they won't come till we're all scalped; but if they do show up it'll be like the last time when they tried to get up Puerta with wagons and got all tangled up like blind dogs in a smokehouse." He looked at his cards after the draw. "Bet twenty bucks."

Riley raised him, and then looked at his cards.

"If they'd leave their damned supply wagons behind and ride after the Indians, they might get something done," the bushy-bearded man said. He tossed in his hand.

Riley won the pot with a flush he had filled by drawing two cards. He raked the chips in absently.

The next day he bought a hammer-headed mule and rode up to have a look at Puerta Pass. Nature had left an easy grade, and travois had left the engineer's stakes. The Mormons would have considered the route a first-class pike, but everyone in Sweetwater had assured Riley that only a few wagons had ever worked all the way across. He guessed some people just didn't know luck when they saw it.

Before he left for Denver he hired four teams and ten men to clear out the worst obstacles on Puerta. In three days the long-striding mule took him to Denver, and there he found the territorial legislature in session in a bar. For five dollars and two rounds of drinks the legislators gave him a franchise to operate a toll road on Puerta Pass. He spent one night playing poker and came to the conclusion that Denver poker players were the poorest in the world. Winning was getting sort of monotonous.

When he got back to Sweetwater, there was a road of sorts up the pass. Riley was smoking a good cigar and waiting at the toll gate when the army came up the pass ten days later.

"What the hell is this?" a broad-beamed colonel on a black horse wanted to know.

"One dollar per horse, three dollars per wagon," Riley said, puffing a fine white cloud of smoke.

The colonel gave the impression of drawing his saber. "Have that gate opened at once!" he ordered a lieutenant, who twisted around to look at a sergeant who was already picking troopers for the job.

"Force that gate," Riley said, "and you'll prove to yourself that eagles have wings, Colonel. This toll road was built by private means, with the blessing of the government of the great territory of Colorado under powers granted by the Government of the United States of America, which in turn derives its authority—"

"My God, a lawyer!" the colonel groaned. He cursed for quite a spell, and his face showed that government was no more comprehensible to him than to anyone else. But in the end he signed for a hundred men and twenty wagons, and all the while he kept giving Riley a dark court-martial stare. "What were you during the war?"

"Infantry private, C.S.A." Riley grinned. "Have a cigar, Colonel."

"I'll be damned." The colonel took the cigar and rode away.

Three days later the cavalry was back again, the colonel having learned that the Utes he sought were now in the Upper Arkansas Valley. Four days later they were over the hill again, and the colonel came back up the road with his command. By then Riley had a tent and a case of good whisky. The colonel had a drink.

Troopers came and went. Army wagons came and went. The army seemed to be supplying the cavalry in two places at the same time. Riley's hip pockets began to bulge with papers signed by the colonel. Between times he fished and drank whisky and felt a little ashamed when he thought of Boone Adams all alone at the Poor Boy with the leaky bellows and the Joe McGee wheelbarrow.

And then one day the colonel came down the pass with all his command. "Some fool went and made peace with the Utes before we could catch up with them," he said.

Riley shook hands with him and gave him three bottles of whisky. He was going to miss the colonel. Travelers were now using the road in increasing numbers but collecting a miserable thirty or forty dollars a day began to bore Riley. Then, too, there were some people who always claimed they were going to a funeral, which gave them the right to use the toll road without charge. Riley didn't like to argue about such a solemn point, even when one man used the excuse six times.

One day Riley went to the owner of the biggest saloon in Sweetwater. "The toll road is a good thing," he said. "Some day the railroad will come this way, and that's the only good route over the range. They'll have to buy it. I'd wait till then; but I'm fed up with the country, and my mother back in Maine is awful sick, so for a measly ten thousand dollars—"

"I'm pretty well fed up myself," the saloonman said, "although my mother lives in Tennessee." He shook his head sadly. "You can't tell about railroads, Riley. Railroads are funny things. I remember a town down in Texas where we expected the railroad to hit, and. . . ."

They settled on four thousand dollars. A party of dudes who fancied themselves as poker players hit town that night, and Riley won two thousand more; so he knew he still had the grasshopper pinned down.

A horse trader told him that a man of his ability should not be caught dead riding a hammer-headed mule, but Riley was fond of old Hammerhead by now, for the mule had bitten him only once and managed to kick him only twice, so he turned down all offers to trade and rode Hammerhead into Denver a second time.

"A few hours later, and you wouldn't have caught me in town," a high official of the War Department told Riley. "I can authorize prompt settlement of your toll-road charges. You're a lucky man, Mr. Winslow. If you hadn't caught me, it might have taken months, more likely years; but, as it is—"

"I jump with the grasshopper," Riley said.

After a few days he was doubly sure that Denver poker players were the world's worst. And then he had a fling at roulette in the Elephant Casino and broke the bank. He bought the place for twenty-five thousand dollars, attracted to it irresistibly because the checks were inlaid with beautiful blue grasshoppers.

For almost a month people waited five-deep to put their money on the tables in the Grasshopper Casino. During that time the government paid off Riley's toll-road charges. He rode high. Everything he touched became money. He considered buying into a bank. And then one night a swamper filling lamps set fire to a five-gallon can of coal oil. The Grasshopper Casino made a hot, brisk fire, and a Kansan watching it go said that a place with a name like that ought to burn, by cracky.

Everybody got out with his life and it seemed that everybody also got out with pockets full of checks, most of which Riley knew full well had come from racks abandoned by cashiers. But he paid off and he still had several thousand dollars left. The next day a government official presented him with a letter which said he had been overpaid nine hundred dollars on the toll road.

"It's best to settle now," the man said. "It might take the government months, or even years, to collect if you contest the matter, but some day they will collect. It's better to adjust the matter now, don't you agree?"

Riley agreed and adjusted.

He sold the lots where his casino had stood and went up the street to tangle with the world's poorest poker players. They had learned something from watching him, he decided, when he went broke three hours later. He kept feeling his pockets. He couldn't believe it. He was actually broke.

A dumpy little man with ragged red whiskers approached him timidly and asked if he owned the mesa south of where Sweetwater used to be.

"What d'you mean—used to be?"

"Somebody made a big strike farther west. There's no one left at all on the creek." The man blinked apologetically, and his whiskers twitched with his words. "I've always had a hankering to start a little cattle ranch, so I thought—"

"That's exactly what I had in mind for that mesa myself," Riley said. "Last week I almost bought the cows, but then I got word that my mother back in Maine is very sick, so for a thousand dollars, say—"

"Oh, my!" the little man said. "That's way out of my class. I was hoping for a reasonable price."

Riley settled for three hundred dollars and a sturdy gray horse. For fifty dollars he sold to a gambling house the sack of inlaid checks, all but a pocketful of yellow ones with the beautiful blue grasshoppers in the center. These he kept for luck.

The wheelbarrow cost him fifty bucks. It did not have a steel bed, and it was more suitable for light gardening than mining; but still it was better than the one at the Poor Boy. He bought, too, a brand-new bellows for the forge. The sturdy gray pack horse carried both items easily, until fifteen miles from Denver, the animal developed something that looked to Riley like a wonderful case of the blind staggers. Riley camped at once, picketing the horse to the wheel of the barrow. The gray appeared to recover, and it showed no concern at all over the fact that it was due for a quick trade.

Old Hammerhead's squeals woke Riley in the night. By the light of a low moon Riley fired three shots at figures scooting along on swift ponies. And by the light of the same moon he saw the wheelbarrow bouncing across the stony ground on the end of the picket rope tied to the gray, and the gray wasn't staggering a bit at the moment.

The Indians cut the rope but not soon enough. At dawn Riley trailed down fragments of the wheelbarrow. There was nothing worth picking up. He flipped a yellow check at the wreckage and hoped that when the gray staggered its last stagger, it would fall smack on an Indian horsethief of any tribe or any description.

Grasshoppers were jumping everywhere in the fall-crisp grass when he rode into the valley of the Sweetwater. He met a railroad survey crew and asked the chief-of-party, "Where to?"

"First to Sweetwater," the chief said. "That'll be the division point, and then we'll run her up the old toll-road grade on Puerta."

"*Old* toll-road grade? Hell, that road's barely a pup," Riley said.

"It's old now," the chief said. "The railroad bought it from a saloonman for fifty thousand dollars."

"Is that a fact?" Riley rode up the valley with the bellows behind the saddle. He flipped yellow checks with grasshopper inlays at real grasshoppers.

Sweetwater had moved, sure enough. It was now up on the mesa, and it was a booming place. A timid little red-whiskered man was watching carpenters building a hotel. "How's your sick mother back in Maine?" he asked Riley.

"Much better. How's the cattle business?"

The man pointed at two milch cows browsing along the edge of the street. Riley bought the drinks.

"There *was* a little flood on the creek," the little man said. "The saloons moved up here, and after that the rest of the town just naturally followed. You had a pretty good townsite laid out here, Mr. Winslow."

"I have an eye for such things," Riley said. He fixed a stern look on the little fellow. "While you didn't actually lie about the town moving, you did give me the impression that everybody had moved on to a strike in the mountains."

"Oh, there's a strike all right, a rich one on the Little Beaver. Lincoln Camp, where there used to be some placer workings, I understand."

Riley stayed one night in Sweetwater, playing poker. He couldn't win for losing. During the night somebody stole the bellows. He looked all over town, but he couldn't find it. He went on to Lincoln Camp.

The place was swarming. A miner told him three Englishmen had made the strike. "They didn't know nothing. They made a blind buy on the Jim Dandy claims from a man they met on top of Jingling Mountain. The claims weren't even in the gulch. They were on a hill. It so happened there had been a flood here that ran everyone out of camp. It also uncovered a rich vein of gold on the ground the Englishmen bought. They've had an offer of a hundred thousand dollars already."

"Bless me," Riley murmured, and bought the drinks.

"Them Englishmen had horseshoes in their pockets," the miner went on. "They no sooner were here than some freighter got lost and blundered down the mountain with the finest layout of mining equipment you ever seen. They bought the whole works, except the forge. It's the kind with a blower on it, a regular jim dandy."

Riley winced at the description. "Who's got the forge?"

"The freighter went into business with it. He gets two bits a head for sharpening steel."

Under a lean-to in the trees the freighter was a busy man. He recognized Riley at once.

"How much for the forge, blower and all?" Riley asked.

"I'll sell you a claim on the hill for five thousand, not more'n a half-mile from where the Englishmen made the strike, I'll swap horses or trade boots, but this here forge is a money-maker I can't part with."

"I passed two wagonloads of them on the way up here," Riley said. "How much for the forge?"

"It's worth five hundred, but I'll take four."

"Two hundred."

"Three hundred and the saddle on that mule."

The saddle was Riley's pride, but he had to take something back to Boone Adams. "If I throw in the saddle, how will the mule pack the forge?"

"For fifteen bucks I'll give you a packsaddle."

"Make it ten," Riley said.

After a half-hour Riley knew that Hammerhead was not going to have anything to do with a packsaddle.

"I used to own that mule," the freighter said. "Never could make him wear a packsaddle. I'll tell you what I'll do—trade you straight across for that little sorrel over there. She's a great pack horse."

The little sorrel had one hip high in the air and the other braced against a tree. "What happens if you move that aspen?" Riley asked.

"When she packs she packs," the freighter said. "When she rests she rests. She's a jim dandy on the trail."

"I'm tired of that word," Riley said.

When Hammerhead saw what was happening, a bitter, ornery expression came into the mule's eyes. It hurt Riley to part with Hammerhead, but he had to take the forge back to Boone, so he made the deal.

The sorrel was a packer sure enough; she went right along until, at the top of a rocky pitch a few miles from Baker City, Riley stopped to light his pipe. It was a large grasshopper lighting on the sorrel's cheek that started all the trouble. She knocked Riley flat and went bucking down the hill. The packsaddle slipped, and the forge came dangling down the side.

Riley found fragments of cast iron for a mile before he caught up with the mare tangled up in the trees. Even the packsaddle wasn't much good then, so he cut it loose and went on into Baker City.

Sam Tully said: "You're back a little earlier than usual this year. Have a good summer?"

"One of the best," Riley said, and bought the drinks.

It was not long afterward that Hammerhead clattered up the street, dragging a broken halter rope; and then the freighter who owned him arrived a little later.

"You spoiled that mule," the freighter said. "He pried up hell, kicking and biting all my horses, and then he busted loose."

"I forgot to tell you," Riley said, "when he raises hell he bites and kicks. I'll tell you what I'll do—I'll trade the sorrel back for the mule."

The freighter spat and bought the drinks. "I got to have something for my trip down here."

"You can have the packsaddle."

"I saw it. Give me the sorrel and thirty bucks to boot, and you can have the hammerhead back."

"Make it fifteen." Forty dollars was all Riley had.

"Thirty. And I'll throw in the halter on the mule. That's my figure." The freighter stood so firmly on the point that Riley finally had to pay.

When the freighter was gone and Hammerhead was leering through the window with a triumphant smirk, Sam Tully said, "Boone done drew all the dust you left behind the bar."

Riley said, "He always was a spendthrift."

When a poker game started that afternoon Riley jumped in with his ten bucks. He lost it in one hand, having a miserable little straight beaten by a flush.

Golden aspen leaves were floating on Spikebuck Creek when he rode bareback up the mountain, singing a song to the mule.

"Well, you're back," Boone Adams said. He was glad to see Riley, but at the moment he was busy tinkering with the wobbly wheelbarrow. There were a few more patches on the bellows above the stone forge, and a good deal more rock over the dump. "Looks like you had a lucky summer, Riley. That's a stout-looking mule you got there."

"It was a good summer." Riley had one yellow chip left. He spun it through the air to his partner. "Would you believe that was once worth a hundred dollars?"

Boone examined the check curiously.

"Streak widen any?" Riley asked.

"Not yet, but it will," Boone said absently. "That's a good-looking chip, Riley. It reminds me of something. Luck is a grasshopper. A man jumps—"

"You could be right," Riley said.

The Singing Sands

There were three passes ahead and their names were like the rhythm of a chant, Mosca, Medano and Music. The alliteration kept running in Johnny Anderson's mind as his tired pony chopped through the rabbitbrush, across alkali flats where the dust rose thin and bitter in the windless air. Like magic words that would kill the trouble behind, the names chased each other; but every few moments Anderson looked across his shoulder at the long backtrail.

Jasper Lamb was doing the same thing, twisting wearily in the saddle, squinting his bloodshot eyes at the gray distance. He was a middle-aged man, slouching, leanly built. For a year Anderson had prowled the mountains with him. They had never faced any severe test until now; and now Anderson was wondering if he had picked the right partner. Lamb was not showing the proper concern about things.

Anderson worked his lips and ran his tongue around his mouth to clear dust and the cottony feeling that had been in his mouth ever since he knew there were men on their trail. "Which pass, Lamb?"

"Medano, I know it best." Lamb glanced at the heavily loaded mule he was towing. The mule was the strongest of the three animals, but it would not be hurried.

Each mile seemed to bring them no closer to the mountains with their golden streaks of frost-touched aspens. Looking backward at the space they had crossed, Anderson was uneasy because of the very emptiness. He said hopefully, "Maybe we threw them off when we made that fake toward Poncha Pass early this morning."

"I figured on wind," Lamb said. "There ain't been any. We've left a

147

trail like a single furrow ploughed across a field. The wind blows like old Scratch here sometimes, but today it didn't." He had come out during the Pike's Peak bust, cutting his teeth on the mountains and losing his illusions at the same time, so now he did not rail against luck or the weather. "They'll be along."

Johnny Anderson was young. He had passed his twenty-second birthday the week before when they were making their final cleanup on their placer claim in the San Juan. He wasted energy cursing the vagaries of the weather; but half his anger was fear as he saw how Lamb's buckskin was limping. The horse had thrown a shoe in the rocky foothills just north of the Rio Grande the night before. Anderson tried to weigh the limp against the distance yet to go; and then he turned to look behind.

There was no dust far back. Mosca, Medano and Music. . . . He studied immense buff foothills ahead. He had never seen their like before but he was not greatly interested.

He asked, "Who are they, do you suppose?"

Lamb did not waste motion in shrugging or any other gesture. "You saw some of the toughs there in Baker's Park when we stopped overnight. Pick any bunch of them."

"We made a mistake!" Anderson said. "We shouldn't have stopped there, and then we guarded the panniers on the mule too close. We should have dumped them on the ground like they didn't amount to nothing. We made another mistake when we slipped out of there by night. We—"

"Sure, we made mistakes." Lamb leaned ahead to feel the shoulder of his horse. "We come out of the San Juan with a loaded mule at the end of summer. Noody had to be smart to know what we're carrying." He kept watching the buckskin's shoulder. "We made our pile in a hurry, boy. I mistrust too much good luck."

Anderson let the thought grind away for a while. "Is your horse going to make it?"

"I doubt it, not without he rests and I try to do something for that tender foot." Lamb looked at the unshod Indian pony under Anderson. It cut no figure at all beside the buckskin. It rode hard and its gait was uneven but the mustang mark was there and there were guts in the pony for many miles yet. Lamb watched it for a moment with no expression on his bearded, dusty features.

Slowly the great pale brown hills came closer. No trees, no rocks broke the rounding contours. The ridges were sharp on the spines, delicately molded. The shadings of the coloration flowed so subtly into each other that Anderson could not tell whether the hills were a quarter of a mile away or two miles. The whole mass of them seemed to pulse in the still heat. Anderson's sudden loss of distance judgment gave him a queer feeling.

When he looked behind once more and saw only lonely vastness, the claws of fear began to loosen and the hills began to capture his attention. A gentle incline led the two men among the pinon trees. The pitchy scent of them was warmly strong. Lamb swung his sore-footed horse into a broad gulch and soon they were riding on a brown carpet that flowed out from the skirts of the hills. Pure sand.

The pack mule balked the moment its hooves touched the silky softness. It sniffed and held back on the tow rope, but at last Lamb urged it on ahead. Riding in an eerie silence broken only by the gentle plopping of hooves, the two men struck a course to turn the shoulder of the dunes where they ended against the mountains.

"That's the biggest pile of sand I ever saw! " Anderson said.

In the strike of the afternoon sun the sweeping curves of the hills blended into a oneness that robbed Anderson of depth perception. There were moments when the dunes had only height and length. He estimated the highest ridge at seven hundred feet, but it seemed so far away he guessed that a man could not reach it in a day.

Staring at the dunes, he forgot for a time the threat behind him— until Lamb stopped the buckskin suddenly. The dust was out there now, standing like thin smoke above the rabbitbrush on the way that they had come. As they watched, the first wind of the day came out of the southwest. The claws hooked in again and the tightness returned to Anderson's stomach.

He rode to the rear of the pack mule, thinking to urge it into greater speed when they started. Lamb's calmness stopped him. With one eye almost closed so that the side of his mouth was raised in the semblance of a smile, Lamb was slouching in the saddle and studying the dust as if not sure of the cause of it. He scrubbed the scum from his teeth with his tongue.

"There were five of them before," he said. "Guess there's still that many. You know something, Andy? They swung away this morning to get fresh horses at Pascual's ranch." Lamb eyed Anderson's wiry scrub. He glanced to the right, past cotton woods and pinon trees, up to where Mosca Pass trail came down in a V of the mountains. "Medano is still best for us. Once we hit the Huerfano, I've got more friends among the Mexicans than a cur has fleas."

"Let's go!"

Lamb swung down. "My horse won't last two miles."

"He's got to! We'll get to the rocks and stand 'em off."

"We might do that with Indians, yes." Lamb lifted the buckskin's left forefoot and looked at the hoof. "These are white men, Andy." He let the hoof drop. "They know what we got." He walked to a cottonwood at the edge of the gulch.

"White men or not, by God—"

"I ain't aiming to die over no gold," Lamb said. "I've got along too many years without it. I ain't figuring to let them have it either." He grinned and his toughness was never more apparent. "Just wait a spell. The wind is coming."

"Out in the valley it would have helped, but here, when we hit the trees—"

"Wait," Lamb said.

The wind reached them after a while. Strong and warm it came out of the southwest. There was an odd rustling sound and the sand lay out in streamers from the ridges of the dunes. It was difficult to tell about the dust cloud, but Anderson knew it must be closer.

All at once Anderson realized that the tracks he and Lamb had made in the broad gulch were gone. Unbroken sand that lay in gentle waves like frozen brown water covered every mark they had made since entering the gulch.

Lamb led his buckskin and the mule toward the dunes. The idea ran then in Anderson's mind that they would lose their pursuers by circling through the hollows of the hills; but when the animals struck the first ridge and began to labor in the shifting, slippery sand, he knew his thought was wrong.

They ploughed over the ridge and dropped into a small basin where the ground was bare. All around the edges of the hollow the sand was skirling, running in tiny riffles, and up on the great hills above them it was whipping from the spines in two different directions.

Lamb took the mule close to the side of the bowl where the sand came down steeply. He began to take the gold from the panniers. It was in wheels, circular pieces of buckskin gathered from the outside edge and tied with thongs. When the first few sacks dropped at the edge of the sand Anderson cried a protest.

"I'd rather fight for it!"

"I'd rather live," Lamb said. "We're not going to get clear unless I ride the mule. We'll get a little fighting even then. Give me a hand."

Each sack that thudded down was a wrench at Anderson's heart. He could not remember how easily the gold had come to them from a rich pocket in the San Juan; he could only estimate the weight of each sack as it fell at the edge of the fine silt.

"Not all of it, for God's sake!" he cried.

Lamb kept dropping the buckskin sacks. "Take what you want but remember you're riding a tired horse. Even Indian nags play out, Andy." A few moments later when Lamb saw his partner stuffing sacks under his shirt, he said, "It'll be here when we come back, son."

It was not the words, but sudden wild music, that brought Anderson's head up with a jerk. It was a weird and whining sound, the bow of the wind playing across the sand strings of the ridges high above. Anderson listened only long enough to recognize what the sound was. It was mocking, discordant. He stuffed more gold inside his shirt.

When the panniers that had held almost two hundred pounds of weight were flapping loosely against the mule, Lamb's voice snapped across the wind with the crack of urgency, "Rake the sand down on top of the stuff while I shift my saddle to the mule."

Soft and warm, the sand slid easily under Anderson's raking hands. When he had covered part of the long row of sacks the wind had already concealed the marks where he had clawed. They climbed from the hollow, pausing on the ridge to peer through a brown haze at the dust still coming toward them. Anderson turned then to look into the little basin. All marks were gone, but he did not trust the smooth quickness of the sand.

"Maybe we could stand them off here," he said.

"Maybe we could die of thirst here, too." Lamb pointed across the shallow sand to the edge of the gulch. "It was six hundred and ten long steps, Andy, from that cottonwood with the busted top. Sight above the tree to that patch of gray rocks on the mountains. You got it?"

Anderson tried to burn the marks into his mind. He stared until he found a third point of sighting, the smoke-gray deadness of a spruce tree between the cottonwood and the patch of rocks. Six hundred and ten paces from the cottonwood. He could never forget this place.

Out in the rabbitbrush the riders had dropped into a swale. Only the dust they had raised behind them was visible. Lamb swung up on the mule and the mule tried to pitch him off. "I hope we never have to eat this devil," he said, "as tough as he is." He rode down the slope and into the broad expanse of shallow sand, towing his limping buckskin.

Anderson had difficulty in mounting. His shirt bulged with weight and his boots were full of sand. The hills were singing their high, queer song. He rode away, twisted in the saddle to watch his tracks; and he saw them drifting into smoothness almost as quickly as he made them. The treasure was safe enough but he worried because there seemed to be a gloating tone in the singing sands.

Now the dust was much closer and the fear of men was greater than all other worries.

Beside the eastern shoulder of the hills they crossed ground where water had carried brown earth from the mountains. The earth was cracked and curled upward in little chips. They let the animals drink when they hit the first seep of Medano Creek.

"Now we got our work cut out," Lamb said.

Medano Pass was rocky. The wind was funneling through it cold and sharp. Now the pursuers gained in earnest, for Anderson's pony began to lag and the hobbling buckskin began to lay back stubbornly on the lead rope.

From a high switchback Anderson saw the riders for the first time. Five of them, the same as before. "Let's get rid of the damned buckskin, Lamb!"

"About another mile and then we will."

When they came to a place where the trail was very narrow above a booming creek, Lamb said, "Drop a sack of gold here, Andy. The lead man will have to get down to get it. Every minute will help."

"Drop one of your own."

"I got only one," Lamb said patiently.

The gold was a terrible weight around Anderson's middle but he would not drop a sack. Nor would he part with it when he had to dismount to lead his pony up steep pitches. The sides of the horses were pounding. They stopped to rest at the top of a brutal hill. They could hear the sounds of the men behind them. Anderson tried to pull off his boots but the sand had worked so tightly around his feet and ankles that he could not get the boots off, and he was afraid to spend too much time in trying.

On a ledge above a canyon Lamb stopped again. He took the panniers from the buckskin, dropped a heavy rock into each of them, and hurled them away. He stripped the packsaddle and threw it by the cinch strap. Anderson heard it crash somewhere in the rocks out of sight. In the next stand of aspens Lamb took the buckskin out of sight and turned it loose.

He seemed to be gone a long time. Anderson stood beside his trembling pony with his rifle ready, watching the trail. Lamb returned. His face was grim with the first anger he had shown since the pursuit began. He took his rifle and walked down the trail. "Go on," he ordered. "I'll be along directly."

Anderson went ahead on foot. There were seven shots, flat reports that sent echoes through the rocks. Anderson stopped, waiting, afraid. Presently Lamb came trotting up the trail. Blood was dripping from his left hand and his shirt was ripped above the elbow. He whipped the blood off his hand and said, "Get on, don't wait for nothing. Not far ahead they got a chance to flank around us if we stop to pick flowers."

On the next steep, narrow pitch Anderson dropped a sack of gold. It was a place where horses would have to hold in a straining position against the grade while the lead man got down. It was not much, but maybe it would help. Four more times he picked his spots and dropped more sacks.

Twice more Anderson went back on foot with his rifle. There were fewer shots each time.

Sunset dripped its colors on the mountains and they flamed with the hue that gave them their name, *Sangre de Cristo,* Blood of Christ. The colors died and the cold dusk came. Again Lamb went back on the trail and his rifle made crimson flashes. They passed the place where a Spanish governor had camped an avenging army two centuries before. They went over the top and the necks of the animals slanted downward.

It was dark then. A wind that came from vastness was running up the mountain. To Anderson, the pass had been the obstacle, and now they were across it. He breathed relief. The magic words, Mosca, Medano and Music came again; but moments later he forgot that it was his life he had worried about, and he thought of the gold they had left in the sand, and of the sacks of gold they had dropped on the trail. At least he had not thrown away everything; there were two sacks yet inside his shirt.

A pale moon rose, throwing ghostly light on the rocks. Far below the timber was a black sea. It was still a long way to the Huerfano, and there were things like weariness and hunger.

Lamb said, "Hold up a second."

In the dead stillness they heard the sound of hoofs sliding on stones on the trail behind them. The men were still coming. Not knowing who they were made it worse for Anderson. Their persistence chilled him. Lamb was a dark form near the head of the mule. "One of those three knows this trail." he muttered.

There had been five men. Anderson did not comment on the difference.

Lamb listened a moment longer. "They're on a shortcut that I didn't care to try." For the first time he sounded worried. He mounted and sent the mule down the trail on the trot.

The clatter of stones came loudly on the higher benches of the mountain.

Lamb set a dangerous pace, cutting across the sharp angles of the switchbacks, sending rocks in wild flight down the slopes. They made a long turn to the left and entered timber on the edge of a canyon where a waterfall was splashing in the moonlight. At the head of the canyon the trail swung back to the right. They were then in dense timber where the needle mat took sharpness from the hoofbeats of the horses.

"Hold it," Lamb called back softly, and then he stopped.

Above the canyon they had skirted, where the trail lay in Z patterns against the mountain, Anderson heard the riders. Suddenly there was an eerie quietness.

Lamb said, "Just ahead of us the trail is open to the next point. They can reach us good from where they are." He led the mule aside. "Put your horse across first but don't follow him too close."

Anderson pulled his rifle free. From the edge of the timber the trail ahead lay against cliffs of white quartz. It seemed starkly exposed and lighted. He peered up the mountain. The shadows were tricky among the huge rocks and he could make out nothing. But then he heard a tired horse blow from somewhere up there in the rocks.

He prodded his pony into the open. It went a few slow paces and stopped. With savage force he bounced a rock off its rump. The animal jumped and started on at a half trot.

Anderson ran. He heard the crashing of the rifles and from the corner of his eye he saw their flame. They seemed to be a long way off but yet he heard the smack of lead against the cliffs beside him. The pony was almost to the point when its hind legs went down. It screamed in agony and pawed its way along the ledge. It reared halfway up,twisting. Anderson saw the glint of moonlight on steel where the leather was worn off the horn, and that was when the pony was going into the canyon.

A man on the mountainside yelled triumphantly, "We got the mule!"

Then Anderson was across. He fell behind the rocky point and shot toward the sound of the voice. The horses were moving up there in the rocks now and someone was cursing. Anderson rammed in another cartridge and fired.

The mule came with a rush, nearly trampling him before he could roll aside and leap up. He caught the bridle with a desperate lunge when the animal would have jogged on down the trail. Soon afterward Lamb skidded around the point. He knelt and fired. "No good," he muttered. "Two of them got into the timber on foot." He reloaded and stood up. "Now let *them* try that trail."

If there had been a taunt or a challenge from the black trees, Anderson would have been sure he was fighting men instead of some determined deadliness that would follow him forever. But the trees were silent.

"Take the mule," Lamb said. "He'll stay with the trail. By daylight you'll be seeing sheep. Ask the first herder you come to how to get to Luis Mendoza's place. Wait for me there."

"We'll both—"

"I was ramming around these mountains when you was still wearing didies," Lamb said. "Listen to what I say, boy. Get to hell out of here with that mule. That's what they're after. They think the gold is still on it. We *want* 'em to think so because one of these days we've got to go back after it. Go on now."

Anderson gave the mule its head and let it pick its way down the trail. He was a half hour away from the point when he heard the first shots rolling sullenly high above him. In the bleak, cold hours just before sunup, he heard more shooting. And then the mountain was silent.

The two sheepherders sitting on a rock beside their flock in a high meadow eyed the mule keenly. "Luis Mendoza?" They looked at each other. One of them pointed toward the valley. It went like that all morning, whenever Anderson stopped at adobes on the Huerfano. The liquid eyes sized up the mule and him, and weighed a consideration; but when he asked the way to Luis Mendoza's place, there was another careful weighing and he was pointed on.

The hot sun pressed him lower in the saddle. Sweat streaked down through the dust on his face, burning his eyes. At noon on this bright late-fall day he came into the yard of an adobe somewhat larger than the others he had passed. Hens were taking dust baths in the shade. There was a green field near the river, and goats upon a hill.

From the gloom of the house a deep voice asked, "Who comes?"

In Spanish Anderson said, "I am the friend of Jasper Lamb."

A little man walked from the house. His hair and mustache were white. His legs were short and bowed. From a nest of wrinkles around his eyes his gaze was like sharp, black points. He said, "You are followed?"

"We *were* followed."

"And Lamb?"

"He is in the mountains yet. He will come." Anderson wondered if he ever would.

The little man said sharply, "I am Luis Mendoza. Lamb is like my son. Do not doubt that he will be here. And now, you are welcome."

Thereupon a half dozen Mexican men of various ages appeared. One of them said, "Yes, it is the mule of Jasper Lamb."

"I have eyes." Mendoza's Spanish flowed rapidly then as he gave orders. Four men rode away, going slowly, chattering, obliterating the marks of Anderson's coming. He knew that if any of the three pursuers got past Jasper Lamb and reached the Huerfano, there would be only shrugs and muteness, or lies, to answer their questions.

"Go back for Lamb," Anderson said.

"He will be well, that one," Mendoza answered.

"He's wounded."

"That has happened before, also. Now we will take off your boots."

One of the pursuers did come in late afternoon. Lying on a pile of blankets on a cool dirt floor, Anderson heard the man ride up. "I look for a stolen mule, Mendoza."

Anderson tried to judge the enemy by the voice. A young man, he thought; and he knew already that he was a dangerous, determined man.

"Of that I know nothing."

Anderson clutched his rifle and started to get up. A broad Mexican sitting across the room from him shook his head and made cautioning gestures with his hands, and all the time he was grinning. After a moment Anderson recognized the wisdom of silence. For one thing, his feet were so scraped and sore and swollen from the sand that had been in his boots that he doubted if he could get across the room.

The man outside said, "The mule came this way. It had a heavy load. The man was young, with sandy hair."

"A *gringo* perhaps," Mendoza said lazily. "They do not stop for long on the Huerfano. The climate sometimes makes them ill," his voice slurred on gently. "Very ill."

"He could be in your house."

"I do not think so. My sons do not think so. My nephews do not think so."

There was a long silence.

"This stealer of mules is gone toward the Arkansas long ago, I think, although I did not see him," Mendoza said. "It is a long ride, my friend, and you are late now."

"Many things are possible," the pursuer answered, fully as easily as Mendoza had spoken. There was no defeat in his tone, but a cold patience that made Anderson wish he could get him in the sights of a rifle for an instant. "It could be that he is gone toward the Arkansas, and it could be that he is in your house, in spite of what all your sons and nephews think. Since the vote is in your favor, Mendoza, I will go toward the Arkansas myself."

"May God go with you," Mendoza said politely.

The man rode away. After a time Anderson dozed and then he woke, clutching where the weight should have been inside his shirt.

"At the head of your bed, *señor,*" the man across the room murmured.

Anderson found the sacks and dragged them against him, and then he slept until sometime in the dead of night when he heard a terrible shout, soon followed by laughter.

Lamb had arrived. He was shouting for wine.

Anderson and Lamb stayed three weeks on the Huerfano. Lamb had married Mendoza's oldest daughter ten years before. She had died in childbirth a year later. These were facts Anderson had never known before.

It was a simple, easy life here in the hills. There were sheep in the upland country, with old men and young boys to watch them. Maize and squash grew in the fields. Anderson did not know where the wine came from but it was here, and every night there was dancing at Mendoza's place.

Quite easily Lamb fell into the routineless drift of the life. He slept when it was hot. He hunted when he was in the mood, ate when he was hungry, and during the long, cool evenings he danced with the best of them on the packed ground in front of Mendoza's house. He was no longer the cool, efficient man who had directed the running fight across Medano. He acted as if he had forgotten the gold lying at the foot of the great dunes.

"We can get it any time," he told Anderson. "What's the rush?" It seemed to Anderson that he was casting around for an excuse. "It's best not to go back there anyway until that last fellow gives up. Only a week ago one of Luis' cousins saw him heading back over the pass."

"Why didn't Luis' cousin shoot him?"

"Why should he? Why should anyone on the Huerfano ask for unnecessary trouble? They can scrape up family battles enough to keep 'em busy all their lives, if they want to." Lamb went away to take a nap.

The change in him puzzled Anderson. Or was it a change? Lamb would have a man believe that he didn't care about that gold. Suspicion narrowed Anderson's mind. He fretted over the delay. He brooded about Lamb's motives; and he worried about the cold-voiced man who had followed the mule even after his companions were dead.

One day he could bear impatience no longer. He told Lamb he was going alone to the dunes.

"Hold your horses. The big *baile* comes off day after tomorrow. We'll leave then." Lamb sighed.

They gave two sacks of gold to Luis Mendoza. It was too much, Anderson thought, but when Lamb parted with his sack carelessly, Anderson felt that he must match it. They rode away on good horses, towing the mule as before. Anderson was in his own saddle, brought down from the mountain by one of Mendoza's sons two days after the Indian pony had gone over the cliff. There were new elk hide panniers on the mule, and they surely must be advertising the purpose of the trip to every Mexican on the Huerfano, so Anderson thought.

"We'll go up the Arkansas and over Hayden Pass and then swing down to the sand hills," Lamb said. "It's possible that fellow caught on to the fact the mule was traveling light. He may have somebody waiting on Medano."

Anderson said, "I don't favor this running in circles."

"I don't favor trouble, particularly not over a bunch of damned metal that grows wild in the mountains."

"That's what brought you out here in the first place."

"Yeah. Well, it was different then," Lamb said. He was unusually silent, almost surly, during the first two days on the trail.

They watered the animals on San Luis Creek when they came down to the floor of the inland plateau. Thirty miles away the dunes were a pale brown mass. Once again they seemed to be no closer after hours of dusty traveling. As if in a stupor, Lamb stared at the sunset on the *Sangre de Cristo*.

Anderson wanted to travel as far into the night as it took to reach the dunes but Lamb overrode him. They camped. Anderson did not sleep well. He kept his rifle close and was sensitive to all of Lamb's small movements and sounds. During the night Lamb rose to go out to the animals when the mule fouled up his picket rope. He came back to the camp slowly, a lean, tall figure slouching through the night.

Anderson held back the trigger of his rifle and cocked the piece silently. Afterward, when Lamb walked past and settled into his blankets with a grunt, Anderson let the hammer down again, and lay with the tightness ebbing slowly out of him.

It seemed to Anderson that they lagged when they started down the valley the next day. At last he cried, "You're in no hurry, damn it!"

"I ain't for a fact." Lamb gave him an oblique glance. "There's kinds of grief that I don't care to hurry into."

"That last man, don't worry about him."

"I ain't," Lamb said. "I'm worrying some about the other four."

They approached the northern end of the dunes. After they encountered the first shallow drifting of sand out from the skirts, they rode for almost ten miles beside the hills before they reached the broad gulch at the mouth of Medano Creek.

Anderson felt a constriction of breath. He wanted to gallop ahead. Nothing was changed. He saw the narrow-leaf cottonwood with the broken top and from a wide angle the gray rocks on the mountain. Mosca, Medano and Music. . . . He wanted to shout.

They left the horses at the cottonwood. Lamb was silent, almost sullen, as if there were no pleasure in this. He stayed at the cottonwood while Anderson led the mule out to the ridge and then part way up the side. When Anderson stopped to look back, he was pleased to see that his trail lay straight behind him and that he was almost in direct line with the sighting marks. He had to shift only a few feet until he had them lined up, the snag-topped cottonwood, the dead spruce and the gray rocks.

He called then to Lamb to start his pacing. Anderson counted the steps as his partner came toward him. Three hundred and fifty across the shallow sand, another hundred to where Anderson waited. The two men went together up the ridge. It seemed higher than before. The total was six hundred steps when Anderson whirled around to take another sighting. They were dead in line.

"Six hundred and ten?" he asked, and his voice cracked on the edge of panic.

"That's right," Lamb answered, and a man could read anything into his tone.

Anderson kept plunging on, but he knew already, and it made him savage. There was no ridge. He was climbing a slope that led on and on toward the deceptive hollows and troughs of the soft, pale sand. The basin was gone. He was a hundred feet above the gold on sand that ran like water.

He sighted again and then he turned and ran up the dune until his lungs ached and his leg muscles became knots of fire. He fell, staring along the surface of the wind-etched slope. Far off to his left there was a hollow, swooping all the way down to natural ground, but the basin with the gold was deeply covered. There was trickery in this; he had known it when the hills sang their song to him.

Anderson got up and staggered back to where Lamb was standing by the mule. "It wasn't six hundred and ten steps, was it?"

Lamb shifted his rifle. "Just what I said, Andy."

"Tell me the truth!" Anderson cocked his rifle and swung the piece on Lamb.

"Our gold is covered up," Lamb said. His squint was at once understanding and dangerous. "We're standing smack on top of it. Lower that barrel. It's full of sand."

Anderson let the barrel of his rifle tip down. Sand poured out in a silent stream. He let the tension off the hammer. "You knew the wind would cover it up, Lamb!"

"No, I didn't. I never realized how much this sand moves."

"We'll dig it out!" Anderson cried. "I don't care how deep it is!"

Lamb sat down. "We'll play hell trying to dig it out." He scooped his hand into the dune. Not far under the surface the sand was dark from dampness. He watched the fine dry grains from the top slide back into the hole. "It took a million years for the wind to make these hills. I guess the wind has got a right to do with them as it pleases. We'll never be able to dig ten feet down."

"Oh yes we will! Underneath it's damp. It'll hold. We'll start at the toe of the hill and tunnel. We'll line the tunnel with boards. We'll—"

Lamb shook his head. "Let me show you something." He dug with his hands, gouging long furrows downslope. The dark sand under the surface was damp for a short time only before the air dried it, and then it sloughed away. "Your boards wouldn't help much, if we knew where to get them. They'd dry out brittle. They'd crack and the sand would pour through the cracks and knotholes. If we were lucky enough to make twenty feet, one day the whole works would cave in on us."

"You act like you don't want to get the gold," Anderson accused.

Lamb looked out on the valley, toward the blue mountains on the edge of the San Juan. He was silent for a long time, a dusty, stringy man with a sort of puzzlement in his eyes. He said, "This gold is sort of used now. It ain't like brand new stuff, somehow. Even so I guess I'd stay and try to get it back, if I thought there was any chance."

"What do you mean, it's used?"

"I killed four men because of it. I lost a good buckskin horse."

"It was our neck or theirs!" Anderson said.

"Sure. I know that." Lamb frowned. "I ain't saying gold is bad, you understand, but it can cause you a pile of grief. I take it as an omen that the wind covered this mess of it up." Lamb rose. He smoothed with his feet the furrows he had made. "Let's move on."

"And leave a fortune just a hundred feet away from us?"

"It's the longest hundred feet God ever created, Andy."

"You don't want the gold?" Anderson asked.

"Not that, exactly. If we could get it, I'd take my share of it, but I'm kind of relieved that we can't get it."

Anderson licked his lips. "Suppose I get it out by myself?"

"I give my share to you right this minute. Now, let's go. We'll have to hump to get a tight camp set up in the San Juan before winter." He started down the dune.

"Then it's mine!"

"Sure, it's yours forever, Andy. Come on."

"You won't come around claiming half of it after I get it out?"

Lamb stopped and swung around. "You don't mean you're going to try?"

"I'm not going to run away from a fortune."

"We'll find another one," Lamb said.

"No! I know where this one is."

An hour later Anderson was in the same place, sitting with his rifle across his knees. He allowed that an obstacle stood between him and the treasure but the proximity of the gold outweighed all other considerations. He watched the dust where Lamb was riding away. Lamb might be trying to trick him. Lamb could have lied about the number of steps from the cottonwood.

Darkness came down on the great valley that had been a lake in ancient times. Purple shades ran in the hollows of the dunes, and the crests of the ridges looked like the black manes of horses struggling toward the sky. A mighty silence lay on the piles of sand that had been gathering here for eons.

Anderson was still sitting on the sand above the treasure. He rose at last, sticking his rifle barrel down into the dune. When he went across the shallow sand to where his horse was tied in the cottonwoods, the animal stamped and whinnied. It could wait. Anderson found a dead limb. He used it to replace his rifle as a marker. He counted his steps back to the cottonwood. They were a few less than Lamb had said.

That night he camped on Medano Creek, waking a dozen times to listen to small noises. The dunes were huge, taking pale light from the ice points of the stars. At dawn he was riding through the pinons, searching for a less exposed campsite. He found it near a spring in a narrow gulch that looked out on the dunes. From here he could see part of the mouth of Medano Gulch, and he could see the marker he had left on the dune. He built a bough hut near the spring, fretting because it seemed to be taking time from more important work.

That afternoon he killed a deer, standing for several moments after the shot, wondering how far the sound of his rifle had carried; and then he was in a fever to get back to where he could watch the dunes.

There had been wind that morning. The marker was standing above the sand by eighteen inches or more. Anderson experienced a quick leap of hope; the wind had built the dunes, the wind had hidden the gold, and the wind could also uncover it again. It was a great thought.

Before evening the marker was almost covered. At dawn it was gone.

Without eating breakfast Anderson hurried from the trees and paced across the sand, taking sightings. Scrabbling on his hands and knees, he found the limb a few inches below the surface of the dune. He knew that he could always locate the spot but the limb was a tangible mark that gave him more of a link with the treasure than anything he carried in his mind. He set another marker at the base of the dune, a huge rock, three hundred and fifty steps from the cottonwood.

Sitting in his camp that afternoon, he worried about the loss of landmarks. The gray rocks on the mountain might change or slide away, the cottonwood and the dead spruce might blow over. He returned quickly to the broad gulch and set a row of rocks fifty paces apart, burying them on solid ground below the sand, in a line which pointed toward the treasure.

Now he felt better. Rocks were solid and heavy; they would not blow away. Going back to his camp in the evening, a brand new doubt struck him: suppose the wind uncovered his line of rocks. Anyone riding past would wonder why they had been placed so. The extensions of the thought worried Anderson until late in the night. He rose and went down the hill to have a look.

He put his face close to the sand, sighting. The surface was gently rippled. He could not see any stones, not even the large one he had left exposed purposely. He felt that his presence protected the gold; he was loath to leave. For a long time he stood shivering in the night. When he finally started back to his camp, a light wind swept down through the pinons. It was a dawn wind, natural; it came every morning and had nothing to do with the great winds that had built the dunes. But Anderson felt that it was a deliberate betrayal, and so he went back to the edge of the sand and stayed there until the wind died away.

During the days and weeks that passed he grew hollow-eyed and gaunt. He begrudged the time it required to get meat when he was out of food. His rest was never unbroken, disturbed by dreams of a powerful wind that swept the sand away to the rocks, leaving his sacks of god lying in a long row where anyone could see them. That happened over and over, and then he dreamed of running down the hill to find himself entrapped in waist-deep sand among the trees. He struggled there, while out on the flat men were riding without haste to pick up the sacks. And then he would waken, trembling and almost ill from frustration.

Light snows dusted the valley. Whiteness lay in the grim wrinkles of the *Sangre de Cristo* and the dunes sparkled in the frosty air of early morning; but the snow never lasted long upon the sand. A season of winds followed. They gathered out of the southwest, twisting into crazy patterns when they struck the dunes. Sometimes Anderson saw sand streaming in four directions on ridges that lay close to each other.

When the wind was at its strongest he never heard the singing. The sounds came only with diminishing winds or when the blow was first rising. High-pitched music skirling from the ridges, running clear and sharp, then clashing like sky demons fighting when the wind made sudden changes. Anderson heard the singing at times when he stood at the foot of the dunes in still air, sensing the powerful rush of currents far above.

Sometimes, crouched in the doorway of his hut, he watched the queer half daylight of the storms and read strange words into the music. There was something in the sounds that wailed of lostness and of madness, of the times after centuries of rain had ceased, when the earth was drying and man was unknown.

Each time the wind ceased, while his ears still held music that could never be named or written into notes, Anderson went down the hill to see what changes had been made.

The dunes were never the same and yet they were always the same, soft contours on the slopes, wind-sharpened ridges, hollows that went down to natural earth, white streaks where the heavier particles of sand gathered to themselves. A million tons of sand could shift in a few minutes but nothing was really changed.

The wind did as it pleased; it did not do Anderson's work for him. Sometimes his limb marker was buried twenty feet deep; sometimes he found it lying ten feet lower than it had been. He always put it upright.

Long snows fell upon the valley. Deer came down from the hills. On clear days Anderson saw smoke at distant farms where pioneers were toughing out the winter. He thought of Lamb, snug by now in some tight, red-rocked valley of the San Juan. Lamb probably was searching for gold again, not really caring whether he found it or not. The thought infuriated Anderson.

Anderson was on the dunes one day when a wind, running steadily along the surface of the ground, began to eat into the side of the slope that covered the sacks. Tense and choked-up, he watched it, first with suspicion, and then with hope. Faster than any tool man could ever create, the numberless hands of the wind scooped sand until a rounding cove appeared. Anderson's largest marker rock sat on bare ground now. The cove extended, an oval running deeper and deeper into the side of the dune where his gold lay.

Anderson followed the receding sand as a man would pace after a falling tide. He counted until he knew he was within fifteen steps of the gold. Whirling around the edges of the cove, digging, lifting, the wind took sand away until Anderson knew he stood no farther than ten feet from the first sack. He could not stand inactive any longer. He began to burrow like an animal, and the wind worked with him effortlessly. He shouted incoherently when his hand closed on soft buckskin. The first sack.

It became an evil moment. Somewhere on Mosca or Medano or Music, or perhaps all three, there was a sudden change. The wind now came from a different direction. Sand poured down the slope faster than Anderson could dig. It grew around his legs, covering them. Sand rippled down the surface of the dune. It fell directly from the air. Cursing, half blinded, Anderson dug furiously. He might as well have been scooping water from a lake with his hands.

He was forced back as slowly as he had come. The cove filled up again. He stood in the wide gulch at last, on shallow sand where there never seemed to be appreciable change.

Almost exhausted, he stumbled away, muttering like a man insane. The wind began to lessen and the dunes sang to him, singing him back to his miserable hut of boughs among the pinons. He threw the sack of gold inside and lay by the spring until he was trembling from cold.

That night there was no wind. He crouched over his fire, and his eyes were as red as the flames that blossomed from the pinon sticks. It was no use to wait on the wind, for the wind would only torture him. He must do everything by his own efforts.

The next day he rode to a farm in the valley. The snow lay unevenly where ground had been ploughed, a pitiful patch of accomplishment, considering the vastness, Anderson thought. There was a low log barn, unchinked. A black-bearded young man came to the doorway of a one-room cabin with a rifle in his hands.

"I'm a prospector," Anderson explained. "I'm looking for some boards to build me a place. Been living in a bough hut."

"Build a cabin." The farmer's dark eyes were watchful, but they were also lonely.

"I lost my packhorse and all my tools coming over Music."

The man shook his head. "I've got an axe and a plough—and that's about it. Come spring, my brothers will be back with some things we need—I hope." He studied the shaggy condition of Anderson's horse. "Come in and eat."

The cabin was primitive. A man must be a fool, Anderson thought, to try to make a farm in this valley. The farmer's name was George Linkman. His loneliness came out in talk and he wanted Anderson to stay the night. From him Anderson found out that there was a man about ten miles east who had hauled a load of lumber from New Mexico the fall before and hadn't got around to building with it yet.

Ten miles east. That put the place close to the dunes, somewhere against the mountains.

Anderson rode away with one suspicion cleared from his mind: Linkman was not the man who had followed him and Lamb to the

Huerfano. Linkman's voice was much too deep. But who was this man against the hills close to the dunes? Anderson was uneasy when he found the place at the mouth of a small stream, and realized that it was not more than two miles from his own camp.

He was reassured somewhat by the fact that the log buildings were old. There had been more cultivation here than at Linkman's place. No one was at home. He saw the pile of lumber, already warping. He stared at it greedily.

The man came riding in from the valley side of the foothills. He was a stocky, middle-aged man, clean shaved, with gray in his hair. His faded mackinaw was ragged. He greeted Anderson heartily and asked him why he hadn't gone inside to warm up and help himself to food.

"Just got here," Anderson said. *The voice. . . .* No, it wasn't the voice of the man who had come to Mendoza's place. That man had been young.

The farmer's name was Burl Hollister. While he cooked a meal he kept bragging about the potatoes he had grown last summer. There was a little hillside cellar still half full of them to prove his boast. Nothing would do but Anderson must stay all night with him.

By candlelight Hollister talked of the new ground he would break next spring, of the settlers who would come to the valley in time. Anderson nodded, watching him narrowly. This place was too close to the dunes, but of course it had been here long before Anderson and Lamb made their terrible mistake in the hollow of the sand.

Anderson brought up the matter of lumber and tools, speaking guardedly of a streak of gold he had discovered on Mosca Pass.

"Tools I can spare," Hollister said slowly, "but that lumber—that's something else. I figured to build the old lady a lean-to kitchen with it before she comes back in the spring. I was aiming to surprise her. This place ain't much for a woman yet, but in time—"

"You could get more lumber before spring." Anderson drew a sack of gold from his shirt. There was not much in the sack, perhaps a pound and a half, for he had left most of it in the buckskin pouch he had recovered from the dunes.

After some hesitation Hollister untied the strings and dipped his fingers into the yellow grains. "Good Lord!" he breathed. "Is that all gold?"

"You could buy more lumber, Hollister."

"Tools, yes" the farmer murmured. "I can spare tools, but dog-gone, it's a long haul to get boards here." He kept pinching the gold between his thumb and two fingers. "Is this from your claim on Mosca?"

Anderson did not answer too hastily. "No, that came from the San Juan. I don't know yet what I have on Mosca."

"All of it for the lumber?"

Anderson nodded.

Not looking up, Hollister said, "All right."

He hauled the lumber and tools the next day to the bottom of the hill below Anderson's camp. Hollister brought also a bushel of potatoes. He spent most of the morning digging and lining a tiny cellar to keep them from freezing. When that was done he said, "I'll help you carry the boards up here."

"You've done enough," Anderson said. "I've got to level off a place here first."

"You're welcome to stay with me till spring."

"Thanks, but I'd rather be closer to my work."

Hollister nodded, staring across at the dunes. "Sort of pretty, ain't they?"

"Not to me. There's too much sand," Anderson said, and then he began to worry about the implications of his statement. He was glad when Hollister left.

Now that he had the lumber, Anderson began to doubt that it would serve his purpose. He had planned to work only at night but desperation was growing in him. In the spring riders would be coming to Medano and Mosca constantly. It was better to take a chance now on Linkman and Hollister, so far the only men who knew he was here.

But he retained caution. Until he knew how the lumber would serve, he would not try to tunnel directly toward the gold. He started a hundred yards away from his line of rocks, in a direction at a right angle to the treasure. He drove short boards into the sand, overhead and on the sides of his projected tunnel. Then he shoveled, framing more lumber to support the board as soon as the sand fell away from them. Sand poured through the cracks and between the warped edges where the boards did not fit tightly. He nailed more lumber over the cracks. In a month of brutal labor he made ten feet. And then one day when he was shoveling back, he heard a cracking sound. He got clear just before the tunnel collapsed.

He was standing with a shovel in his hand, too spent to curse, when Linkman rode up. Anderson did not hear him until the farmer was quite close, but when he saw the long shadow of the horse upon the sand, he dropped his shovel and leaped to grab his rifle.

"Hey!" Linkman cried. "What's the matter?"

Anderson lowered his rifle, but he kept staring at the visitor, who was looking curiously at the ends of boards sticking from the sand.

"That's a funny place for a potato cellar." Linkman tried to smile but he was too uneasy to make it real. He fumbled on, "I thought your mine was up on Mosca."

Anderson did not say anything. He saw the slow breaking of something in Linkman's expression, a fear, a disturbed sensation that Linkman tried to conceal. The man could not have made himself more clear if he had put a forefinger to his temple and made a circular motion.

"I was just riding around," Linkman said vaguely. "I guess I'll be going. I was just scouting for a place to get some firewood." He rode away.

Anderson went back to his camp. When he knelt at the spring he knew why Linkman had thought him mad. His beard was matted, his eyes hollow and bloodshot, his lips tight against his teeth. He was jolted for a few moments, and then he drank and turned his mind once more to the problem of the treasure.

It struck him suddenly. He would build his tunnel in the open, where he could make the boards tight and the framing strong. He would build sections that would fit together snugly, large enough for a man to crawl through easily. The next time the wind gouged out a hole in the direction of his gold, he would have his sections ready to lay in place. Let the damned wind cover them. The tunnel would be there, even if it was under two hundred feet of sand.

There were omissions in his plan that he did not care to dwell on at the moment; overall, it was a beautiful idea and that was enough. He rose to cook a meal and was annoyed to find he had no meat.

He found the horse tracks when he was hunting deer in the pinons above his camp. He spent the whole afternoon chasing up and down the hills until he knew that someone had been watching him, not only recently but for a long time. Instead of fear, he felt an insane fury that made him grind his teeth.

That night another gale came out of the southwest, coursing toward the high passes. Restless in his cold hut, Anderson heard the howling of it; and later, the singing of the sands when the wind began to decrease.

Clean morning sunlight on the great buff hills showed Anderson that they were unchanged. The ends of the boards from his collapsed tunnel were hidden now, and for the hundredth time his limb marker above the gold was covered. For several moments he was motionless.

There were forces here that he could never conquer, a challenge that would lead him to wreckage. Lamb had known what he was doing when he wasted not a moment, but rode away. For the first time Anderson felt an urge to leave, but he knew that the wind could undo what it had done; and if he went away, he might be haunted forever by the thought that what he had waited for happened one hour, a day, or a week, after he quit.

He went down the hill and began to build the sections of his tunnel lining. He piled them on the shallow sand. He built them so that one man could drag them into place when the time came. It was not heavy work but it tired him more each day. He went at it with desperate urgency, thinking that the wind might choose a time to dig toward his treasure when he was unprepared.

Dizzy spells began to bother him during the three days it took to build the boxes. He had been eating scraps, or very little; and his mind had been burning up the resources of his body. This he realized, but time might run away from him, and so he staggered on at his work, resting only when his vision darkened.

Utterly spent, he finished the boxes one afternoon when there was no wind. He slumped down behind a pile of them, letting his hands fall limply into the fine sand.

Sleep struck him like a maul. He dreamed of the running fight across Medano, of the easy life on the Huerfano. He trembled in his sleep, a young man who was old and gaunt. A voice roused him slowly.

"Anderson! Anderson! Where are you?"

Groggily, Anderson tried to come out of his exhaustion. He thought he was back on the floor of Mendoza's house, with his feet swollen and scratched. The last pursuer had come across the pass and was inquiring about him and the mule.

"Hey, Anderson! Don't tell me you've got lost in one of those sluice boxes."

Anderson stared at his boots. There was no doubt of it: the voice was that of the man who had survived the chase, the same cool voice of a young man who would not give up. Anderson's rifle was in one of the boxes. He could not remember which one.

His muscles dragged wearily when he rose. He could not believe the man sitting there on the horse was Hollister.

"Sleeping in the middle of daylight!" Hollister grinned. His clean shaved face was bright. His gray hair showed below the frayed edges of his scotch cap. He frowned at the boxes. "You're a long ways from water with those sluices, Anderson"

Hollister was the man. Now that Anderson could separate his voice from his appearance, he was able to get rid of the inaccurate picture he had built of Hollister. Anderson moved around the boxes until he found his rifle. He remembered the flight across Medano long ago. It was Hollister's fault and his fault that the gold was here.

Hollister said, "You've worked yourself plumb string-haltered, Ander—" He stopped, staring into the muzzle of Anderson's rifle. "What's the matter?"

"You're the man that followed me and Lamb to the Huerfano! You're no farmer. You've been watching me ever since I've been here."

Hollister kept his hands on the saddle horn. He looked at Anderson gravely. "The farm belongs to a man who wanted to go back to Kansas for the winter. I'm the man, all right. Now there's just two of us. The wind got your gold, didn't it, Anderson?"

Anderson stepped away from the boxes, edging to the side so that if Hollister made his horse rear the act would not interfere with the shot. Anderson was ready to kill the man. He wanted to. All he lacked was some small puff of provocation.

Hollister gave him none. He sat quietly, moving only his head. "When I came back over the pass, I found the panniers and the packsaddle you threw away. There was only one place where you two could have covered your tracks that day—here. I knew you'd come back.

"There's two of us, Anderson. You're as well off as you were before. I'm much better off, thanks to your partner." He gave the thought time to grow. "You left the gold here. The wind covered it. Your partner should have known better, but of course we were pushing you hard and you didn't have much choice. There's ways to get at it, Anderson. How deep is it?"

Anderson did not answer. He still wanted to kill Hollister but he knew he could not do it.

"The two of us can get it out of there," Hollister said. "I know a way." He looked at the boxes. "That won't work. You figure to make a tunnel of them, don't you? The sand will blow in one end and pour into the other. I know a better way, Anderson."

He was bargaining only because the rifle was on him, Anderson thought. But no, Hollister must not be sure of where the treasure lay.

"I've got every ounce of every sack you dropped on Medano." Hollister said. "That goes in the split too. You know where the rest is. I'm not sure. You can't get it out. I know a way. I could have killed you, Anderson, months ago. If I had been sure of where the sacks were, maybe I would have." He smiled. "That's all in the past now. There's gold enough for ten men."

Anderson grounded his rifle. "You know a way to get it out?"

"Yes."

That was the bait, Anderson thought, the bait that would bring the deadfall crashing down on his neck. But belief began to grow in him. The thought that he could trust Hollister became more important than any idea the man had about recovering the treasure.

"Think about it," Hollister said. "You've no one to ask about me. I'm an odd man inside. When I give my word, Anderson, before God, it's good." He turned his horse and rode away. The faded mackinaw covering his broad back was an easy target all the way to the cottonwoods.

Anderson had believed him while he was here, but now the worms of suspicion began to twist and turn again. For a week Anderson did not go down upon the sands. He stayed in camp or hunted, and he saw no more fresh horse tracks on the hills. The winds came, piling sand in a long, curving ramp against his boxes, and the wind uncovered the boards where he had experimented with a tunnel. There was something ancient and ghostly in the look of the lumber sticking from the dune.

He knew with a dreary certainty that men could not defy the work of a million years of wind. The caprice of the gales would expose the treasure when the time came, but that might be a century from now.

There was also the thought that it could be tomorrow, and that was what held Anderson, gnawed with the fear of defeat only, no longer dreaming of what gold could buy. It struck him that if he could transfer the burden of worry, which in a way was exactly what Lamb had done, then he might be free.

He rode to see Hollister.

The man was sitting by a warm fire, smoking his pipe. "Out of potatoes, Anderson? The darned things are beginning to sprout. It must be getting near spring."

Near spring. Months of Anderson's life had flowed into the sands. He had lived like a brute.

"You look some better," Hollister said. He spoke like a neighbor being pleasant but knowing that there was bargaining to come.

"This way of yours to move the sand. . . ." Anderson let it trail off. There was no way to move the sand. His own ideas had been sure and clear about that once, but now he knew better.

"Yeah?" Hollister's eyes tightened.

"You've got the sacks I threw away on Medano?"

Hollister nodded.

"For them I'll tell you where the rest is, and you can have it all—if you can dig it out."

Hollister cocked his head. "I'd rather have you working with me—for half of everything."

"You're afraid I won't tell the truth? I thought Lamb had lied to me too, Hollister. He didn't. He paced the distance. I recovered one sack of gold, right where it was supposed to be."

Hollister rubbed his lips together slowly.

"One sack is all. The wind will break your heart, Hollister."

"I can beat it."

"Give me what I left behind on the pass. The rest is yours."

Hollister's eyes were bright. "Let's go up and take a look at the dunes."

The hooves of the horses made soft sounds in the broad gulch. The full weight of the hills bore on Anderson and he wondered how he had ever been fool enough to think he could outwit the dunes. He knew better now and he had learned before his mind broke on the problem.

"They're yours, Hollister."

The older man's satisfied expression threw a jet of worry into Anderson. Maybe he was selling out too cheaply. It was an effort to stick with his decision.

Hollister said, "Your sacks are buried just inside the door of the potato cellar."

Anderson pointed to the limb on the dune. He told Hollister about the rocks under the sand and the sighting marks and the number of steps from the tree.

"I knew most of that from watching you," Hollister said, "but I wasn't sure. Why'd you start the tunnel over there?" His gaze was sharp and hard.

"I did that after I knew you were spying."

Hollister knew the truth when he heard it. "It would have saved me gold if I had killed you, wouldn't it?" In the same conversational tone he went on, "I'm going to bring a ditch down from Medano. I'll flume it through the sand and let the water wash away what I want moved."

Water would seep into the sand. It would run out of cracks in the flume, causing the sections to buckle. The eternal wind would work easily while Hollister was floundering and cursing his broken plan. Anderson had never felt sorry for himself. Now he had sympathy for Hollister.

"Don't come back," Hollister said. "We've made our bargain. I'll kill you if you hang around or come back."

Anderson went up the hill to his camp. The first signs of spring were breaking on the edges of the valley. He hadn't noticed them before. He stared for a while at the bough hut. It was a hovel unworthy of a Digger Indian. *I stayed in that all winter.*

He took his camping gear and kicked the hut apart.

Out on the sand, Hollister was walking slowly. He had found the line of rocks. He turned and sighted, and then he looked at the boards where the wrecked tunnel had been. There would always be in his mind, Anderson knew, doubt that Anderson had told the truth. The sand would defy him, the winds would mock him, and the singing on the ridges would jeer him.

When Anderson rode away, he saw Hollister dragging the boxes with his horse, dragging them up to where he would build a flume that would break his heart. The struggle of the horse and man against the sand was a picture that Anderson would never forget.

He found the sacks in the potato cellar where Hollister had said. He opened each one and ran his hand inside and afterward looked at the grains of gold clinging to his cracked and roughened skin. The sand had done that too.

He stuffed the sacks inside his shirt. At once the weight was intolerable. Perhaps somewhere out on the floor of the valley where there was no sand to blow over it. . . . No, gold was not to be buried. He would put it inside the pack on his horse. Half of it was Lamb's.

Anderson hesitated and then he dropped one bag on the floor. He thought it was a small enough price to pay for transferring a crushing burden. He rode away, going toward the purple mountains of the San Juan Basin. For a while the tug of the treasure of the dunes was still strong, but he kept going until at last he knew beyond doubt that he had made a good decision.

At sunset he turned to look back. Against the high range the buff hills were small, pale, beautiful, changeless. Anderson raised his eyes to the crimson glory flaming on the summits of the Blood of Christ Mountains, watching quietly until the color seeped away; and then he rode on, knowing that tonight he would sleep as he had not slept for months.

The winds still sing across the dark manes of the sand dunes, wailing, if the ear can understand, of the man who lived for thirty years in a little hut among the pinons. He dressed in cast-off garments that ranchers brought him. He raised dogs that ran wild, eating them when times were lean. He was crazy as a bedbug, for he talked of gold he was going to wash from the sands The wind alternately covered and uncovered the rotting sections of a flume he had tried to build around the shoulder of the dune.

He said that the wind knew a great secret and that four times the wind had almost showed him the secret; and then in the next breath he would curse the wind with such insane vehemence that people were glad to get away from him. There was something vicious about the old man, but there also was something pitiful and lost in the record of his life.

On a bright fall day when the aspens on Medano were golden streaks against the mountains he died on the sand with a shovel in his hands. George Linkman, a pioneer rancher, found him there with the hungry dogs whining and edging closer to him. Linkman shot the dogs. One yellow cur went howling across the sand almost to the rotting trunk of a huge, fallen cottonwood before it died.

There had been a strong wind the night before. When Linkman carried the old man toward the trees to bury him, he saw a line of rocks, a solid line of them, running from where the dead dog lay to the base of the first dune. It appeared that the crazy old devil had tried at one time to build a dam to catch the floodwaters of Medano Creek in the spring.

The next time Linkman came by the dunes—he was an old man and his riding days were numbered—he observed that the wind had covered the rocks once more.

The Man Who Made a Beeline

He crossed a range of flinty hills on a one-eyed calico mule named Gabriel, leading a sorrel packhorse with a load that was compact and very heavy. In late afternoon he came into a tremendous valley touched by the first frost-fire of autumn.

Ahead of him the mountains had pulled the sun down, shattering its strength into crimson pennants that ran to the ends of the horizon. The mighty barren peaks, rising up to bar farther progress to the west, caught all of his awareness, while he rode for a mile with the grass rustling against his stirrups.

"The Sunset Mountains," he murmured, and that was their name from then on.

On the third day he found what he wanted, enormous granite boulders against a hill on the south side of the valley. Their hardness made his drill steel ring and when he cleaved the first one with black powder it separated with a cracking, grainy sound and showed a clean hard face of blue.

Building stone, monumental stone, the most even-textured in the world. To Brady Sedgwick it was more beautiful than gold—it was strength and dependability.

He was a tapering column of a man with an unruly mane of jet-black hair, the powerful, square hands of an artisan, the shoulders of a quarryman, and with an expression of grave reserve in his deep-set eyes.

He paused in his work to look upon the valley, all autumn gold and waving grass, running west to the violent colors of the scrub oaks twenty miles away. The town should be at the forks of the river and

177

the buildings should be solid structures. Here was the granite for them.

On the river a half mile from him the bleached pole framework of Indian lodges said that men had been in this valley long before Sedgwick. There was no sign that white men had ever been here.

Sedgwick was content. People would come; no place like this would be overlooked much longer. He worked. He knew the grain of rock and, to the inch, the dimensions of stones that could be made from a given block of granite. He drilled plug-and-feather holes and split out building stones on lines that broke to his wedge taps cleanly.

The sorrel packhorse grew fat on the crisp grass. The calico mule grew sleek, whirling with bared teeth toward any unknown sound that came from its blind side.

Sedgwick was not lonely—he had ridden by himself from Vermont. He worked. When it was necessary, he shot one of the deer or elk that came from the river every morning, or one of the skimming antelope that abounded in the valley. Once he made a net of poles and a blanket and scooped from the river fifteen pounds of trout in two tries.

At dusk, one day, the blond giant came up from the river. The mule gave the warning. Sedgwick rose from where he was striking a fire with flint and tinder.

The man's flat hat lay on the back of his neck, held by a thong around his throat. His hair was a tangled mass of curls. His face was grim. He carried lightly a rifle that must have weighed eighteen pounds. It was the way he came, swishing the grass aside and driving in a hard beeline, that made Sedgwick wonder.

For just an instant the man looked at the quarry work and then he jerked his head to stare once more at the horse and the mule, belly deep in forage. When he spoke, his teeth showed as brown and strong as those of a healthy horse.

"You by yourself?"

Sedgwick nodded.

"Can I ask your help?"

"Yes. What is it you need?"

"Over there where the steep hills come down from the east." Something bitter and terrible lay on the man's face for a moment.

"Do I need my rifle?" Sedgwick asked.

"I never go anywhere without mine."

Sedgwick found his rifle leaning against a block of granite. It was not loaded—it seldom was, except when he stepped out from camp to hunt. Something in the steady look of the blue-eyed giant made Sedgwick thumb away a spot of rust upon the barrel. He began to load the rifle.

"You have the right look about you," the blond man said, "but your rifle wasn't loaded and you had to look three times before you even knew where it was." It was in the nature of a question.

"A loaded gun is like a lock upon a door. Out here I've felt no need of either."

The man watched Sedgwick curiously. He gave an outer appearance of calmness, this stranger, but he swung around with savage impatience when Sedgwick was ready to go.

"Frank Pickett."

"Brady Sedgwick."

They did not shake hands. When they went downhill at a fast walk, the calico mule began to follow.

"A mule has some sense," Pickett said so bitterly and with such obscure significance that Sedgwick knew something was grinding brutally inside him.

It was after dark when they crossed the river. Frantic trout bumped against Sedgwick's legs. The mule went up and down like a dog afraid of getting its feet wet, and then it made a running jump.

"What's the mule's name?" Pickett asked.

"Gabriel."

They walked for another mile. Sedgwick knew they were going as straight as men could travel. An early moon poured ghostly light upon the valley, making shadows out of nothing. Sedgwick saw, then, the mark in the grass where Pickett had walked on his way to the quarry. They went over the gentle hills, across small creeks, through shallow swamps, and through the stands of willows in the same straight line.

"You heard when I shot my deep-hole today?" Sedgwick asked.

"Yes."

"You can't see my quarry until you get across the creek."

"I heard your blast."

And he had not veered a fraction, Sedgwick thought.

"You saw the smoke too?"

"No," Pickett said. "I said I heard the blast."

Something terrible drove a man who would go in a dead-straight line even if he could not see his destination. Sedgwick watched the tireless intensity of Pickett's long strides. They must have come five miles already.

The heavy stand of native hay thinned down and wore away beneath their feet. They came to bunch grass and then that gave way to stones and soon they were close to the flinty hills that ran up to the low range of barren mountains which defended the east end of the valley.

Gabriel moved in closer to them, walking abreast, keeping his good eye on the unknown side of the night.

Pickett stopped suddenly and turned around. The moonlight gleamed on his sweating face. "It was my fault," he said harshly. "I'll say that now." He turned and strode on in the same motion, walking in the same straight line until they came to sagebrush at the foot of a steep hill. "Here," he said.

There was a wagon on its side. The white canvas of its top made a huge spot of lightness against the gray shadows. Gabriel jumped nervously. Somewhere close a dog snarled in a low, deadly tone.

"It's all right, Hornet," Pickett said. "Be quiet." The dog was somewhere in the shadows under a pinion tree. The menace of its tone changed to warning. It did not leave its place beneath the tree.

There were four horses and they were dead in the harness. Somewhere close on the hill coyotes yapped. The dog's growl then was sheer ferocity.

Pickett walked around the dead team. "I tipped it high enough with my back under it but that was all I could do."

When he went around the wagon Sedgwick saw what Pickett meant. The woman lay beneath the hind wheel. The heavy rim was on her chest. There were blankets under her head and she appeared to lie in peaceful sleep but her face was whiter than the moonlight.

"I lifted it five times," Pickett said. "But she couldn't move. I had to let it down five times. She smiled at me and told me not to worry. And then she died."

Sedgwick ducked under the tilted wagon box. He locked his hands across his stomach, set his boots against the flinty ground and tried to straighten his back. He knew he was a powerful man. The boards, pressed into his back, creaked. They lifted. The long muscles of his legs grew rigid and his neck tightened into iron.

The wheel did not move.

All the while his eyes were on the white face. She was a beautiful woman. Dark curls above her forehead stirred when a light breeze ran from the pinions.

When Sedgwick's trembling muscles forced him to relax, although the wheel had not moved, he knew the agony that Pickett had suffered.

He twisted his boots against the ground. "Once more."

This time he strained until he thought the blood would burst from his body. The wheel came up slowly. The wind ruffled the gingham dress. Pickett put his hands under the woman's arms and pulled her out gently, lest even now she could be hurt.

Under the tree the dog whimpered.

Pickett spread the blankets and put the woman on them, then folded them carefully over her. He left her face uncovered.

"She used to sleep like that," he said, "with a little smile." He stood up slowly. His hands came down at his sides. "Nancy," he said.

He walked away into the sagebrush, looking up the hill. "We came down a hundred worse than that. She drove some of them herself. Three sagehens got up right in the worst of it. The team had seen a million sagehens but this time everything went wrong. Where did I make the mistake, Sedgwick?"

"You made no mistake. The thing happened. How long had you been married?"

"Two years," Pickett said absently. "No, I made a mistake. I should have made her walk down the hill. Maybe I should have told her to jump when it started. Maybe—"

He talked on. The self-recrimination would pass in time, Sedgwick thought. Pickett was not the man to wallow in any weakness. He was too young and forceful for that.

Gabriel snorted at the dead horses. The dog growled. A few moments later the cry of a baby came from under the dark pinion. *Christ in heaven!* Sedgwick thought. The dog began to whine anxiously.

But it snarled when Pickett stumbled toward the tree. Pickett kept talking to it, coaxing it. Five minutes passed before the dog allowed him to crawl under the tree.

"How old?" Sedgwick asked.

"Six months yesterday. She threw him when we were going over. He lit in the sage and was only scratched a little. It's all right, Hornet, be quiet." Pickett straightened up with the child in his arms. The dog walked at his knee, snarling low. "It was always her dog, Sedgwick. After Jim was born, sometimes I could hardly get near the kid."

The baby's cries were loud and lonely and demanding. It was, Sedgwick thought, at least a hundred and fifty miles to any kind of settlement where he had last seen a woman. Six months old. Why, damnation! Sometimes babies nursed for two years.

"Gabriel lets no one ride him but me," Sedgwick said. "I'll go back and get the horse."

"What for?"

"So you can ride back to a town."

"What for?"

"For the baby, man!"

"No," Pickett said. "I'll not go back."

Tomorrow he would, Sedgwick thought, when the grief began to clear from his mind.

"I'll get the horse anyway."

"Save the trouble," Pickett said. "When we first saw this valley from the flint rims over east, she couldn't take her eyes away from it. She said we'd settle here and that our kids would grow up here. We're here, all of us. We'll stay."

"You can go back and get the kid when he's—"

"No," Pickett said. "He's not going back."

Sedgwick was silent. Tomorrow it would be different. And then he remembered the hard, straight line of Pickett's travel to and from the quarry. No, it would not be different tomorrow.

The baby cried the rest of the night.

When the fall sun was just beginning to warm the ground the next day they buried Nancy Pickett on top of the hill. With a bar and pick they pried stones from the ground to cover the mound. Pickett made a cross of oak from the wagon tongue. That worried Sedgwick, this crippling of the wagon. Gabriel and the horse could have pulled it light to wherever Pickett chose to settle.

Pickett put no letters on the cross. His grief was frozen in him, Sedgwick thought, and he did not want others to wonder idly about this grave in days to come.

"I can make a granite marker, Pickett."

"No."

The baby cried most of the time. Hornet crouched beside him, worrying. The dog was a heavy, low-slung brute with yellow streaks, like pitchpine, running through his black coat. When the grave was covered heavily with rocks, Hornet would not leave, not even when Pickett took the baby away.

"Come on, you!" Pickett said. The dog did not move. Pickett gave the child to Sedgwick and raised his rifle. "Maybe this is best, after all."

"Wait!" Sedgwick cried. "Let me try."

He talked to Hornet as he sometimes talked to the mule. The dog raised its head from between its paws and studied him from yellowish eyes. "Let's go, Hornet." When Sedgwick walked away the dog followed. From that day it never growled at Pickett again and neither did it show him the least affection.

At the wagon Pickett warmed a thin gruel he had tried to give the baby that morning. A second time the baby would not take it.

"It would give him the scours anyway," Sedgwick said.

"What'll I feed him then?"

"Milk." Sedgwick looked steadily at Pickett from under his dark brows. "Shall I go get the horse for you?"

"You heard what I said about that. No!"

Pickett cut the harness from the horses. Three of them had broken their legs, Sedgwick observed. All of them had been shot in the head. Pickett hurled the scraps of harness on top of the wagon. Deliberately he piled there, also, three pieces of furniture that had been thrown through the canvas top. He set the pan of gruel on a cherrywood dresser.

He struck fire into powder spilled on crumpled canvas and blew until the cloth flamed. He put a pistol in his belt. He carried his son in the crook of one arm, his heavy rifle in the other. He walked away on the same dead course he had made last night.

Blood was thick and black around the heads of the horses. Their eyes were sagging into ugly pits. Smoke drifted across them. Sedgwick walked away. Gabriel came out of the sage and followed him, keeping his sound eye cocked toward the powerful dog walking at Sedgwick's left knee.

Smoke rose high as the fire grew to a crackling roar. On the Sunset Mountains Sedgwick saw the first whiteness of coming winter. The baby was crying again.

That afternoon in Sedgwick's camp, among the litter of blue stones, the baby's cries were not so loud. It sucked its fingers and whimpered with hunger and exhaustion. Pickett held it, pacing about like a madman.

From a miscellany of vague, unwanted things he had heard and seen while crossing the plains Sedgwick remembered scraps of conversation among women in an emigrant camp where he had stopped to talk about the trail ahead. *"My Billy was chewing bacon when he was seven months. They say the savages give their young'uns a broth from dried buffler meat long before they can crawl. . . ."*

Sedgwick went to a boulder where he had tried to sun-dry strips of deer meat. Varmints had taken most of it and the jays had carried some away but there were still a few strips dried into the rock like old leather. He pried them loose with his knife and brushed the grains of granite away with the blade. He wiped the face of one of his striking hammers with his sleeve and used another hammer to pound the meat.

When it stuck to the hammers he scraped the thin sections off with his knife and put them in a frying pan and made a broth. He thought it must not be too hot, so he kept feeling it with his fingers, but his fingers were so calloused he could not tell whether the broth was too warm for a tiny baby.

Pickett tried it with his fingers. It was about right, he guessed. Sedgwick whittled a spoon. The baby choked when they tried to feed it. Pickett held it upside down and Sedgwick patted its back. They tried again to feed it from the spoon and again it choked and caused them both to stumble over each other's feet as they tried to help it. It cried.

"Hold him a minute!" Pickett said. He searched his buckskin shirt, inside and out, to find the cleanest spot. He cut a patch from it with his knife, folded the buckskin over his little finger and then looked at it. "That's seven times too big!" he cried.

Sedgwick whittled down the handle of the spoon. They wrapped the buckskin around that, then dipped it into the broth and put it in the baby's mouth. He sucked greedily, striking the air with his tiny fists when they took the sop away to dip it in broth.

It was slow work but it seemed to be doing the trick. While Sedgwick was not hopping between the fire and the baby to keep the broth warm, he pried three granite blocks into a *U* and lined the cavity with grass.

An hour and a half passed before the baby fell asleep in the middle of a sucking sound. Pickett and Sedgwick looked at each other solemnly. They nodded. Most carefully the father put the child in the granite crib. Jim gurgled. He protested against something, and then he threw up everything he had eaten and began to scream.

"Oh, hell!" Sedgwick said. "We've poisoned him!"

They bumped heads, getting the baby from his bed. He vomited some more. They wiped his face off with handfuls of grass. He wailed.

"They do that sometimes," Pickett said. "Give him more broth. He's got to eat." His eyes were wild. "I think they do it sometimes."

Sedgwick pounded meat on a bullset. He made more broth and eyed it with suspicion. They fed the child again. He was as greedy as before, and once again he fell asleep. Pickett put him between the stones. They looked at him uneasily. He moved. They held their breaths. He rolled on his side and belched, and then he grunted and went back to sleep.

They tip-toed away. Hornet lay down at the open end of the granite blocks.

Chapter 2

It was after sundown then. They were sweating and Sedgwick was more weary than if he had worked all day.

"When did you eat last, Pickett?" The man had eaten no breakfast or dinner.

Pickett shook his head, thrusting the question away. He walked along the hill, looking far across the valley toward the crumpled breaks that hid a burned wagon and a cross on a bleak escarpment.

He should have wept by now, Sedgwick thought. Something in him had to give way to break his harshness.

"You want some supper, Pickett?"

Pickett did not answer.

Several times during the night Sedgwick saw him by the fire, pounding meat with the handle of his knife. His face was stony. It did not relax even when he was looking at the baby.

Before dawn Sedgwick rose. With one hand on Gabriel's neck, with his rifle straight down beside his leg, he kept the mule between him and deer standing at the river, angling toward them slowly. He killed a buck, gutted it beside the icy water, and carried it back to the quarry. He and Pickett spent the day building drying racks and slicing meat.

"You think I was crazy to burn the wagon, don't you?"

"Yes."

"Everything in it would have reminded me of what I did!"

"You did nothing, Pickett. It happened. The child will remind you forever, anyway."

"I'll salvage nothing from the wagon."

"So be it," Sedgwick said. There was good iron under the ashes at the foot of the hill, and iron, like granite, was the strength of the world. But let the iron rust into the earth.

They made a broth that day from the liver of the deer. They fed it in small portions to the baby, feeling their way toward what a tiny stomach could stand and what it could not stand. Each time a feeding proved successful they looked at each other soberly and breathed normally again.

They kept the drying rack full. The golden sun of Indian summer worked with them. Hornet was a fierce guard whenever they moved fifty feet from camp. At other times he caught cottontails in the grass. He formed a friendship with the mule, learning early to approach always on Gabriel's seeing side.

Besides the squares of patching for their rifle bullets, the only cloth in the camp was on or around the baby. They learned that the natural processes of a baby occur frequently and when least expected, and that one diaper is a poor minimum to cope with nature.

They struck upon the idea of dry grass to bolster their lack of cloth. The sharp edges of the grass and brittle seed stems turned parts of the infant red and made him scream. They rubbed the reddened parts with deer fat, and since there was only one pot in camp, and that a cooking vessel, one of them was trotting back and forth to the river all the time.

Hornet began to understand the sequence of events. Something happened to the baby, and then the human beings did something to comfort him. Hornet took the responsibility of barking when the first act occurred. Since his nose was keen he often sent the warning when he was many feet from Jim, then raced to his side and barked some more.

"The damned didie ain't going to hold out," Sedgwick said.

Pickett looked at the white crests of the Sunset Mountains. "We can't spare any part of the blankets. There ain't enough as it is."

"My buffalo robes won't work."

Pickett cut off one of his pants legs. The buckskin served until it had been washed once, and then the edges of it dried in hard curls and the baby howled.

It occured to Sedgwick one day that he had not touched a tool for a long time, that the shelter he had planned to build was still unbuilt. He looked at Pickett drying a triangle of cloth over the fire. The two of them could lick six average men at once and here they were bound down by a handful of life, on the trot or worrying every minute of the day and parts of the night.

Sedgwick thought that he could bark, if he set his mind to it in earnest, an instant before Hornet, so attuned had he become to Jim's needs.

The whole business was one of the wonders of the world.

"I'm out of blasting powder, Pickett. We can get some where that railroad was building about two hundred miles east."

Pickett nodded. "Go ahead."

"We can both go."

"No."

"Why not?" Sedgwick asked. "The valley will still be here. Besides, we don't own it, you know."

"We own it from here to that red Pinnacle over there," Pickett said. "You and me and Jim. Let any man say we don't."

"We do then. We can come back to it."

"Go ahead, Sedgwick."

"You go for powder then. I'll take care of Jim."

"No," Pickett said. His sandy beard was curling from his jaws now. His face was massive, grim.

"You're afraid I can't take care of Jim?" Sedgwick asked.

"Not at all. There's towns, Sedgwick. Women are coming out this way. I don't want to see one."

"You're not the man to live alone, Pickett. She's gone. Even without the baby, you're not the man to live alone. Marrying again won't be forgetting her. You—"

"The hell it won't! Any woman's hands on that baby or any woman making up to me will be something I can't stand. Jim is all I got left of her, Sedgwick."

"You've got yourself, you damned fool! That baby might die here or anywhere—"

Pickett's fist swept up. Sedgwick did not feel the blow but he knew that the world turned dim for a moment. He felt his hips strike the ground. He saw his boots in the air before him. Except for his hands thrown behind him in an automatic gesture he would have rocked over on the back of his head. He doubled his legs under him and leaped up.

"What I meant is—"

Pickett knocked him down again. "Don't ever say the baby might die!"

"You fool! " Sedgwick rose. He dodged a blow coming at his face. He struck Pickett in the ribs as hard as he could. He drove his fist into the curling beard, against the tight-clamped mouth. The impact felt like iron. Pickett sprawled on the ground. He was up in an instant.

They hammered each other like men gone mad. They crashed together head-on, locking grips and trying to twist each other to the ground. They kneed each other and tried to bite. They fell across one corner of the granite crib. Hornet slashed at both of them viciously.

They were rolling downhill, holding each other by the shirt and chopping short blows with their free hands, when the frightened cries of the baby came to them.

Together they leaped up and ran to the crib. A blanket folded on the edge of the blocks had been knocked over the child's face. He was striking at it and yelling. Blood dripped from Pickett's knuckles as he reached down and plucked the blanket away. Jim opened his mouth for another bellow and then he stared and made a grunting sound.

Pickett wheeled and walked into the rocks, going as straight as the bore of a rifle until he came against a huge boulder and had to turn.

When he was out of sight Sedgwick lay down, cradling his face on his arms, gasping. He could not recall that he had ever been struck so hard before, and now all the pain of it was springing to full life. After a while he rose and staggered to the river.

Pickett was building a fire when Sedgwick returned. Jim was asleep.

"There's a spring not over a hundred yards back in the rocks," Pickett said. "We haven't explored this place very well, Sedgwick."

Sedgwick grunted. They fried antelope steaks and ate them without speaking. Sedgwick wiped the frying pan out with grass and hung it on a limb stub. He passed his tobacco pouch to Pickett. They smoked their pipes, watching the long dusk run across the valley.

"I lose my temper," Pickett said. "I'm a fool sometimes." He paused. "But I'm not going out and neither is Jim."

The next morning they began to build a cabin. Sedgwick had dreamed of a structure of immense logs laid on a deep foundation of granite—but there was no time for that. They built with aspen logs, with the base log on the ground.

It seemed that Hornet barked for help every time their attention was concentrated on some detail.

"That river is too far away," Pickett said. He made a bucket of sorts from a deer hide and a frame of small poles. They filled it at the spring. The bucket leaked and it had a bad odor, but so did everything else about the process for which they used the bucket.

"That damned didie just ain't going to last forever," Pickett said. "What do Indians use?"

"I never raised an Indian kid in my life," Sedgwick said. "I shot my bolt when I remembered the story about making broth from pounded jerky."

Sometimes they got in almost a full hour's work at one lick before having to do something for the baby.

One day after Hornet had barked, Pickett said, "That dog is smart enough to take care of Jim by himself—if he only had hands instead of paws.

Those were the first complimentary words Sedgwick had ever heard Pickett say about his dead wife's dog, but Pickett spoke grimly, with a sullenness underlying his expression. His resentment against one evil moment of accident on a rocky hill was yet strong and fresh in his mind. Sedgwick guessed he was trying to forget by not forgetting.

Some men clung to memories and grew maudlin; but Pickett was slashing savagely at all his memories.

Unless he laughed some day and put everything behind him and turned to another woman, he would go mad. And if Jim died. . . . It twisted something in Sedgwick to think that such a thing could happen. He left the pile of mud and grass he was daubing into cracks between the logs and went swiftly to see if Jim was all right.

The baby smiled at him crookedly and tried to stuff grass into its mouth.

They roofed the cabin with poles, covering them with a mat of grass, first, and then dirt. They built a fireplace of granite blocks, lining the inside of it with mud and sticks to keep the stone from cracking. They made a window of hide scraped thin, so thin in spots that air as well as light came through.

Their doorway was extra large. They had to duck only six inches to go through it. Across a frame of poles they lashed wet hides to serve as a door.

Under a warm Indian summer sun they finished the work one day at noon. Sedgwick held the baby up to the see the cabin. Jim choked on a piece of grass he had stuffed into his mouth. He began to spit up. Long after Pickett had pulled the grass from his mouth the baby cried, holding his breath so long between outbursts that they were sure he was strangling. They hopped around, patting Jim's back, yelling at each other to do something.

After a while Jim grew tired of crying and grabbed the fringes of Sedgwick's jacket. They sat down then, looking soberly at each other.

By then the calico mule had gone into the cabin, standing just inside the doorway, with his good eye rolling at them defiantly. It took Sedgwick an hour to coax him out. He laughed about it, but Pickett's face was as bleak as ever.

They saw the Indians when Gabriel squealed and Hornet barked. There were ten of them, broad, dark-faced men on ponies. They came along the hill from the west with eight dogs walking stiff-legged before them. Far up the valley, on the river, another group was coming.

One of the biggest curs ran in at Hornet, and then all the rest followed. The Indian dog went up like a striking stallion. Hornet stayed low to the ground and shot under him and broke his hind leg with one crunching snap and twist. Then the rest of the pack were on Hornet, covering him completely.

A second dog went spinning away, howling, with its stomach ripped. The Indians sat their ponies and watched with interest.

Pickett had his rifle in his hand. Sedgwick, once again, could not remember just where his rifle was. He went forward and began to kick dogs rolling in the grass. He sent two grunting away with their tails low. The rest gave up and ran behind the ponies. Throwing foam and blood from his muzzle, Hornet trotted back and stood beside the baby's crib.

Sedgwick raised his right hand. A broad-faced, powerful Indian returned the signal. He spoke, but Sedgwick did not understand the words. Utes, he guessed—this was their stamping grounds. The leader tried another language.

"Spanish," Pickett said. "Almost, that is." He listened and then he answered. The Indians swung down and came into the camp.

They grunted among themselves when they saw the baby, and then their sharp brown eyes looked all around. They peered into the cabin. One of them made the universal sign for woman, then pointed at Jim.

Sedgwick pointed at the sky.

The Indian forgot the matter at once. He began to examine one of the granite blocks, running his hands over it curiously, poking at the round marks of plug-and-feather drill holes. He asked a question. Sedgwick shrugged.

Pickett said, "He wants to know where the gun is that shot those holes in solid rock."

Sedgwick picked up a drill and a hammer and made motions with them. At once the Indian lost interest. The band went away a half hour later, riding to the river. Some time later the other group up the valley reached the framework of cones, spread hides around them and built fires.

"Rojo's band," Pickett said. "He's the one that did most of the talking. Utes. They're on their way to the big hot springs to winter." He gave Sedgwick a hard look. "Not because of them but on general principles I think you ought to keep your damned rifle loaded and know where it is, Sedgwick."

They moved Jim into the cabin that evening. He fell asleep soon after they fed him broth. Hornet lay down in the doorway.

"Let's mosey down there and find out something from the squaws," Pickett said.

"About didies?"

"Yeah. That one won't last—How long does a kid wear one, anyway?"

"For a long time." Sedgwick scowled. "I think."

They were welcome in the Ute camp. There was no ceremony about their coming. Most of the men were squatted around a fire eating buffalo ribs.

Rojo's pointing finger said, *Help yourselves.* . . .

After he had stuffed himself Sedgwick thought he must remember to roast the next fat meat he and Pickett cooked instead of searing it in a pan. Pickett's beard was smeared with grease. Like Sedgwick, he kept rolling his eyes at every young Ute scampering about. The girls wore skirts, the boys wore breech clouts, and the toddlers of both sexes wore little or nothing.

"There must be a baby around," Pickett said.

He began to talk to the chief, stumbling along in Spanish as he tried to make his request clear. Quite obviously Rojo did not understand. Pickett pointed toward the quarry. He indicated the approximate length of Jim with his hands. He tried to imitate a baby's cry.

The Utes stared at him and then they stared at each other.

Pickett made motions about his loins. He grunted. Some of the older children came close, peering, grinning. A squaw carrying water stopped to watch and giggle. She went on and motioned to three more women. They all looked at Pickett and giggled.

His face utterly serious, Pickett started again. He made a rocking movement with his cradled arm, and then he held his nose. Once more he made the motions around his loins. Whether the Indian men understood or not, Sedgwick saw humor rising in their eyes. They grunted at each other and laughed.

They could laugh and the women could giggle, but Sedgwick knew he could not, for this was a deadly serious matter to Pickett.

Sedgwick rose, wiping the grease from his beard with the back of his hand. "I'll look." Carrying his rifle he strode around the camp, peering into the lodges. An old woman spoke harshly to him and waved him away when he stuck his head in the last one. The Indian children followed him on the tour.

He went back to the fire where the men were. "There ain't a baby in the place!" he said disgustedly.

Pickett was looking at the bucks as if they were the stupidest creatures alive. He rose suddenly and walked to a squaw. The other women edged in, grinning. Pickett tried his Spanish. The squaw shook her head. He pointed at a naked child. He made a cradle of his left arm and rocked it as if it held a baby. The squaw watched him with suspicion.

"Hell!" Sedgwick said. "They carry 'em on their backs, Pickett." Pickett pointed to his back. He made bouncing movements with his shoulders. The women did not follow him. He stood on spraddled legs and made the motions of putting on a diaper. The squaws giggled. The children went through the motions of putting on diapers. They squealed with laughter. Pickett cursed and looked helplessly at Sedgwick.

There would be a time, Sedgwick thought, when this would be funny, but the time was not now. He grabbed a naked child and carried it forward. He held it in one arm and indicated the portions where a diaper would be needed.

An old squaw shook her head. She pointed vaguely across the creek, behind the lodges, anywhere outside the limits of the camp. The men rocked with laughter. Sedgwick put the boy down.

"They know what I mean!" Pickett said wickedly. "They're making fools of us." He picked up his rifle and walked away in a dead-straight line.

It was then a young woman Sedgwick had not noticed before walked through the group of women. She was taller than any of the rest. Her face was brown, not dark, her features more cleanly defined. Her braids glistened in the firelight.

She touched the sleeve of Sedgwick's shirt. She pointed to her buckskin skirt. He made the same motions putting on a diaper that Pickett had made.

The young woman nodded.

"It scratches him." Sedgwick dug at his thighs and made a grimace of pain. The Indian children shrieked with laughter.

Once more the woman touched his shirt, rubbed the blackened buckskin between her fingers. She made chewing motions with her mouth. She indicated her skirt and nodded.

Softer buckskin, sure! Sedgwick grinned. He pointed to the woman's skirt and held out his hands. He meant: give me some buckskin like that. The young squaw spat at him, her face angry. She wheeled around and walked away. He stood there with his hands still spread, and the camp roared with laughter.

Sedgwick picked up his rifle and left.

Pickett was lying on one of the buffalo robes in the cabin. "What do they know about raising babies?" he said.

Chapter 3

Sedgwick took off his boots and lay down, and then he rose immediately to go out and put the frying pan over the broth kettle which would have to be heated during the night. He put more wood on the fire. He stood for several minutes, looking toward the Indian camp.

When he went back in he said, "There was one squaw down there that wasn't bad to look at."

"Go back then," Pickett said.

"I would, but she's sore at me." Long ago Sedgwick had sneered at the thought of men who looked with favor on Indian women. That was long ago. "Why don't you take Jim down there tomorrow—"

"No woman is going to touch him!"

"I'm sick of hearing that. The best thing you could do for yourself and Jim is to take out with those Utes when they leave. The hot springs they're going to is not far from the railroad." No more than sixty or seventy miles, Sedgwick estimated.

Pickett was silent.

"I think I'll go out and get some things we need. We're going to be short—"

Pickett sat up quickly. "So I walked into your camp uninvited, and ate your salt, and took half of your robes. Here!" Something heavy struck the wall beside Sedgwick and fell on his leg. He picked it up, a leather bag. "There's four hundred dollars in that," Pickett said. "Go buy what we need."

"I didn't mean it that way, Pickett."

Stubborn silence was the only answer.

They were digging out the spring the next day, so that they could cover it against freezing. Hornet came to Sedgwick, disturbed but not excited. He whined and trotted back through the rocks toward the cabin. The two men watched him out of sight and then they jerked their heads toward each other.

"There's nothing wrong with Jim," Sedgwick said, "or else the dog wouldn't have left him. And he would be raising the roof if there was anything amiss."

They went back to work. Hornet came again, whined, and trotted away. A few moments later they heard him give a soft bark, unlike any of his other signals. They snatched their rifles and ran.

The woman who had felt Sedgwick's sleeve last night was standing outside the doorway with the baby in her arms. Hornet was sitting at her feet, looking up at her and whining.

"Put him down!" Pickett said.

The woman looked at him steadily. She made no move.

"Put him down!" Pickett's blue eyes had turned pale and murderous. There was no reason in them.

"Wait!" Sedgwick cried. "She doesn't understand." He stooped slowly, his eyes on the woman. He pretended to lay something on the ground.

With a swift yet gentle motion, the woman placed Jim in the grass. Pickett cocked his rifle and raised it. Sedgwick was ready and waiting. He swung the barrel of his rifle against Pickett's head. The man dropped like a cut rope. *If he's dead he deserves it,* Sedgwick thought.

He walked toward the cabin. Two riders were coming up the slope, he observed, and down by the river the Indians were breaking camp. The woman picked up the baby. Hornet leaned against her skirt and sat there with his yellow-blazed face happy.

She pointed at herself and then at Sedgwick, and then she pointed at the ground beneath her feet. Her braids were shining, her brown face calm, and there was a steady question in her eyes.

Me and you and here. There could be no mistake about it, but Sedgwick went through the same signs, pointing toward the cabin instead of the earth. She nodded. Jim clutched at a bright binding on one of her braids. Sedgwick jerked his thumb toward Pickett. He pointed then at Jim.

The Indian woman's eyes blazed. She shook her head. Once more she had misunderstood his signs.

Even Hornet had recognized that she was what Jim needed,

Sedgwick thought. He blinked. The baby's face was shining clean. He realized how filthy it had been before. But it was not just Jim. . . . She stood tall in her beaded buckskin garments. Sedgwick realized at last that they were not the clothes she had worn last night. These were her best.

The two people here on the edge of the great valley with the Sunset Mountains running white across the long western horizon needed now no common language. An Indian woman, tall, with a waiting question. A powerful man in blackened buckskins. Man and woman understanding things the human race knew before it was articulate.

"The baby ain't mine."

She could not understand, of course, but Sedgwick had been talking to himself anyway.

"If it was just me— "

The two riders stopped twenty feet away, Rojo and a solemn old man with a wrinkled face. Rojo asked the woman a question. She answered without looking at him. He spoke to Sedgwick, who could only shake his head. The old man made a speech in a thin voice, pointing back the way the Utes had come, making other gestures that Sedgwick did not understand.

Pickett said, "He's telling you that— "

Sedgwick swung around. Pickett was sitting up, steadying himself against a rock.

"—that her man was killed. She had a child that died last spring. She is half Cheyenne and a trouble-maker in the camp. Rojo is her uncle. He doesn't even want one pony for her. She wants you."

"What do you think, Pickett?"

"She asked you, not me."

Pickett's voice raised no objection. At this one moment he was, Sedgwick sensed, the man he must have been before his wife's death. He was still half stunned, but some natural quality in him was functioning. But it had required a blow that should have cracked his skull to make the change. After a while he would rise and his mind would gather in all the thoughts that made him walk in a hard line.

Tomorrow, a week from now, remembering too much of what he wanted to remember, he might raise his rifle again. No impact from the outside would make Frank Pickett whole again; the change would have to come from him.

Sedgwick looked at the woman and shook his head. He pointed toward the Indian camp. The hides were gone from the cones now, and the bare frameworks looked gray and lonely.

For an instant the question in the woman's eyes changed to a plea, and that was when words would have struck deep into Sedgwick—but she had no words.

She put Jim down and walked away. The Indian men wheeled their ponies, and all three went back down the slope toward the figures moving away from the river. Hornet whined.

Pickett got up and sat on a rock, holding his head in his hands. When Sedgwick took Jim inside the cabin, he saw the folds of soft buckskin lying on the edge of Jim's nest of grass and a small stone jar that held a grease which looked and smelled like mutton tallow. When he changed the baby's diaper he found packed inside it fine-rubbed, rotten wood, which shook loose easily from the buckskin.

Pickett came to the doorway. "I'm going hunting."

Sedgwick watched him go across the valley, walking as a man should, with little detours now and then to look at things that might be of interest. His course took him toward the flint escarpment to the east, and Sedgwick saw him gradually moving faster, and then he was making no detours.

When Pickett returned that evening he came as he had come the first time, driving straight and hard.

Yes, Sedgwick thought, *It was well that I shook my head and pointed her away.* But if she had spat at him or shown anger it would not be such a hard remembrance.

It was the warmest, longest fall that Sedgwick was ever to know in the valley. Snow kept getting lower on the Sunsets and the edges of the river were scalloped with ice every morning, but after sunrise it was gone.

One day Sedgwick saddled Gabriel and put the packsaddle on the horse. He picked up the bag of money that had lain in the corner of the cabin ever since Pickett threw it.

"I'll be back when I get here, Pickett. What do you want, providing I can find it somewhere?"

"Nothing," Pickett said.

There was no name to the town. Pickett thought it was the most barren place that could have been selected. The inhabitants, sixty of them, said the railroad would have to come this way, but if it did not, they had built flimsily and could move quickly.

During his second day in town a train of fifteen wagons jolted in and camped by a treeless creek where the stale and almost lifeless water made Sedgwick remember the clear-running river in a distant valley.

He went that night to listen to a meeting in the camp. There had been dissension on the trail and it was still strong in the company, and now the members were going to elect another leader. Sedgwick had seen wagon trains on the plains, and not one that knew where it was going, how to get there, or whom to obey.

The argument began fiercely. Sedgwick watched a woman standing alone beside the front wheel of a wagon. Her hair was golden, her face small and square. She seemed to look with disdain upon the wrangling of the men.

A bearded man slouched through the night, with a rifle in one hand and a jug in the other. He stopped beside Sedgwick, looked him up and down, and held out the jug. Sedgwick drank.

"How was the beaver hairing-up?" the man asked.

"I'm no trapper."

"The hell you ain't! Obadiah Brandon can smell a thousand campfires on you. Drink with me. I've heard the talk of fools ever since I hired to guide this train across. Don't tell me I didn't smell you right!"

They sat down and drank together, while the wagon company argued. "My name is Sedgwick. I come from a valley at the foot of the Sunsets." Sedgwick described it.

Brandon described it much better. "I been through there fifty times. There ain't no beaver left. And I never heard the mountains called the Sunsets either."

"I said I was no trapper."

"Don't argue about it! You look and smell all right to me, so you're going to be a trapper until we've handled a jug or two." Brandon drank. "Listen at 'em!"

"Where are you taking the train?"

"We started to California. I don't know where we're going now. Half of them split away on the Smoky Trail and went for Oregon. Now the rest got seventeen different places in mind. Listen at 'em."

"Who's the woman by the wheel?"

"Beth Denton. Her husband died of cholera afore we cleared Kaw country. There's other widders in that mess, and old Barclay McCune's two girls that oughta been married up afore we started. More females floating loose—" Brandon raised the jug.

"They're going alone?"

Brandon passed the jug. It was getting light. "They got cousins and fathers and brothers. They ain't alone exactly." He staggered up and went away to find another jug.

Sedgwick walked to the edge of the firelight. He stood a head higher than any man there. The women, all except Beth Denton, stood in groups near the shadowy wagons. He heard an infant fretting.

Beth Denton noticed him. She watched him until Brandon came up with another jug and pulled him away.

"Bring them to the valley," Sedgwick said.

"What for? You want to ruin it? You want to see it ploughed up and all the beaver scared away—"

"There's scarcely any beaver now."

"Yeah," Brandon said. "I have a drink or two and I think it's forty years ago." He pulled Sedgwick down and began to talk of places and times that Sedgwick had never known. Vast distances, the winds and the rains and forgotten days of an early West ran through Brandon's voice. He came to the point of weeping, and saved himself each time by using the jug.

"Bring them to the valley," Sedgwick said. His own voice was thick now.

"It's only a hundred and fifty miles or so," Brandon muttered, "and then I'll be shet of 'em. You and me can go back to Brown's Hole then, Sedgwick. We'll get ten kegs of Frenchy's whiskey—"

"I can't go this winter." Brandon, in a way, was like Pickett, dreaming of something lost, but Brandon would be all right when he was sober. "Bring them to the valley."

Brandon rose and staggered through the circle of men, thrusting them out of his way. He began to tell about the valley at the foot of the Sunsets. At first it seemed to Sedgwick that he was exaggerating, and then Sedgwick began to realize that the description was true.

"You're raving drunk, Brandon!" a black-bearded man shouted. "Shut up and get out of here. You have no place in this meeting."

"Shut up yourself!" Brandon roared. "I've listened to a pack of idiots all the way from Leavenworth! Now I'll talk, and I never tell a lie, drunk or sober—not to fools that want to believe lies, that is."

He talked. When he had finished, the wagon company was silent. If they had had seventeen places·to go before, now they had an eighteenth. It was not long before there was another hot discussion. Brandon waved the jug around his head and stalked away.

Beth Denton's voice cut clearly across the heavy man talk. "Let that tall man who put Brandon up to this step out here and give his reasons for wanting us to go where Brandon said."

Many of the men had not noticed Sedgwick before. They did now. They bade him come forward.

"What have you got to sell out there, mister? We ain't buying land."

"I've got none to sell." Sedgwick was drunker than he had thought. He tried to answer questions and accusations, and all the time he was conscious that Beth Denton was watching him as if he were a liar of the worst sort. How could he tell them how much Pickett and the baby needed a woman, which had been the basis of his whole idea in the first place?

When they fell to arguing among themselves and forgot him, Sedgwick walked over to Beth Denton. He tried to bow and almost pitched on his face.

"It's the truth," he said.

"You have nothing to sell?"

He forgot the granite that had held him in the valley. "Just loneliness, Mrs. Denton. Just a valley full of that."

She watched him quietly, then walked away.

Brandon grabbed his arm. "Let's get out of this pow-wow, Sedgwick. They make more noise than squaws fighting over buffler guts!"

When Sedgwick and Brandon stumbled across the creek, half dragging their rifles, Sedgwick saw Beth Denton watching him from where she stood with a group of women. That was the last he remembered of the night.

He woke up in the morning with badger hair in his mouth, or something worse. He and Brandon were on the ground with a broken jug between them and a buffalo robe chest high over them. Brandon sat up and scratched. His beard was shot with gray. His cheekbones were knobby.

"I was kicking high for a spell," he said, "but it always ends. I can't find what I've left behind me in no jug. You're right good company, Sedgwick."

Sedgwick sat up. The world rocked. He worked his mouth and spat. He wondered if he had made a fool of himself and if Beth Denton had seen him.

"That was a good fight we had until those fools dragged us apart," Brandon said.

"Fight?"

"A regular tooth-and-toenail rassle. They ruint it. You sure you want those folks in your valley, Sedgwick?"

"Bring them all if they'll come."

"The second time you flung me clean across the crick I thought maybe it wouldn't be a bad place for me. I ought to settle somewhere, in a sort of way."

"Bring the wagons, Brandon, and half of what I own out there is yours."

"I don't want land. I just want a place to say is home. There's a thousand places but I can't go back to them all, not any more. I'll see if I can bring the wagons to you."

Sedgwick got up. He found himself so stiff and bruised that he could hardly stand.

"It were a good rassle," Brandon said. "But I'm getting too old for it."

Before Sedgwick left the camp he stopped where Beth Denton and two older women were cooking at a fire. "What is the best food for a baby about seven months old?" he asked.

The women stared at him.

"It has no mother?" Beth Denton asked. Her eyes were gray, Sedgwick observed. She had a clean, strong jawline and a sturdy neck.

"No mother and there's no other woman near."

"In that valley?"

Sedgwick nodded.

"Bring it out of there," one of the older women said. "Mrs. McCune is nursing a baby two months old."

"I can't bring him out. We've been giving him broth from pounded deer meat. Is that all right?"

The women exchanged glances. "Indian mothers do that, I've heard," one of them said quickly, "but you'd best bring the child—"

"I can't." Sedgwick walked away.

He loaded the packhorse with his purchases and rode toward the Sunsets. At every campfire he saw Beth Denton across the flames from him; and then sometimes the face of the Indian woman looked at him with the plea in her eyes that had turned to stoniness just before she put the baby down and left.

The closer he got to the valley the more he cursed Pickett.

He was sniffling on the fourth day and his bones ached and his head was stuffy. He gave no thought to such a minor affliction. By the time he reached the valley it had passed away, excepting his runny nose.

Pickett was sitting on the chopping block. He helped unload the packhorse without speaking. Hornet came out and barked around Sedgwick's legs, and then followed Gabriel down into the grass when the mule was free.

"Jim all right?" Sedgwick asked.

Pickett nodded. "I half expected you to bring somebody back with you. I'm glad you didn't try it."

When they carried the supplies inside Sedgwick picked Jim up and carried him around the room, tickling the baby's face with his wiskers. Jim grabbed Sedgwick's beard and laughed.

A week later Jim cried fretfully all night. He ate his broth and could not keep it down. His face was flushed. He began to cough. They kept him warm, so warm the cabin was a stuffy trap. They sponged his face with cool water on a buckskin swab. They rubbed his chest with melted tallow from the stone jar. They cut up one of the woolen blankets Sedgwick had brought back.

Every time Sedgwick warmed one of the squares of cloth to lay on Jim's chest, his throat contracted when he saw how tiny the piece of blanket was.

For three days they scarcely left the cabin. Jim grew worse each day. The heat of his tiny body frightened Sedgwick. They dribbled warm water into Jim's mouth by gently squeezing a piece of buckskin.

When the baby slept it was fitful sleep, and then his dry coughing woke him to cry plaintively.

Neither man slept more than a half hour at a stretch. Whether roused by noise or not, they found themselves leaping to alertness after brief rest, to go across the room and kneel beside the baby.

There came a night when they were sure he was slipping away from them. Pickett had spoken very little. His face was gaunt, his eyes were brooding hollows, and he was as close to utter madness as he would ever be.

"What can we do?" he asked.

Sedgwick said, "We can pray."

They knelt on the dirt floor and asked a Man who loved little children not to take this one. Sedgwick thought of things he had done which he did not like to remember now—but Jim had done nothing.

Sedgwick threw himself beyond the logic of a hard, independent man who felt no need of help for himself—and he believed and yet he did not believe, knowing that death could go through the walls of the cabin easier than sound.

Pickett got up slowly. "Did He hear us?"

"We asked. That's all we can do."

Sedgwick did not know what he thought, for faith is a filmy, tenuous quality and yet strong enough to rip a rock apart.

He shook his head. "We asked, Pickett."

Pickett turned savage. He grabbed Sedgwick's shirt. "There's something we can do to save him! We just don't know what it is, that's all!" He flung Sedgwick aside. He knocked the door out of the way and leaped outside.

"Where you going?" Sedgwick cried.

"I'll ask Nancy! She'll tell us what to do!" Pickett plunged down the hill. There was a light snow on the ground. Sedgwick was only then aware that it had fallen.

"I'll find out!" Pickett's voice came streaming back as he raced toward the flint hills in a straight line.

"God help him." Sedgwick went back to do what little there was to do for Jim.

All night the small breath of life flickered on the rim of outer darkness. Sedgwick muttered prayers and did everything else that he thought could help.

When dim light was showing on the scraped hide of the window Pickett stumbled in. Something had burned out of him. His face was haggard but his eyes were clear and quiet and his expression was no longer set against himself.

"He's gone?" he asked softly.

Sedgwick shook his head. "Not yet."

"I asked her. I knelt by the rocks and asked her. I was a crazy man, Sedgwick. There wasn't any answer. How could there be? She's gone. She's been gone all this time and now I know it. It wasn't my fault, altogether. It just happened." Tears ran down Pickett's gaunt cheeks and tangled in his beard. "I know now that Jim can die too. Do you think he will, Sedgwick?"

"I don't know."

They knelt beside the baby and waited. It was full morning when Pickett put his fingers on Jim's forehead and felt the baby's face. It was cool. Jim woke up. They gave him warm water until they were afraid to give him any more. He fell into a restful sleep. Hornet came from a corner where he had lain like dead for a long time. He crouched beside the baby, panting in the heat.

Pickett wept then, with his face raised and unashamed.

Sedgwick went out on the hillside. The sun dried the tears on his cheeks. Already the thin snow was melted.

After a while Pickett came out and began to chop wood. "You put up with a lot from me, Sedgwick."

Sedgwick shook his head. It seemed like nothing now. He looked at his granite blocks. He had thought that any structure should be based on something as solid and strong as granite. The thought was still sound, but he knew, also, that there were things more powerful and lasting than stone.

Pickett rubbed his thumb along the ax. "We've let this blade get dull, Sedgwick." And then he said, "How soon do you reckon he'll be all right to go out of here?"

"Let's don't rush things, Pickett."

The wagons came two weeks later. There were five of them, stringing down from the flint hills. Pickett grabbed Jim and held him up.

"Look there, Jim! Look at the wagons!"

The baby grabbed Pickett's beard.

From here the wagons looked all alike. Sedgwick wished he had not been so fuzzy-headed one morning that he had neglected to observe some distinguishing feature of the Denton wagon.

"Well," Pickett said, "let's go down there."

"Let them get camped first, man!"

Obadiah Brandon rode up the slope not long afterwards. The granite blocks gave him a start. His mouth fell open when he saw Jim. "I seen the grave. How come the wagon got burnt?"

"I burned it," Pickett said, neither angry nor defensive. "Those folks figuring to settle?"

Brandon gave Sedgwick a quick look that slurred easily into casualness. "I reckon they be." He squinted toward the rocks. "Would you boys mind me putting up some kind of hut right close? As I remember, there's a spring back there in the rocks."

"You're welcome," Pickett said. He held Jim up. "Did you ever see a healthier kid than him?"

Brandon stared dubiously. "I reckon not." He scratched his head. "Several unattached females came along. The McCune twins." He looked slyly at Sedgwick. "One or two others, too."

"Mrs. Denton?" Sedgwick asked.

Brandon studied a moment. "I believe she did." He laughed. "When we going to have another rassle, Sedgwick?"

"When I'm as old as you, you grizzly bear."

In the evening Pickett and Sedgwick rode down to the camp. They had scrubbed Jim with warm tallow wiped off with soft buckskin. He was wearing a fresh diaper with rotten wood packing, and he was wrapped in a new blanket.

The women crowded in at once. They had Jim out of Pickett's arms before he was fair dismounted. Sedgwick saw Beth Denton and observed that she was wearing a dress that no woman would wear while the wagons were traveling.

Jim began to bellow. A woman said, "Take off your poke bonnets, you ninnies. Anyone would know it ain't used to having bonnets looming over it."

The woman was right. Jim stopped crying when the women took off their high bonnets.

"Why, look how clean he is!"

"I swear he looks healthy! Who could believe it?"

"Meat broth! Land of Goshen—"

"We give him marrow too," Pickett said. "He really gums that up. It's good for the bones—and things." There was a solemn expression on his face but it was a proud and happy kind of soberness. Sedgwick saw the dark-haired McCune twins watching Pickett with sparkling, sly intensity.

For one sharp moment that caught him hard Sedgwick remembered dark hair that had been moved by a breeze running down a steep hill on a moonlit night that now seemed deep in the past. Complete forgetting by him or Pickett would be unnatural, he thought, but the bitter moments of the past could be distilled into strength to meet the future. He was sure that Pickett understood that now.

Sedgwick talked to men who were full of questions about the valley. His eyes kept straying to where Beth Denton stood with the rest of the women. She held Jim for a time and then she passed him to one of the McCune twins. She glanced casually at Sedgwick when she strolled away.

Sedgwick left a man in the middle of a question. Beth Denton was standing near the front of her wagon. He bowed and said, "The first time I saw you I couldn't do this very well."

Her expression was grave but there was a hint of laughter behind her eyes. "So I noticed, Mr. Sedgwick."

"That dress—"

Hornet cornered a brindle dog under a wagon. The night was filled with snarls and howls. Almost at the same time an ox made the error of lumbering up on the blind side of Gabriel. The mule began to squeal and kick ribs loose. Sedgwick ran to help get the trouble under control.

She was still by the wagon when he returned. "You have a strong vocabulary, Mr. Sedgwick. I wonder what the baby's first words were?"

"Both Pickett and I are hoping there will be more gentleness around Jim before long, Mrs. Denton."

"Oh?" She smiled. "You speak for Mr. Pickett too?"

"Let him take care of himself."

One of the McCune twins cried, "Good heavens! What's this inside his—I thought for a minute—"

As one veteran lecturing to others Pickett began to explain the advantages of fine, rotten wood inside a diaper.

The laughter of the women overwhelmed him. He looked at the dark-haired girl holding Jim and smiled.

Sedgwick said, "Mrs. Denton, would you care to look at the valley from that little rise yonder?"

"I saw it from much higher than that this afternoon, Mr. Sedgwick, when there was light enough to see it, moreover. But if you insist—"

They stood beside the river on a small knoll a hundred feet from the camp. The laughter and the talk flowed out to them. And then, for the first time since he had known him, Sedgwick heard Pickett laugh. It was the most joyous sound of all.

Shortly afterward Sedgwick saw Pickett leave the baby with the women and walk off with a group of men.

Someone said, "There's one jug left that Obadiah Brandon never knew about."

Out of the darkness across the river Brandon yelled, "Get it out, Barclay. I'll be right over!"

Sedgwick said, "This will never be a lonely valley again."

It had a personal sound, the way he meant it, and although Beth Denton did not answer he was sure she understood.

The Bounty Killers

They were bounty hunters, Frank Moxon and Dave Delaplane, men who took deputy sheriffs' commissions anywhere they could get them, and who then rode forth to collect the reward money on the heads of wanted men.

Now they were in South Fork, after a man who had changed his name to John Sevier, who was worth two hundred and fifty dollars dead or alive back in Kansas. It was not much, but Moxon said it would help pay their expenses on to Durango, where there was bigger game.

For ten years, Moxon had been a bounty hunter, which was a long time to keep shaving close to death, but he liked it. He was a big man with heavy, bitter features and a sharp stillness in his flat gray eyes. He was well known, well hated, which were the reasons he had been reecognized at the livery in South Fork before he swung out of the saddle. It was said that Moxon had never yet collected the reward on a live man.

Delaplane was new to the business; he had done one job with Moxon. From the door of the livery, the only one in town, Delaplane watched the old man who had recognized Moxon hurrying down the street to spread the news.

"Let him do his best," Moxon said. "I like people to know I'm around."

They were going down the street to the sheriff's office when a man carrying a single boot came from the mercantile across from them. He had been laughing about something and the humor was still on his face. It was crushed out suddenly under a terrible awareness as he stared at Moxon and Delaplane.

The moment hung on a glittering point, and then the man turned quickly on the red stones of the flagged walk and went up the street and into a building with a small sign that said *Boots*.

"Another one knows you," Delaplane said.

"He ought to," Moxon smiled. "That's the man we came to get, John Sevier."

Through the dust-scummed window of the sheriff's office, Delaplane caught a glimpse of a heavy-featured man sitting inside. Moxon said, "All right, Delaplane," and went through the doorway.

Delaplane stood by the wall, at the side of the open doorway, watching the town. Things were beginning to buzz a little now. Men hurried in and out of the saloon directly across from him, studying him, asking each other quick questions.

The voice inside the sheriff's office was slow and heavy, like the face Delaplane had seen briefly through the window. "This warrant is sort of old, isn't it, Moxon?"

"Murder warrants don't run out."

"I know something about the law. You know what I mean." Papers rustled. "This thing would have rotted away if it wasn't for you, Moxon."

"No doubt about it. Cigar?"

"Keep it." The sheriff's voice was flat with disgust. "How come you're this far away from the big money?"

"A little here, a little there," Moxon said. "It happens we're going on into the San Juan after some big ones, but I always like to pay expenses on the way. You've got some rough poker games in this country, Sheriff."

They went on sparring. The sheriff was getting the worst of it, beginning to lose his coolness. Moxon liked to work that way, asking his direct questions only after he had a man trapped and angry. So far, the name of the wanted man had not been mentioned. Moxon would get to that in his own way, slowly, deliberately, with a cruel relish.

Without looking, without wanting to look, Delaplane knew this sheriff was no match for Moxon. Pretty soon the sheriff would deny ever hearing of a man named John Sevier, most likely.

Delaplane watched the town. Moxon had said Sevier was a man who had run once but who would not run again. Moxon was generally right about men; but still, Delaplane kept one eye on the bootery.

To reach South Fork, he and Moxon had crossed two mountain ranges, and then they had ridden through cattle country and through farming land. The town was on the edge of both. There seemed to be plenty of business here. Before the old man had spread his news, Delaplane had seen men moving leisurely, criss-crossing the street to talk to each other.

About half the buildings were of stone or sand brick. Water ran in a small ditch at the edge of the flagged walk. There was just the one saloon. Delaplane decided it was the air of permanence that gave the town its slow look and made it different from all other small places along the frontier of the mountains on the west.

He tried to build contempt against South Fork, a half dead one-streeter with a lone saloon. He wished Moxon would get to the point so they could do their job and leave the place.

The sheriff's voice had lost its calmness. He was saying, "Men like you don't give a damn for anything human. When you lay that stinking money on a bar don't it bother you, Moxon? Don't you look back and remember how you made it?"

"My way suits me fine," Moxon said. "If you don't understand me, neither do I understand men like you who think they're the grandfathers of some two-bit dump like this."

"What do you mean?"

"You keep bragging of what a clean, peaceful little village you've got here, but when I show up to help you keep it that way, you get all edgy."

"This town don't need any of your kind of law, Moxon."

"All law's the same. Brother officers, ain't we?"

"No, by God!" the sheriff said.

"Do you want to see my commission?"

"I know about you."

Moxon laughed quietly. The aroma of his cigar drifted out to Delaplane. It was a fifty-center, and because of what the sheriff had said, Delaplane remembered how Moxon had spilled silver on a bar to buy a handful of them. The money had looked like any other money, and the bartender had not used tongs to pick it up and drop it into his till.

That money had come from making a dangerous living, from carrying out justice decreed by law. Moxon and Delaplane were only the working instruments of an institution hated in some degree by all men.

Delaplane spat on one of the flagstones. The spittle spread through the dust film, and the wetness brought out the red of the stone. He stared at it for a moment and then he raised his eyes again, watching the bootery with tough alertness. To hell with the softness of up-country sheriffs. Grandfathers of a two-bit dump.

Inside, Moxon got to his point. "Is John Westrum here?"

"I don't know of anyone by that name in the whole county."

"That's reasonable," Moxon said. "Do you know him by the description on the dodger?"

"No."

"Do you want to look again, Sheriff? It's ten years old. I don't look like I did ten years ago. Would you say you do?" Moxon's voice was soft and mocking.

"I don't know anybody by that description."

"We heard he took up bootmaking, Sheriff."

There was a pause. "So?"

"He did well under his new name, John Sevier. Maybe his reputation for making boots spread farther than was good for him."

"Yeah?" the sheriff said, and Delaplane knew by the sound of his voice that he was beaten.

"As a matter of fact, you're wearing a pair of Sevier boots, Sheriff," Moxon said. "How do they fit?"

Delaplane watched a woman going up the street with two boys who looked like twins. Premonition touched him as the three made steady progress past the fronts of buildings. One boy ran to the edge of the walk to go around an awning post. The other bumped against the woman in his hurry to dart back and do as his brother had done.

The three of them went into the bootery. Cold-eyed, and thoughtful and no believer in hunches, Delaplane knew that he had been right about the woman and the two boys from the start.

He heard the sheriff saying, "Sure, I knew about him! He killed the wrong man in a political mess, but it was a fair fight. They forgot about it back there in Kansas when things changed, didn't they?"

"They didn't change the warrant. It stands."

"Two hundred and fifty dollars, Moxon! There's real bastards you can go after that are worth ten times that much. Look—"

"I do my job, whether they're big or little. It's a matter of law, Sheriff. That's what we have to have to bring the West under control."

"Law hell! If I thought like you, I'd throw my badge away right now. He's been here nine years. He married a good girl and he's got two kids. There ain't a person in this town that won't go the limit for him."

"It's your job to see that they don't, Sheriff. Sevier is my man. You're bound by your oath to uphold me."

Delaplane watched the woman and the two boys come out of the boot shop. She had them by the hands now, and they were dragging back, looking over their shoulders. She looked straight across at Delaplane. She turned as if to go back inside and it was then Delaplane caught a glimpse of Sevier, shaking his head slowly, pointing his wife away.

The door closed and the woman hurried down the street with the two boys. They would have run around the awning post again but she dragged them on. From where he stood, Delaplane judged that she was not a pretty woman.

She looked across at him again. No, she was not pretty. Delaplane received an impression of whiteness and a mouth caught with fear.

Moxon and the sheriff came out. Mildly surprised, Delaplane observed that the sheriff was a young man, fleshy, with blue, worried eyes. He gave Delaplane a quick look and Delaplane read him as a man with sand and competence enough for the duties of an average lawman's office; and as a man who would not have lasted a full evening as a deputy marshal, say, in some of the places where Delaplane had carried a badge.

The deficiency was more apparent because the sheriff was close to Moxon, who was lean and hard of body. The set of Moxon's lips was making puckers between the scar lumps of a powder burn near the corner of his mouth. His eyes were bright with cruel mirth.

"I'll try," the sheriff said, "but I know he won't give up to you, even when I promise that some of us will go along to see that nothing happens to him like happened to some others who gave up to you, Moxon. You've had too damned many prisoners jump you or try to escape a few miles out of town."

"Is that a fact?" Moxon said gently. "You're young, Sheriff. You've sat in a chair in this God-forsaken place without much chance to learn anything, so this one time I'm going to let your remarks pass."

Moxon's eyes had congealed like glacier ice. Delaplane watched the sheriff. He expected the sickening change that came to most men when Moxon hit them with his rank, deadly spirit, but the sheriff looked back at Moxon steadily, pale with anger. Then the sheriff left the walk and angled in a slow walk toward the bootery.

The whole town watched him go inside.

Delaplane said, "Suppose Sevier does decide to give up?" There had been no doubt about the attitudes of the wanted men on Delaplane's first job with Moxon; they had sent word to Moxon to come and get them if he could.

"Sevier will be like the last three," Moxon said. "He'll stand up." He was pleased with the thought.

"He's got a family. Maybe he'll decide to go back and stand trial. The chances are he'd be cleared if he did."

Moxon shook his head. "There's no money in it if you have to ride five hundred miles with a prisoner. I thought I made that clear to you at the start, Delaplane."

"Yes, you did." Argument was useless. Certain facts had been clear all the time, but Delaplane had not dwelled on them before. Perhaps he would not have been in doubt now if Moxon had denied the sheriff's charge about killing prisoners. Delaplane took a long look at Moxon. No man could be utterly dead inside, completely ruthless, no matter what kind of reputation he had made.

Delaplane did not think Moxon was that way in spite of all that was rumored about him.

In their lonely camps on the way to South Fork, Moxon had talked for hours at a time, half puzzled, half angry because men hated him. He could not understand and it seemed that he was trying to break through his lack of comprehension so that he could, perhaps, walk carelessly on a street like this and be hailed in friendship, instead of being stared at in fear and hatred.

Those two emotions were in the air now as men watched Moxon and Delaplane. *Bounty hunters, killers, bastards with no souls, no decency, no fairness.* Delaplane had heard the words brushed across Moxon's name before he had ever seen the man, and now the men across the street were saying the same words of Delaplane.

The sheriff came out of the bootery. Delaplane knew by the way he hesitated, glancing down the street as if he held some forlorn hope of finding aid, that Sevier had refused to give up.

"There you are," Delaplane said. He saw the years before him, a hundred situations like this; but the softness of the men across the street angered him and he threw their rage back at them when he said, "Let's get it over with."

"Not so fast, son," Moxon said. "Be slow and easy. Word gets ahead, and the next job is half done for you when you get there."

Moxon liked every moment of it; the hostile attention of the town, the stubborn, beaten manner of the sheriff as he walked toward them, the fact that Sevier was inside his shop, watching, maybe cringing, breaking up with fear.

"Let's get it done!" Delaplane said.

Moxon smiled. "You've got to learn patience."

The sheriff came up. He gave Moxon a long stare. "He won't go back."

"Too bad," Moxon said gently.

"To you he's worth two hundred and fifty miserable dollars. That's all you want, Moxon, so—"

"Easy, youngster, I warned you once. You're about to suggest a bribe. No honest lawman—"

"I'm damned sick of *you* talking about law, Moxon."

"Have a bartender mix you something for that, Sheriff. Maybe it'll settle your stomach." Moxon put his flat, merciless stare on the sheriff, who crossed the walk heavily and went on into his office. Without turning, Moxon said, "I want affidavits of his identification, Sheriff. You can get it done for me in advance, or I'll have to trouble his wife about it afterward."

The man inside did not answer. Moxon relit his dead cigar. The men of the town had deserted this side of the street. Moxon looked over at them with his bitter smile. "They yell their heads off for law and order, but they're always thinking it's for someone else. When it hits close to home they get indignant as hell. The world is full of pious fools, Delaplane."

Silent men were dangerous. Those across the street were noisy, without direction. They reminded Delaplane of excited children. Watching them, he said, "This Sevier ain't worth much, Moxon. Couldn't we sort of overlook—"

"No. You can't do it, not even once. Go over to the saloon and get something to eat and come back here."

The flatness of silence followed Delaplane into the saloon, but once he was through the doors he heard the chattering outside resume. He gave the men inside quick appraisal; they were like the men outside. He ordered a beer and then he began to make a sandwich of ham at the free lunch counter, waving away flies.

"Dave Delaplane! How are you, Dave? "

Delaplane swung around. For an instant he did not recognize the smiling man with his hand out. It was Frankie Caldwell. He was heavier than he had been in the old days in Granada and the whiskey flush that had grown on his face there was gone. Delaplane said, "Hello, Frankie." He ignored the outstretched hand and went back to making the sandwich.

"What are you doing out this way, Dave?"

"Just riding." Delaplane glanced over his shoulder at Caldwell. The same amiable weakness lay about the man's eyes and mouth. Caldwell was living proof that all Texas trail hands were not hell dogs with a double set of teeth. He had come up the trail three times before he had decided to stay in Granada.

For a while everyone in Granada had assumed that Caldwell was a ring-tailed wonder. He was appointed deputy marshal and he had lasted three days, until a run-of-the-mill tough took his pistol away and threw him out of a saloon. After that Caldwell found his level, a drunkard and an odd-job man around livery stables and saloons. Everybody had liked him, including Delaplane, until Delaplane grew hard enough to understand that liking weakness was a mistake tough men did not allow themselves to make.

"It's sure good to see you," Caldwell said.

The bartender thumped Delaplane's beer on the bar. Some of it slopped over. Delaplane gave the man a sharp look and saw a stubborn, hostile face. He slid a silver dollar into the wetness where the beer had spilled. The bartender knocked it back toward Delaplane with a snap of his forefinger that was like a sentence of contempt.

Caldwell said, "What's the matter, Sam? Dave is a friend of mine." He said it as if it meant something and the assumption irritated Delaplane.

"He came here with Frank Moxon."

Caldwell stared at Delaplane. "You're with Frank Moxon! No, Dave."

Delaplane felt like slapping Caldwell aside. He tossed the sandwich back toward the free lunch trough. Some of the ham and pickles fell out and dropped into the sawdust of the floor. Caldwell picked up the glass of beer and nodded toward a table in the back of the room.

Delaplane walked back to the table with Caldwell and sat down. "What the hell's on your mind, Caldwell?"

"You happened to be riding this way and fell in with Moxon, is that it? You're not really working with him?"

"Why not?"

"That bounty hunter! Not you, Dave!"

Delaplane stared at Caldwell. "Still a drunkard, Frankie?"

Caldwell shook his head. "I'm working off and on, learning to be a stone mason. You shouldn't be with Moxon."

"It's a man's job. What's the matter, are you afraid someone will take my pistol away from me?"

The jibe brought no shame to Caldwell's face. "I wasn't cut out for being a lawman, any more than you're cut out to be a cold-blooded killer."

"I'll run my own business," Delaplane said.

"That Moxon—he's the lowest kind of scum. Killing for money. I saw him take a man in Dodge once, and it was murder. Moxon enjoyed it."

"Go over and reform him."

Again, the jeer at Caldwell's courage had no effect on him. The change in him from the old days was puzzling, but he was still a weak man to be held in contempt. All at once something like pain touched Caldwell's features. In a quiet tone he asked, "You didn't come here after Sevier? My God, no! You're not here after John Sevier?"

"Why not?"

Caldwell showed horror. "Everybody here knows about him, Dave. When the time is right he's going back to Kansas and be cleared. He's got a wife and kids. He's—"

"He should have gone back before now."

"He couldn't! Even in a fair fight you don't kill a politician's brother and then throw yourself on the mercy of the politician's court."

"I know what happened. I know about Sevier."

"And you're still going to take him?"

Delaplane nodded.

"Let me tell you about him." Caldwell talked and Delaplane received a picture of a well-liked, respected family man against the background of a town that had its evils and troubles, but in far less degree than the places Delaplane was used to.

Delaplane knew then why he had looked with dislike upon South Fork: He was lonely and did not fit and he resented the fact. Maybe that was why Moxon was so bitter too, with a resentment so great that no town would ever want him. Delaplane's joining with him had not brought a halving of loneliness but rather a doubling of it for both of them.

"Don't go ahead with it," Caldwell said.

"He can give up."

"He won't. What man in his right mind would? Moxon never delivered a live prisoner to any sheriff."

"No man is as black as he's painted."

"You're going ahead with it?"

Delaplane rose. He took the beer with him and set it before the bartender. The man's hatred was a steady, smoldering quality. Deliberately, the bartender took the glass and dropped it, beer and all, into a trash barrel at the end of the bar.

At the door Delaplane looked back at Caldwell. He saw contempt in the man's expression. That was something, a weak, gutless character like Caldwell showing contempt of anything. It was puzzling; it was also disturbing. Delaplane went across to Moxon.

"The sheriff talked to Sevier again," Moxon said. "Walk past the place and take a look inside."

Time was running toward sunset. A big south window gave light on the cobbler's bench. Sevier was working. He did not look at the window when Delaplane passed. Delaplane's impression was of youth, of big, strong hands, of a long face and thick brown hair. There was a pistol belt lying on the bench before Sevier.

Beyond the shop Delaplane paused, giving a long glance to the men, now silent, who were watching from down the street. He went past the bootery again and Sevier did not look up from the boot he was working on.

The twins had brown hair too. Two hundred and fifty dollars. . . .
At manhood they would be worth two hundred and fifty dollars
apiece. It was a crazy thought that made Delaplane uneasy.

He went back to Moxon.

"He's alone in there, working on a boot."

"Pretending to, you mean?"

"No," Delaplane said. "He's really working."

A strange expression came to Moxon's face, the puzzled anger, the
lack of understanding. "Damn him, he ought to be quaking in his
boots right now."

"Look, Moxon, just this one time, why can't we—"

"No!" Moxon reached inside the door of the office and hauled out a
rifle. "The sheriff's personal long-gun." He gave it to Delaplane.
"Some pious idiot will bring a horse to the back of his shop. They
always try it. Cripple the horse just before it gets there. I'm going to
eat."

Moxon went to the saloon, ignoring the men who fell back to give
him room. Delaplane moved up to a hardware store. There was vacant
ground on the up-street side of the bootery and wide fire gaps between
the buildings down-street from the bootery. Delaplane put the rifle
butt softly into the clay between two flagstones and waited.

He saw it coming. With over-done casualness the townsmen saun-
tered up the street and broke into little groups, obstructing his clear
view through the fire gaps to the alley behind. But they left open
spaces between their heads and he saw the woman leading a blue roan
up the alley.

It was Sevier's wife.

Some of the townsmen, over-tensed with their little act, turned to
look behind them when the horse passed, and their companions
jabbed the offenders with low words and elbow blows.

Delaplane went quickly into the hardware store. He grabbed the
first chair that he saw and ran back to the walk. He stood on it with his
rifle quartered across his body, and now he could see above the heads
of every man blocking the gaps between the buildings. The move was
prompted more because he had been challenged than because he
thought Sevier actually was going to make a run for it.

The way the man had sat, not looking up, working carefully at his
bench. . . . No, Sevier was not going to run.

After a time the woman came from the shop. Her head was high, her body straight, but she broke suddenly and slumped. A gray-haired man leaped to put his arm around her and helped her down the street. Another man went into the alley and led the horse away. The groups broke up, beaten.

Delaplane sat down in the chair. He did not understand the weakness in his legs. Sevier could have made his break. He should have. He would have been hard to hit.

In fact, Delaplane knew he would have missed.

Now the townsmen were in a large group below the saloon. The sheriff was there. The whole mass was astir with some activity, crowding, talking, reaching their hands toward the sheriff.

Silence struck them momentarily when Moxon came from the saloon. Long striding, tall, with the scarred side of his mouth cocked in a half smile, Moxon came up to where Delaplane sat.

"A chair, huh?" Moxon said. "You're catching on. Easiness always puts the fear of God into them."

Delaplane stared at him. "Did you pay in the saloon?"

"Did the bartender try to pull that on you, too?" Moxon grinned. "Yeah, I paid, and he took the money, after he gave it a moment's thought." He looked toward the bootery. "He's about ready to come out like a brave man. All you have to do, Delaplane is to watch for another brave fool in that mess of magpies across the street."

"I want to let Sevier go."

The flat gray eyes lay intently on Delaplane. "No, you don't," Moxon said.

The sheriff called, "Moxon!" He was hurrying up the street with four men.

"I've seen this happen before, too," Moxon said. He laughed gently.

There was serious hopefulness in the faces of the five men. The sheriff did the talking. "We've more than doubled the reward, Moxon. Take it and leave town."

The money was in a salt sack. Moxon reached out and took it. "Five hundred, huh?"

The faces of the townsmen brightened. Standing now, Delaplane felt relief, and at the same time, sickening disgust for Moxon. It had been only a stall to run the price up when Moxon had refused before to let the sheriff mention a bribe.

Moxon hefted the sack. His smile bunched the scars on his cheek.

He spread his fingers and let the money drop to the walk. "Ten times that much wouldn't bribe me. I earn my money."

It was the truth, Delaplane knew. Money or love or anything human beings could offer would never turn Moxon from the pleasure of twisting and tormenting the souls of men, nor from the joy of killing men. Delaplane no longer had any understanding left to give Moxon; all he knew was that Moxon was fundamental, terrifying evil.

Sevier came from the bootery, tall and young and deliberate. He stood with the sunset on him, buckling around him a pistol belt.

The sheriff said, "John! Wait!" He started to run toward Sevier. He made two steps before Moxon clipped him in the side of the head with his pistol. The sheriff fell with the toes of his boots in the ditch beside the walk. Moxon dropped his pistol back into the holster.

Habit made Delaplane swing toward the townsmen with his rifle half raised. They fell back. Moxon gave him a curious intent look, noting his action but staring longer than he needed to observe that alone.

"All right, Delaplane." Moxon cocked his head, smiling as he looked across at Sevier. He walked toward Sevier, who had come to the edge of the walk on his side of the street, waiting.

"Don't, Moxon," Delaplane said. "Not this time."

Moxon did not turn or hesitate. "Keep your eye on them."

Delaplane dropped the rifle. It clattered loudly on the red stones. He took three quick steps away from it on the balls of his feet.

Moxon said, "Keep your eye on them, son. Pick up your rifle." He did not turn. His voice was under cold control.

Delaplane was expecting Moxon to make a simple quarter turn as he drew his pistol, but Moxon pivoted the other way, a half turn that brought him around ready to shoot. He was dead on the place where he had heard the last sound from Delaplane.

The tick of time it took Moxon to shift his aim to where Delaplane now stood was the same instant Delaplane used to shoot Moxon through the heart. Delaplane saw Moxon's pistol fall. The bitter, hating smile lived on a split second and then it too crashed down with the falling of the man himself. And all the townsmen came racing.

Delaplane saw Sevier's wife running toward her husband, with the twins bumping along far behind her. The boys lost interest in their father before they reached him; they ran, instead, to see what was going on across the street where all the crowd was gathering.

Caldwell came through the press and took Delaplane away. Delaplane walked for a time still gripping his pistol before he thought to put it back into the holster.

"You fooled me," Caldwell said. "What changed your mind?"

Delaplane thought of a man working at a bench when death was waiting for him, of a white-faced woman, of two boys running around an awning post, of the loathing in a bartender's eyes, of money in a salt sack falling on red stone, of Caldwell pleading for a man's life; and he thought of Moxon trying to curse away his terrible loneliness around a campfire, which was the worst memory of all.

There was no glib explanation, so Delaplane said, "I don't know."

He walked down the street with Caldwell and he observed that there was some kind of strength in the man after all.

Due Process

It was maybe two weeks after old Ute Henderson died of the slow fever at his home place on the Little Peralta.

Spring roundup was on, which meant for four-five days crews from the five outfits in the southern part of the valley would headquarter at the big holding corrals not far from Joe Tonso's saloon and store.

Those of us who could get away in the evening after work would go up to Tonso's, which didn't mean we got roaring drunk every night. We didn't have that kind of money, and Tonso didn't give that kind of credit. We did get together for a little fun and talk.

This particular evening the fun was out. Obadiah Smith showed up and as usual he was trying to start trouble. He was a whopper-jawed, scorpion-eyed cuss who fancied himself as a gunfighter. We doubted that he was, but none of us cared to find out the hard way, and that of course made it easier for him to be a bully.

Obadiah's specialty was pushing Mexicans around. He worked for Burt Hamlin, who didn't have any Mexican riders, but there was a fair sprinkling of them in other Peralta Valley outfits. They always tried to avoid Obadiah.

This time it was Ragged Hudnall, one of Obadiah's own crew, that Obadiah was giving trouble. "Take a man like you, he don't have the guts for gunfighting," Obadiah said.

"You're right," Ragged said.

"Sure I'm right!" Obadiah swung a look around the room. "And the rest of you are the same way."

"Yep," Clum Bronson agreed, and the rest of us just tried to pay no attention. Obadiah was having one of his streaks. The best thing to do was let him run.

Not getting any rise out of us, he tried Joe Tonso. "This is a fine two-bit dump you run here, Joe."

Tonso was slopping glasses in a bucket behind the bar. "I guess you could call it that."

"I am calling it that!"

"Suit yourself," Tonso said.

Nothing makes a bully meaner than lack of resistance. Obadiah was trying to figure who to abuse next when Pistol Pete showed up, getting as far as the doorway before he saw Obadiah. Pete was a grinning, bandy-legged little Mexican who worked for the Circle T, a good rider, and about as harmless as they come. We'd nicknamed him because of the big old horsepistol he always carried. Nobody had ever seen him shoot the gun and some of his nearest friends claimed it was too rusty to go off anyway.

There he was in the doorway, grin wiped out by the sight of Obadiah.

"Come on in!" Obadiah said.

"I think maybe I have some business somewhere."

"Come on, come on! I'll buy you a drink."

Pete's big-toothed grin winked on and off as he came up to the bar. Tonso eyed Obadiah and said, "Don't start no trouble."

"Who's going to start trouble? You worry too much." Obadiah grabbed Pete's arm and hauled him over close, pouring him a drink. Obadiah raised his own glass. "To Pistol Pete, the terror of the Peralta!"

"Si," Pete said, straining to be agreeable. All he wanted was to get out the quickest way he could. He gulped the whisky.

"Another one," Obadiah said. "We'll drink to all the dirty, chili-picking greasers I'm going to wipe out one of these days."

Pete tried to grin. "Gracias," he said, and drank and started to leave.

Obadiah spun him around and threw a glass of whisky in his face. That was one of Obadiah's favorites. He liked to blind a man, gun-whip him down and stomp him into the floor.

I grabbed a singletree off the wall.

Obadiah reached for his gun. No hurry. He grinned as he watched Pete standing with his eyes squinched shut and whisky running off his face.

That was when Pete, blinded and scared, hauled out his rusty old cannon and fired. Talk about roar! Pete was blanked out by the powder smoke.

The slug knocked Obadiah back. He doubled over and hit the floor on his face, deader than a slunk calf.

We stood there with our mouths open.

Pete dropped the gun and ran. He hit the side of the door going out, bounced off and kept going. He was on his horse and away before we grasped the full fact of what had happened.

Tonso came trotting from behind the bar and got down beside Obadiah. "He's done for."

"He had it coming," Ed Glassman said.

Some of the boys carried Obadiah outside into the moonlight and put him alongside the wall.

"He was bought and paid for a long time ago," Tal Hunter said.

We went back inside to talk about it.

Nate Matlock showed up a few minutes later, leading Pete by a rope around his chest and arms. "I was on my way here when I heard the shot. I met Pete, riding like a wild man. He wouldn't stop, so I went after him and roped him. What's going on?"

We told him.

Nate said, "This calls for a little investigation."

"Never mind that lawbook you stuck your nose into once," Glassman said. "There's no problem here."

Nate paid him no attention. "Why'd you run away?" he asked Pete.

Pete cut loose in Mexican so fast and furious that only Tonso could understand. "He says he was afraid the Hamlins would start a war of extermination against the Mexicans in the valley on account of it. He was going to warn them."

Pete nodded vigorously, cut loose again. "He says he thought you were bringing him back here to hang him," Tonso interpreted.

Nate took the rope off. "The facts seem clear. Self-defense—but of course we'll have to take it to a jury."

"Why?" I asked.

"Proper procedure," Nate said. "Due process of law."

Ragged grunted. "Hell! Let's just bury him."

Obadiah's pistol was on the bar. It had fallen out of the holster while we were carrying him outside, and someone had picked it up. "Is that the full extent of the search of the deceased?" Nate asked.

"That's his gun, yep," Tonso answered.

"We'll defer further action along that line." Nate was sure taking charge. "Right now, as a coroner's jury, it's up to us to determine the cause of Smith's death."

"He was shot," I said. "Dead center, by a slug big enough to knock over a buffalo."

Nate shook his head. "Hearsay. Set down, all of you, and let's have the evidence properly presented."

"You mean we haul Obadiah back in here?" Ragged asked.

"That won't be necessary. I want each man to tell carefully and honestly his version of what occurred."

"You don't talk that way all the time," Glassman growled. "What's bit you, Nate?"

"His ma used to stack lawbooks on his chair so's he could set high enough to reach table," Ragged offered. "I think his learning seeped in the wrong end of him."

Nate laughed with the rest of us, but he was some serious when he got started on legal matters. Before long he had things going his way. No wonder Pete got nervous, what with everyone so solemn, and one after another telling how he had killed Obadiah.

Pete decided we were working up a hanging, so he made a break for it. Clum tripped him. We made Pete go sit on a keg of salt pork while we completed the inquest.

Nate announced the finding. "One Obadiah Smith was killed by a bullet fired from a pistol in the hands of Pistol Pete, and the whole mess was self-defense."

"That was a heap of talking to get around to something that even Tonso's hound knew beforehand," Ragged observed. "Now, where do we get our pay?"

"Pay?" Nate shook his head.

"I was on a jury once and I got paid," Glassman argued.

"This wasn't exactly a jury, not the kind that gets paid, leastwise," Nate said. He thought for a while. "Well, I guess each man, including Pete, can have one drink."

"Who pays?" Tonso asked quickly.

"The court will take the matter of payment under advisement," Nate said.

Tonso grunted. "That means I'm stuck for the drinks." He set them out.

I didn't drink, and when I asked for a can of tomatoes, Tonso balked. "You get whisky, or nothing."

Whisky was two bits a shot. Tomatoes cost one buck a can. "All right, give me a cigar," I said. I didn't smoke, either, so I gave the dried-out black stogie to Pete.

Pete still wasn't sure that we weren't going to hang him. The cigar seemed like a last gesture. Once more he started to light out, but someone hauled him back and Tonso at last got it into his head we weren't holding anything against him.

"It's getting late," Ragged said. "We got plenty of hard work again tomorrow, so let's bury Obadiah and get out of here."

"It's not that easy," Nate said. "There's certain legal aspects yet to be taken care of. Tonso, give us your best lantern."

We assembled around the deceased. He didn't look very good in the moonlight.

Nate said, "You know, we haven't actually proved him dead."

"Huh!" I said. "I'm satisfied."

"We really ought to have a doctor say so."

"I hear there's one about seventy miles south," Glassman said. "Go get him, Nate."

"I'll have no levity," Nate studied Obadiah. "Yeah, I'd say there's no doubt about it."

"Where do we bury him?" Ragged asked. "Or does that take another court session?"

"The deceased will have to be thoroughly searched in the presence of witnesses."

"Help yourself," Tonso said.

"Get a pencil and some paper, Joe," Nate ordered. He looked at me. "You're appointed to do the searching."

"Who appointed me?"

"I did."

"I just resigned the appointment!"

"Court order," Nate said. "Get on with it before you're held in contempt."

Everybody else was quick to support him.

I rustled through Obadiah's pockets quick as I could. Found a Mexican dollar, a Piper knife and some crumbly twist tobacco.

"There's a bulge under his shirt," Nate said. "Proceed with the examination of the deceased."

"Why don't you just call him Obadiah? I'm getting sick of that deceased stuff."

"Proceed," Nate said.

Around Obadiah's waist was a money belt of fine leather. It was heavy. When I gave it to Nate, he ripped some stitches with his knife and out popped a twenty-dollar goldpiece.

We went inside where the light was better. Sewn around the belt in little flat pockets were twenty-three more.

"By Ned, he's robbed a bank somewhere!" Ragged said.

Nate looked stunned like the rest of us. He said it would be proper, we still being a jury, to allow certain expenses from the money while deliberating.

We deliberated for three drinks around. For me it was a can of tomatoes.

By that time the jury was some loosened up and ready to deliberate in earnest, but Nate called a halt to further expenses. "How much is his horse and rig worth?"

It was a good outfit. We decided on a hundred and ninety bucks. Glassman said make it two hundred to keep things even.

"His pistol?" Nate asked.

"Twenty bucks," Clum Bronson said, "holster and all."

We agreed that it was a fair price.

"What happens to his stuff?" Ragged asked.

Nate scowled. "That's what I'm trying to figure out. Does anybody know of any relatives?"

Glassman snorted. "He never even had a friend!"

Hunter said, "We got a better idea where he went than where he come from." He hefted Obadiah's pistol. "I *would* give five bucks for this."

"I guess anyone would," Nate said, "but that ain't the way we're handling this business."

"How are we handling it?" I asked.

Nate cleared his throat. He sort of drew himself up, which wasn't hard, since he was about six feet three to start with. "Gentlemen," he said, like he was addressing Congress, "we've got an estate on our hands."

Danged if he didn't make it sound pretty important, but Ragged grunted disgustedly. "Estates are houses and a lot of land and money in a bank and that sort of stuff."

Nate shook his head. "Everything Obadiah left is his estate, money, horse, gun—the whole works. We will have to apply the due process of law to the handling of it. I'm hereby declaring myself administrator and the rest of you deputy administrators."

"Deputies?" Pistol Pete looked uneasy. As a matter of fact, none of us was much taken with the word.

"What's this here administrator thing?" Ragged asked.

"That means we take care of everything Obadiah left until it can be disposed of in a legal way for the benefit of his estate, or heirs."

"How can you benefit the estate by disposing of it?" Clum asked. "And if Obadiah ain't got no heirs—"

"Objection overruled!" said Nate.

"Sounds simple enough," said Glassman. "Let's divvy up the works and be done with it."

Nate looked like he'd been hit in the belly with a corral pole. "We've got to follow proper procedure!"

"Yeah? Well, you name it," Ragged said.

Nate hemmed and hawed. "I'll have to take it under advisement."

"How long does this here advisement last?" Tonso asked.

"Until our next session tomorrow evening."

In the meantime, Nate would be doing the same work as the rest of us, and getting just as dirty and sweaty, but he made it sound like he was going off to a high-paneled room somewhere to throw a study on all the law that had ever been written.

"I don't want Obadiah laying around out there until tomorrow evening," Tonso said.

We buried Obadiah down in the gulch, where we could do more bank caving than shoveling.

The next night there at Tonso's, Nate said to me, "I've set four drinks per man as the expenses of each meeting. That means you get one can of tomatoes, or equivalent value in place of four drinks."

"You sure must have been thinking hard today."

"The session is in session," Nate said. "Who's got an idea about Obadiah's estate?"

"I think we ought to consider everything careful before we make any moves," Tonso said.

Glassman snorted. "You're boarding Obadiah's horse and getting paid for it, and making twenty-four cents on every two-bit glass of whisky we drink. We could set on this case all year and you'd be happy."

"I'll have no personalities!" Nate said. "What I want is ideas."

Tonso's blue hound came in and lay down with a sigh near the door.

Hunter said, "Let's sell the whole estate to Tonso here, and—"

"Fine!" Glassman nodded. "What do we do with the proceeds?"

"Lemme finish, damn it! Turn the whole works over to Tonso. Then he provides free drinks for any cowboy that shows up, until the estate is gone. Of course he don't say beforehand that the drinks is free."

Offhand, that sounded like a fine idea. Tonso was nodding agreeably.

"What happens after everybody in the valley finds out about the free drinks?" Nate asked.

"Be quite a rush," Hunter admitted. "But—"

"I know who'd be leading the rush," Glassman said. "What with you staying on the Bragg place all summer, and the rest of us out in the hills in cow camps."

"Calling me a drunkard, huh?" Hunter came around and took a swing at Glassman.

Glassman jumped back and fell over the hound, which let out an awful howl. Nate grabbed Hunter. "Order! Order! We ain't going to have none of that around here!"

"He called me a drunkard!"

"You wanta be cheated?" Glassman yelled.

We didn't get nowhere that night.

As a matter of fact, we didn't get nowhere the following night either. There were some pretty fair ideas about getting rid of Obadiah's estate, but Nate put the kibosh on all of them. We began to call him Old Proper Procedure, and we were getting about as disgusted with him as we were with Obadiah for getting himself killed.

When we were going out to the horses, Ragged proposed, "Let's take the estate and send Nate somewhere to study law."

"Yeah," Hunter said. "Maybe to Europe."

"She is a long way from here," Pistol Pete ventured.

We rode back toward camp.

Ragged said, "You brought on this whole thing, Pete. There ought to be some way we could make you responsible."

"No, no!" Pete said.

"I got it!" Hunter yelled. "All that money Obadiah had proves he was wanted somewhere for robbery. There's a reward out for him, sure as shooting, and it's a cinch it amounts to as much as the estate. Pete killed him, so Pete gets the estate."

That sounded like straight thinking. But Nate said, "There's no proof there was a reward. Even if there was, rewards ain't paid out of a man's estate. Motion overruled."

Hunter got sore. "I quit!"

"You'll be in contempt," Nate warned.

Hunter paused. "What's that?"

"Not showing proper respect for a court and legal procedure."

"Where the hell is the court? You mean us arguing and gabbing every night in Tonso's?"

"We're law, every one of us. We've got to act like it. We're responsible for our actions to the Territorial Courts."

"I quit," Hunter said, but it sounded pretty weak.

"Bury the money in a hole," Pete said. "We shoot the horse. Bury him too. On top we put the lariat so it will turn into a snake if anyone makes to dig."

"Yeah," Ragged said, "and we throw Nate in with the rest of the stuff."

"We ain't burning nothing," Nate said. "We're going to settle this thing all legal and proper."

We had one more night to go. After that, we were going to be scattered all over the Peralta until fall. I didn't see much chance of getting the estate settled.

When we went back to Tonso's that last evening, there was a six-horse team in the corral and a wagon with a hunk of rock on it that must have weighed six tons. My back ached just from looking at that stone.

Tonso introduced us to Jake Foley, a rawboned fellow with a face about like the rock on the wagon. We'd heard about Foley. He'd taken up a claim near Dirty Billy Springs and spent his time blasting.

"Mr. Foley here," said Tonso, "is on his way to sell a gravestone to Ute Henderson's widow."

Ragged began to laugh. Nate rammed him in the ribs.

"What's so funny?" Foley asked.

"I didn't tell him," Tonso said.

Nate took the floor, naturally. "Ute Henderson was married to an Indian, Foley. She and her family got up and left when he died. Far as we know, they took Ute along to bury him somewhere in the rocks up high."

"Why, I'd heard he was one of the leading citizens around here!"

"Reckon he was," Nate said, "but that's what happened to him. You won't be selling no rock down there, Foley."

"Stone." Foley eyed us all with suspicion.

Tonso set out the first round of our expenses. "I persuaded Mr. Foley to wait until you boys had a chance to talk to him about buying his rock for—"

"Stone," Foley said. "For whom?"

"Obadiah Smith," Tonso finished.

"Buy a rock!" Clum said, outraged. "What for? The country's full of rocks."

Nate set his glass down. "A stone for Obadiah! Tonso, I think you've got it!"

"Got what?" Hunter asked.

"We'll use the money to buy a stone for Obadiah," Nate said. "That will settle our problem."

Naturally, he didn't want Foley to know it was an estate because the price of everything always goes up where an estate is involved.

Foley said, "Was this Smith a leading citizen?"

Hunter choked on his whisky.

"You could say that," Nate admitted.

You could, sure enough. It was a hell of a lie but you could say it.

"I never heard of him," Foley said.

"You hadn't heard that Ute Henderson was married to a squaw," I said. "There's probably quite a lot you ain't heard."

"Sure!" Tonso said. "If you ever got away from your quarry you'd have heard of him. It'll be a fittin' monument—"

"They don't make the kind of monuments Obe ought to have," Glassman said. But maybe Foley's rock will do."

"Stone."

Nate asked, "How much were you figuring on getting from Ute's family?"

"Maybe seventy-five dollars."

"Maybe we can come close to that," Nate sighed.

"The price is not everything." Foley showed considerable doubt. "My stones are not just something to be sold. They're cut to last for centuries, and I'm rather particular where they get put."

Trying to run the price up, I thought.

"Fine a piece of granite as I ever quarried."

"We'll pay your price," Nate said.

Foley got a stubborn expression. "It'll have to be a worthy place."

"Right down in the gulch," Hunter said.

Foley looked horrified. "Down in a gulch!"

"We'll work it out," Nate said hastily. "How much?"

"Who was this Obadiah?" Foley asked.

"What's the difference?"

"I'm not placing a stone on the grave of some drifting gambler." Foley was a Vermonter, we found out later. He had narrow views.

Foreseeing the end of court expenses, Ragged was crowding the bottle. "Obadiah was no gambler. He was a loud-mouthed, no—"

"One of us, one of our friends," Nate cut in.

You could see Foley wasn't much impressed with our bunch. That man had a whale of a pride in his granite.

"How did this feller die?" Foley asked.

"I shoot him!" Pete said.

Foley scowled. "I don't like the sound of this. I don't think this corpse was the kind I'd respect."

"What's that got to do with us buying your rock?" Ragged shouted. "We got the money."

"Stone," said Foley.

"I can show you a million tons of the same just by going to the door!"

"Not like mine," Foley said. "Mine is a piece of the finest blue granite. Not a flaw in it."

"Whatever it is, we'll buy it," Ragged grunted. "All you want for it is money."

Foley's blue eyes turned angry. "Money is never the most important consideration in the placing of monumental stones," he said coldly. "My father and his father before him refused large sums to set their stones on the graves of immoral people."

"Who said Obadiah was immoral?" Nate sounded indignant. "You insulting his memory?"

Foley didn't back up. "How did he happen to be killed by him?" He jerked a chin at Pete.

"I will show you how I killed him," Pete said. "He—"

"Never mind that!" Nate smiled at Foley. "Pete's like a kid. Kinda excitable. Might even say he's not quite all there. Why, he wouldn't shoot a magpie."

"Not Pete!" we all cried.

Pete looked a little confused. He started spluttering Mex.

"What's he saying?" Foley asked.

"Telling how he killed twenty-two Injuns single-handed," Nate said. "See what I mean about him being a little off?"

Foley said, "If he's crazy, why do you let him carry a pistol?"

"A toy," Nate said. "Worthless." He stepped over and grabbed Pete's gun. We'd examined it after Obadiah was killed, and found only two caps on the nipples.

The odds were a hundred to one that Pete hadn't even cleaned it since the shooting.

Nate tipped the cannon up and began pulling the trigger. It clicked three times. "See there?" he said, and should have quit right then, but he went one click too far and the gun like to lifted the roof off.

Tonso's hound let out a howl.

"How could a man kill another man with a gun that hits once out of five times?" Nate snorted. He tossed the pistol back to Pete.

"Four times," Foley said. He coughed in the powder smoke, eying the roof. "I guess you've proved your point."

"So you'll sell us the rock—the stone?" Nate asked.

Foley frowned. "How *did* Obadiah die?"

"Caused by something that he was born with, I think," Nate said.

"Sure, he had that trouble all his life," Ragged said.

Foley eyed us narrowly. "He wasn't a sinful man?"

"Good to his horse," I said. "Always took off his hat around women." Those were facts, everything on the good side I could remember.

Some could lie better. They built Obadiah up considerable. He'd been polite, thoughtful, helpful and honest. Before they went too far, Nate shut them off, and just in time, for Foley said dryly, "I never put a stone on the grave of a saint before."

"We'll have to admit that on occasion he did use swear words," Nate said.

"I do a mite of that myself," Foley admitted.

"He was thrifty," Tonso said. "He saved money."

"Ah!" said Foley.

"How much for the rock—the stone?" Ragged asked.

"I won't go less than seventy-five dollars."

"A measly seventy-five bucks for a stone for a man like Obadiah?" Hunter said in an outraged tone.

"I can get a larger one, but that will take time."

"The one outside will do," Nate said, "but we feel that we'll have to spend more for it. One hundred dollars."

"Two hundred," I said.

"Three hundred bucks!" Glassman yelled.

Tonso whacked the bar with his hand. "Four hundred!"

"Four fifty!" Ragged shouted.

"One thousand boocks!" Pete howled.

"Told you he was crazy," Nate said.

Foley figured we all was. He walked out.

"We're not joking!" Nate yelled. "This is serious."

We followed Foley outside, all of us trying to make him believe us. In all my life I never found a man so hard to give money to.

After Nate got us shushed, he talked to Foley over by the wagon. Tonso figured up the bar expenses and a buck and a half for boarding the horse, and came up with a figure that was the entire estate of Obadiah.

"It's our final offer," Nate said. "I can't be responsible for what the boys might do if you don't accept."

We looked tough as we could, although I'm sure that didn't influence Foley in the least.

"Is there something sinful or unlawful about this?"

"Believe me," Nate said, "we're straining ourselves to be as legal as we can."

"It's a damn funny offer." Foley thought for a long time. "But I'll take it."

We all breathed with relief.

"I'll show you where the grave is, so you can start setting the stone tomorrow," Nate said.

"In a gulch?" Foley shook his head. "No stone of mine will be placed on loose ground."

Dead or alive, that Obadiah was nothing but trouble.

"You've already made the deal!" Ragged raged.

"Oh, no! The sale of a stone includes the setting, and if I don't have solid ground I don't sell."

Ragged threw his hat on the ground. "It's fifteen feet down to solid ground in that wash!"

Foley said stonily, "No deal."

"What *do* you want?" Glassman asked.

"Rocky ground." Foley glanced at the point of the hill above Tonso's. "That looks a good place."

"The guy ain't buried there," I protested.

"Move him," Foley said.

Hunter groaned. "By God, up there's all solid rock!"

"Good. My stone will set well in a place like that."

Nate said, "Your stones ain't more important than the people themselves."

"They are to me."

We went back into Tonso's to argue about it. There was no shaking Foley. He wasn't going to set his stone on loose ground, and we couldn't dig a hole in rock.

"You move him, Foley," Ragged suggested. "You're getting enough for the stone to move all the graves from here to the mountains."

"I'm a stonemason, not an undertaker."

Nate had been thinking like sixty. "Foley, ain't it proper to set monuments on land to someone lost at sea."

"Yes."

"All right, put Obadiah's monument on the hill."

You could see that Foley was pretty favorably taken. "You claiming his grave is lost?"

"Yep!" Ragged said. "We buried him at night. I doubt that any of us could say where he's at."

Hunter tried to mess that up. "I know right where he is."

"Not me," I said.

"Me neither," Ragged grumbled. "First big rain—"

Hunter was stubborn. "I kin find him."

Foley shook his head. "The man is right. There's deceit in this. I won't be a party to it."

There we were, stuck fast against Foley's pride and hard morality. We looked to Nate, but all he said was, "I think I'll remove all restrictions on the expense limit."

The expenses began to flow pretty fast. Foley was right in there, holding his own. His face got red, but I couldn't see that he was loosening up much.

The conversation had got pretty loud and it had extended to about everything under the sun. It was then that Nate brought us back to business. "We'll have a vote to determine whether the grave is lost or not."

Everyone of us except Hunter voted that it was lost beyond reasonable finding, whatever that was.

"No, sir!" Hunter said. "I'll show you where it is."

He lurched away from the bar and started out. He fell over the doorsill and lay there groaning.

"I accept that as evidence that he was incompetent to vote," Nate declared. "Therefore, the grave of Obadiah Smith is lost by unanimous action of this group."

"Second the motion!" yelled Pistol Pete. He was learning something, though not much, about democratic procedure.

We looked at Foley.

"I agree," he declared, solemn as an owl.

"It is, therefore, fitting and proper that Obadiah's stone be erected on a suitable hill in the vicinity where he was last seen," Nate said. "All those in favor—"

"Aye!" we yelled.

"No more expenses," Nate said.

"Hell, I was just beginning to understand law," said Ragged, who could hardly walk by now.

"And what do you want as the inscription?" Foley asked. He took two cuts at the last word before he got it right.

Nate said, " Obadiah Smith, 1881. That's enough."

We all wanted to add something. "In Memory of" or "Rest in Peace" or "He Was a Good Man." I thought "He Died Game" would be pretty good.

Hunter staggered up and came back to the bar. He'd skinned both shins on the high log sill and was feeling ill used. "Just put 'To Hell With Him'!"

Nate had his way. Nothing but the name and date.

We sold Obadiah's gun to Tonso for twenty bucks, and added that to the gold. It was somewhere close to four hundred and fifty bucks, a heap of money for a stone, but getting that estate settled was a big relief.

We'd overlooked something. There was still the horse and the rig, which we'd appraised at two hundred. Tonso called that to our attention.

"You know, of course, Foley, that a horse is involved in the deal," Nate said.

"No, I don't know it." Foley had all the gold before him on the bar. The way he was staring at it, you could tell that his conscience and principles were having a real rough time. "I don't know nothing about a horse. I don't want nothing to do with it."

"You have to take the horse," Nate said.

"I don't even have to take this money." Foley weaved a little, but his eyes were hard and steady. "It's too much."

"The horse is extra for cutting the inscription," Nate said.

"No! That's included."

I had a feeling that it wouldn't take much for Foley to shove that pile of gold back at us.

"I'll buy the horse and rig," Tonso said, "but I won't go any two hundred. I'll go seventy-five."

"It's a deal!" Ragged said.

"No, it ain't," Nate said. "We set the price at two hundred, and that's what we'll get."

Tonso shook his head. "Not from me."

"You ain't shoving the horse off on me either," Foley said.

I tell you that Foley was a hard man to deal with.

But Nate wagged his finger at Foley. "In payment for services to the estate of Obadiah Smith you have just accepted one bay horse, with saddle and bridle, for two hundred dollars."

"Not me," Foley said. "You'll have to do something else with the horse."

"Would you deprive the late lamented of the esteem the world should render by leaving him in an unmarked grave?"

"The grave is lost," Foley said. "I ain't depriving him of nothing."

"You just sold the horse," Nate said.

"Huh?"

"You just sold it to Tonso here for seventy-five dollars. Give him the money, Joe."

Tonso counted out seventy-five dollars and added it to Foley's pile.

"There," Nate said. "Nobody can say it's sinful to lose money on a deal."

"Hah!" said Foley. "That's even more sinful than making too much." Way he stared at that pile of gold on the bar, the more he looked like a dog with a mouthful of bad meat and no place to spit it.

Suddenly he heaved up tall as he could and glared like we was the scum of the earth. "I confess to greed," he said. "I was swayed by the power of gold, but now I renounce the whole deal."

We stood drop-mouthed.

"I will not be a party to deceit and trickery!"

"Nobody asked you to shoot your grandmother," Ragged growled. "Just take the money."

"No!"

Nate cut in smooth and fast. "Of course on transactions of this kind, we do expect a contribution to our cause."

"The wages of sin—What cause?" Foley said. The way he tightened up, you could tell he was not only a hard man to give money to, but a tougher one to take it away from.

"Church fund," Nate said.

"There ain't no church."

"Of course not," Nate said. "That's what our fund is for, to build one." He looked Foley hard in the eye. "I suggest that you contribute all but seventy-five dollars of that money to the fund."

Foley wrassled with that. "I haven't the right."

"Now you're obstructing justice and law."

"That's the first I've heard of any law around here."

"We've got it. You're obstructing it."

Foley counted out seventy-five dollars, put it into his pocket. "For the stone." He shoved the rest away from him. "Do what you wish with it."

"No," Nate said. "We gotta have your statement you're contributing it to the church fund."

"It wasn't mine! I've refused it."

"You took it once. Now you're giving it to the church."

"All right!" Foley yelled. "I'm giving it to the church!"

Nate shoved the money at Tonso. "Deposit this with the rest of the church funds."

"How much have you got?" Foley asked.

"I haven't counted lately," Tonso said, "but it's coming along."

A sudden quiet fell over us. The thing was done.

Smith's monument is still on the hill where Foley set it. You'd be surprised at some of the yarns told today about how come it to be there, about that great pioneer Obadiah Smith.

Hell, maybe he was! His money built the church.

My Brother Down There

Now there were three left. Here was the fourth, doubled up on his side at the edge of the meadow grass where the wind had scattered pine needles. His face was pinched and gray. Big black wood ants were backing away from the blood settling into the warm soil.

Jaynes turned the dead man over with his foot. "Which one is this?"

Holesworth, deputy warden of the State Penitentiary, gave Jaynes an odd look.

"Joseph Otto Weyerhauser," he said. "Lifer for murder."

Deputy Sheriff Bill Melvin was standing apart from the rest of the posse. He had been too deep in the timber to take part in the shooting. He watched the little green State patrol plane circling overhead. It was a windless day. The voice of the mountains spoke of peace and summer.

Joseph Otto Weyerhauser. Spoken that way, the words gave dignity to the fugitive who lay now on the earth in the pale green uniform that had been stolen from the wash lines of a little filling station a hundred miles away.

Sid Jaynes was a beefy man with dark eyes that glittered. Jaynes had not known who the convict was and he had not cared. The green pants and shirt, when Weyerhauser tried to run across the head of the little meadow, had been enough for him.

"He played it like a fool," Jaynes said. "He could have stayed in the timber."

"You made $12.50 with each one of those shots, Jaynes." The deputy warden's voice ran slowly and deliberately.

"Let the State keep their twenty-five bucks," Jaynes said. "I didn't come along for that." His rifle was a beautiful instrument with a telescopic sight. The dead man lay beside a sawed-off shotgun and a .38 pistol taken from a guard he had slugged with a bar of soap in a sock. "Why didn't he stay in the timber, the damn fool?"

"They're all city boys, " Warden Holesworth said. "He was heading for the highway."

It put you on the wrong side of your job to make a comparison between the dead man's short-range weapons and the rifles of the posse, Deputy Bill Melvin thought. Weyerhauser had been one of four prison escapees. He had taken his big chance with the others, and here the chance had ended.

That was all there was to it; but Melvin wished he did not have to look at Weyerhauser or hear any more from Jaynes, who was always the first man to reach the sheriff's office when the word went out that a manhunt was on. Jaynes, who ran a garage, never came when help was needed to find a lost hunter or a wrecked plane.

Sheriff Rudd spoke. Sheriff Rudd was a veteran of the open-range days of men and cattle. He stood like a rifle barrel, tall and spare. His face was bony, with a jutting nose.

"There's three more," the sheriff said. "All tougher than Weyerhauser." He squinted at the green plane, now circling lower in the trough of the mountains. "Call that flyer, Melvin. He's buzzing around this basin like a bee in a washtub. Tell him to get up in the air. Tell him about this and have him call the patrol station over the hill and see if anything has popped there."

Deputy Melvin started back to the horse with the radio gear. Jaynes called, "Ask him if he's spotted any of the other three."

Melvin paid no attention.

"One twenty, ground party, Stony Park."

"Ground party, go ahead."

"Get some altitude. You're making Sheriff Rudd nervous."

"What does Rudd think I am? There's a hell of a wind up here. What happened?"

"We got Weyerhauser. Dead. Call Scott and Studebaker on the road blocks."

"Stand by," the pilot said.

Melvin leaned against the mare. She moved a little, cropping grass, switching her tail at deer flies unconcernedly, while Melvin listened to the plane call across the mountains. Jaynes's sleeping bag was on the crosspieces of the pack saddle, put there to protect the radio from branches.

Jaynes walked over. "Has he spotted—?"

"I didn't ask," said Melvin.

"Why not?"

"He would have said so if he had."

"Well, it won't hurt to ask. Maybe—"

"Go collect your twenty-five bucks, Jaynes."

"What do you mean by that?"

Jaynes did not understand. He never would.

"Ground party, One twenty," the pilot said. "Negative on all road blocks and patrol cars."

"Thanks, One twenty. Call Studebaker again and have an ambulance meet us at the big spring, east side of Herald Pass, at one this afternoon."

"Okay." The plane began to climb. Melvin watched until it gained altitude and shot away across the timbered hump of Herald Pass.

"That's a hell of a note," Jaynes complained. "Guys like me come out here, taking time off from our business just to do what's right, and you don't even ask whether he's spotted the others or not."

Melvin pulled the canvas back over the radio. "Four times twenty-five makes a hundred, Jaynes. What are you going to buy with all that money?"

"I give it to the Red Cross, don't I!"

"You mean that first twenty-five you knocked down—that little forger? I remember him, Jaynes. He came out of a railroad culvert trying to get his hands up, scared to death, and you cut loose."

Jaynes was puzzled, not angry. He said, "You talk funny for a deputy sheriff, Melvin. You sound like you thought there was something nice about these stinking cons. What are we supposed to do with them?"

Melvin went back to the posse. Deputy Warden Holesworth had searched the dead man. On the ground was a pile. Candy bars, smeary and flattish from being carried in pockets; seven packs of cigarettes.

"One down and three to go," Jaynes said. "Where do we head now, Sheriff?"

Sheriff Rudd looked around the group. Two or three of the men sitting in the grass had already lost stomach. Rudd named them and said, "Take that sorrel that's started to limp and pack Weyerhauser up to the highway."

"At the big spring on the east side," Melvin said. "There'll be an ambulance there at 1 o'clock."

"I've got to get back myself," the deputy warden said. "Tomorrow I'll send a couple of guards out. We can fly in Blayden's hounds from up north—"

"I don't favor hounds," the sheriff said. "Keep your guards, too, Holesworth. The last time you sent guards we had to carry 'em out. You keep 'em sitting in those towers too much."

"That's what they get paid for, not for being Indian guides and cross-country men. To hell with you." They grinned at each other. Then Holesworth gave Jaynes another speculative glance and helped lift Weyerhauser on to the lame horse.

That left seven in the posse. They divided the cigarettes. Small ants went flying when someone gave the pile of candy bars a kick. One chocolate bar, undisturbed by the boot, was melting into the earth beside the other stain.

Two days later Sheriff Rudd cut the trail of three men whose heel-prints showed P marks in the center. Rudd swung down and studied the tracks, and then he took the saddle off his gelding.

"What's the stall?" Jaynes asked. "That's the track of our meat, Rudd."

"A day and a half old, at least. Give your horse a rest." The sheriff sat down on a log and began to fill his pipe.

Melvin walked beside the footprints for several steps. He saw the wrapper of a candy bar lying on the ground. Four days on candy and desperation. The poor devils. Poor devils, hell; the candy had been stolen from the filling station where they had slugged a 60-year-old man, the desperation was their own, and they were asking for the same as Weyerhauser.

Melvin looked up at the gray caps of the mountains. They ran here in a semicircle, with only one trail over them, and that almost unknown. If these tracks with the deep-cut marks in the heels continued up, the fugitives would be forced to the forgotten road that led to

Clover Basin. From there the trail went over the spine at 13,000 feet.

It was a terrible climb for men living on candy bars. Melvin went back to the resting posse, saying nothing.

"Clover Basin, maybe?" Sheriff Rudd asked.

Melvin nodded.

"Why haven't the damn search planes seen them?" Jaynes asked.

"There's trees and rocks, and the sound of a plane engine carries a long way ahead." Bud Pryor was a part-time deputy, here now because he had been called to go. He was a barrel-chested man who could stop a barroom fight by cracking heads together, but he didn't care much for riding the mountains. And he didn't care at all for Jaynes.

"Any other stupid questions, sharpshooter?" Bud Pryor asked Jaynes.

The sheriff got up. "Let's go."

They rode into the first of the great fields of golden gaillardia at the lower end of Clover Basin. The buildings of the Uncle Sam Mine hung over the slope at the upper end like gray ghosts. Rudd stopped his horse. The others crowded up behind him.

Motion started at the highest building and sent small points out on the slide-rock trail. "Hey!" Jaynes cried. Both he and Melvin put glasses on the tiny figures scrambling over the flat gray stones. Two men in green uniforms. Two men who ran and fell and crawled upward toward the harsh rise of Clover Mountain.

Jaynes let his binoculars fall on the cord around his neck. He raised his rifle, sighting through the 'scope. Some sort of dedication lay in his glittering eyes, some drive that made Melvin look away from him and glance at the sheriff.

Rudd, however, without the aid of glasses, was watching the fleeing men on the eternal stones of Clover Mountain.

Jaynes kicked his horse ahead. "Come on!"

"Get off and lead that horse a while, Jaynes," the sheriff said. "You've knocked the guts out of him already the last few days."

"There they are!" Jaynes gestured with his rifle.

"And there they go." Rudd got down and began to lead his horse.

"Now what the hell!" Jaynes twisted his face. "They're getting away—farther out of range every second!"

"They're a mile airline. It'll take us the best part of two hours to reach the mine," Sheriff Rudd said with weary patience. "And then it will be dark. Go on, Jaynes, if you want to, but leave that horse behind."

"It's mine."

"You'll leave it behind, I said."

Jaynes looked through his 'scope and cursed.

"Three came in here," Bud Pryor said. "Go on up and kick that third one out, Jaynes. He's there."

"How do you know?" Jaynes's voice was not large.

Pryor's thick lips spread in a grin. He was still sweating from the last steep hill where they had led the horses. "Gets chilly mighty quick in these high places, don't it?"

Rudd started on, leading his horse. It was dusk when they closed in on the bunkhouse of the Uncle Sam Mine, working around from the rocks and coming closer in short rushes to the toe of the dump. Jaynes and Melvin went up the dump together until their heads were nearly level with the rusted rails that still held rotting chocks.

"I'll cover you from here," Jaynes said. "This 'scope gathers light so a man can't miss."

Melvin raised his head above the dump. An evening wind drove grouse feathers across the yellow waste toward him. He saw a rat scurry along the ledge of a broken window and then sit still, looking out. Inside, two or three others squealed as they raced across the floor.

Melvin scrabbled on up and walked into the bunkhouse. Two rats carrying grouse bones ducked through holes in the floor. One half of the roof was caved in but the other end, where the stove sat with its pipe reduced to lacy fragility, was still a shelter.

The stove was warm.

Here, for a time, three men had stayed. They were city-bred, and so this man-made shell seemed the natural place to take shelter. No outdoorsman would have sought the rat-fouled place, but the escaped prisoners must have received some small comfort from it.

Instinctively they had huddled inside this pitiful ruin for the security that all pursued mankind must seek. And now, caught by the dusk and the silence, looking through a window at the mighty sweep of the high world, Bill Melvin was stirred by a feeling for the fugitives that sprang from depths far below the surface of things called logic and understanding.

"What's in there?" Jaynes called.

Melvin stepped outside. "Nothing."

Jaynes cursed. He climbed to the dump level and stared at the dim slide-rock trail. He fondled his rifle.

Pryor's voice came from the lower buildings, high-pitched and clear, running out to the walls of the great basin and echoing back with ghostly mockery. "Nothing in any of these, Sheriff!"

"Let's get on the trail!" Jaynes yelled.

"Come down here," Sheriff Rudd said, and both their voices ran together on the darkening rocks around them.

Melvin and Jaynes rejoined the others. Melvin was dead-weary now, but Jaynes kept looking at the slide-rock, fretting.

"We can't get horses over that slide-rock at night," Rudd said. "And maybe not in daylight. We'll camp here tonight."

"And all that time they'll be moving," Jaynes objected. "Are you sure you want to catch them, Sheriff?"

"They'll be feeling their way down the worst switchbacks in these hills," Rudd said. "On empty stomachs."

"Like hell!" Jaynes said. "They've been living like kings on grouse."

"One grouse," Melvin said.

"They must be getting fat." Rudd pointed to the floor of the basin. "We'll camp down there and give the horses a chance to graze."

"And make this climb again in the morning," Jaynes said disgustedly.

Dew was gathering on the grass when they picketed the horses. All the chill of the high-country night seemed to have gathered in the enormous black hole. They ate almost the last of their food at a fire built from scrubby trees.

Jaynes cleaned his rifle before he ate. He rubbed the stock and admired the weapon, standing with the firelight glittering in his eyes.

"What will that pretty thing do that a good Krag won't?" Bud Pryor asked.

Jaynes smiled and let the answer gleam in the reflection of the flames.

"Somebody will have to start out tomorrow for grub," the sheriff said. "How about it, Jaynes?"

"I can live on the country," Jaynes said.

"Yeah." The sheriff unrolled his sleeping bag. "One hour each on guard tonight. Not at the fire, either. Stay out by the horses. I'll take it from 3 till dawn."

Jaynes peered into the darkness. "You think the third one is around in the rocks, huh?"

"I think the horses can get all tangled up. The third man went over the hill a long time ago," Rudd said.

"How do you know that?" Jaynes asked.

"Because I'm betting it was Marty Kaygo. He's the toughest and the smartest. He wouldn't sit in that eagle's nest up there, hoping nobody comes after him."

"Kaygo, huh? What was he in for?" Jaynes stared toward the gloomy crest of the mountain.

"He killed two cops." Rudd took off his boots, pulled his hat down tightly, and got into his sleeping bag. "He killed them with one shot each." The sheriff was asleep a few moments later.

Jaynes set his rifle on his sleeping bag and began to eat. "Who are the other two?"

"Don't you even know their names?" Melvin asked.

"What's the difference if I don't?"

Maybe Jaynes was right. It had to be done, one way or another; names merely made it harder. "Sam Castagna and Ora L. Strothers," Melvin said. "Castagna used to blow up rival gamblers for a syndicate. Strothers specialized in holding up banks."

"Ora L. That's nice and gentle, a con having a name like that," Jaynes said.

"Don't you give him the right to have a name?" Melvin asked. "Don't you give him the right to be a human being?"

Jaynes looked blank at the anger in Melvin's voice. "What is it with you, anyway? You and Rudd both talk like it was a crime to send those bastards rolling in the grass."

Rolling in the grass. That was exactly what had happened to Weyerhauser when Jaynes's second shot ripped through his belly.

Melvin walked away from the fire suddenly, into the cold dark layers of the night. The possemen were sacking out. Jaynes squatted near the fire alone, eating, a puzzled expression on his face. Bud Pryor, stripped down to long underwear and his boots, came over and stood beside the flames for a few minutes, warming his hands.

Dislike of Jaynes and a sort of wonder mingled on Pryor's fleshy face. He parted his thick lips as if to speak. But then he left the fire and settled into his sleeping bag, grunting.

The night was large and silent. Up toward the knife edge of Clover Mountain two men had scrambled across the rocks, crawling where slides had filled the trail. Two men running for their lives.

Melvin kept seeing it over and over.

Castagna's sentence had been commuted to life just two days short of the gas chamber. Strothers had never killed a man, but he was cold and ruthless. Marty Kaygo, who must have gone across the hill before the others, was in debt to the law 180 years. This was his third escape from prison.

They were all no good, predators against society. But. . . . In the solemn night, with the tremendous peace of the mountains upon him, Bill Melvin stared uneasily at the line which must run from crime to punishment.

Ordinarily, he did not allow himself to be disturbed like this; but Jaynes, scraping the last of his supper from a tin plate, had kicked over the little wall that divided what men must do from what they think.

"I'll take the first watch," Melvin said.

Jaynes came out from the fire. He spoke in a low voice. "It's only 9 o'clock. Barker's got a flashlight. We could slip up on the slide-rock trail—there's patches of snow there—and see for sure if they all three crossed."

"Why?"

"If one is still here, he'll try to slip out of the basin tonight. We could lay out in the narrow place and nail him dead to rights."

"I'll take the first watch." Melvin walked deeper into the night, trembling from high-altitude fatigue, mouthing the sickening after-taste of Jaynes's presence.

"Why not, Melvin?"

"Go to bed!"

Sometimes a healthy man does not sleep well at great altitudes, and so it was with Melvin this night. When Jaynes relieved him, Melvin heard the beefy hunter going down the basin past the horses. He knew that Jaynes would make for a place where he could command the narrow entrance to the basin, and that he would lie there, patiently, his rifle ready.

Melvin wondered if his eyes would glitter in the dark.

Jaynes stayed his watch, and the watch of the man he did not waken for relief.

Dawn slid across the peaks. Light was there when dew and gloom were still heavy in the basin. The sheriff and Pryor cooked the last of the bacon and opened the last two cans of beans.

Jaynes saddled up and led his horse toward the fire before he ate. "What kind of rifle was it this—what was his name, Kaygo?—stole at the filling station?"

"A .30-06," Rudd said. There were pouches under his eyes this morning, and he looked his years. He stared through the smoke at Jaynes. "New one. He took five boxes of shells, too, Jaynes. They're hunting cartridges."

"I've got a few expanding noses myself," Jaynes said. "Let's get started."

Rudd spat to one side. "You're like a hog going to war."

Bud Pryor laughed. The other manhunters stared at Jaynes or at the ground. They seemed ashamed now, Melvin thought, to be a part of this thing. Or a part of Jaynes.

Pryor said explosively, "I'll go in after chow today, Sheriff. Me and Jaynes."

"No!" Jaynes said. "I can live on the country. Me and Melvin can keep going when the rest of you have to run for a restaurant."

Rudd said to Pryor, "You and Barker, then. It's closer now to Scott than it is to Studebaker, so we'll split up after we cross the hill. Try the radio again, Melvin. Maybe nobody will have to go in."

"No contact," Melvin said, later. "When we get to the top, we can reach out and make it."

They took the slide-rock trail from the dump at the side of the bunkhouse. In passing, Melvin noticed that the grouse feathers were almost entirely blown away.

Seventy years before, jack trains had used the trail; but now the years had slid into it. The posse led their horses. Sparks from steel shoes in the stretches where the ledge still showed drill marks; a clattering and a scramble, with the horses rolling their eyes when they had to cross the spills of dry-slippery rocks.

In the snowbanks, the tracks of three men; and one man had gone about a day before the others.

There lay the ridge, half a mile ahead. On the left, where they traveled, the mountain ran down wildly to ledges where no human being would ever set foot.

They lost the little radio mare. She slipped and fell and then she was threshing over and the slide-rock ran with her. She struck a ledge and was gone. The rocks kept spilling down a thousand feet below.

Rudd patted the neck of his frightened gelding. "There went a damn good little mare."

Jaynes said, "They don't exactly give those radios away, either. My sleeping bag cost 62 bucks."

The came out on the wedge-top and went down three switchbacks to let the horses take a blow out of the wind. A dozen lakes were winking in the sunlight. The mountains on this side ran in a crazy pattern. Every major range in the United States runs north and south, with one exception; but from the pinpoints where a man must stand, the north-south coursing is often lost or does not exist at all.

There was no highway in sight, no smoke, just the vast expanse of timber with the gray-sharp slopes above and the shine of beaver meadows where little streams lay separated from each other by ridges 8000 feet high.

"A regiment could hide out down there all summer," Rudd said. "But these guys will most likely keep running downhill, hoping to hit a highway sooner or later."

Jaynes's rifle was in his hands, as usual when he was on foot. He pointed with it. "I know every inch of that country. I've fished and hunted all through it."

"Don't be a fool," Sheriff Rudd said. "I rode that country before you were born, and I discovered a new place every time I went out. And I could do the same for 100 years." Rudd shook his head. "Every inch of it. . . .!"

Jaynes said, "I can find any tenderfoot that tries to hide out down there." He patted the stock of his rifle.

"Goddamn you, Jaynes! I'm sick of you!" Melvin cried. "Keep your mouth shut!"

Jaynes was surprised. "Now what did I say? Have you got a biting ulcer or something, Melvin?"

"Let's go on down," Rudd said.

Melvin's stomach held a knot that eased off slowly. For a moment he had seen the land without a man in it, forgetting even himself as he stood there on the mountain. But Jaynes would never let a man forget himself for long.

In the middle of the morning the green plane came over and circled them. The pilot was calling, Melvin knew, but they had no way now to listen or call back. After a while the plane soared away over the green timber and drifted on toward Scott.

They struck the timber. Fallen trees lay across the trail, slowing the horses. There were still three men ahead.

"Planes, radios, horses—what the hell good are they?" Jaynes said irritably. "In the end it comes down to men on foot closing in on each other."

"Like you closed in on the Uncle Sam bunkhouse, huh?" Pryor asked. "Hand to hand, tooth and toenail."

"Strip down to a breechclout, Jaynes," Rudd said. "I'll give you my knife and you can go after Kaygo properly."

Barker said, "Yeah, why don't you do that, Jaynes? You big-mouthed bastard, you."

Barker had little imagination. He was a sullen man who would kill the fugitives as quickly as Jaynes. All that motivated Barker now, Melvin thought, was a desire to transfer the cause of his hunger and weariness to another human being. Jaynes had already been marked by him as a target.

"I don't understand you guys, so help me," Jaynes said.

Melvin felt a flash of pity for him; the man really did not understand. What made Jaynes tick probably was as obscure as the forces that had sent the men he so greatly wanted to kill into a life of crime. Somebody ought to be able to figure it out. . . .

The big buck flashed across the narrow lane in a split second. The smaller one that followed an instant later was going just as fast. Jaynes broke its neck with one shot.

The thought of fresh liver relieved some of Melvin's dislike of Jaynes. "Nice shooting, Jaynes."

"Thanks."

"I'll eat that thing without skinning it," Bud Pryor said. He had his knife out already and was trotting ahead.

Jaynes sat on a log and cleaned his rifle while Pryor and Melvin dressed the buck. Jaynes had merely glanced at it and turned away.

"He's larded up like first-class, grass-fed beef," Pryor said. "Lucky shot, Jaynes."

"I seldom miss a running target." Jaynes spoke absently, looking ahead at the trees.

Pryor sent Melvin a helpless look. "It sure looked lucky to me."

"No luck at all," said Jaynes. "It's simple if you have the eye for it."

Pryor made a motion with his knife as if to cut his own throat. He and Melvin laughed. For a few moments Jaynes was no problem to them.

"Sling it on a horse," Sheriff Rudd said. "We can eat when we get to Struthers' sawmill set."

"Struthers? That's one of the men we want," Jaynes said.

"Different spelling," Rudd said. "Jumbo Struthers has been dead for forty years, and the sawmill hasn't run for fifty-two years."

"We could dig him up," Pryor said grinning, "so Jaynes could shoot him."

For the first time Jaynes showed anger. "Why do you keep digging at me? What are we out here for, anyway? You act like there was something wrong in what we're doing."

"We're here to bring back three men, dead *or* alive," Rudd said. "Let's go."

The trail expanded into a logging road, with live trees trying to close it out and dead trees trying to block it. Mosquitoes came singing in from a marsh on the left. Already tormented by the snags on fallen timber, the horses shook their heads as the insects buzzed their ears. Pryor kept swinging his hat at blowflies settling on the carcass of the deer. "The good old summertime," he said. "How'd you get me out here, Sheriff?"

"You were getting fat, so you volunteered."

The small talk irritated Jaynes. "We're not making much time," he said. Later, after a delay to lever aside a tangle of dead jackpines, he went ahead in a stooping posture for several steps. "One of the boys ain't doing so good all at once."

Melvin studied the tracks. One man had started to drag his leg; a second one was helping him. The third track was still older than these two. Farther down the road a punch mark appeared in the soil. One man was using a short pole as a cane.

Jaynes wanted to race away on the trail. "We'll have that one before long!"

"Hold up." The sheriff stopped to fill his pipe. "I'd say the fellow twisted a muscle or sprained his ankle trying to jump that tangle we just cleared out. The other one will leave him, that's sure."

"The old ranger lean-to in Boston Park must be pretty close," Jaynes said. "Half a mile, I'd say."

"About a mile," Rudd said.

Melvin knew about it, the big lean-to sometimes used by fishermen and hunters. Man had made it, and the fact would seem important to the men ahead. Considering the tracks of the injured fugitive, Melvin wondered whether the convict would last to Boston Park.

"If he's bunged up as bad as it looks, he's likely ready to quit," Rudd said.

"He won't give up," Jaynes said. "He'll make a stand."

The sheriff narrowed his eyes at Jaynes. "Why will he, if he's hurt?"

"If he's been left at that lean-to, he's the loneliest man in the world right now," Melvin put in.

"Yeah?" Jaynes kept edging ahead. "I'm not walking up on that hut to find out how lonely he is."

"Nobody is," Rudd said. "When we get close, two men will take the horses. The rest of us will cut off into the timber and come in from all sides of the lean-to. He may not be there at all."

The lean-to was set between two trees on high ground, clear of the swamp that edged the beaver ponds. Generations of outdoorsmen had piled boughs along the sides and on top until the shelter was a rust-brown mass. That it had not been burned by a careless match long ago spoke tersely of the nature of the men who came far into the mountains.

Melvin and Sheriff Rudd came to the edge of the trees a hundred yards apart. They waited for Pryor, on the right. Barker and Jaynes were to ease out of the trees on the left, Barker to cover the back of the shelter, Jaynes to prevent escape farther to the left.

There had been a fire recently among the blackened stones before the lean-to. Fine ashes stirred there, lifting to a little wind that rolled across the beaver ponds and whispered through the tall swamp grass.

Melvin saw Pryor come to the edge of the trees and signal with his hand. Barker slipped to the cover of a windfall behind the shelter. He wagged his rifle.

Inside the lean-to a man cleared his throat.

Melvin sank to one knee behind a log.

The sheriff said, "Come out of there! You're boxed. Walk out with your hands up!"

"I can't walk," a voice replied.

"Come out of there. We'll rip that place apart with bullets if I have to ask again."

The brittle needles scraped against each other. A chunky man whose face was black with beard came on hands and knees from the hut. He was wearing a soiled, torn green uniform, too small for him. One pants leg was gone below the knee.

"Toss your pistol away," Rudd ordered.

"No gun." The man clawed against one of the trees. He pulled himself erect. "No gun, you stinking, dirty—" He started to fall and made a quick grab at the crosspiece of the shelter.

A rifle blasted from the edge of the timber beyond Barker. The man at the lean-to fell. He was dead, Melvin was sure. "Watch him! Watch him!" Jaynes called. "It's just his arm."

Melvin and the sheriff walked in then. The man had been shot through the left hand, a thick hand, by a soft-nosed hunting bullet. The palm was torn away and the fingers were spread like the spokes of a shattered wheel. The man rolled on his side and put his broken hand under his arm.

"My leg is cracked before." He cursed. "Now look at it!" The leg was really broken now; it had twisted under when the man fell. Melvin searched him and found two packs of cigarettes.

Barker came around the hut. Jaynes arrived on the run. "I could just see his arm when he grabbed for his gun!"

"He grabbed, all right," Sheriff Rudd said. "To keep from falling on a busted leg."

"Oh!" Jaynes stared down. "It looked to me like—"

"Shut up." Rudd yelled at the timber where the two men were holding the horses. "Bring 'em on!" There was a first-aid kit on Melvin's horse.

"Which one is this?" Jaynes asked.

"Sam Castagna." Suspected of seven murders, convicted of one, sentence commuted to life. "Where's Strothers, Sam?"

"Run out on me." With his face against the brown needles Castagna tried to spit explosively. It merely dribbled from his mouth and hung in his black beard. He cursed in Italian, glaring up at Jaynes.

Barker said, "No gun anywhere around the hut. They had two sawed-offs and two .38 pistols, besides the rifle Kaygo swiped at the filling station."

The horses came in at the trot. Pryor circled the swamp and plodded through the grass. He looked at the wounded man. "Castagna, huh? Nice boy who likes to put bombs on carstarters. The other two are still going down the trail, Sheriff."

"Straight to a highway," Rudd said. "Let's patch him up and move on."

"I'm going to eat here," Pryor said, "if you have to leave me. I'm going to beat the blowflies to some of that deer." He began to build a fire.

Melvin and Barker made splints for Castagna's broken leg. They wrapped his hand. He watched them stolidly. When they pulled his leg, he ground his teeth and sweated. Melvin got him a drink of water afterward.

"Thanks," Castagna held the cup in a trembling hand, slopping part of the water down his chin and into the thick black hairs at the base of his neck.

"Where's Strothers and Kaygo, Castagna?" Jaynes asked.

Castagna looked hungrily at the meat Pryor was roasting on a green limb. He lay back on the ground and closed his eyes. There was a depression under his head and it caused his face to tilt straight into the sun. Melvin took off his coat and rolled it under the wounded man's head.

They squatted around the fire, rotating cutlets chopped from the loin with a hand ax, too hungry to bother with a frying pan. Blood from half-raw meat ran down their chins when they chewed.

None of us is far removed from the wolf, Melvin thought; but there is a difference between men like Rudd and Sam Castagna. There has to be. Yet where was the difference between Castagna and Jaynes, who cleaned his rifle before he ate?

Melvin glanced at the gleaming weapon, laid carefully aside on the dry grass. He felt an urge to hurl the rifle far out into the beaver pond.

Sheriff Rudd ground his meat moodily. "I never used to stop when I was on the chase. We stop to gorge ourselves while a desperate man keeps going. The difference is he *has* to get away and we don't *have* to catch him."

"Him? Who do you mean?" Jaynes asked. "Why don't we have to catch him?"

"Oh, hell," Rudd said. "Gimme the salt, Barker."

"I don't understand what—" Jaynes said.

"Before we leave here, Jaynes, you throw into that pond every damn hunting bullet you got," Rudd said. "I'm going to watch you do it."

They all looked at Jaynes. He could not grasp the reason for their hostility. "Shells cost money. I'll use that old coffee can over there and bury them under the lean-to. Next fall I'll be through here hunting."

"Do that then," Rudd said. "Every damn soft-nose you got." But Rudd seemed to find no satisfaction in the trifling victory.

He knew he was only scratching at the surface, Melvin thought.

The sheriff twisted around toward Castagna. "Some deer meat, Sam?"

"Yeah. Yeah, let me try it." Castagna ate greedily, and then he lost everything before they could get him onto a horse.

The green plane was cruising southwest of them. A few minutes later it came over Boston Park, dipping low. It went southwest again, circling six or seven times.

"Uh-huh," Rudd said.

"He must be over the Shewalter Meadows," Jaynes said. "That's all down-timber between here and there."

"Not if you know the way from the sawmill set." Rudd swung up. "Catch Castagna there if he starts to fall."

There were still two sets of mantracks down the logging road. Just before they reached the sawmill site they found a sawed-off shotgun laid across a log, pointing toward one of the sawdust piles near the creek. Under it an arrow mark scratched in the black soil pointed in the same direction.

"Now that's a cute trick," Jaynes said. He sighted through his 'scope at the sawdust piles, age-brown mounds blending into the wilderness. He was suspicious, but he was confused.

"It reads to me that Strothers wants to quit, and wants to be sure we know it," Rudd said.

"Suppose he's still got the pistol? Suppose it's Kaygo?" Jaynes asked.

"Most likely Kaygo is over there where the plane was circling,"

Melvin said. Kaygo had left the others at the Uncle Sam Mine. The sheriff, at least, was sure of that, and Melvin had accepted it. Still, he did not like the quiet of the sawdust piles, warm and innocent-looking out there by the creek.

Rudd said. "Come on, Melvin. The rest of you stay here. Take Castagna off the horse and let him lay down a while."

"I'd better—" Jaynes said.

"Stay right here," the sheriff said.

Rudd and Melvin leaped the creek and tramped upon the spongy surface of the sawdust piles. In a little hollow of the shredded wood they found their man, asleep.

His blond whiskers were short and curly. The sun had burned his face. His green shirt, washed recently in the stream, was spread near him and now it was dry. His heavy prison shoes were set neatly together near his feet.

"Strothers, all right," Rudd said. "Wake up!"

The man was snoring gently. He jerked a little but he did not rouse until Rudd tossed one of the shoes on his stomach. Strothers opened his eyes and yawned.

"What kept you so long?" he asked.

Cold and deadly, the bulletins had read; he had never killed a man, but he had always entered banks prepared to kill. He had studied law, and later, engineering. It was said that he could have been successful in either. Now he sat on a pile of sawdust in the wilderness, ready to go back to the isolation cells.

"Local yokels, eh? I didn't think those lazy bastards of guards would come this far. Got anything to smoke, Constable?"

"Where's Kaygo?" the sheriff asked.

Strothers yawned again. He felt his feet. "Talk about blisters!" He began to put on his shoes. "Why, Marty left us at a rat hole on the side of a cliff day before yesterday."

"We know that," Rudd said.

"That's why I mentioned it." Strothers reached toward his shirt.

"Hold it!" Melvin picked up the shirt. There was no weight in it, nothing under it. He tossed it to Strothers, who rose and began to put it on.

"Where's the other .38?" Rudd asked mildly.

"The other? So you got Weyerhauser. Can I have a smoke?"

Melvin lit a cigarette and tossed it to Strothers. The sheriff and his deputy glanced quickly at each other.

"I don't know who's got it," Strothers said. The horses were coming out of the timber.

He saw Castagna. "Did you ask Sam?"

The sheriff's eyes were tight. He spoke easily, "Sam's clean. You look clean. So Kaygo's got it. Why'd you give up, Strothers?"

"Too much of nothing here. No future." Strothers grinned, dragging on his cigarette, watching the horses from the corners of his eyes. The surface was smooth, but there was steel savagery underneath. Castagna was a bully who had graduated to bombs on starters and bundles of dynamite against the bedroom walls of gambling kings; Strothers was everything the long F.B.I. reports said.

"You could have given up with Castagna," Melvin said.

"That two-bit character! I play it alone." Strothers puffed his smoke. "Do I get some chow?"

"Yeah," Rudd said. "Half-done venison."

"Raw will be fine, Constable."

"Walk on over toward the horses," Rudd said. "When I say stop—stop."

"Sure, Constable. Just don't stall. I want to get home as soon as possible. I'm doing some leather work that can't be neglected."

Not the usual bravado of a petty criminal—Strothers was too coldly intelligent for that. He was spreading it on lightly for another purpose. He wouldn't have much luck with Rudd, Melvin knew. Let him find it out.

Strothers limped ahead of them. "When my last blister broke, that was when I decided to hell with it."

"Right there, Strothers," Rudd said, when they were twenty feet from the horses. With the exception of Jaynes, the posse was relaxed. The first heat of the chase had been worn from them, and this third easy victory coming toward them was nothing to cause excitement.

Rudd nodded at Melvin, making a circle with his finger in the air. Melvin walked wide around Strothers and freed his lariat from the saddle.

"The great big Strothers, he comes easy," Castagna said sullenly.

Strothers ignored Castagna; his eyes were on the rope in Melvin's hands. Barker and the others looked at Strothers dully, but Jaynes sensed what they did not. He pushed his 'scope sight down and raised his rifle.

"Never mind!" Rudd said sharply, standing several paces behind Strothers. "Put that rifle down, Jaynes. Drop your pants, Strothers."

Strothers smiled. "Now look, Constable. . . ." He was watching the loop in Melvin's hand.

And that was when Rudd stepped in and slammed Strothers to the ground with the butt of his rifle. Melvin drove in quickly then. Strothers was enough for the two of them for a while, but they got his arms tied behind him at last.

The little automatic, flat, fully loaded, was tied with strips of green cloth from Castagna's pants leg to the inside of Strothers's thigh. Castagna cursed bitterly, clinging to the saddle horn with his one good hand.

"Why didn't you search him right at first?" Jaynes demanded angrily.

"It takes more steam out of them to let them go right up to where it looks like it's going to work," the sheriff said. "Build a fire, Pryor. We may as well eat again before we split up."

Strothers chewed his meat with good appetite. He had struggled like a wolf, but that was done now and his intelligence was at work again. "What tipped it, Constable—the cigarettes?"

"Partly," Rudd said. "You wouldn't have left both packs with Sam unless you figured to be with him soon. That wasn't too much, but I knew you would never go back down the river and let them say Ora L. Strothers was caught asleep and gave up without a fight. You really were asleep, too—on purpose."

"Sure. I got the nerve for things like that. It made it look real." Strothers's good nature was back, but he was not thinking of his words. His mind, Melvin knew, was thinking far ahead now, to another plan, setting himself against walls and locks and ropes and everything that could be used to restrain a man physically, pitting his fine mind against all the instruments of the thing called society.

There was a lostness in him that appalled Melvin. Strothers was a cold wind running from a foggy gorge back in the dawn age of mankind. The wind could never warm or change or remain confined. Compared to Strothers, Sam Castagna was just a lumbering animal that knocked weaker animals out of the way.

"You would have taken Castagna with you, if you could have knocked a couple of us off and got to the horses?" Melvin asked.

"Sure," Strothers said. "We planned it that way."

That was talk to be repeated in the prison yard, to be passed along the corridors of the cell block. Talk to fit the code. But not to feed the vanity of Ora L. Strothers, because it was a lie. Let Castagna, lying feverishly on the ground in Melvin's jacket, believe what Strothers said. Castagna had been left behind to build up the illusion that desperate men would surrender without a fight. That he was injured and had to be left was not primary in Strothers's mind; it was merely helpful coincidence.

"Which one of us was to 've been first?" Melvin asked.

Strothers wiped his lips. "You, I thought. Then I changed my mind." He glanced at Jaynes.

"Yeah," Jaynes said. "I read you like a book. I wish you had tried something, Strothers."

The two men stared at each other. The antagonism that separated them was as wide as the sky.

"I'll bet you're the one shot Sam," Strothers said. "Did you shoot Joe Weyerhauser, too?"

Jaynes did not answer. Watching him, Melvin thought: He lacks the evil power of Strothers's intelligence, and he lacks the strength of natural good. He doesn't know what he is, and he knows it.

Strothers smiled. "I've taken half a million from the banks and never had to shoot a man. You, Snake Eyes, you're just a punk on the other side because you don't have the guts and brains of men like me, How about it?"

Jaynes leaped up. His wasp voice broke when he cursed Strothers. He gripped his rifle and stood with the butt poised to smash into Strothers's face.

"Whoa there, Jaynes!" Sheriff Rudd said, but it was not he who stopped the rifle. With his legs tied and one arm bound behind his back, Strothers looked at Jaynes and smiled, and Jaynes lowered his rifle and walked away. After a few steps he turned toward the creek and went there, pretending to drink.

Barker and Pryor stared at Strothers. "Don't call *me* any of your names," Barker growled.

Strothers looked at him as he might have glanced at a noisy child; and then he forgot them all. His mind was once more chewing facts and plans, even as his strong teeth chewed meat.

If this man had been led by Marty Kaygo, what kind of man was Kaygo? thought Melvin.

Rudd said, "I'll take everybody in but you and Jaynes, Melvin. Do you feel up to staying on the trail?"

There was no place where a plane could set down to pick up Castagna. Two and a half days out, Melvin estimated. Rudd would need five men to keep an eye on Strothers day and night. They were out of food, too.

"All right," Melvin said.

Jaynes had overheard. He came back from the creek. "I'm staying, too."

Strothers smiled.

"I'll send the green plane over Shewalter Meadows three days from now," Rudd said. "With grub. Now what else will you need?"

"Send me another coat," Melvin said. "Send Jaynes another sleeping bag. We both better have packs, too."

The sheriff nodded. He put Strothers on a horse and tied him there. They lifted Castagna to the saddle again. He was going to suffer plenty before they reached the highway. Castagna looked at Melvin and said thickly, "Thanks for the coat."

Strothers smiled at Melvin from the corner of his eyes. The smile said: Chump!

A hundred yards down the creek a logging road took off to the left, and there went the tracks of Marty Kaygo. Melvin and Jaynes walked into second-growth timber. The sounds of the horses died away. Under his belt Melvin was carrying the pistol he had taken from Strothers.

Jaynes said, "I damn near smashed that Strothers's ugly face for him."

"Uh-huh."

"You can't hit a man tied up like that, not even a pen bird."

"No."

"Of course not," Jaynes said.

The road began to angle to the right, along a ridge.

"This won't take us straight to where the plane spotted Kaygo," Jaynes said. "Let's cut into the timber."

"I'm staying with his tracks. I don't know what that plane was circling over."

The road turned down the ridge again, on the side away from Shewalter Meadows. Kaygo's tracks were still there, but Jaynes was mightily impatient. "I'm going straight over the ridge," he said.

"Go ahead."

"Where will I meet you then?"

"At the Meadows."

"You sure?" Jaynes asked doubtfully.

"This old road runs into one hell of a swamp before long. I'm betting he went to the Meadows, but I'm going to follow his trail all the way."

They separated. Melvin was glad. He wanted to reduce the chase to the patient unwinding of a trail, to an end that was nothing more than law and duty; and he could not think of it that way so long as Jaynes was with him.

Where the swamp began, Kaygo had turned at once up the ridge. There was something in that which spoke of the man's quality, of an ability to sense the lie of a country. Most city men would have blundered deep into the swamp before deciding to turn.

Jaynes was right about down-timber on the ridge, fire-killed trees that had stood for years before rot took their roots and wind sent them crashing. Melvin went slowly. Kaygo had done the same, and before long Melvin noticed that the man had traveled as a woodsman does, stepping over nothing that could be walked around.

Kaygo would never exhaust himself in blind, disorderly flight. What kind of man was he?

Going down the west side of the ridge, Melvin stopped when a grouse exploded from the ground near a rotting spruce log. He drew the pistol and waited until he saw two others near the log, frozen in their protective coloration. He shot one through the head, and five more flew away.

Now an instrument of the law had broken the law for a second time during this chase; but there were, of course, degrees of breakage. A man like Strothers no doubt could make biting comments on the subject.

Melvin pulled the entrails from the bird and went on, following Kaygo's trail. The man had an eye for terrain, all right. He made few mistakes that cost him time and effort, and that was rare in any man crossing unfamiliar, wooded country.

A woodsman at some time in his life? Melvin went back over Kaygo's record. Thirty-five years old. Sixteen of those years spent in reformatories and prisons. An interesting talker. Athletic. Generally armed, considered extremely dangerous. Approach with caution. The record fell into the glib pattern of the words under the faces on the bulletin board in Rudd's office.

Gambles heavily. If forced to work, seeks employment as clerk in clothing store. . . . There was nothing Melvin could recall to indicate that Kaygo had ever been five miles from pavement.

The sun was getting low and the timber was already gathering coolness in its depths when Melvin came out on a long slope that ran down to the Meadows, two miles away.

Where the sun still lay on a bare spot near a quartz outcrop Melvin stopped, puzzled by what he saw. The mark of the steel butt-plate of Kaygo's rifle and the imprint of his shoes, one flat, the other showing no heel print, said that Kaygo had squatted near the ant hill; four cigarette butts crushed into the ground said that he had been here for some time.

Coolness had diminished activity of the ants, but they were still seething in and out of their dome of sand and pine needles; and Kaygo had squatted there for perhaps an hour to watch.

It was Melvin's experience that some perverseness in man causes him to step upon ant hills or kick them in passing. This one was undisturbed. Kaygo had watched and gone away. Melvin had done the same thing many times.

What if I have and what if he did also? he asked himself. Does that change what I have to do? But as he went on, Melvin kept wondering what Kaygo had thought as he squatted beside the ant hill.

Near dusk Melvin lost the trail where the wide arm of a swamp came up from the drainage basin of the Meadows. But Kaygo was headed that way, Melvin was sure. One gentle turn too far to the left, back there on the long slope, would have sent Kaygo into the ragged canyons near the lower end of the Meadows.

He must have spotted the place from the top of Clover Mountain; but seeing from the heights and finding from a route through timber-choked country are two different things.

Kaygo had a fine sense of distance and direction, though. I can grant him that, Melvin thought, without feeling anything else about him to impede my purpose. The purpose—and Melvin wondered why he had to keep restating it—was to bring Marty Kaygo out, dead or alive.

On the edge of Shewalter Meadows, where the grass stood waist-high to a man all over the flooded ground and the beaver runs that led to the ponds out in the middle, Melvin stopped behind a tree and scanned the open space. There was only half-light now, but that was enough.

Beavers were making ripples in the ponds and trout were leaping for their evening feeding. The Meadows lay in a great dog-leg, and the upper part was cut from Melvin's view by spruce trees and high willows. The best windfalls for sleeping cover were up there, and that was where Jaynes would be, undoubtedly.

Let him stay there tonight alone. Sooner or later Melvin would have to rejoin him, and that would be soon enough. Melvin went back into the timber and cooked his grouse. He ate half of it and laid the rest in the palm of a limb, head-high.

The night came in with a gentle rush. He dozed off on top of his sleeping bag, to awaken chilled and trembling some time later. The night was windless, the ground stony. Melvin built up the fire and warmed himself by it before getting into his sleeping bag.

Dead or alive. The thought would not submerge.

One Kaygo was a vagueness written on a record; Melvin had learned of another Kaygo today. They made a combination that would never give up.

If Melvin had been here just to fish and loaf, to walk through the dappled fall of sunshine in the trees, and—yes, to be caught away from himself while watching the endless workings of an ant hill; to see the elk thrusting their broad muzzles underwater to eat; to view all the things that are simple and understandable . . . then, he knew, he would be living for a while as man was meant to live.

You are Bill Melvin, a deputy sheriff. He is a man called Kaygo, an escaped murderer.

Dead or alive. . . .

He came from dreamless sleep when the log ends of the fire were no longer flaming but drizzling smoke across a bed of coals. He felt the presence near him by the rising of the hackles on his neck, from deep memories forgotten by the human race.

Carefully, not breaking the even tenor of his breathing, he worked one hand up to the pistol on the head shield of the sleeping bag.

The man was squatted by the fire with a rifle across his knees. His hair was curling brown that caught a touch of redness from the glow of embers. The light outlined a sandy beard, held steady on wide cheekbones, and lost itself in the hollows under massive brown arches. The man's trousers were muddy, at least as high as the knees, where the fabric was strained smooth by his position. They might have been any color. But there was no doubt that the shirt was green.

The face by itself was enough.

It was Marty Kaygo.

He was eating what was left of Melvin's grouse.

He turned the carcass in his hands, gnawing, chewing; and all the while his face was set toward the shadows where Melvin lay.

Slowly Melvin worked the pistol along the edge of the ground until, lying on his side, he raised it just a trifle. The front sight was a white bead that lined across the coals to Kaygo's chest. Melvin's thumb pushed the safety down.

Long rifle cartridges, just a spot of lead that could sing over space and kill. Kaygo, the cop-killer. Speak to him, tell him to put up his hands and let his rifle fall. If he swung the rifle to fire, the pistol could sing and kill.

From where came the whisper that fire and food must be shared even with a deadly enemy? From the jungle all around that might pull them both beneath its slime an instant later?

The sabre-tooth and the great reptiles were out there in the night. And men were men together, if only for a moment. The jungle was not gone, merely changed.

Melvin let the pistol rest upon the ground.

Marty Kaygo rose. He was not a tall man. Even in his prison shoes he moved lightly as he stepped to a tree and replaced the carcass of the grouse. He grinned, still looking toward where Melvin lay.

And then he was gone.

Melvin lay a long time before he fell asleep again.

When he rose in the bitter cold of morning, he went at once to the dead fire. There were the tracks. He took the grouse from the limb. One leg was untouched.

Staring out to where the first long-slanting rays of the sun were driving mist from the beaver ponds and wet grass, Melvin held the chilled grouse in his hands.

What's the matter with me?

The truth was, Jaynes was Melvin and Melvin was Jaynes, great developments of the centuries; and Kaygo did not fit where they belonged. But. . . .

Melvin shivered.

He went out of the timber into the sunshine, and he sat down to let it warm him while he ate the rest of the grouse. There before him, leading through the gray mud out toward the wickerwork of the beaver dams, were the tracks of Kaygo. He had crossed the boggy ground by night, walking the beaver dams above deep water, returning the same way. It was not an easy feat even in daytime.

I wish I could talk to him, Melvin thought. I wish. . . .

The shot was a cracking violation of the wilderness quiet. It came from somewhere around the dog-leg of the Meadows.

Melvin went back to the camp site and got his gear.

Before he turned the dog-leg, he saw Jaynes coming toward him. Jaynes stopped and waited.

"What the hell happened to you, Melvin?" There was blood on Jaynes's shirt.

"I followed his trail, just as I said I would. You shoot a deer?"

"Yeah. That's one thing there's plenty of here. Kaygo's around. I saw his tracks in the upper part of the Meadows last night. We'll get him. I know every inch—"

"Let's get at the deer."

They roasted meat, and then Jaynes was impatient to be off.

"Just hold your steam," said Melvin. "We've got another two days before the plane drops chow, so we're going to start drying some of this meat."

"There's lots of deer."

"We'll dry some of this. We don't know where that plane will drop our supplies, or what they'll be like when we get to them. And you're not going to shoot a deer every day, Jaynes."

They cut the meat in thin strips and laid it on the gray twigs of a fallen tree until the branches were festooned with dangling brown meat. Camp-robber birds were there at once, floating in, snatching.

"How you going to stop that?" Jaynes asked.

"By staying here. I'm going to do some smoking with a willow fire, too. Take a turn around the Meadows. See what you can find out. You know every inch of the land."

"I'll do that." Jaynes took his rifle and strode away.

He was back at noon. "Where'd you camp, Melvin?"

Melvin told him.

"Well, he was there, this morning. He crossed the swamp and went back the same way. He's in the timber on this side somewhere. He's getting smart now about covering his tracks."

"What's he eating?" Melvin asked cleverly.

"I don't know, and I don't care. He slept one night under a windfall. Where'd he learn that, Melvin?" Jaynes was worried.

"I think it must come to him naturally. He's probably enjoying more freedom right now than he's had in his whole life."

Jaynes grunted. He eyed the tree that was serving as a drying rack. "Hey! Do you suppose we could pull him in with that?" He looked all around at the fringe of trees. "Say we go down into the timber on the other side and then circle back to that little knob over there. . . . About 325 yards." Jaynes rubbed the oily sheen of his rifle barrel. "One shot, Melvin."

"You think he's hungry enough to try it?"

"He must be."

"The birds will scatter our meat."

"Part of a lousy deer, or one jailbird! What's the matter with you, Melvin?"

The venison was not going to cure before the plane came in and Melvin knew it. He had stalled long enough.

They went a half-mile beside the lower Meadows. On the way Jaynes stepped sidewise to jump into an ant hill and twist his feet; and then he went on, stamping ants loose from his shoes. "He must be hungry enough by now."

They went back through the timber and crept behind a log on the little hill across the field from their camp. The smoky birds were having a merry time with the meat.

Now Jaynes was patient. His eyes caught every movement across the park, and his position did not seem to strain his muscles. They stayed until the shadows lowered cold upon their backs. It was then that they heard the rifle-shot somewhere in the lower Meadows, two miles away.

"He's got his own meat." Melvin laughed.

Jaynes rose. "What's so damn funny about it?"

Melvin had wrapped his undershirt around a venison haunch, but the blowflies had got to it anyway. He brushed the white larva away.

They roasted meat and ate in silence.

Marty Kaygo was still around Shewalter Meadows. They cut his sign the next day, and they found where he had killed the deer. The convict was here, and it seemed that he intended to stay.

Jaynes was infuriated. And he was speechless for a while when they returned to camp that night and found that Kaygo had stolen Melvin's sleeping bag.

"Who are the tenderfeet around here?" Melvin laughed again.

"You don't act like you want to catch him! By God, I do, and I'll stay here all summer to do it, if necessary!"

"To catch him?"

"To kill him! I'm going to gut-shoot him for this little trick!"

"You would have, anyway." There was no humor now in Kaygo's stealing the sleeping bag.

The plane came in on the afternoon of the third day. Clouds were scudding across the peaks and the pilot was in a hurry to beat out a local storm. He banked sharply to look down at the two men standing in the open dryness of the upper Meadows.

He went on east, high above the timber. They saw him fighting a tricky wind. On the next bank he kicked out the box. The parachute became a white cone. Lining out with a tailwind boosting him, the pilot sped away toward Scott.

"If he had any brains he'd've stayed to make sure we got it," Jaynes said. "Typical State employee."

. A great wind-front flowing in from the mountains struck them with a chill that spoke of the rain soon to follow. Melvin watched the plane bouncing jerkily in downdrafts above the canyons. "The pilot's all right, Jaynes."

"Look at that thing drift!"

They knew for sure after another few moments that the box would not land in the upper Meadows. Melvin said, "Wouldn't it be something if it lit right at Kaygo's feet?"

"Big fine joke, huh?"

They trotted across the creek and down along the edge of the Big Shewalter to keep the 'chute in sight. They were a long way from it when they saw it splash into the water near the opposite side of the flooded area. An instant later the rain boiled down on them.

"I hope they had sense enough to put the stuff in cans." Jaynes turned up the collar of his jacket.

The ponds were dancing froth now. Through the mist they saw Kaygo run from the timber and wade out after the box.

Jaynes dropped to one knee. He pushed his 'scope down and began to click the sight-adjustment. "Eight hundred yards," he muttered. His rifle bellowed with the thunder on the mountains. "Where'd I hit?"

"I couldn't tell."

The first hard blast of rain was sweeping on. Jaynes fired again, and this time Melvin saw the bullet strike the water to the left of Kaygo, chest-deep now, towing the box to shore with the shroud-lines of the chute.

"About five feet to the left," Melvin said.

Kaygo sprawled into the grass when the next shot came.

"That did it," Melvin said.

"No! He ducked."

Kaygo raised up. Skidding the box over wet grass and mud, he reached timber while Jaynes tried two more shots. Over that distance, through wind and rain, Jaynes had performed well—but Kaygo was still free.

Kaygo's boldness was worth applause, but Melvin felt only a bleak apathy. The end had been delayed, that was all.

"Come on!" Jaynes said.

"Across that open swamp? No, thanks. We'll work through the timber."

"He's got our stuff!"

"He's got a rifle, too."

The box had been fastened with wing-nuts, easy to tap loose. The packs Melvin had asked for were gone, and the jacket, and about three-fourths of the food. Melvin estimated. The sleeping bag had been unrolled. Rain was filtering through the pines on a manila envelope containing a note.

They peered into the gloom of the wet forest. It was no time to press Kaygo hard, and they both knew it.

While Jaynes raged, Melvin read the note.

"Rudd started in at noon today with big posse. He says not to take any chances. He says there were *two* .22 pistols and a hunting knife taken from the filling station."

"That's a big help!" Jaynes cursed the weather, the pilot, and the stupidity of circumstance.

"I told you on Clover Mountain I was sick of you, Jaynes. Now shut up! You're lucky Kaygo didn't slice your sleeping bag to pieces or throw it into the water."

"I'm fed up with you, too, Melvin! You didn't even try to shoot a while ago. You act like the stinking louse is your brother!"

My brother. The thought plowed through Melvin, leaving a fresh wake. It was not fashionable to speak of men as brothers; you killed your brother, just like anybody else.

They plodded toward camp, carrying the cans of food in their hands. The labels began to soak off. Melvin finished the job on the cans he was holding.

"That's smart," Jaynes said. "Now what's in them?"

"You're right, they're no good to us any more. A hungry man has to know what he's getting." Melvin began to hurl the cans into a beaver pond, until Jaynes pleaded with him.

"Then shut your mouth for a while!" Melvin cried.

They went on to camp through a cold rain that soaked into Melvin's soul.

"Soup!" Jaynes said later, when they sat under a dripping tree before a smoking fire. "Kaygo's back in the timber having hot coffee and canned chicken."

Jaynes could not destroy everything, for he had the unrealized power to give laughter. Melvin began to laugh while Jaynes stared at him angrily. Was it the sound of laughter, as well as the smell of fire, that caused the monsters of the long-ago jungle to raise their heads in fear?

"I said I'd get Kaygo if it took all summer. You sit here and laugh some more, Melvin. *I'll get him!*"

They found the second pack the next morning, empty, hanging on a tree. "He's cached part of the grub somewhere," Jaynes growled. "He couldn't have put it all in one pack. Smart! He did it in the rain, and now we can't backtrack him."

But they could trail him in the fresh dampness. Kaygo had realized that, too; he had gone far south of the Meadows, and on a rocky ridge they lost his trail. The ridge was a great spur that ran down from Spearhead Mountain, bucking through lesser cross-ridges arrogantly. The lower end of it, Melvin knew, was not eight miles from the highway.

"Maybe he's clearing out," Jaynes said. "He read that note about Rudd. He knows he's going to get it. He's headed for the highway now. Somebody else will get him, after all we've done!"

"Pathetic, ain't it?" Melvin looked at Spearhead Mountain. "Maybe he went that way. He likes mountains."

"What do you mean?"

"Nothing you'd understand. He's gone toward Spearhead, Jaynes."

"The highway! I'm going after him, Melvin. If I don't cut his trail by the time I hit Bandbox Creek, I'll come back. Don't sneak off this time and camp by yourself. He could have walked right in on you that night."

"Yes, he could have killed me, I suppose."

Jaynes's eyes narrowed. "Those tracks beside your fire the next morning—one of yours was on top of one of his, Melvin. He sneaked in while you were asleep, didn't he? And you were ashamed to mention it to me! It's a wonder he didn't take your rifle and sleeping bag right from under you. I'll mention that to Rudd when he gets here."

"You do that, Jaynes." Harlan Rudd had shared food and fire with outlaws in the old days, and he was not ashamed to talk about it now that he was sheriff. "Get out of my sight, Jaynes, before I forget I'm a brother to you, too!"

"Brother?" Jaynes gave Melvin a baffled look before he started down the ridge.

There was something Kaygo could not have known about this ridge: It appeared to be the natural route to Spearhead, but higher up it was a jumble of tree-covered cliffs.

Melvin stayed on it only until he found where Kaygo had slipped from his careful walking on rocks and left a mark which he had tried to smooth away. Then Melvin left the ridge and took a roundabout, but faster, route toward Spearhead.

He went too rapidly. In mid-afternoon he saw Kaygo far below him, between two curving buttresses of the mountain. The fugitive was not pushing himself.

While Melvin watched through his glasses, Kaygo removed the stolen pack and lay down in a field of columbines, pillowing his head on the stolen sleeping bag. The wind was cold on Melvin's sweating skin as he hugged his vantage point behind the rocks.

Jaynes might have made a shot from here; he would have tried, although the range was 400 yards greater than yesterday across the Big Shewalter. Melvin knew his own rifle would do no more than scare Kaygo down the hill.

Like hunting sheep, he thought. You have to wait and try to make them blunder into you.

Kaygo lay there for an hour. He was not asleep. He moved occasionally, but mostly he lay there looking at the sky and clouds.

He was wallowing in freedom; that was it. Damn him! He would not do what fugitives are supposed to do. He insisted on acting like a man enjoying life.

My brother down there, Melvin thought. Yes, and I'll kill him when he comes near enough on the saddle of the mountain.

Kaygo rose at last, but he did not go. He stretched his arms to the sky, as if he would clutch a great section of it. Then he sat down and smoked a cigarette.

The sweat was tight and dry on Melvin. The wind scampered through his clothing. Of course I have to kill him, he told himself. He's found something he loves so much he won't be taken from it any other way.

Kaygo went up at last. Melvin slipped behind the rib of the mountain and climbed steadily. The wind was growing quiet now. There was a sullen heaviness in the air. It would rain again today.

Melvin was far ahead when he took a position among rocks that overlooked the saddle. He could see Kaygo, still in no hurry, coming up the harder way, coming over a red iron dike that had made the notch on Spearhead back when man clutched his club and splashed toward refuge as the clamor broke out in the forest.

It was his job. Society paid him, Melvin reminded himself. Climb faster Marty Kaygo. You will have your chance to go back where you belong, and when you refuse the job will be done quickly.

The air grew heavily quiet. Melvin blinked when he heard a tiny snap and saw a blue spark run along his rifle barrel. He rubbed his hand against his woolen shirt. His palm crackled with pinpoint sparks and the fibers of the sleeve tried to follow the hand away. He stroked his hair and heard the little noises and felt the hair rising.

All this was not uncommon on the heights in summer when a storm was making, but Melvin had never experienced it before. It gave him a weird sensation.

Kaygo came into the saddle when the air was fully charged. He jumped when blue light ran along his rifle barrel. He was then two hundred yards from Melvin. He would have to pass much closer. Kaygo stared in wonder at his rifle, and then at the leaden sky.

He held up his hunting knife. Sparks played upon the point. Kaygo laughed. He raised both knife and rifle and watched the electricity come to them.

A little later he discovered steel was not necessary to draw static from the swollen air. Kaygo's fingers, held aloft, drew sparks. He did a dance upon the rocks, shouting his wonder and pleasure. Strange balls of light ran along the iron dike and the air was filled with a sterile odor.

This day on Spearhead Mountain, Marty Kaygo roared with joy.

Melvin had never heard laughter run so cleanly. Laughter from the littered caves above the slime; laughter from the tree-perch safe from walking beasts; laughter challenging the brutes. . . .

It did not last. The rain came just after the first whistling surge of wind. The bursting air cleared.

Kaygo trotted easily for shelter, his head lowered against the pelt of ice. He came straight toward the rocks where Melvin lay. There was a clatter somewhere behind Melvin, granite slipping on granite, but he had no time to wonder.

"Kaygo!" he yelled. "Drop it!"

The man threw up his head as he ran and he brought the rifle up, not hesitating.

My brother, Melvin thought. That held him one split second longer, with his finger on the trigger and his sights on Kaygo's chest.

Another rifle roared behind him. Kaygo's legs jerked as he tried to keep running. He went down and his hands reached out for the wet stones. That was all.

Jaynes came limping through the rocks. "I hurt my knee, but I got him, rain and all!"

Melvin could not rise for a moment. He felt frozen to the rock. At last he came up, slowly.

"You were right," Jaynes said. "He took the hard way. After I left you I got to thinking that was what he would do."

They went across the stones to Kaygo. Jaynes turned him over. "Heart. I said I didn't miss running shots, not very often." That was all the interest he had in Marty Kaygo; and now that vanished, too.

Jaynes slipped the pack from the dead man's back. "Steal our chow, would he! Grab your sleeping bag and let's get out of here. Rudd and the others can take care of the chores now. Four for four, Melvin."

"You're counting Strothers?"

"I wish that big-mouth had tried something."

The rain was the coldest that ever fell on Melvin. He unrolled the sleeping bag and covered Kaygo with it, weighting the sides with stones.

Jaynes started to protest, but near the end he helped. "I guess even Kaygo deserves something. He wasn't a bad-looking character at that, was he?"

All this time Melvin had not looked at Jaynes. Now he picked up Jaynes's rifle. Deliberately, Melvin began to smash it against a rock. He splintered the stock and the forestock. He bent the bolt and he battered the 'scope until it was a twisted tube hanging by one mount, and he continued to beat the breech against the rock until the front sight ripped his palm and the impacts numbed his wrists.

He dropped the rifle then and stood breathing hard.

Jaynes had cursed loudly at first, but then he had stopped. The hard glitter was gone from his eyes.

Now, in the voice of a man who lives with splinters in his soul, Jaynes said, "By God, you're going to buy me a new rifle, Melvin. What's the matter with you, anyway?"

Melvin said nothing. Then together they started down the rain-soaked mountain.

Bibliography of Western Publications by
Steve Frazee

Novels

Range Trouble (as Dean Jennings). New York: Phoenix Press, 1951.
Shining Mountains. New York: Rinehart, 1951.
Pistolman. New York: Lion Books, 1952.
Utah Hell Guns. New York: Lion Books, 1952.
The Sky Block. New York: Rinehart, 1953
Lawman's Feud. New York: Lion Books, 1953.
Sharp the Bugle Calls. New York: Lion Books, 1953.
Cry Coyote. New York: Macmillan & Co., 1955.
Many Rivers to Cross. New York: Fawcett Gold Medal, 1955.
Spur to the Smoke. New York: Permabooks, 1955.
Tumbling Range Woman. New York: Pocket Books, 1956.
He Rode Alone. New York: Fawcett Gold Medal, 1956.
High Cage. New York: Macmillan & Co., 1957.
Running Target. New York: Fawcett Gold Medal, 1957.
Desert Guns. New York: Dell Books, 1957.
Rendezvous. New York: Macmillan & Co., 1958.
Smoke in the Valley. New York: Fawcett Gold Medal, 1959.
A Day to Die. New York: Avon Books, 1960.
Hellsgrin. New York: Rinehart, 1960.
The Alamo. New York: Avon Books, 1960.
More Damn Tourists. New York: Macmillan & Co., 1960.
A Gun for Bragg's Woman. New York: Ballantine, 1966.
Fire in the Valley. New York: Lancer, 1972.

Collections

The Gun-Throwers. New York: Lion Books, 1954.
The Best Western Stories of Steve Frazee. Carbondale, IL: Southern Illinois University Press, 1984.

Juvenile Novels

Walt Disney's Zorro (novelization of TV play). Racine, Wisconsin: Whitman Books, 1958.
Year of the Big Snow. New York: Holt Rinehart, 1962.
Killer Lion. Racine, Wisconsin: Whitman Books, 1966.
Lassie: The Mystery of the Bristlecone Pine. Racine, Wisconsin: Whitman Books, 1967.
Lassie: Lost in the Snow (The Secret of the Smuggler's Cave, Trouble at Panter's Lake.) New York: Golden Press, 3 vols., 1979.